KT-160-016

A Cotswold Killing

REBECCA TOPE

Allison & Busby Limited
12 Fitzroy Mews
London W1T 6DW
allisonandbusby.com

First published in Great Britain by Allison & Busby in 2004.
This paperback edition published by Allison & Busby in 2017.

Copyright © 2004 by REBECCA TOPE

The moral right of the author is hereby asserted in accordance with the
Copyright, Designs and Patents Act 1988.

All characters and events in this publication,
other than those clearly in the public domain,
are fictitious and any resemblance to actual persons,
living or dead, is purely coincidental.

All rights reserved. No part of this publication may be reproduced, stored
in a retrieval system, or transmitted, in any form or by any means without
the prior written permission of the publisher, nor be otherwise circulated in
any form of binding or cover other than that in which it is published and
without a similar condition being imposed on the subsequent buyer.

A CIP catalogue record for this book is available from
the British Library.

10 9 8 7 6 5 4 3 2 1

ISBN 978-0-7490-2183-2

Typeset in 10.5/15.5 pt Sabon by
Allison & Busby Ltd.

The paper used for this Allison & Busby publication
has been produced from trees that have been legally sourced
from well-managed and credibly certified forests.

Printed and bound by
CPI Group (UK) Ltd, Croydon, CR0 4YY

684040646831

REBECCA TOPE is the author of three bestselling crime series, set in the stunning Cotswolds, Lake District and West Country. She lives on a smallholding in rural Herefordshire, where she enjoys the silence and plants a lot of trees, but also manages to travel the world and enjoy civilisation from time to time. Most of her varied experiences and activities find their way into her books, sooner or later.

rebeccatope.com

For Diana

LEICESTER LIBRARIES	
Askews & Holts	29-May-2017
	£7.99

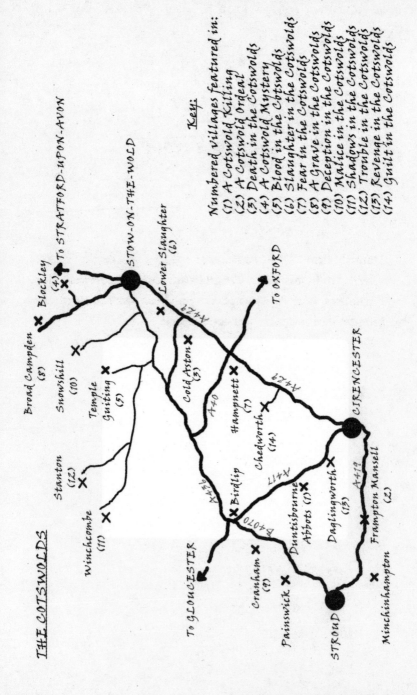

THE COTSWOLDS

To STRATFORD-UPON-AVON

Broad Campden (8)
Blockley (4)
Stanton (12)
Winchcombe (11)
Snowshill (10)
Temple Guiting (5)
STOW-ON-THE-WOLD
Lower Slaughter (6)
Cold Aston (3)
Hampnett (7)
Chedworth (14)
Birdlip
Cranham (9)
Painswick
Duntisbourne Abbots (1)
Daglingworth (13)
CIRENCESTER
Frampton Mansell (2)
Minchinhampton
STROUD
To GLOUCESTER
To OXFORD

A424
A429
A40
A417
A436
B4070
A419

Key:

Numbered villages featured in:
(1) A Cotswold Killing
(2) A Cotswold Ordeal
(3) Death in the Cotswolds
(4) A Cotswold Mystery
(5) Blood in the Cotswolds
(6) Slaughter in the Cotswolds
(7) Fear in the Cotswolds
(8) A Grave in the Cotswolds
(9) Deception in the Cotswolds
(10) Malice in the Cotswolds
(11) Shadows in the Cotswolds
(12) Trouble in the Cotswolds
(13) Revenge in the Cotswolds
(14) Guilt in the Cotswolds

Author's Note

Duntisbourne Abbots is a real village, as are the others referred to in this story. The pubs and churches are real. But the houses, farms and people have all been made up, and any resemblance to reality is a coincidence.

Chapter One

The pain in Thea's finger was intermittent, but sharp. She prodded, then nibbled it, making it hurt more. There was something so wincingly vulnerable about the flesh beneath a fingernail, like the underbelly of a turtle – protected by hard tissue because of its exquisite sensitivity. It was the ideal spot for a torturer's attention, and Thea gave a little groan of satisfaction as she focused on it. Hepzibah cocked an interested ear, but didn't budge from her sunny spot in the doorway.

It was almost time to set out. The cottage would have to be secured, everything turned off and tidied up. She wouldn't be back again for three weeks, by which time dust would lie thick on all the surfaces and junk mail be silted up behind the front door.

Shaking her finger, she gathered up her bag, laptop, coat and mobile phone. Hepzibah sighed. 'Sorry, babes,' Thea told her. 'Got to hit the road. Shame about the weather.'

Woman and dog boarded the Golf with some reluctance. It was very warm inside, from sitting in full April sunshine.

Thea stashed her laptop securely between two leather bags on the back seat and paused to run through her mental list of necessities one last time. Her greatest dread was boredom, as she spent the coming three weeks in charge of a house and smallholding with assorted animals and responsibilities. Surely there would be afternoons and evenings where everything was exercised and watered, and there was little to do but read, walk or play Scrabble online.

'Let's just hope we get some sunshine,' she muttered.

The route ran westwards, along the A40 as far as Burford, then the 429 to Cirencester. Her goal was the Cotswold village of Duntisbourne Abbots, where a Mr and Mrs Clive Reynolds were shortly to leave for a luxury cruise of the Caribbean. Because they had two labradors, a small flock of rare breed sheep, a fear of intruders and plenty of money, they had availed themselves of Thea's services as a house-sitter.

They did not know, and Thea did not tell them, that this was her very first commission. Never before had she agreed to occupy a stranger's home, in return for money, a well-stocked freezer and a fragile trust in her competence.

She was not by any means a stranger to the area. Her own home was in Witney, an easy drive away. If Duntisbourne became impossibly dull, it would be feasible to escape back to the cottage for a few hours in her garden or drop in on one of her friends.

'It won't be dull,' her friend and neighbour Celia had assured her. 'After all, I thought the whole point of doing it was to get a change of scenery and meet some new people. It's not as if you need the money.'

The money, actually, would be rather welcome. The

Reynoldses were paying her an impressive £630 for her services, and that was not to be sniffed at, the way her shares had slumped in the past year or so. It would pay the Council Tax for six months, if nothing else.

Another sharp pain stabbed through her finger as she pulled the car door shut. It was the long finger on her left hand, and she scrutinised it with a detached interest. She'd painted her nails a vivid pink that morning, the colour representing the medium level of discomfort in her own private code.

Although she was familiar with the Cotswolds, she had never before been to the precise area of her house-sit. She was pleased to see it matched up to the parts she did know, as she meandered down the A429 towards Cirencester. Scattered on the tilting hillsides were the distinctive stone houses and barns that typified the region. Creams, yellows, natural shades of beige and grey characterised stone that was not to be found anywhere else in Britain. Woodwork was painted black or brown or white, but never anything primary or startling. Cotswold buildings, like the sheep, evidently regarded colours as signs of corruption or contamination. Let the flowers offer up a few brave splashes of pink or purple if they must – they were beyond control – but that was as far as it went. Even the vivid black and white buildings of Herefordshire or Worcestershire were too much. Here, the original hues provided by the earth itself were the obvious and rightful choice, and the attentions of the world's discerning visitors provided ample confirmation.

The spaniel curled prettily on the passenger seat, and hardly moved for the duration of the journey. They made good progress, skirting Cirencester and getting onto the broad sweep of the dual carriagewayed A417. A disappointingly featureless road, where the traffic rushed blindly through a corridor carved into the landscape. Strange rocky terraces bordered both sides of the road for part of the way, the sandy tints presenting an incongruous desert landscape, suggestive of heat and drought, whatever the actual weather. Only when she turned off as directed did Thea suddenly feel she was in genuine Cotswold territory again.

The scenery, in late April, was almost ludicrously English. White may-blossom, some of it drifting on the roadsides, mixed with the yellow faces of celandines and the occasional mauve of a wild violet. The fresh green of new leaves and lush grass in the verges carried an optimism that Thea could not ignore. There were months of summer ahead for her to enjoy. It had been a wet and windy winter, frustrating for her and Hepzie alike, and its passing was something to celebrate – or so she tried to convince herself. Celebration was still an uncomfortable concept, a year on from her catastrophic loss.

The lanes narrowed dramatically within a few hundred yards of leaving the main road, closing in on her, swallowing her up. The open vistas she'd noted on the road down to Cirencester had now vanished.

Clive Reynolds had given careful directions, which turned out to be indispensable. Tiny country lanes dived off at strange angles, down steep slopes. Trees on both sides made them dark and mysterious; it was impossible to see more than a few yards ahead. There was a strong sense of venturing into alien territory.

It was two minutes to two when Thea drove through the

gateway to Brook View House. The handsome wooden gate stood wide open, the gravel drive looked recently raked, and two mature beech trees dominated the manicured lawn that sloped away to the left of the house.

'Wow!' Thea nudged the dog. 'Have a look at this.'

It hadn't been necessary. Hepzie was already sitting up and scanning the scene. Her long tail wagged enthusiastically. A man Thea recognised appeared in the front doorway of the house, wearing a grey Aran jumper, surely too hot for the spring day. The dog's tail slowed and stopped.

'Hmm,' said Thea, as she turned off the ignition.

'This is the thermostat,' Clive Reynolds told Thea, pausing to ensure he had her full attention. It was the ninety-third thing he'd shown her, or so it felt. He'd raised a disapproving eyebrow at her lack of notepad and pencil. 'I hope you'll be able to remember it all,' he'd said.

'Oh, I'm sure I shall,' she assured him. 'Especially as you've already made so many helpful notes.'

The 'helpful notes' amounted to five single-spaced pages of A4, immaculately produced on a computer, with bullet points and underlinings. Thea had quickly come to the conclusion that Clive Reynolds was a typical senior civil servant, accustomed to giving orders and extremely fond of making lists. His wife, who he persistently referred to as 'Mrs Reynolds' was tall, stiff-necked and narrow-eyed. She did not appear comfortable with the idea of leaving her house in the care of a stranger.

Thea had provided references when requested to do so, and had met the Reynoldses two weeks earlier, in a tea shoppe in Burford. She had not overtly confessed to her total lack of experience, but led them to believe it had been some time since she last undertook such a commission. It was only when she mentioned her brother-in-law as a potential referee, who happened to be a superintendent in the West Midlands police and known, at least by reputation, to Clive Reynolds, that she seemed to pass muster. Oh, yes – one of us, she could see him thinking. And, as always, her appearance helped.

Thea had known she was beautiful for the past twenty years. Before that she had been a plain schoolgirl, with poor skin and insufficient flesh. Leaving home and discovering men had worked a transformation: by some inexplicable chemistry, she had developed into a woman who attracted people of all ages, both genders and most races. She took no credit for it, often found it hard to take seriously, but nonetheless exploited it to the full.

Even now, in her early forties, it persisted undiminished. She took care to get her hair expertly cut, to smile at people – and that was about it. Nature did the rest, however unfair that might seem to other women. She just happened to have pleasing cheekbones, a wide mouth and nicely arched eyebrows. As usual, the magic had worked on Clive Reynolds.

When she further divulged, with downcast eyes, that her husband, Carl, brother to James-the-policeman, had died in a very unpleasant traffic accident, just over a year ago, the sympathy vote clinched the deal. A good-looking widow in her early forties with such respectable connections had to be all right. In fact, by the time the pot of tea was drained, she had the impression the Reynoldses thought she was rather a catch.

'Feel free to pop along to the next house up the road' – he told her now, waving an arm to indicate the direction – 'and introduce yourself to Helen. She told me to mention it. I think she feels a bit bad for not being up to holding the fort herself.'

Holding the fort was going to be a somewhat more arduous task than Thea had anticipated. She was to monitor the temperature in every room, as well as the humidity, and ensure that all twenty-six house plants were kept in peak condition. She must be sure to always be in when the postman came, in case there was something to sign for. She must make a meticulous note of every telephone message, with date and time. She must memorise the security code on the burglar alarm, because they were absolutely emphatic that it must never ever be written down anywhere. If it didn't rain, she would have to water the garden and keep the pond filled to a certain level. Failure to observe this requirement could lead to deleterious consequences for the water lily.

The dogs were both neutered male labradors, named Bonzo and Georgie, and fantastically well trained. To Thea's eye they seemed virtually lobotomised. Hepzibah did her usual female trick of lying on her back and displaying a clean pink underbelly as soon as she saw them, but quickly righted herself in the face of their humiliating lack of interest.

The labradors had a whole page of the notes to themselves, and the sheep even more. These comprised a small flock of shaggy Cotswold ewes, with a clutch of pretty lambs at their heels. Despite the lengthy notes, which had side-tracked into interesting but irrelevant descriptions of the breed, their requirements seemed mercifully straightforward.

On the tour of the outside acres, Clive drew Thea's

attention to the good-sized brook running around two sides of the sloping field, which could just possibly be host to infant brown trout if conditions were optimal. A pool had formed in the bottom corner of the Reynoldses' property, providing the sheep with easily accessed drinking water. 'Not that they use it very much,' he added. 'Sheep drink remarkably little.' The putative trout would, however, be jeopardised by the sheep trampling the water too vigorously if they did go down to drink, and could she please check daily that the water was still running freely. If not, then she might take a spade and clear a way for the flow. They stood at a little distance from the pool, which Thea examined with some pleasure. It looked quite deep in the middle, and was edged with vegetation – brambles especially. It was eight or ten feet across in each direction, and seemed highly unlikely to run dry, whatever the weather.

'Did you make it?' she asked, aware of something unusual in its formation.

'Let's just say I gave nature a helping hand,' he said. 'We've had cattle and horses here from time to time, and they need a lot of water. I dug it out to this depth, to help save a bit more for them. It's perfectly all right to do that.'

Thea wondered at the defensiveness, suspecting a minor breach of waterway regulations.

There was an odd mismatch between the obsessive attention to detail, the desperate need to control every nuance of life at Brook View, and the personality of Clive Reynolds himself. He was careful in his demonstrations, but not unduly so. His wife let him get on with instructing the house-sitter, apparently unconcerned that he might omit something or get a detail wrong. The pickiness was all in the written pages, which Thea carried with her as they moved from point to point, making sure she understood what was where. Despite a dawning fear that there would be considerably more work than she had anticipated, she found herself liking Clive. She sensed a fragility about him, a look in his eye of appeal and vulnerability, that sat uneasily with the hearty civil servant façade.

Promptly at four, Mr and Mrs Reynolds departed for Heathrow and their evening flight to Barbados, casting one last joint glance over their shoulders. Thea waved brightly, standing on the gravel for a full minute, in case they could still see her through the hedges. When she was sure they'd gone, she went back into the house and closed the door. 'Well,' she said to the three dogs, as they all stood watching her. 'There's just us now.'

This statement remained true for less than five minutes. The younger of the labradors turned towards the door with a rumbling growl before Thea heard anything. Then, as the rattle of gravel underfoot came to her ears, all the dogs became agitated. Before anyone could knock on the door, she had pulled it open.

The man standing there was almost comically rural. Not merely mud-stained and ill-dressed, but somehow from another age as well, despite his relative youthfulness. The material of his trousers was thick, his jumper evidently hand-knitted. Strands dangled from the cuffs where they were coming unravelled. His boots were ankle-high, with laces threaded through eyelets. The bottoms of his trouser legs were bound with hairy bale string, revealing green socks between trouser and boot that could also have been made by hand. Around his neck was a bizarre scarf, patterned in purple and yellow, possibly made of silk. Thea watched in fascination as he shyly played with it. The labradors sniffed him thoroughly, but seemed to bear him no ill will.

The gardener, she decided, despite there having been no mention of such a person. 'Hello?' she said.

'Afternoon,' he smiled, not so much shy as *unpractised,* she decided.

'I'm Joel. They've gone then, have they?'

His accent was so impeccably Oxford English that Thea wanted to laugh. A mad thought that he must be part of a local theatrical company entered her head. She cast a quick glance up the lane, wondering whether there might be more like him, putting on some sort of strolling play, going from house to house.

'Yes, they went five minutes ago,' she said. 'I'm Thea Osborne.'

Without missing a beat, he asked, 'Doro or An?'

Equally deftly, she said, 'Neither. Nor Ale. Just Thea, pure and simple.' It wasn't the first time some variation on this question had been asked, but there had been a friendly intelligence in this man's way of doing it. It made her feel warm towards him.

'This your dog?' He bent to pat the spaniel's soft head.

'That's right. I'm afraid she's called Hepzibah, for reasons I can't properly explain. She seems to be settling in fairly well.'

'It's refreshing to see a long tail on a cocker – though not everybody would say so around here, even now.'

'She certainly wags it enough.' Thea refrained for the moment from pursuing the implications in that 'even now' remark. Already she was hoping there'd be time for further conversation with this very strange young man.

'Here on your own, are you?' he asked, glancing past her into the house as if scouting for a husband or friend.

'Just me and the dog,' she nodded. It had felt like a perfectly benign question.

All the time, she was examining his face, waiting for some explanation as to why he was there. He looked to be in his middle thirties, hair growing thickly on top, cut short at the sides. Clean-shaven, blue eyes, reasonably tall. His hand, playing with the dog, was narrow with long fingers. 'Are you their gardener or something?' she asked, when she could bear the uncertainty no longer.

'Gardener?' He stared at her. 'No, of course I'm not the gardener. I'm Joel Jennison. I'm from the farm across the lane.' He waved an arm in the general direction of the roadway behind him. 'Barrow Hill, it's called. I'm a neighbour. Gardener!' he repeated the word with scorn.

Thea did not apologise. It seemed a perfectly reasonable mistake to have made. But it was nonetheless embarrassing, if only because she no longer knew where to place him. English society persisted in pigeonholing people according to accent, income, education and connections. And clothes. If Joel Jennison had wanted her to place him accurately, he should have put on a clean sports jacket and cord trousers before coming to the door.

She managed a half-shrug, a kink at the side of her mouth, to indicate confusion, but said nothing more. Bonzo, the older labrador, lost interest and trudged heavily back into the house, head and tail slung low.

'I thought I should come and say we're just over there if you need anything,' the farmer blurted. 'I expect you'll be all right – those daft sheep have all lambed by now, and been wormed. But one thing I need to tell you is that the shearer's coming on the 10th, and it's usual for the Reynoldses to send theirs over to be done at the same time. Did they mention that?'

The 10th of May seemed a long way off, and Thea filed it in a deep mental recess. She was still struggling with the man's accent.

'Not that I recall,' she answered to his question. 'It might be in the notes.'

'Well, you won't have to do anything much. We'll come and fetch them, and bring them back again for you. Clive must have taken us for granted, as usual.'

Thea said nothing. Hepzibah had pottered off across the sweeping lawn, and Thea rather fancied going with her on a detailed exploration.

'Well, milking time,' said Farmer Jennison. 'Just thought I'd show my face. You're welcome to come over for a cup of tea any time. My old dad lives with me, and he always likes a visitor. Best time is just after dinner. Two-ish.'

Thea's confusion deepened. He was shy, she realised. And single. And motherless. And busy. And against the docking of spaniels' tails. 'That's really nice of you,' she said. 'Thank you very much. Let me get sorted out here for a few days, and maybe I'll take you up on the offer sometime in the middle of the week. Should I have your phone number? Then I can call and make sure it isn't a nuisance for you.'

He laughed. 'Don't do that. Just take pot luck. Bye, then.'

She watched him go, his walk unself-conscious in the cracked old boots. She wondered whether she would recognise him if she ever met him in Cheltenham, dressed in a suit and tie.

She didn't go back into the house, but followed Hepzie's paw-steps over the lawn. Her instinctive eye for the history of a place revealed that the garden was not in fact of any great antiquity. Despite the beech trees, which were perhaps fifty years old, there was ample evidence that this garden had not long ago been part of a field. A lot of stonework and fencing had transformed it into classic rural grounds, closely resembling something from a television gardening programme. All the basic rules had been observed: frame the distant view; bring everything together with careful design; aim for variations in height to maintain interest. There were seats, pathways, pleasing curves and a riot of different botanical textures. The pond had a trickling water feature over artistically arranged rocks, which provided a constant background noise that Thea expected she would quickly grow accustomed to. *We leave it on night and day*, Clive had told her. *Jennifer's very insistent about that*. He hadn't even shown her where the switch was to turn it off.

The only surprise was in the generous size of the lawn. Lawns were not fashionable these days, and there was no suggestion that the Reynoldeses had a number of ball-game-playing teenage sons.

A wide five-barred wooden gate opened into the field containing the sheep, but this was not the favoured access. 'We hardly ever use this one,' Clive had said. Another similar gate led from the gravelled yard on the other side of the house. It was through this portal that Thea was to approach the sheep. A small barn stood close by, in which their winter fodder was stored.

Clive had given extra verbal orders regarding gates and dogs. 'We prefer the dogs not to go into the field together. There's always a risk that they'll run off and get into trouble with neighbouring farmers.

'This time of year everybody's very sensitive about lambs, and you can never completely trust two dogs out on their own.' The written notes just said *Exercise B. and G. in garden. Walks at your discretion, on leads.*

There had not, however, been any outright ban on using the garden gate, and Thea did so now, though minus the labradors. She and her own dog took a short stroll that way, admiring the bluebells growing in the copse on the other side of the brook, and listening to the piping song of a solitary starling perched in an alder. There was a buzzard mewing a field or two away. Everything seemed peaceful, the air mild and sweet-scented.

'We're going to like it here,' Thea told the spaniel.

Chapter Two

A page of instructions dealt with procedures for the end of the day. Check all electrical items unplugged was typical. Surely, Thea thought, nobody did that these days? There were circuit-breakers and fail-safe systems, which meant the house was protected against lightning strikes, or whatever it was Clive Reynolds was afraid of. Sitting at the kitchen table, the list in her hand, she came to a decision. She would not unplug everything unless there was reason to expect a thunderstorm.

Make sure the road gate is closed and fastened. Test security lights when it gets dark. Bring flower tubs into conservatory if frost is forecast. Clearly she was going to have to pay close attention to the weather forecast every evening.

The list was unflagging. *Check that the sheds are both locked. Watch the dogs when you put them out, and be sure they've passed water. Close and fasten all downstairs windows.* Only downstairs? How very sloppy. And there was much, much more.

It all made her feel weak and irritated. Until then, she hadn't thought of herself as idle or careless, but compared to Clive Reynolds she was a total slob. She had done almost none of these things before leaving her own house for three whole weeks. Well, she resolved, she was in charge now, and as long as everything was intact when their owners returned, they would never know how she'd achieved it. For a start, she had no intention of checking the stupid security lights.

Even in a pruned form, the tasks took forty minutes. She missed the weather after the news on television, but a glance at the sky reassured her that there would be neither frost nor lightning. The dogs slumped uncomplainingly into their big plastic beds, lined with very clean blankets (*Wash the dogs' bedding every third day*) and showed no sign of missing their people. Hepzibah watched Thea closely for clues as to her night-time fate. Sleeping on the bed was her most favoured option, but she would, if necessary, settle for a nest on the floor close by. Thea had carefully sidestepped the issue when granted permission to bring her own dog, and the Reynoldses had mercifully neglected to mention it. 'As you've been such a good dog, I think we'll smuggle you onto the bed,' she said. 'So long as you stay on your blanket.'

The bed was comfortably soft, the room situated at the back of the house, on a corner, was neutrally furnished and decorated, with two casement windows overlooking the back garden and field. Before settling down, Thea threw one of the windows wide open, wondering whether the rising sun would waken her. As far as she could work out, it faced roughly north-eastwards. At least there should be a fine dawn chorus, with so many places close by for birds to perch

24

and sing. As she leant for a moment on the sill, she was very conscious of the water feature in the corner of the garden. The trickling waterfall, powered by electric pump, sounded loud in the still of the night. Thea worried that it might keep her awake, but her fears were unfounded. She dropped off within five minutes of switching out the light.

Three distinct things woke her in the night. Firstly there was the recurrent throb of her finger. Before going to bed, she had probed it again, with a needle she'd brought with her in a small emergency sewing kit. Afterwards it was quite a lot more painful. In the night, with no distractions, it hurt more than ever. She indulged in a few habitual thoughts of Carl, who was dead. Forgetting Carl was not an option; neither was letting the anguish of losing him fade. Carl, who had been her mate, her comfort, her unquestioned permanent partner. Big and gentle and good and wise. The universe had never quite recovered from his loss. Secondly, Hepzie stirred two or three times, changing position, and pressing more closely against Thea, through the duvet. Giving the dog her own blanket, on top of the duvet, had been a mistake. It made Thea too hot. So she sat up and extracted it, throwing it on the floor. 'We can wash the duvet cover,' she said. 'Which we'd have to do anyway, I suppose.'

Thirdly, there was the scream from outside. A sudden rising human-sounding scream, so startling and incongruous that Thea could not quite believe she'd heard it, through the layers of sleep. She'd been dreaming about sheep, and a sudden surge of water and a gate that wouldn't open. Downstairs, the labradors did not bark. Thea switched on the lamp beside the bed. Outside, after that single wrenching sound, there was silence, except for the constant splashy trickle of the garden waterfall. Hepzibah jumped off the bed and went to the window, standing on her hind legs, but still not tall enough to see out. She squeaked anxiously, but showed no sign of being able to hear or smell anything significant. Thea did not leap out of bed. She didn't get up at all. She gazed at the open window, seeing nothing outside but dark grey sky, and re-ran the sound in her head, trying to persuade herself that it had been made by a rabbit or a bird. Her own semi-rural cottage was not immune to night-time slaughter, or the mating calls of foxes.

They could often be quite alarming.

But this had been different. This had penetrated more deeply, freezing her with fear. It had been something awful, unearthly. She should get up and do something about it. Even if she'd lived in the middle of cacophonous night-time Manhattan, she'd have surely felt compelled to investigate a sound like that.

So why didn't she at least lean out of the window and see if there was any suspicious movement? Or phone the police. Or send the dogs out to sniff around. Somebody out there was in severe distress. Probably in the field left under her charge. She was being paid to act responsibly and ensure that all was well.

But there had been no further sound, apart from odd rustles and the burble of the water feature at the end of the garden. She had been asleep and might easily have mistaken some innocent wild animal for a human being. Perhaps, even, there was a local person of reduced capabilities, given to wandering at night and screaming. To make an outcry would be embarrassing, if this was so. There must be other houses and farms within earshot, anyway. Let somebody local take control.

The time was three forty-five. The dead of night. Outdoors at such a time was an alien place. Whatever might be going on out there was part of a different sphere of existence. Besides, she'd obediently locked and barred the doors, set the burglar alarm, bedded the dogs – to try to unpick all that would probably trigger the alarm and lead to further humiliation. And besides again, the security lights hadn't gone on. That clinched it. No burglar. Nothing untoward creeping up to the house – even foxes generally triggered the damned things.

Finally, and selfishly, she concluded that she was safe and snug where she was. Whatever might have happened out there had happened, and by now there would probably be little help for it. Nobody was shouting for help, or screaming with pain. It had surely been an animal. Rabbits could shriek their heads off as the fox grabbed them. There might be badgers fighting amongst themselves, or one of the buzzards catching a shrew or some other protesting prey. It could, she concluded, be almost anything.

So she invited the spaniel to jump back onto the bed, pulled up the duvet and quite quickly went back to sleep.

It wasn't so much that she forgot the events of the small hours when she woke at seven thirty – it was more that she had so many tasks to perform that there wasn't time to think about it.

Open front gate for postman. Make sure dogs go out, and reward them afterwards with small biscuit (top shelf, left hand cupboard – tin labelled MARKIES*). If dry, open windows. Thursdays, leave £10 in tin box to the right of the front door for the Veggie Box people. Outside, check sheep for problems. If sunny, open greenhouse vents.* And so forth.

However, by nine thirty, she had counted the sheep from the yard gate, since they were obligingly scattered over the upper part of the field; persuaded the unenthusiastic labradors to make a tour of the garden, and ticked off six further items on the list. For the moment, there seemed to be nothing more to do. She had the rest of the morning to herself.

The day being dry, the obvious choice was to walk down the hill to the village. There was a public footpath covering the half-mile or so between Brook View and the centre of Duntisbourne Abbots, which Thea found to be maintained to near National Trust standards, as soon as she climbed the stile on the other side of the road from Brook View's front gate. The walk took a leisurely fifteen minutes, Hepzibah running cheerfully along before her.

The village buildings on the whole were modest in size, giving the sense of an old settlement surrounded by fertile hillsides. Every roadway leading to the village centre was steep and twisting, with no clear vistas. Most of the houses escaped being overlooked by any of the others, producing a sense of solitude and secrecy that felt strange in the middle of a village. The morning was cool and cloudy and the only sign of life was the aural evidence of a Sunday service going on inside the church. The organ played and snatches of thin human voices drifted through the air. Four or five cars were parked near the lychgate, suggesting an influx of churchgoers from the surrounding countryside.

The church itself – a broader building than the usual simple design – boasted an inviting graveyard, surrounded by stone cottages; a bigger house looked down from a slight elevation, and the roadsides were already getting shaggy with spring growth.

Fastening a lead to Hepzie's collar, Thea walked past the church and along a road that could possibly claim to be the main village street, wondering whether she was going to encounter any inhabitants. A door banged shut somewhere, and a baby cried briefly. A dog barked and a car approached. Still there was no sign of a human being, no pub or shop or post office. The village hall was a small old stone structure, which could well have been a tiny local school originally. The whole place was beautiful, timeless and secretive. A well known name on the tourist circuit, featured on toffee tins and jigsaws, epitomising rural England, it seemed to be turning its back firmly on Thea's intrusion. With a sense of desolation, she turned round and started back the way she'd come. At least Joel Jennison had welcomed her, she consoled herself.

On the path, about halfway along, she encountered a young couple, and found herself staring eagerly at their faces. They seemed to be about twenty, a boy and a girl, walking side by side, but not touching. Both were taller than average, and thin, but not alike in any other ways. The girl had light brown hair, round shoulders and blemished skin. The boy's eyes were sunken, his cheeks hollow. Neither appeared to enjoy a healthy diet or much fresh air.

'Morning,' said Thea, and Hepzie ran up to them, performing her usual ecstatic wagging dance around them. The boy bent down to pat her, but the girl shrank away.

'Hi,' muttered the boy. The girl said nothing. Thea was past them before she had a chance to say more, besides which they had not appeared to be in a talkative frame of mind.

A shadow seemed to attach itself to her, as a result of the encounter. Her own daughter was of a similar age to this couple, which perhaps made her all the more interested in them. But none of her daughter's friends had this look of sickness about them; this air of debility. Perhaps there was some sort of convalescent home close by, or even a hospice. She wondered, uneasily, whether the pair had AIDS.

By a predictable chain of reasoning, her mind returned to the scream in the night. It was disgracefully remiss of her not to have gone out and investigated it, at first light if not when she heard it. She ought to do a careful circuit of the Reynoldses' acres, just in case something lay dying on a fence or in a gin trap, or . . . or what? She could imagine nothing that would continue to cause genuine concern by daylight. Whatever it was would have long ago disappeared from sight. All the same, if she made her patrol, and found nothing, she would know not to worry if the same thing happened again. Just another night-time noise, she'd be able to tell herself comfortably.

Thea was not a nervous person. On a practical level she had found several positive aspects to living alone. The logic was simple: If I can survive Carl's dying, then I must be able to survive anything was the gist of it. She worried about the inevitable day when Hepzibah would die – but in the nature of things that was ten or more years off, and easily deferred as a cause of concern. She trembled for the safety of her daughter, now and then, but Jessica was robust and never seemed to get into serious difficulties. A final year student at Durham, she already had a job to go to in September – fast tracking up the ladder of the Police Force, earnestly encouraged by her delighted uncle. Then, Thea suspected, the worries would really begin.

She did not fear for her own safety. Forty-two might not be any age these days but she believed the best was already behind her. Nothing could ever be as carefree and contented as the years with Carl had been, even if she hadn't quite understood that at the time. Now there wasn't much left to lose, and if she could finish each day with a small mental sigh of satisfaction, that was the best she could ask of life.

The Reynoldses' field was about nine acres in area, the garden almost another acre. There was dense hedge around three sides of the property, and somewhat scrubby woodland adjacent to the fourth, which marked the eastern boundary. This woodland lay the other side of the brook, which in places cut a ravine at least ten feet deep. A sturdy fence barred the way to any man or beast bold enough to scramble down into the brook and up the other side. 'The locals call this a dingle,' Clive Reynolds had said. 'But I think that's over-stating the case, myself.'

Dingle or not, it was pretty, with trees growing down to the water's edge. In a corner of the field the ground flattened out, offering Clive the opportunity to create the small pool he'd shown Thea the day before. Wild violets and bluebells grew vigorously in the hedgerows, along with white blossoms on blackthorn bushes.

Thea walked slowly down the wooded side, peering into the brook from time to time. Hepzibah zig-zagged across the field, following multifarious scents, enjoying the freedom. They had left the unambitious labradors in the garden, as Clive Reynolds had ordained. 'They're not too keen on long walks,' he'd said. 'Just leave them to potter about round the house and garden.'

The clouds had lifted and thinned, giving way to a gauzy covering that allowed warmer air through. Birds sang.

She reached the corner, where the watering hole was. The sheep clearly didn't use it much, as there were few footprints in the soft ground. Only the imprint of two human feet were visible, aligned neatly side by side and parallel. 'Must be where Clive stood yesterday, when he showed me around,' she muttered, somehow not quite believing it. She didn't think they had gone so close to the water – and if those were Clive's footprints, then where were her own?

It seemed almost an answer to her question when something bobbed in the water a few feet away that, when she looked, turned out to be the sole of a Wellington boot. How uncharacteristically untidy, she thought, before taking a closer look.

The boot was not upended, but lying nearly horizontal in the water. A lateral-growing bramble obscured her view, and she moved sideways to see better. There was something else sticking out of the water, a couple of feet away from the boot. Something brown and sodden.

The whole picture hit her in a rush. Once recognised,

it burnt itself into her mind, like a brand. It was a human body, half submerged in the pool, wearing boots, and with the cloth-covered buttocks partly out of the water. The torso was wedged under another lateral bush, impeding the flow of the brook as it came down the side of the field. The head was invisible, the water opaque. Everything was in shadow, with a large ivy-covered tree cutting out the light. Thea stepped into the pool, intending to drag the thing out, but, feeling her boots sink into soft mud and finding the body far too heavy, she panicked. Water came over the tops of her boots, she slithered helplessly, and ended up sitting beside the body in twelve inches of very cold water.

Frantically she pushed herself backwards onto the comparative security of the not quite so muddy field. Where was the dog?

Useless thing – shouldn't it have known there was a dead body here, just by its sense of smell?

She sat there for a moment, wiping her hands on the scanty grass, trying to think. It was a man, drowned in the little pool. He hadn't been there yesterday, and it was unthinkable that he had got there by accident. It had, she decided with some reluctance, almost certainly been his dying scream she had heard in the night, and failed utterly to respond to.

Her clothes stuck to her disgustingly when she stood up and tried to run back to the house. Her feet squelched in the water-logged boots. The dog ran round her, thinking it was a game. The back door was still locked, so she had to circle the house and go in through the front, left irresponsibly on the latch. For a moment, she had no idea where the telephone was. The hall was quite narrow and L-shaped. Kitchen, living room, dining room and study all opened from it. After a few seconds' thought, Thea moved heavily to the study, leaving wet footprints and muddy drips on the beige carpet. In the study, on a very nice antique desk, sat a telephone, which also served as a fax machine. She remembered, belatedly, that there was also a normal instrument attached to the wall in the kitchen.

No time to change her mind, she decided, simultaneously aware that time no longer mattered to the body in the pool.

Chapter Three

The police – two male uniformed officers – asked her to show them the body, and whether she had any idea what had happened, or who the man was, as they stood on the edge of the pool assessing the situation. Nobody moved to lift the body clear, once it was established that there was no prospect of saving his life. 'Didn't you try to lift his head free?' one of them asked Thea.

'No,' she admitted. 'He was obviously dead already, and I couldn't get a proper foothold. He seems very tightly wedged under there.'

'Do you know who it is?'

'No, of course not. His face is under water. I'm a stranger here. I don't know anybody.' Her voice was rising, and she was still in her wet clothes.

'Hmm,' they said.

'I'm afraid I've messed up a piece of evidence,' she confessed, looking at the ground. 'There were footprints here, but I think I sat on them.'

'Probably belonging to the deceased,' one man said.

'Mmmm.' Thea tried to offload the niggles she felt about the matter. If the police weren't bothered, then why should she be? But she couldn't resist a close examination of the pool's edge, which only confirmed that she had indeed obliterated the marks she had seen in the mud.

'Well, leave it to us, Madam,' she was dismissed. 'We'll come and talk to you later. You go and get yourself into some dry clothes. But keep the ones you're wearing to one side, if you don't mind. We might want to examine them.'

Thea shivered. Did they think she'd drowned the wretched man?

They let her walk unaccompanied back to the house, speaking urgently into their phones, waving their arms about, and gingerly stepping into the pool. The sheep watched from the top end of the field, and Hepzibah ran sniffing to and fro until Thea called her in.

Vehicles began to arrive, and Thea was required to direct them before getting a chance to change her clothes. They drove through the gate from the yard into the field, having got out to test the feasibility of this. 'You might not be able to get all the way,' Thea warned them. 'It's rather soft at the bottom. And can you keep the gate closed? The sheep'll escape otherwise.' She wondered whether she ought to try to pen the animals into a shed or barn, out of the way, but when no objections were made to her orders concerning the gate, she abandoned the idea.

From the house, she could not see much. She assumed they were examining the whole surrounding area before removing the body from the pool. They seemed to take hours over it, and Thea was dismayed at the mess they were making of Clive Reynolds' field.

36

And not just the field. After a time, men in white coveralls started crawling over the garden, too. Thea felt invaded and powerless. It was like a scene from a film, the uniforms sinister and inhuman. People who dressed like that became robotic, following orders and trampling sensibilities. They might seize her dog, wreck Jennifer's borders, or accuse her of cold-blooded murder.

She didn't quite know why she did it, but something prompted her to seek out the switch for the water pump, in the utility room at the back of the house. The noise of the constant running water had irritated her earlier in the day when she exercised the dogs, and somehow she assumed it would interrupt and distract the search for clues. She found a likely-looking switch, in the on position, and reversed it. Then she went to the front door to listen. All was blessedly quiet. It occurred to her that she might enjoy better quality sleep if she left it off for the duration of her stay.

Neighbours materialised – if *neighbours* was the right word. Only three other dwellings were closer in proximity than half a mile, and yet there were soon nine or ten people gathered in the road outside Brook View's wide-open gate. Most of them seemed to have come on foot. Thea, finally changed into clean trousers and a fleecy sweatshirt, stood uncomfortably on the gravel near the front door and foolishly scanned the crowd for a familiar face, feeling at bay.

The stares directed at her did not look friendly. Nobody tried to speak to her. They seemed content to wait out there until the facts of the matter became apparent. Nobody ventured through the gate, or showed any signs of impatience.

It gradually dawned on Thea that their behaviour was

strange. Why were they not more curious? More surprised? It was as if they'd slipped into a routine that had taken place before. They knew already how to behave. She could almost believe she heard the word *again* muttered amongst them. It wasn't absolutely obvious what was going on in the Brook View field, but Thea supposed that anybody could have made a pretty good stab at guessing. Four vehicles had grouped together towards the end of the field, invisible from the road. Another arrived as the people stood there – a Renault Espace, containing two men in suits. Thea waited for them to turn in through the gate, and bent down to speak to the driver.

'They're down there,' she pointed. 'I'll open the gate for you.'

That done, she walked down to the front gate. 'Hello,' she said, addressing a middle-aged woman wearing a Barbour jacket. 'I'm Thea Osborne. I'm house-sitting for the Reynoldses. I hadn't bargained for anything like this.' And she forced a silly laugh.

'Like what?' said the woman.

'Well – somebody's died down there.'

Another woman snorted. 'Course they did. That's the undertaker's van, come to remove the corpse.'

'Looks as if he drowned,' said Thea, wondering if it mattered what she said, but too anxious to make human contact to care.

Nobody responded to that, apart from a gentle collective sigh that seemed to pass through the group like a melancholy breeze.

'We know who you are, anyway,' said the first woman.

'Clive told us you'd be here.' She didn't meet Thea's eye, but fixed her gaze on the yard and the field beyond. Thea felt sidelined.

'I suppose we'll have to contact them. They'll be on their ship by now, probably. I've got all the numbers and everything.'

'You leave them,' said a younger man with dark curly hair and a London accent. 'They've deserved this holiday. No use bringing them back.'

'It won't be up to us, Martin,' the Barbour woman said. 'It'll be completely out of our hands. Clive and Jennifer were here until yesterday, so the police probably will want to speak to them.'

Thea didn't like the sound of this. 'Oh, I can settle that,' she blurted. 'I mean – I know there was nothing in the pool yesterday, just before the Reynoldses left. Anyway,' she announced without thinking, 'I *heard* it happen. In the night.' Too late, she realised her folly. The briefly gratifying flare of attention from everybody within earshot was followed by acute self-reproach. The scream in the night was bound to be vital information, best confined to the ears of the police. Had one of these people been responsible for the death? Was she endangering herself by her careless honesty? Anything seemed possible at this juncture. She forced a giggle. 'At least, I *thought* I did,' she added.

Another silence met this shift of position, and she scanned the group, registering each face in turn, still hoping for some sign of friendship or concern. She found a pleasant-looking older man, sporting a grey beard; a woman standing close to the man previously addressed as Martin, who seemed impatient, clapping her hands together; a tall younger woman with a woolly hat pulled down low over hair that was apparently bright red; two further middle-aged women with old-fashioned perms and handbags; a teenaged boy leaning on a bicycle; and a pale-faced girl of about twenty, who frowned her bewilderment at being involved in such strange events.

The bearded man approached the girl, and put a gentle hand on her arm. 'Monique – you shouldn't be here. Martin, take her back.'

'Hang on a bit, Harry,' said the Londoner. 'I want to hear what's been going on. Susanna can do it, if she's going in a minute. Monique's all right, anyhow.'

The young woman with the woolly hat turned her head slowly to give Martin a thoughtful look. 'Fine by me,' she nodded. 'I've seen enough here.' She held out a hand to usher the girl away, pausing to nod at the Barbour-jacketed woman.

'Thanks,' Martin said. Then he added, 'Paolo's probably up by now – he'll watch out for her.'

The woman beside him drew closer, as if needing some comfort. Without looking at her, he threw an arm around her shoulder. Thea noted this public display of couplehood, in her efforts to fix the whole group in her memory. There were some moments of silence, during which the boy on the bike gave up the vigil and set off down the lane with a few preliminary wobbles. 'Careful, Johnny!' called one of the handbag ladies.

The bearded man swung his arms a few times, and then said to the group in general, 'I think I'll be off, if that's all right?'

Nobody answered, and he walked away, presumably to a car parked out of sight.

Mumbling some excuse about the dogs, Thea retreated to the house, and paced the hall, biting at her damaged finger. She had no idea what would happen next: would she be sent home almost before the job had begun? Would she have to make a statement at the police station? Could she have saved the man if she'd gone rushing out in the night, when she heard that dreadful scream?

It seemed an age before the procession of vehicles began to leave the field, presumably conveying the body to the mortuary, and the scraps of evidence, photographs, observations all packed up for forensic analysis. She went outside again, to watch them go, noting that all but three of the onlookers had dispersed. Two uniformed officers were walking across the gravel towards her. Time at last for her interview, she guessed.

Before escorting the policemen into the house, Thea saw the man called Martin step forward to obstruct the passage of one of the police cars. He bent down to speak to the driver through the window. 'Can you tell us who it was?' he asked, speaking loudly as if his was the voice of the whole assembled throng.

'Looks like Joel,' came the reply. 'Have to get identification, of course. But it's no secret – Joel Jennison's gone and got himself killed.'

Thea felt ridiculously upset. The only person to have spoken to her since she arrived, and he had to go and die on her. She took it personally; all the more so because she had lain there in bed, ignoring his scream while he was dying. She was criminally at fault, and everybody in the village would know it, thanks to her thoughtless remark. With a sensation of confessing to a piece of culpable negligence, she told the story to the policemen.

'And what time would this have been?' asked one.

'Three forty-five,' she said. 'Or a few minutes before that.'

'You were afraid to go and see what had made the noise, is that right?'

She hesitated. How simple it would be just to agree with this explanation. Women were cowards, everybody knew that. Nobody would blame her for cowering nervously under the bedclothes, in a strange house, all alone.

'Not really,' she said. 'It was more that I didn't think I'd find anything. And, quite frankly, I doubt if I would have gone right to the corner of the field in the pitch dark. I don't know the layout properly, and would really not have known where to look. But now, of course, I wish I had.' She smiled wanly at them. 'Poor man.'

'You didn't know him, I take it?'

'Well, funnily enough, he came to see me yesterday. He's the only person locally who I had met. He seemed very pleasant.'

'He came to see you?'

'Yes. Five minutes after the Reynoldses left. He was just being friendly, introducing himself.' She sighed. 'I feel as if I've walked into something very unpleasant.'

'More than you know,' agreed the policeman who'd done most of the talking, earning himself a tap on the wrist from his colleague and a frowned instruction to hold his tongue.

'He didn't drown himself, did he?' Thea ventured. 'Not if that scream was really him. Somebody pushed him in and held him down in the water. Horrible.' She shuddered.

'We can't say,' said the quieter policeman. 'Now, would you give us the contact numbers for Mr and Mrs Reynolds, please.'

'Are you going to bring them home?' She didn't know whether she wanted a yes or a no to that. It would be frustrating to be sent packing now, leaving everything in such turmoil, forever wondering exactly what had happened and why. On the other hand, she couldn't pretend to like Brook View and its environs very much, on first impressions. It seemed cold and strange. And a sudden death during her first night was hardly an auspicious beginning.

'That won't be up to us,' he said.

Thea watched them leave, and then went into the house. One vehicle remained, and white-coated officers still moved like ghosts around the garden and field, scanning the ground at their feet. The sky had grown cloudy and she was alarmed to discover that it was already half past two. She must have missed any number of instructions since the morning. If nothing else, she was supposed to take the labradors for a stroll to the end of the garden and back. *If interested, you might throw them a ball or a stick*. Whose interest, she wondered, was hypothecated? Hers or the dogs'?

She was also hungry. Plans to make herself a good lunch of ham and salad, ready provided in the Reynoldses' fridge, went by the board. Instead she cut two slices of bread and made a ham sandwich, eating it standing up, restlessly moving around the kitchen.

Could the local people really be as unwelcoming as they seemed? Were they perhaps merely stunned and concerned by what had happened? Could be if she made the first approach, things would be different. What had Clive said? *Do go and call on Helen*, he'd suggested with a wave towards the top of the hill. Right, then. That's exactly what she would do.

Helen, it turned out, lived on a very tidy little farm with four large horses in the roadside field. They looked like Arabs to Thea's uncertain eye. She walked up the drive with Hepzie on the lead and admired the property before her.

The house was at the yellower end of the Cotswold spectrum, with a pale grey tiled roof and three proud dormer windows, leading Thea to visualise the attic rooms inside, no doubt of interesting shapes, the ceiling sloping down to the low window. Such rooms were the stuff of children's stories, the windowsills often at the exact height for a child to curl up comfortably and look out on the world. There was something old fashioned and safe and magical about Helen's house. There had been no name on the gate, nor any she could see attached to the house. No need, she assumed. Everybody would know it without a label.

A sturdy porch shielded the front door, and a low stone wall separated the small front garden from the farmyard. Aubretia was just coming into flower along the top of the wall, and an ancient stone trough was filled with tulips and hyacinths almost at the end of their blooming.

A casual inspection would conclude that this was a house at least two hundred years old, on a working farm, unchanged for generations. A closer look would reveal the absence of muck and mud; the manicured garden; the large new Subaru parked in the open end of a barn where a tractor ought to be. This place had been gentrified, with a vengeance. No milking cows or pigs or noisy roosters here. Just very expensive horses, perhaps some undemanding sheep and a few distant fields rented out for pasture. The man of the house probably worked as a software consultant, the woman, if she worked at all, would be a designer of some sort.

Thea blinked rapidly, thinking herself into the appropriate frame of mind to deal with the people she expected to encounter. Then she activated the clanger of the large bell suspended from the porch. It made a pleasingly loud noise.

A woman opened the door, instantly identified as the one with the Barbour jacket in the road outside Brook View's gate earlier in the day. 'Oh!' said Thea. 'It's you!'

The woman smiled, a genuine friendly smile, and held out her hand. 'Helen Winstanley,' she said. 'Do come in. And bring that dear little dog.'

Chapter Four

The lounge appeared to be newly decorated in a calming dove grey with pink woodwork. The Chinese carpet was blue and grey and white. The furniture was shiny and did not look very comfortable. 'Try this one,' said Helen Winstanley, patting an armchair. 'It's better than it looks.' She didn't even glance at Hepzibah, as the spaniel crossed the expensive carpet and flopped down on a pristine sheepskin rug in front of the empty grate.

'Tea?' she asked in the next breath. Thea thanked her, wondering whether a maid would bring it. It was the sort of lounge that would be nicely set off by a maid.

Instead, the woman disappeared, saying she wouldn't be long. Thea remained in the chair, feeling no compulsion to explore or even to read the spines of a shelf of books beside the fireplace. She was much too weary and emotional for that.

It was the smile that did it, she decided. Until then, she'd been braced for a cool reception, rehearsing how she would explain herself. The amicable manner of her temporary neighbour had disarmed her, and suddenly the events of the day caught up with her.

'So, you must be feeling you got more than you bargained for,' Helen said, having returned with a tea tray and poured out two cups. 'It must be utterly bewildering.'

'Unreal,' Thea admitted.

'Somebody's been very clever with the timing, that's for sure.' When Thea didn't immediately answer, Helen gave her a straight look. 'Don't you think?' she prompted.

'That poor man. He seemed really nice.'

'You met him?' The question came fast and sharp, as if a different person had spoken.

'Yesterday. He knocked on the door only a few minutes after the Reynoldses left. Came to introduce himself, he said.'

'Did he indeed?' Helen proffered a cup of tea, and as Thea went to take it with her left hand, she accidentally stubbed her sore finger on the saucer. 'Ooh!' she moaned, snatching it back. Her hostess almost dropped the whole thing.

'What's the matter?'

'My finger.'

'Let's see.' The woman took Thea's hand without further permission. A pair of spectacles dangled round her neck on a gold chain, and she fitted them onto her nose before examining the finger. 'It's right in the nailbed,' she said. 'I can see something black. Look – there's something in it.'

Thea pulled away, but didn't break the connection entirely. 'I don't think there is,' she said. 'That's where I stuck a needle down it. It's left that mark.'

The air seemed to grow colder around them. Helen tightened her hold on Thea's hand. 'That's a new one,' she said. 'Inventive.'

Thea smiled. 'What is it with you, then?'

'Feet, mainly. Stones in shoes.'

Thea gave a sympathetic moan. 'What happened?'

Helen shrugged. 'Daughter. Drugs. In and out of our lives, never knowing what to expect next.' Thea could feel the tears gathering, the throat thickening.

'My God.'

'And you?'

'Husband. Died a year ago. It's getting a bit better. I suppose.'

Mutually, they agreed to leave it there. After all, the whole point of hurting yourself was to distract from the deeper pain. If you talked about it, that negated the exercise. The surprise was in finding a fellow sufferer so easily. Thea had not expected that.

'Clive Reynolds suggested I come to see you,' she said. 'I'd never have known anybody lived up here otherwise.'

'He wanted me to do what you're doing. I nearly said I would, until I began to realise just what was involved. I hope he's paying you well – it can't be easy.'

'It's all right. Or would have been without a body in the brook. You came down to see,' she almost accused.

'That's right, I did. Virginia in the village phoned me, and said something was going on. I think she phoned most of the people who were there.'

'Why?'

'It's the sort of thing she'd do. Makes her feel important, I guess.'

Thea reminded herself that this was a small village, where the fate of one of its inhabitants impacted significantly on everybody else.

'Can you tell me who all the people were?' she asked. 'I've got their faces etched on my mind.'

'Why bother? You won't see many of them again.'

'I might. And I'm curious. The nice-looking man with the beard, for instance.'

'Harry. He's a widower.' Helen seemed to have a sudden thought. 'I should phone him. He'd gone before they said it was Joel, hadn't he?'

'Yes, I think so. Why do you need to phone him?'

'He's Joel's uncle. I ought to be sure he knows.'

'He didn't suspect, then?'

'Probably he did, yes. Nobody said anything, but I guess we all knew who it was likely to be.'

Thea felt giddy with the threads of local history that she couldn't hope to grasp. 'Well, just tell me who the others were. The two women with the perms?'

'Virginia and Penny. They're neighbours. Stalwarts of the village; WI, Parish Council, that sort of thing. They run the gossip network.'

Thea moved to the front window. 'Hence the phonecall, I presume. Can you see Brook View from here?'

'Not quite. But I can see a stretch of road, look, just beyond the house.'

'The girl with the woolly hat?'

'Susanna. She probably came with Martin and Isabel. She works at their place on a Sunday, quite often.'

'Monique?'

Helen's face closed, as if swept by a thick curtain. 'Just a foreign student. Staying with the Staceys.'

'The Staceys being Martin and Isabel? The chap with the London accent?'

'Right. They're your next neighbours down the road. Fairweather Farm.'

'That's everybody then, I think. Except the boy on the bike.'

'Johnny Baker. I doubt if you'll see him again, either. He's Virginia's boy, actually. Her youngest.'

'Goodness. She looked too old.'

'She's younger than she looks. About fifty-five, I suppose. Johnny's fourteen.'

Thea shrugged, accepting that the family histories of the villagers would never really matter to her. 'Well, thanks for explaining,' she said.

'It must be strange, walking into something like this. Aren't you scared?' Helen examined her with blatant curiosity.

'Not really. Put it down to lack of imagination.'

Turning the conversation to Helen, Thea discovered that James Winstanley was away, appearing as Guest Speaker at a Conference in Beijing. 'Something to do with the internet,' she added, confirming Thea's original guess as to his line of work.

'When did he leave?' Thea asked, aiming for casual interest, rather than a clumsy attempt at establishing the man's alibi. After all, the police were presumably going to be asking the same thing.

Helen was not deceived. 'He actually left quite late yesterday. His flight was supposed to go at eight this morning, so he spent the night in a hotel near the airport. And yes, I spoke to him last night and everything was going according to plan.'

'You don't know if the flight took off on time then?'

Helen cocked her head slightly to one side. 'I don't keep close tabs on him. He travels all the time. I lose track of where he's meant to be.'

Helen's own work, when she described it, sounded equally irregular and unpredictable. 'Oh, I do all sorts of things,' she said, with an airy flip of the hand. 'Never did decide what I wanted to be when I grew up.'

She freely disclosed that she and James had lived in this house for eight years. Their daughter had been eleven, and due to start secondary school. Thea was tempted to ask more about the unnamed daughter, but was somehow diverted to her own Jessica, of whom she indulged in some boasting.

'And you like it here, do you?' she asked, after a short lull.

'Love it. Honestly – it suits me perfectly. I always felt embarrassed at having money while still being a bit unambitious in my tastes.'

Thea gave a snort, half sceptical, half sympathetic. 'That's not how most people would regard living here.'

Helen grimaced. 'That's probably true. I blame the City fatcats and their seven-figure bonuses. They're wrecking it for everybody else, buying five-bedroom country cottages and only coming down one weekend a month, to make sure the security systems are working. I'm here full-time, I haven't got a security system worth the name, and I don't shop in supermarkets.'

'You're a freak,' Thea laughed, sensing they were creeping closer to the real reason for Helen living where she did. Not the friendly people or the Cotswold stone, but the essential Englishness of the area, was what appealed. There were few places left that could claim the same amalgam of unself-conscious qualities which went back to Roman times and had not changed much since. Thea herself could recognise it when she saw it, but would have been hard pressed to articulate it. Something stoical and judgmental of perceived weakness in others; values which placed a premium on ancient skills such as stonework and preparing good food. An automatic respect for the law, which was provoked to rage when these laws were manifestly unjust. People who felt most comfortable with a strong leader, and who became insecure when expected to work out their own destinies.

'Are you very friendly with the Reynoldses?'

'Not terribly. They don't socialise particularly. You could say we share a basic outlook on life, I suppose. But I can tell you that they won't be too keen to come home early. Jennifer's been looking forward to this trip for more than a year. She takes it as her hard-earned compensation for a very gruelling time.'

'Oh?'

'Well, it can't hurt to tell you, I suppose. You're not likely to gossip, are you? You see, Clive had been having an affair with some woman he worked with, apparently for ages and ages. Jennifer never suspected anything – didn't want to see what was under her nose, probably. Then it all blew up, around Easter last year, and she had a breakdown. It was quite dramatic: she went wandering round the lanes at night, sobbing and swearing. She came all the way up here, more than once. Totally out of her mind, for a bit, poor thing.'

'Another one for the club, then,' Thea murmured, hardly aware that she'd spoken out loud.

'You might say that,' Helen nodded quickly. 'Anyway, Clive got her into some smart psychiatric place, dropped the other woman, and became Jennifer's abject slave.'

'Did that work?' Thea was sceptical. 'Did the other woman move away?'

'It all seemed to settle down well enough. I never knew who the other woman was, to be honest. They managed to keep everything quite discreet, as far as I'm aware.'

'So that's the lowdown on the Reynoldses. Poor things. It sounds like a rocky time for them.'

'These things happen. Jennifer came to me for a couple of heart-to-hearts, and each time she was feeling much better than the last. I think they've been more or less back to normal for the past three or four months. Since Christmas, I suppose.'

'Have they got any children?' Thea mentally scanned the walls and shelves in Brook View, and failed to recall any family photographs or evidence of grandchildren.

'Two boys. One's in the airforce, and one emigrated to Canada. Neither's married, but the Canadian one has a long-term girlfriend. They don't come visiting much.' Helen's gaze became unfocused for a moment. 'You might say they were the lucky ones,' she mumbled.

Thea remembered the errant daughter, and said nothing, until she also remembered the sick-looking youngsters on the footpath that morning.

'Is there some sort of hospital around here? Clinic, or something?' she asked.

'What? No, of course not. What makes you ask that?'

Thea explained about her encounter.

'Oh, they'll be from Fairweather. Martin's got a big herb-growing operation there, and employs loads of casual workers. Mostly students. They all look half dead, don't you find?'

Thea thought of her robust daughter, and mentally disagreed. But there didn't seem any grounds for arguing, so she kept silent. It was, in any case, definitely time to go. Hepzibah, who had been peacefully enjoying the sheepskin, stood up, almost before Thea had thought the thought. It was wonderful to have such a telepathic dog. It made a person feel cherished and attended to, twenty-four hours a day.

'Are you going to be all right?' Helen asked her, with seeming sincerity. 'All alone in that house, knowing somebody's just died outside?'

'The house is like Fort Knox,' Thea said. 'And I can't imagine there'll be a repeat of last night. I always think the safest place to be is where some big disaster has just happened.'

That was when Helen dropped the bombshell. 'Then you don't know?' she said. 'Nobody's told you that there was another death in that field, two months ago?'

Thea let Hepzie run free on the way home, risking the occasional car passing them on the road. The dog was obedient enough for it to be a very minimal risk, and the grass verge was wide enough most of the way for her to run safely off the tarmac. It was much easier to think if you didn't have an eager spaniel pulling you along.

The story Helen had told was a simple one. On February 22nd, in the early morning, the Reynoldses had been awoken by the sound of a gunshot outside. Clive, it seemed, had dashed fearlessly outside in pyjamas and bare feet, managing to catch a glimpse of a figure running across the field and pushing though the hedge between the Brook View field and the one to the west of it. The odd burrowing action necessary to penetrate a hedge which was demonstrably sheep-proof had been the most vivid part of the tale.

'But who was it that was killed?' Thea demanded.

'Paul Jennison. Joel's older brother,' Helen replied with a sombre face, before continuing with her account.

Fibres had been retrieved, footprints preserved. The gun had been Paul's own, and only his fingerprints were on it. Many people queried Clive's testimony and asserted it must have been suicide. But forensic work demonstrated that the angle and distances were entirely incompatible with self-annihilation. This left a broad spectrum of hypotheses, ranging from his having put the gun down for some reason, during which careless moment his attacker stole up and snatched it, to his willingly handing it over to someone he knew and trusted.

'My God! Then it must be some sort of family feud? Surely that much is obvious now that Joel's been killed. And there must be some pretty strong suspicions as to who's doing it? Surely there must be . . .'

Helen shook her head firmly. 'I don't think so. The Jennisons have been perfectly ordinary farmers here for forty years or more. They've never upset anybody, never had any scandal attaching to them. It's an absolute mystery.'

Thea had smiled her scepticism. 'Well, that can't be true,' she said. 'I mean, the bit about them never upsetting anybody. It sounds to me as if somebody is very upset indeed.'

Now, walking past the entrance to Barrow Hill, her thoughts turned to the poor old man, bereft of both his sons. It was too much to contemplate, the double grief, the sense of victimisation he must be feeling. Almost, she turned into the farm track, wanting to go and offer some solace, some word of human sympathy. But she didn't. She'd never met the man. He might be crazed, or sedated. Joel's doorstep promise of ready hospitality from a man who 'liked visitors' was quite irrelevant now. How might he react if a strange woman showed up, claiming to have heard his dead son's final despairing scream?

The gate to Brook View was open, and a police car sat reproachfully on the gravel forecourt. 'Oops,' Thea muttered.

The same two policemen she'd spoken to earlier emerged from the vehicle. 'Sorry to trouble you again, madam,' said the talkative one. 'Just a few more questions, if that's all right.'

His diffident manner calmed her anxieties. 'Of course,' she smiled. 'Come in. I'm sorry I wasn't here.'

'We thought you'd just gone for a walk, seeing your motor's still here,' he said.

'That's right.' She led them into the house, dodging the labradors, who came bounding out much more friskily than usual. They had been shut in rather a long time, she supposed. Maybe they weren't quite as lethargic as she'd first thought.

The policemen wasted no more time. They repeated to her the statement she'd made to them earlier, and then went on, 'Can you give us a definite assurance that the body was not in the pool yesterday afternoon?'

Thea blinked. 'Absolutely,' she said. 'But surely you can gauge the time of death, and settle that once and for all?'

'Probably.' He looked away from her, tapping his teeth with his pencil. 'You see, we need to decide now whether or not Mr and Mrs Reynolds should be brought home.'

'So, if Joel was alive when they got on their plane, they

can carry on with their cruise?' Thea impressed both herself and the police officers with her rapid grasp of the essentials.

'Well, yes. We'd still want to ask them some questions, and three weeks is a long time, but if we can be satisfied they're not pertinent witnesses, we can maybe speak to them on the phone.'

'Have they left port yet?' Thea couldn't work out the time frame, allowing for the flight and the several intervening time zones.

'There's another hour or two,' said the policeman. 'After that, it would get rather complicated.'

'Well, you can let them have their holiday,' she said, wondering whether they would really decide the matter on the basis of what she told them. 'If the scream I heard was Joel, then they must have been somewhere over the Atlantic at the time.'

'Now – that scream,' prompted the quieter man. 'Would you say it was a cry of pain? Or something else?'

Thea sighed. 'I was asleep, you see, when it came. I only heard a sort of echo. You know – the memory of it, after I woke up. And that makes it really difficult to describe.'

'Try,' he urged her.

'Well, I would say it was a cry of fear more than pain. But then you have to wonder whether somebody would shout out with fear, don't you? Imagine it – you're out in the dark at three in the morning. In somebody else's field. You know there's only a woman in the house, so you're not too worried about being confronted. Then some other person hits you, or pushes you or waves a torch in your face. Well, you wouldn't shout, would you? You'd talk more or less normally, or call out in words. You wouldn't howl.' She looked from one to the other, hoping they'd understand what she was trying to explain. 'Do you see?'

They exchanged glances, and said nothing for a moment. Then, 'Well, p'raps it'll be easier to understand when we've got the post-mortem results,' said the spokesman.

'That's right,' said the other.

'Oh!' Thea remembered. 'And the security lights didn't come on. That's another reason I didn't go out to investigate. It made it more likely I'd just heard a bird or a rabbit or something.'

The first policeman wrote this down on his notepad. 'That's very useful,' he said. 'Assuming we can be sure the lights are working? And that they illuminate the part of the house with your bedroom window?'

Thea thought about it. 'That's a point,' she admitted. 'We'll have to check it after dark, I suppose.'

On the doorstep, she asked one final question: 'So what do you think will happen about the Reynoldses?'

'Not for us to say, madam,' said Chatterbox.

There was a lot for Thea to think about that evening, not much more than twenty-four hours after her arrival. The atmosphere had changed completely, though oddly enough not altogether for the worse. The dogs seemed to have recovered from whatever malaise had been keeping them so passive, and were positively manic when it came to their feeding time. 'I know what it was!' she told them, feeling foolish. 'You're missing your mum and dad, after all. And there was me thinking you couldn't give a damn.'

If the theory was correct, then the pain of separation had been short lived. But that was dogs for you. Whatever the explanation, Bonzo and Georgie were much better company that evening. She took them outside and threw two tennis balls for them, which she'd found in a box in the back pantry, with other items that appeared to be dog-related. Hepzibah looked on coolly. She did not chase balls herself, and was not at all sure she approved of her mistress spending time with these big yellow morons.

Out in the garden, the game over, Thea paused to listen. There was scarcely a sound that could be attributed to mankind. A cow bawled in the distance, an evening bird sang its farewell to the day and a breeze swished lightly in the bushes. It was idyllic. Thea's own cottage at home was almost adjacent to the A40, with traffic noise a steady background. Noticing its absence for the first time since coming to Brook View, she acknowledged what an improvement it made. And all the better, she thought smugly, for having turned off the annoying water feature in the corner of the garden.

It was curious, being a stranger to the area. Two murders committed within two months had to be earth-shattering for the inhabitants. She did, undoubtedly, feel sorry about Joel Jennison, who had taken the trouble to call on her so quickly and been so pleasant in his manners. It was hard to believe he'd turned into that sodden mass in the sheep's watering hole, only about twelve hours later.

But Thea was hardened to sudden death. She knew, down to her bone marrow, that it happened; that you could never take life for granted, however secure and safe you might believe yourself to be. Her Carl had been vivid with life – loud, solid, even smelly in a nice way – and he had been snuffed out by a juggernaut. After that, anything was possible.

She went to bed early, taking a resentful care over the

locking-up procedures. She wasn't afraid, she insisted to herself; it was merely that the world outside would expect her to be thorough, and just at the moment it was politic to placate the world outside.

The dog was warm on the duvet again. The one pure uncomplicated element in a life that never stayed serene for long, was her affection for the dog. The softest, most forgiving, most beautiful dog imaginable. Sometimes Thea felt it was her only route to salvation, this feeling she had for the animal.

She slept dreamlessly, and awoke at seven thirty to rain dashing against the window. Wet and windy, she noted. What a nuisance. Did she really have to take the dogs out and count the sheep and open the gate and all the other needless outside tasks she'd been set? Surely nothing could have happened to the sheep during the night – they'd be huddled in the lee of a hedge, five minutes' walk away through the blustering weather. She'd leave them until later in the morning, when conditions might have improved.

Wishing she'd gone to the trouble the previous night of organising teamaking equipment in the room, she pushed back the duvet with Hepzibah rolled up in it. At that moment, the phone rang.

This time, she went straight to the instrument in the kitchen, where a notepad and pencil were within easy reach.

The line was poor, which led her to assume the caller was on a mobile. 'Mrs Osborne?' came a man's voice. 'Is that you?'

'Yes,' she shouted.

'This is Clive Reynolds. I'm calling from my ship. They tell me there's been some trouble.'

'Well, yes . . .' Surely, she thought, he'd been told hours ago? Why had he left it so long to call her?

The line suddenly improved, as if someone had flipped a switch that ought to have been flipped from the outset. Perhaps that's what actually happened.

'Look. I've told the police they'll have to force us to come back – we're not going to volunteer. We've waited a long time for this holiday, and there's a lot riding on it. The man's dead – nothing anybody can do about that. I'm just sorry you've been landed with such a fiasco. That's all I'm calling to say.'

Thea's mind slowly caught up. 'What time is it there?' she asked. 'It must be four in the morning.'

'Something like that. Not according to my body clock, of course. They never sleep on a ship, you know.'

'So you want me to carry on as planned?'

'If you don't mind.' His tone was brisk, giving her little option in her reply.

'I don't mind,' she said. 'Not really.'

'Thank you. That's a big relief to us both.'

She wanted to say something about Joel Jennison, and Helen Winstanley and the silent villagers – but she didn't. 'Bye, then,' she said, replacing the receiver with the sense of a die cast.

61

Chapter Five

The rain stopped at ten thirty, and to make up for her slackness, Thea took the three dogs into the garden, and offered to play with them. She had half expected the police to tape it all off and tell her not to go into it, but evidently they'd examined it to their satisfaction, and given the all clear. The dogs did not seem to be in the mood for much romping, so she gave up, taking instead a slow tour around the beds and shrubs. The garden had a strong appeal, with winding paths leading to an open area shielded by laurels and rhododendrons. She had intended to give the water lily an inspection, but was distracted by the overnight appearance of new shoots in one of the flowerbeds. Too early for a definite identification, nonetheless she was happy to see them. Looking at the whole garden more closely, she found signs of the police search that had lasted most of Sunday. Nothing too destructive, but clearly they had rummaged in borders and beds, breaking off some early flower spikes. They would recover, she knew. Some would even be better for the damage. Plants could teach people a thing or two in that department.

A lot rested on this coming summer, the second of her widowhood. If she was to get through the second half of her life free from misery and guilt, she suspected it would have to be with the assistance of the natural world and its never ending optimistic progress.

In her mid-thirties, Thea had picked up an incomplete degree course, and acquired a BA in History. Very much by accident she found herself specialising in industrial history of the early eighteenth century, developing an interest in transport particularly. Canals and railways caught her interest, and much to her family's amusement she became fascinated by both.

Having graduated, there were no obvious employment opportunities for such a qualification, other than teaching. Thea Osborne was no teacher. 'I'm far too lazy for all that paperwork,' she would say. 'And I'm never going to get the little beasts to behave themselves while I drone on about Brunel and Stevenson.'

The studies were therefore set aside, and Thea got a part-time post in the Bodleian, mostly associated with cataloguing documents. It was dry, undemanding and not very well paid. She stuck with it because it did not significantly interfere with her duties as wife and mother, friend and sister.

When Carl was killed, she had abruptly abandoned the job and never gone back. As the months had passed, it became increasingly unimaginable to return, for reasons that seemed to proliferate. Carl's life had been insured, thanks to a cousin who happened to sell policies and would not be dissuaded. Carl and Thea had been sheepish about it, not seeing themselves as the sort of people who insured themselves. But the eventual payout had provided a safety net that made even part-time work an unnecessary exertion.

Abandoning the water lily to its fate, partly out of guilt at having turned off its splashy water feature, she remembered the Cotswolds, still uncounted. When she went to the yard gate, to make her belated inspection of the sheep, the labradors as well as Hepzibah expressed a desire to go with her. 'Oh, what the hell,' she muttered. 'What harm can it do?' Then caution prevailed, as she remembered Clive's anxieties over sheep worrying.

'Sorry chaps,' she corrected herself, squeezing through the gate without them. 'Better not come with me, after all. For all I know, you're covert sheep murderers.'

Bonzo and Georgie looked at her, tails wagging slowly in unison. Nothing seemed to upset them. Big silly unambitious things – not so different from sheep themselves. She permitted herself the knowledge that she didn't really like them very much.

The day continued to feel aimless and fragmented. It was a Monday, the start of a new week, and there were twenty more days to get through before she could go home again and . . . and what? Nothing really beckoned from Witney, any more than it did from Cirencester or Gloucester or Duntisbourne bloody Abbots.

'Don't get depressed, don't get depressed,' she instructed herself fiercely. 'Think of the new plants growing, the sunny days ahead.' She knew the danger signs – nothing tangible to look forward to, everything feeling futile, grey weather and complete absence of human company. She recalled her flicker of interested anticipation at the sudden appearance of Joel Jennison at the door. A young man, just across the road, inviting her to drop by. It had seemed such an auspicious start. He might have been badly dressed and impeccably spoken, a walking contradiction, but he'd been friendly, and that was the main thing. His death the next morning now felt like a personal slight.

There was Helen, of course. She'd been nice, especially about the finger. But Thea had recognised the underlying neediness of Helen Winstanley. A lost and lonely girl hid just below the skin of the affluent confident woman. And Thea wasn't very good with the lost and lonely.

From hard experience, she knew there was only one remedy when she felt like this. Get busy. Fill your mind with something from outside yourself. Make lists. Meet people. It was what middle-aged Englishwomen had always done when left alone. They bustled, organised, cooked; they rambled and knitted and gossiped. They gave up hope of losing themselves in any sort of intimacy with a man. If he wasn't dead or off with a floozie, he'd be in the pub or watching football on the telly. Admittedly there were the favoured few who seemed to find the perfect bloke, but Thea felt herself to be beyond that sort of compatibility now. She'd forgotten how to do it, how to signal properly, how to submit and flatter.

So – to action! The urge from the previous afternoon to turn down the track to Barrow Hill Farm came back even more strongly. Right, then, she decided. That's what she would do. She would go to the farm where an old man grieved for his two dead sons.

* * *

If she had any expectations, the reality only partly met them. Joel Jennison had called on her in the most agricultural of attire. He had been muddy and unkempt. By extrapolation, it stood to reason that his farm would be something the same, and in most ways it was. There was certainly mud.

The buildings occupied a hollow, at the end of a short rutted drive. The house, greyly unassuming, had farm buildings on two sides and a yard in front. The yard was occupied by a large number of multi-coloured cattle. Thea could see no way of approaching the house other than through the thronging animals. There was the sound of a tractor engine coming from one of the large barns.

She was not wearing waterproof boots, which she realised now was a serious mistake. Underfoot was an unwholesome mixture of muck and mud, to a depth of at least two inches. Her shoes, stout as they might be, were no match for this. She nearly turned back, but that was not her nature. There had to be a way around the muck, and she set about finding it.

Stone walls divided the yard from the house, the house from a field behind it, and the track from the land on either side. The walls were about three feet high in every case. Thea hopped over the one on her right, thinking to circle round and approach the house from the back. Lateral thinking, she told herself smugly.

She was now in a field containing a flourishing crop of young thistles. They snatched at her ankles as she walked through them, but her socks provided protection. This was not a well-kept farm, she concluded. Self-respecting farmers didn't let thistles grow where lush spring grass or newly sprouting corn should be.

There was a gate into the field behind the house, and she climbed over it, enjoying the process. It never failed to remind her of childhood summers spent at her grandparents' home in Wiltshire, where she and her siblings had been taken on lengthy country walks designed to tire them out.

Now there was just another wall between herself and her goal. This field boasted a better crop of grass, wet from the morning's rain. Her shoes were soaked by the time she climbed over the second barrier, beginning to feel that this was enough climbing, and – damn it – she was probably going to have to do the whole thing again in reverse, in order to get back to Brook View.

The house stood uninvitingly before her. There was something stern about it, the windows like the eyes of an offended schoolmaster. There was no door at the back, just a weedy patch of garden and the rusting remains of some sort of farm implement.

The tractor engine had been running constantly since she arrived, but now it was switched off. She headed around the house, hoping to encounter whoever had been working in the shed. Mucking out, perhaps.

The cattle milling about in the yard did not seem surprised to find her popping up on the other side from where she had first appeared. She looked at them, and they looked at her. These were not milking cows, she realised. Most were male, and they were not full-grown. They were penned into the yard, with a large circular contraption full of silage to eat. Their expressions epitomised boredom on an epic scale.

She was now in the walled-off front garden, leaning over the half-sized gate, her back to the house, wondering what to do next. Knocking on the door was the obvious course of action, but she was assuming from what Joel had said that the only person living here was his father. Which meant the person driving the tractor must be the old man. Which meant there wouldn't be anybody in the house. Still, this was all supposition, and a knock might bring some unforeseen result.

It did. The door was opened by a girl of about fifteen. She had red eyes and hunched shoulders. 'Who are you?' she said in a wan little voice, looking past Thea as if to work out how she'd got there, across the filthy yard.

'My name's Thea Osborne. I'm looking after the Reynoldses' house. It was me who found . . .' She didn't know how to phrase it.

Had Joel been this girl's father? Brother? Possibly, though this was stretching it, her *husband*?

'Oh.' The girl frowned. 'What do you want?'

'I wanted to come and say how sorry I am.' The words were not well chosen, but this was the usual cliché, and she couldn't think how else to express it.

'Sorry? Why? You don't know us.'

'No. But I know what it's like when somebody dies suddenly. People often stay away from you, just when you'd like somebody to talk to.'

'Are you talking about Uncle Joel?'

Ah. 'He was your uncle?'

The girl nodded.

'Do you live here?'

'Not really. I live with my mum. We've come to see to Gramps. Mum!' She turned and called back into the house.

Thea began to feel sorely out of her depth. These people were not going to thank her for the intrusion. And she was going to feel extremely silly floundering back through the thistles to regain the homeward track.

Then the girl's mother appeared. She was clean, tidy, made-up and calm. 'Who's this, Lindy?' she asked, with an expression full of forced encouragement and dutiful interest.

The girl didn't respond, so Thea introduced herself again. 'I'm really sorry for the intrusion. I just thought you might . . . well . . .' It sounded weak and silly in her own ears. The truth, and she knew it, was that she'd come in order to keep her own demons at bay. Taking a share in other people's was always the better option.

'Come in. How did you get here? Look at your shoes! Isn't this place abysmal!'

Her accent was almost as BBC as Joel's had been. A strong sense of disorientation descended on Thea as she stepped into the house. Without consultation, she undid the slimy laces of her shoes, and left them inside the door. Something about padding across the hall in purple socks seemed to generate at least a potential for increased intimacy.

Barrow Hill Farmhouse was heavily furnished in a style that could not be neatly categorised. Big old furniture dusty and unpolished. Good quality carpets that had withstood years of feet and grit and animal hairs. Thea noticed for the first time that no dogs had accosted her. Now it seemed there was a strong family preference for cats. At one glance she could count four on various perches around the room. Thank Christ she'd left Hepzibah behind.

Mother and daughter were watching her, their expressions

identical. Thea suddenly felt very silly indeed, to the point where she could think of nothing to say. 'Gosh, well . . .' she floundered. 'I just thought . . .'

'She's staying at the Reynolds' place,' said the girl. 'She must be the woman who found Uncle Joel.'

'That's right,' said Thea.

'Poor you. It must have been a shock.' Lindy's mother had not yet given her own name. 'Everything's in a state here, I'm afraid. Those bloody bullocks in the yard. Gramps won't put them back in the field – says it's too soft for them. It makes living here like being under siege. How *did* you manage?'

Thea tried to laugh. 'I came round the back.'

'You *were* determined!'

'No, not really. I just didn't want to turn back. I should have worn boots. It's my own fault.'

'Lindy, make some tea, will you? There's a good girl.'

Lindy slouched out of the room, and started to run a tap and make a metallic clattering sound.

'You don't live here?' Thea asked.

'Oh no. I was married to Joel's brother. Paul. He was killed in February – did you know? I can't believe history's repeating itself like this. It's really knocked us sideways. It's the end for the farm, of course. Gramps is out there, mucking out the cowshed, pretending everything's all right. They weren't coping before this, not really. Now it's going to be completely hopeless.'

Thea entertained notions of land-hungry neighbours committing murder in order to achieve possession of Barrow Hill.

'But Paul – wasn't he farming here as well?'

'He was until a year ago. Then we moved away to Cirencester. There wasn't enough money coming in to keep us all here. Paul got work at the garden centre, and I went full-time. We were doing all right.'

'I can't imagine what it must be like. Are there other brothers or sisters?'

The woman laughed harshly. 'They'd be pretty scared by now, wouldn't they! No, it was just the two boys. Their mum went off with a fertiliser rep when Paul was fourteen and Joel twelve. I don't think Gramps has been the same since, to be honest.'

'There are milking cows here, is that right? Joel came over to talk to me on Saturday afternoon. He said he'd have to go and get on with the milking. That's going to be hard work.'

'It's impossible. We've found a relief chap to come and take over. They cost a fortune, of course, but Gramps can't do it. Except he did do it yesterday morning, when he couldn't find Joel.'

Thea recognised the indiscriminate babble that came with the shock. All those disconnected thoughts that flew at you from all sides – When? What? How? The compulsion to keep the basic functions operating, the desperate urge to create some sort of narrative to explain events as they hurtled you into a whole new reality. The need to assure yourself that your surviving loved ones were safe, while at the same time resenting them for being the wrong loved ones. She spun on her heel, overwhelmed by the returning sensations and insights, in the presence of another sudden death.

'The poor man. How did he manage?'

'He won't give in. He can hardly stand up for more than a

71

few minutes, with his hip. So he took a stool out to the milking parlour, and rested between each cow. It took him hours, but he got them all done. But he couldn't do it again. We had the relief last night and this morning, but the expense . . . I don't suppose you . . . ?' For a moment there was a flicker of irrational hope on the woman's face.

'No,' said Thea. 'Sorry. I've been on farms quite a lot, but I've never actually milked a cow.'

'Do you do much of this house-sitting?'

Thea smiled. 'Well, actually, this is my first time.'

Lindy came back, with two mugs of tea. 'There's a car coming down the lane,' she said. 'Looks like police.'

'Oh! I'd better go, then,' said Thea. 'I'll be in the way.'

'They'll want to ask more questions,' said the woman. 'They've really got the bit between their teeth now. Trying to work out why both brothers should get themselves killed.' Her tone was bitter. 'Pity they didn't work a bit harder two months ago. All that evidence from the hedge – you'd think they'd have got the bastard right away. But once they'd done the house to house stuff round all the villages, they seemed to give up on it. Said it must have been a poacher from Birmingham or somewhere, and it would have to be a slow, careful investigation, whatever the hell that means. Anyway, this shows how wrong they were.'

'You think it was the same person both times?'

The woman shrugged, but her reddening cheeks made the gesture seem false. However much she knew or suspected, it was not the sort of knowledge conducive to a shrug. Thea gave the matter her undivided attention and came to the quick conclusion that the wife and sister-in-law of two murdered brothers must surely have some ideas as to who and why.

Thea was torn between wanting to leave this bizarre household, and wishing she could stay and hear the full story. 'I'm sorry – I don't think I caught your name,' she said, more as a ploy to regain the woman's attention, as she gazed out of the window.

'Oh – June. I'm June. Look, I think you probably should go. It might upset Gramps to find you here. Come back another day. I'll make sure the yard's clear next time. God! Look at that wretched man. He's up to his ankles in shit.'

Thea put down her tea, untasted. The mug had struck her as disconcertingly unclean. 'I'll go the back way again, shall I?'

'Up to you,' said June, plainly indifferent. Her initial concern had disappeared completely, leaving Thea feeling very much surplus to requirements.

She retraced her steps through thistles that seemed to have grown in the past half hour. What had she learnt in her visits to the neighbours – Helen Winstanley as well as June Jennison? Two very different women, both amiable enough when confronted by a stranger who was only expected to be here for a few weeks. Amiable, but distracted. Their attention had been very much elsewhere, in both cases. Perhaps it was the distraction that provoked Thea's stubborn streak. She wanted to get under their guard, to earn their confidence and learn a bit more about what was going on in this apparently typical English village.

It seemed to take an age before she was hopping over the stone wall back into the lane leading up to the road and the place she was beginning to think of as home. Finding a stretch of wall that was level and not defended by nettles or brambles proved tricky. Just as she'd selected a place, a voice greeted her.

'Will you hang on a minute, Mum says.' It was Lindy, wearing wellington boots, coming through the gate from the mucky yard. 'She wants to ask you something.'

Thea felt weak. Surely she didn't have to make the stupid roundabout journey all over again. 'Don't worry,' Lindy assured her. 'She'll come out here, in a minute. The police want to talk to Gramps. They've gone out to the shippon to look for him.'

Thea waited, beginning to notice the cold penetrating her light jacket. A wind had sprung up and the sky was grey.

June Jennison emerged from the house, and made an assertive passage through the yard, elbowing cattle aside impatiently. 'Oh, thanks for waiting,' she said. 'This is silly, isn't it. I've a good mind to send them out into the field right now. It's not muddy, is it?' She peered over the wall at the thistles. 'They might eat some of those weeds, if we're lucky.'

'They're not donkeys, Ma,' said Lindy.

Thea had a sense of a world on the edge of chaos; the relentless needs of farm livestock presenting a distraction from the pain and shock of a sudden death, forcing the family to continue at least a token imitation of normal processes. But Gramps was supposed to be retired, his hip wouldn't allow him to stand for more than a few minutes, both his sons were dead, and his yard was ankle deep in muck.

'Er . . .' she said, wishing she could just go.

'Oh, sorry. Listen – I do want to talk to you. You must

have been the last person to see Joel, apart from Gramps. I want to know what he said, exactly. Did he mention Paul at all? Did he tell you anything?'

Thea inhaled slowly. June Jennison seemed smaller, out of doors. Much the same age as Thea herself, she was greying and plump. She wore a neat knitted garment that stretched over ample breasts. But she had taken care with her appearance, for all that. There was lipstick and eyeshadow, and nail varnish. Everyone in this family, Thea concluded, was impossible to categorise. Educated, apparently, but by no means affluent; working with their hands, but not therefore artisans. What had Paul been like, she wondered – and when was she going to meet Gramps – Mr Jennison Senior?

'I don't think he told me anything important,' she said. 'He seemed to just want to introduce himself.'

'What time was it?'

'Just after four.'

'But that's *milking time*,' June said with great earnestness. 'He wouldn't have gone visiting then. Was he dressed up?'

Thea had to abort a peal of laughter. 'I think he was in his milking clothes,' she said.

'Then he wasn't just visiting,' June said. 'He wanted to tell you something – to warn you, or ask you for help. Take my word for it, he was there for a very good reason.'

Chapter Six

June's words echoed in Thea's head, as she walked back to Brook View and tried to apply herself to the job she was supposed to be doing. Clive's lists were beginning to acquire a life of their own.

However many times she read them, there always seemed to be some instruction she'd overlooked. *Check telephone for recorded messages* (1571) was one she had failed to obey thus far. Choosing the machine in the study, she lifted the receiver and listened for the broken tone that indicated a message. Sure enough, somebody had called.

Keying in 1571, she listened, pencil in hand, for the recording, which gave its time as 1.30pm on Saturday. Thea had been remiss in not checking for calls earlier. She wondered where the Reynoldses had been when the phone rang, shortly before her own arrival. 'Clive? It's only me. Have you left yet for the great adventure, I wonder? I suppose you must have done. Anyway, just to say I saw the piece in the paper, and hope Jen wasn't too bothered by it. These things happen – nobody's going to think badly of her. Give us a shout when you get back, and we'll have a drink or something. Bye for now.'

Thea dropped the pencil without using it. The caller had not given his name, but she thought she recognised the voice as that of Martin Stacey with his London/Essex vowels. She didn't make a note, not quite sure enough of the caller's identity to say for certain that Stacey had called. The message itself didn't seem to be the sort you needed to pass on, three weeks later, either. She did rather wonder what had been in the paper concerning Jennifer Reynolds, all the same. The woman was beginning to sound like a person rather susceptible to being upset. Hadn't Helen Winstanley implied as much? That the whole point of the cruise was to mollify her, after Clive's regrettable fling? Thea brought Jennifer to mind: tall, narrow-shouldered, stony-eyed. A habit of tucking her small chin into her neck, making her seem stern and critical. Not at all a vulnerable person to be protected from wounded feelings.

Well, it shouldn't be too difficult to find a copy of the local weekly paper – and surely that was the most likely periodical to which the phone message referred? In fact, Thea realised, with a small jolt of pleasure, she could quickly and easily check it on the laptop, which had been sitting where she left it on a chest in her bedroom ever since she'd arrived. A search for 'Jennifer Reynolds' would save her hours of trawling through pages of newsprint. It would be a little task saved for a quiet evening, she decided.

A few minutes later, she had to answer the door to the police again. She had noticed their car arrive and assumed they were returning for another look at the field. It was a surprise when an officer rang the doorbell.

'Mrs Osborne, sorry to trouble you again. We've just

come from Barrow Hill, where I gather you paid a visit a little while ago?' It was the less talkative one from Sunday morning. He had a very short haircut that looked all wrong on his wide head.

'Oh, yes?' She spoke brightly, taking care to present an open expression, eyes wide, slight smile on her lips. 'Would you like to come in?'

'Thank you.' He stepped into the room, but only a little way. His uniform looked unyielding, inhuman. 'So – You didn't see Mr Jennison, did you?'

'You mean the old man? No, he was outside, doing something on his tractor. I spoke to June Jennison and her daughter.'

'She told us,' he nodded. 'She believes you must have more information for us than we've had so far. That Mr Joel Jennison possibly came here on Saturday with something urgent to say to you.' He was speaking slowly, trying to make himself clear as much to himself as to Thea.

'He didn't give an impression of urgency. June thinks what she does because he was wearing his working clothes. I wonder whether she's right? Perhaps he didn't think it was worth changing just to pop over here for a few minutes. Perhaps he'd been delayed by something, so there wasn't time to change.'

'Mrs Osborne, we've had the results of the post-mortem now. Mr Jennison didn't die of drowning. I'm not at liberty to give you the full picture, but I can tell you that he died somewhere else, and was subsequently dumped face down in that pool.'

Thea's eyes grew wider. 'But . . .' She tried to calculate the implications of this news.

'We haven't got an accurate time of death, unfortunately. But it was a considerable interval prior to your finding the body.'

'So . . . What does that mean? What about that scream?'

'The scream *could* have been him. He could have been attacked close to the house, left there for a while, and then placed in the water at a later time. But we found no traces of an attack in the garden or field. There would have been blood loss.' He avoided her eye, wary of her reaction.

Thea was not distressed by the mention of blood in itself, but a renewed stab of guilt assailed her. 'Didn't anybody else hear anything?' She already knew the answer to that. Who could there have been, close enough to the spot at that time of night? The neighbours she had somehow believed must exist were in fact much further afield than she had first thought.

'Not that we're aware.'

A short silence ensued, during which Thea tried to remember whether she had left any questions unanswered. She didn't think she had.

'I had a call from Clive Reynolds this morning,' she offered. 'He doesn't want to come home early, does he?'

The policeman's face remained blank. 'So it would seem,' he said.

'You can't really make him, I suppose? Not unless you think he did it.'

'That isn't strictly the case. If we felt he was an important witness, we could subpoena him.'

'It would be a pity to ruin the holiday for them.'

'Unfortunate,' he agreed.

'So you won't?'

'Not at present, no.'

She could tell it was an awkward situation, probably leading to arguments in high places. It was possible to imagine a Saturday afternoon scenario in which Clive Reynolds doubled back to Duntisbourne, murdered Joel and then somehow zoomed off to Heathrow for his flight. Except . . .

'Joel did do the milking on Saturday afternoon, I assume?'

'According to his father, yes, he did.'

'So we still assume he was alive when the Reynoldses boarded their plane?'

'Within half an hour or so, yes. They finished the milking at seven. Then Joel had his supper as usual, at eight. His dad went to bed at nine. The flight actually took off at nine thirty—'

'So with checking-in and everything, the Reynoldses have to be in the clear.'

'I'm not really at liberty to discuss these details with you,' said the man again. Thea was fully aware that he had already told her more than he should have done. It was amazing what a smile could do, accompanied by an open and innocent demeanour.

'But his brother was shot, wasn't he? Isn't it unusual for the same killer to use different methods?'

He sighed, and switched his weight to the other foot. 'It's very unusual for one person to commit more than one murder,' he said. 'Unless it's someone who goes berserk and shoots a whole schoolful of kids all at once.'

Thea wished she'd invited him to sit down. He seemed jaded, almost bitter, and she felt he was due some sympathy. But it was too late for that. 'I should be getting along,' he said.

* * *

The house plants had been badly neglected for two days, but did not appear to bear any grudges. Leaves spread glossily, stems maintained the perpendicular and incipient spring shoots were evident everywhere. Thea recalled a time in her life when she'd been the proud owner of a windowsill full of succulents and busy lizzies, and warmed to her charges. They were, after all, impressive. The sort of thing you could pay £50 for in a garden centre. She suspected that if she allowed any of them to die, the value would be deducted from her eventual payment. She would dust them and spray them, she pledged to herself, the day before the Reynoldses were due to come home.

Later that evening, she fetched her laptop from the bedroom and booted it up. It was her favourite possession, her link to the world, her entertainment. On it she sent and received e-mail, played games and balanced her accounts. Without it, she could not have indulged her fond and foolish passion for playing online Scrabble.

It was an addiction she seldom disclosed to anybody. She had found an internet Scrabble club, mostly composed of Americans, and she routinely played four or five games a day. She noted unusual words everywhere she went, listing them alphabetically and very often using them to excellent effect. But the competition was fierce, and others in the club frequently used words she had never seen before. She was, she freely admitted, ruined for the real thing with a board and a living breathing opponent who would demand to know what jota or odic actually meant. Who would not take kindly to repeated use of qat and zax and hmm and vav. It was a perversion of the original game, but she didn't care.

She was hooked, and that was that. Too late to go back now.

She used the Reynoldses' phone socket for her modem, aware that this would block any incoming calls, but not concerned. There was always the 1571 thing if anybody needed to leave a message.

Her first game was close, but she won by four points. The second one, played against a person calling himself BeesNeez, started badly, until she managed to place the K on a triple letter square going in two directions, which boosted things nicely. She liked the K almost best of all the letters, investing it with a personality all its own.

Hepzibah sat close to her, but not in physical contact. Thea had to sit up at the small table under the window of the lounge, and the dog was curled on a rug near her feet. Despite calling themselves 'laptops', it had been obvious from the start that to try to use it on a lap was uncomfortable and frustrating. And the battery never lasted very long, so she almost always operated it from the mains. The resulting cables could make working on a lap even more complicated.

BeesNeez had the Q, which he (she supposed it was a he) used to only moderate effect, and then the X, making XENON and OX simultaneously, and Thea felt that failure was inevitable. It was a fifteen-minute game and time was running out. She lost by twenty points, and was unreasonably downcast about it.

She had postponed checking for any e-mails until after the game, saving it as a small treat in the event of losing. For a year now, life had been composed of just such small mood-boosting strategies. Acutely aware of where she stood on the elation-depression spectrum at any given moment, she had doggedly collected these goodies, storing them up and doling them out when required. It worked, but it was not much of a substitute for Carl's ready attention and reliable companionship.

There were eight e-mails: one selling a new penis-enhancing drug; two from desperate Africans wanting a sponsor to get them to the UK; two from an outfit called My Offers, which Thea suspected she had carelessly signed up for two or three years ago; one from Jessica; one from brother-in-law James; and one from somebody wanting her to house-sit in July. She read the last one first – a family living on a few acres near Stroud, with a cat, poultry and elderly pony. Sorry about the rather short notice, but liked the look of her advertisement, and would she please reply quickly.

She sent a brief response, saying the diary was free for July, and she would phone them the next day. Stroud was only a few miles away from her present position, she realised. She might go and see them during the coming week.

This was as good as she could have hoped for. Her two dearest relatives, and the prospect of more work in the pipeline. The spam was quickly deleted, and she concentrated on the messages from real people.

Hi, Momma, wrote her daughter, knowing she hated to be addressed like that. *How's the job turning out? Can't wait to hear all about it. Phone me! I handed in my dissertation this morning! Hooray!! Only five more weeks and then we're free. Still haven't decided what to do with the summer. Advice please? How's sweet Hepzie? Uncle J. says he wants to talk to you – should be an e-mail from him. Gotta go. There's a gig at Collingwood. I'm singing. Aaarghhh! Loadsalove, Jess. xxxxx*

* * *

The message from James, flagged up like that by Jessica, put her in something of a flutter. A kindly man, desperately wounded by his brother's sudden and horrible death, he had put a lot of energy into concern for Thea. Too much, she had eventually realised; it hadn't done either of them any real good. An undercurrent of attraction, a sense of being thrown together in their grief, had made Thea uneasy. James had a wife and career. Thea had no intention of intruding herself into either one – but she was grateful for his abiding presence in her life, just the same. And she was more than grateful for the way he had immersed himself in Jessica's life, listening, helping, encouraging. In that respect he was the personification of the word *avuncular*. Pity it was too long ever to feature in a game of Scrabble.

His message did nothing to assuage her flutters.

Thea – I hear you're in the Cotswolds this week. Forgot just when it was going to be. I never got around to telling you that I know Clive Reynolds slightly. Heard about the dead man in his field – are you involved? Listen, love. Be very careful. There's something going on in your area. Funny people. And I don't mean funny . I'm coming down there on Wednesday. Tried to phone you, but your mobile's not taking calls. Switch it on, there's a good girl. I spoke to Jess, but hope I didn't worry her. Tricky time for her, finals and everything. Anyway, see you on Wednesday. Lock the doors. Love, James.

One of the most irritating things about James was his obsession with security. It went with the job, of course. He spent his working day listening to terrible tales of burglary, mugging, rape and assault, until nobody could blame him for believing the world to be rife with criminal behaviour. Danger lurked in every doorway for him, and even without a dead man in the field, he would have shared Clive Reynolds's cautious approach to doors, lights, gates and dogs. Not that the dogs showed any sign of understanding their role as guardians; they never even woke up when blood-curdling screams shattered the night.

Still, it would be nice to see him, and intriguing to get a new angle on the murder of Joel Jennison. Funny people, hmm? In Duntisbourne Abbots itself, did he mean? Thea found that difficult to credit. There was obviously money in the area, and where there was money, there would probably be a level of anxiety and self-interest beyond the point of comfort. Envy, deviousness, stress – all were obvious concomitants of an affluent lifestyle. Some of these houses were changing hands at half a million pounds or more. Money on that scale had to carry with it a lot of bad vibes, as well as the more normal feelings of pride, complacency and self-indulgence.

Or had he meant something else entirely? Was he talking about a covert drugs cartel operating from one of the cottages beside the church? Or a child pornography ring meeting secretly in one of the local farms? Anything was possible, she supposed, albeit with a large dash of scepticism. Possible, but surely unlikely? In any case, the implication was that Clive Reynolds was on the right side. One of us. He might have been an adulterer, but not, apparently, anything 'funny'.

She took the dogs out into the dark garden, last thing before bed. The garden didn't remain dark for long, with an automatic power-light suddenly blinding them in its beam. *There, she thought. Security lights working perfectly.*

Bonzo and Georgie trotted quite cheerfully from tree to tree, relieving themselves copiously in the process. Hepzibah squatted on the edge of the lawn, and Thea concluded that all was well in that department at least. All three dogs would make it through the night with no urgent calls of nature.

She took a moment to appreciate the evening. The moon was close to full, flickering through fast-moving patchy clouds. For a moment she wondered how come it had been so dark the night before, until she realised there had been a thick cloud cover. It was breezy, and she caught the tang of agricultural activities. Partly it was the sheep in the Reynoldses' field, she suspected. Several of them had mucky bottoms, and Thea had noticed a whiff coming from them at close quarters. Apparently it intensified at night. The only sound was the breeze in the trees, and a car engine almost beyond earshot. It felt calm and safe, and natural. Just the way it had felt that first evening, shortly before the man from the neighbouring farm met his violent end.

It had been a strange day, full of scrappy encounters and elusive wisps of information concerning the Jennisons. She could detect no pattern to anything, including the peculiar existence she was expected to endure for the next three weeks. Every time she thought about it, the period seemed to expand, until three weeks felt like infinity. A glimpse into the future suggested that she would be a very different person by the end of her stay at Brook View.

Chapter Seven

Tuesday arrived noisily. The breeze had turned to something much more businesslike, and the treetops behind the house swirled and bucked alarmingly. Thea tried to calculate their distance from the house, wondering whether the roof was at risk from a falling cypress or beech. She had a feeling that beech trees were particularly susceptible to strong winds, having shallow root systems. Fortunately, both the proud occupants of the sweeping lawn were much too far away to cause concern.

'OK, chaps,' she told the labradors, as she let them out of their night quarters in the back kitchen, 'we'll face it together, shall we?'

Throwing open the front door, she found the wind less awesome than expected. Despite the tossing vegetation and the constant noise, the air on her face was comparatively gentle, and not at all cold. It must be coming from the south, she concluded, to judge from the mild temperature. She held her face up to it, relishing the fresh sensation, closing her eyes and letting it ruffle her short hair. The dogs seemed to be happy out in it, too. Hepzie's long ears flapped, and the feathering on her legs streamed decoratively behind her as she ran across the lawn. 'Better look at the sheep,' Thea muttered aloud, turning left along the side of the house, to the yard and gate into the field.

The sheep were nonchalantly grazing, with their backsides to the wind. Their fleeces were obviously very thick and heavy, hardly ruffling in the airflow. Thea tried to imagine them after shearing, half the size and suddenly clean and white again. How would their own lambs recognise them, she wondered.

She satisfied herself that they were all present and correct, that no trees had yet blown down, and retreated back to the house, with the dogs following her. It was only nine o' clock, and the day began to loom somewhat emptily ahead.

Briskly, she refused to give in to any inklings of gloom. Already she had made the acquaintance of the two closest neighbours, savouring the sense of possibility inherent in a new relationship. The discomforting fact of Joel Jennison's violent demise had probably assisted in forging links, however transitory, with Helen and June. She recalled the group of villagers clustered at Brook View's gate and wondered which of them she might get to know next.

The absence of a local Post Office struck her as a severe deprivation. Where did they go for their gossip? No shop, either, nor even a village pub. What an odd place this must be, where the people jumped into their cars every morning to drive off to work in Cirencester or Gloucester, or else shut themselves into an attic room to labour all day designing software. Young mothers perhaps organised coffee mornings in each other's homes, and the old – well, what did happen to the old? Even the middle-aged might not all have work to go to. What about Virginia and Penny, the village stalwarts who organised the gossip network and turned up at murder scenes even before it was officially a murder scene? Did they sit in the churchyard on a sunny day and reminisce together? Did they gather in that quaint little village hall to play bridge and knit squares for Oxfam blankets? Did they catch a daily bus into town, and bustle about the shops buying goods they didn't need? Thea rather doubted that a daily bus would be on offer, or that more than a scant handful would use it if there was.

All of which indicated that there was only one way to meet people: the way she had so far adopted with some success. She had to go to their homes and knock on their doors. The only requirement was foreknowledge of their names. She had memorised Harry Richmond and Susanna something, besides Virginia and Penny. Plus the Staceys, who had from the outset struck Thea as important. They were neighbours to Brook View, for one thing, Fairweather Farm being only a short way down the lane to the left of the front gate.

Pondering all this, Thea realised she was not constrained by the usual rules of protocol. It didn't matter if she blundered into rudeness or embarrassment. She was only there for three weeks. She had nothing to lose and much to gain. She was, presumably, the object of some curiosity, not least because of the murder. There might also be sympathy for the shock she'd suffered. Plus, if her assessment of daily village life was at all accurate, there would be a number of locals starving for a bit of conversation, during the long quiet hours of Monday to Friday.

One big decision was whether or not to take Hepzibah. It had worked well with Helen, having the dog alongside. It would have been close to disaster at Barrow Hill. But the dog liked wind blowing her ears inside out, and Thea loved her company, so that was decided upon.

They followed the same footpath as on Sunday morning, when investigating the route to the village, before the grim discovery in the pool. Emerging onto the road from Brook View's gateway, they turned left, where to turn right would bring them to the Barrow Hill entrance. Barely twenty yards along, there was a stile on the other side of the road, and the well-maintained pathway, which ran past a farmhouse that had to be the back of Fairweather Farm and two cottages before arriving on the edge of Duntisbourne Abbots.

The farmhouse was substantial, flanked by a stone barn on one side and a newer building on the other, made of steel girders and sheets of corrugated iron. The area between the house and lane was entirely different from that of Barrow Hill, being clean and dry. Thea realised that the proper entrance must lie on the other side of the house, with a driveway opening onto the road at some more distant point. It was difficult to be sure, but it seemed very probable that the land adjoined that of the Jennisons of Barrow Hill. This realisation reminded her of her theory that the murders might have something to do with rapacious neighbouring farmers, greedy for extra acreage.

Whilst Thea paused to assess her courage levels, Hepzibah seized the initiative and wriggled under the gate into the yard. Instantly there was a great flurry of snarling and shrieking, which Thea correctly interpreted as sudden attack from a sizeable black and white collie on her small soft beloved spaniel.

'Hey!' she shouted, struggling to open the gate. 'Stop it!'

Serious dog fights were rare, in her experience. Hepzibah's habit of unconditional submission had so far disarmed every dog she encountered and there had never been a moment's trouble. This time things were different. The collie had the spaniel's long right ear between its jaws, and was shaking it viciously. Blood flew in an arc all around Hepzie's head and she howled at a pitch designed to elicit maximum distress in any listener. Thea became frantic. Somehow getting through the infuriating gate, she kicked out as hard as she could, shouting through clenched teeth. Hepzie was howling at the top of her voice, an unearthly sound of fear and pain which tore at Thea's heart. If the dog was killed . . . if this bloody beast of a collie didn't let go . . . she kicked out again, causing a muffled yelp, but no sign of surrendering its prey.

Desperately, Thea grabbed the aggressor's jaws. It was, after all, only a collie. A Rottweiler or bull terrier might have given her pause. But this was not a breed designed to hang on at all costs. It had long jaws, relatively easy to get a purchase on, and force open. This was what she did, with strength she hadn't known she possessed. With an ominous crack, she achieved her goal, and the spaniel pulled free, still howling and spraying blood from the torn ear.

Fiercely, Thea addressed the collie, before letting it go. 'Now just you behave yourself,' she said, far too angry to fear anything it might do to her. She need not have worried. As she relaxed her grip, she realised she had dislocated or even broken its jaw. Pathetically it sank onto the ground, pawing at its own face and whimpering. 'Serves you right,'

Thea said loudly, while beginning to feel a surge of remorse. After all, Hepzibah had invaded its territory. If this was another bitch – and Thea thought it was – that was a risky act. Too late, she wondered if she ought to have kept the spaniel on a lead.

'What the *hell* is going on?' came a voice from the direction of the house.

Thea looked up to see Helen Winstanley striding towards her. She blinked, trying to work out what was incongruous in that.

'Oh, it's you,' Helen said. 'What's happening?'

'This bloody dog attacked Hepzie. It's torn her ear. I thought it was going to kill her. I think I must have hurt it, making it let go.'

Helen bent down to inspect the collie, and Thea was reminded of how she had bent over her own sore finger, two days before. There was something of the brisk unsqueamish nurse about Helen Winstanley.

'Here, Binnie,' she murmured. 'Let's see then. What've you been up to, you naughty girl?'

'It's her jaw. I had to wrench it open.'

Helen laid firm hands on either side of the dog's face, and lifted it slightly, feeling the joints with her fingers. The dog made an apologetic squeal.

'She's normally as gentle as a new lamb, but she's got pups.' There was no hint of reproach, which only made Thea feel a hundred times worse. She moaned slightly, and only then turned part of her attention to her own bleeding pet, sitting dazedly beside her. As she did so, she became belatedly aware of a wound on her own hand, caused by a collie tooth. She shook it quickly and then forgot all about it.

'Dislocated, I think,' said Helen. She made an abrupt pushing motion with two fingers, and Thea heard the faint click which she hoped was reversing the damage wrought by the earlier one. The dog squealed again. 'It'll probably be OK – just a bit sore. How's the spaniel?'

Thea took a careful look. The long black ear, normally thick and soft with curly hair, was matted and red with blood. Fingering it gently, Thea found a split almost three inches long. 'Quite nasty,' she said.

'Well, these things happen. They'll both survive, which is the main thing. I would offer to show you the pups, but Binnie might take offence. They're not really old enough to be interesting yet, anyway.'

'She's not yours, is she?' Thea looked around her, at the farmhouse, and beyond.

'No. I'm just visiting. But she knows me pretty well.'

Thea wanted to ask a dozen questions, most of them obvious, some of them impertinent. The answers were none of her business.

'Should I speak to her owner? I mean, I have hurt her. There might be vet's bills . . .'

'Oh, he's not here at the moment. I was round the other side, knocking, when I heard all the shemozzle with the dogs. Don't worry about it – I'll put it right for you.'

'This is the Staceys' place, right?'

'Right. Fairweather Farm. Martin and Isabel are bound to come back soon.'

'They won't be very happy about their dog,' said Thea. A whine from Hepzie stirred her to action. 'I think I should find a vet for my own, don't you? I gather the Reynoldses use one in Cirencester. This ear might need stitches or something.'

'I wouldn't be in too much hurry. You'll probably find it'll heal by itself, if you keep it clean. It's already stopped bleeding, look. Has Binnie bitten your hand?'

Thea held it out, and Helen took it in a gentle grip. 'Not very deep. Does it hurt?'

'Hardly at all,' Thea lied. The wound was sending shooting pains up her arm, and her whole hand throbbed.

'Wash it and let the air get to it. It'll probably be all right in a day or two. What a lot of wounded females!' Helen laughed. Thea thought she detected relief and perhaps impatience.

'We'd better go home and patch ourselves up, then,' she said. 'Come on, Hepzie – you'll have to walk. I'm not carrying you.' She addressed Helen, 'She's such a funny shape, all top heavy.'

'She can walk. Serves her right for invading Binnie's territory.' Helen bent down to stroke the spaniel, softening the words. 'She's a sweet thing, isn't she.'

'She's wonderful,' said Thea, aware suddenly of how terrified she'd been that her dog would be killed. She felt shaky and weak at the thought.

Thea and Hepzibah dragged themselves back home, battered and hard done by. It had been a traumatic experience for them both, and Thea closed the front door with a sense of having escaped from something hostile.

Most of the day from then on was spent indoors, despite a burst of warm sunshine at mid-day. Her hand settled down to a dull ache, enabling her to do a little light dusting, sweep the kitchen floor, shake the dogs' bedding out in the back yard, and then turn to her laptop for company. As she'd hoped there was a message from James.

Thanks for directions. Sounds cosy. Should be with you by 10.30am Wednesday. All news then. Have the coffee pot on. Love J. xx

So the housework would not be in vain. Odd how quickly she'd come to feel proprietorial towards Brook View, its condition her responsibility, rather than that of the Reynoldses. She took the dogs out and walked them around the garden, snatching at an occasional weed and admiring the burgeoning clematis that had flung itself handsomely over the garage roof. Evidence of police trampling was plain, but not devastating.

Most likely, the plants would have recovered before Clive and Jennifer got home. And besides, there were plenty of things that were undamaged – not just the clematis but roses, weigelia, great clumps of marguerites, and much more besides. Thea wondered why there'd been no mention of a gardener, nor any specific instructions to her as to weeding or pruning. Wasn't spring a time of intense garden activity? Probably, she concluded, Clive or Jennifer, or even both, insisted on doing the whole thing unaided. And good luck to them, she thought, wondering just which sun-soaked Caribbean island they'd be docking at first.

In the early evening, using her mobile, she telephoned the Stroud people, Julia and Desmond Phillips by name, who had e-mailed her about house-sitting. The woman who answered the phone sounded wildly eager to recruit her. 'Oh, gosh, thanks for calling back. We never thought this would be so difficult. Everybody's booked up for July. We're going to Ireland for a fortnight, from the eleventh. Are you all right with ponies? He's quite old, you see, and crotchety with people he doesn't know. My daughter says she won't come if we can't find somebody to look after Pallo.'

Thea examined her conscience. 'I can't pretend to be an expert,' she confessed. 'But I'm sure I'd be able to manage.' Only then did she ask herself if she actually *wanted* to. Was she yet in a position to assess just how competent and enthusiastic a house-sitter she was turning out to be?

'Well, come and see us. Where are you?'

'Actually, I'm not far from you. I've got a three-week house sit in the Duntisbournes. Where are *you*, exactly?'

'We're actually closer to Minchinhampton than Stroud. Do you know it?'

'I don't think I've ever been there, but I can probably come down and find it one day this week.'

'Oh, yes! That would be perfect. Come one evening, or maybe at the weekend. We're all out during the day.'

'OK, then.' A tremor of caution prevailed. 'Let me get back to you when I've worked out when I can best get away from here. I'll phone you back, probably in the next few days.'

'Well, be sure you do,' said the woman eagerly. 'You sound just what we're looking for.'

Chapter Eight

James was four minutes early. Thea had left the front door ajar, so that she would hear him arrive.

Bonzo gave a single deep *woof* when he heard the car drive in. Thea got up quickly, putting aside the paperback she'd been trying to read. All the morning jobs had been finished before ten, and she hadn't been able to think what else to do. The coffee machine was ready to be switched on, and James's favourite custard creams laid out on a plate, thanks to a quick expedition to a petrol station with a shop attached. Petrol stations were the new village shop, she was beginning to understand. Milk, bread, dog food, biscuits, drinks and other basics were all readily to hand. Thea suspected that this would be her chief source of groceries for the duration of her stay.

The prospect of seeing somebody she knew well was ridiculously heartening. Being amongst strangers was supposed to be liberating; you could adopt any persona and nobody would spot the inconsistencies. And she hadn't been conscious of it being hard work, exactly. It was simply that James was so *wonderfully* familiar. She knew what he liked, what he would say, how he felt. And he knew the same about her. That, she understood, was what mattered most of all.

He almost rolled out of the car in his eagerness to hug her. In one swift catlike movement, he'd emerged from the vehicle and was standing with arms outstretched. Thea laughed, feeling tension drain out of her, and flew into the embrace.

'For heaven's sake,' she gasped, pulling away again. 'It hasn't been *that* long.'

'Seven weeks,' he said. 'If anybody's counting.'

'Oh, well, whatever it is, it's really good to see you. I hadn't realised I was going to want to see a familiar face after only a few days.'

He turned his attention to the house, and the labradors standing in the front doorway. 'It's OK, then, is it?'

She didn't give a direct reply. 'Come and see Hepzie. She's in the kitchen.' Hepzibah and James had a one-sided relationship which Thea wasn't always quite happy about. Since the sudden disappearance of Carl, the dog seemed somehow to have guessed that James was the nearest she was ever again going to get to a proper master. Whilst clearly favouring Thea with Top Person status, she nevertheless lost all restraint when James came visiting. Because he hated dogs jumping up at him, Thea had shut the spaniel into the kitchen ten minutes previously.

'Wait. Let me get my stuff.' He raised a hand in a silent 'Stay!' gesture, and went back to the car. Moments later he emerged carrying a slim black briefcase that Thea thought looked incongruous in a policeman's grasp, albeit a plain clothes policeman. He aimed the plastic rectangle that comprised the electronic key at the vehicle and it obediently clunked in response. Thea bit back the sarcastic remark about locking everything, even out here in rural Gloucestershire.

'Go into the living room,' she told him, 'and I'll put the coffee on and fetch Hepzie. She's had a bit of an accident, so she's not at her best, poor darling.'

It was typical of James that he didn't ask for further detail immediately. Instead he took the door indicated, and disappeared into the Reynoldses' living room. It occurred to Thea at that moment, that he might have been in the house before. Clive had seemed to know the name, and James's e-mail suggested a mutual acquaintance. It gave her a strange sensation, as if the grown-ups had been conferring behind her back, and there was some sort of conspiracy under way of which she had not been informed. At the same time, she knew herself well enough to accept that she was often inclined to a mild paranoia. She had always imagined that people were talking about her, with not-so-benign intentions. It came, she believed, from being born into the middle of a large family. The siblings had been rivals not just for affection, but approval and attention.

'How's Rosie?' she asked, in an effort to recapture a note of realism.

'Rosie is fairly fit,' he replied with a promptness that suggested he'd prepared the words earlier. 'Her back's playing up a bit at the moment.'

Rosie was a slender athletic-looking woman, of slightly less than average height and an almost incredibly sweet nature. Everybody loved her for her wide blue eyes, genuine smile and mischievous humour. She was the embodiment of the policeman's patient wife, listening to James's distressing stories, adapting to his unpredictable working hours, and pursuing her own career as a librarian. But Rosie had a Back.

Her vertebrae did not conform properly to the recognised model, and she suffered crippling pain at times. The courage required simply to get dressed in the morning was sometimes too much for Thea, or even James, to think about. And because she hid it from other people and refused to let it dominate her, Rosie emerged as utterly loveable.

Which was why Thea always made a point of bringing her into the conversation when things between her and James threatened to become overly intimate. Nobody, *nobody*, could ever contemplate doing anything that would hurt Rosie.

Which was also, in a way, why James's understated words – *her back's playing up a bit* – actually meant that she was suffering horribly.

'Oh, Lord,' said Thea, with profound sympathy.

'Well, that's how it goes. Look, I'll have to go before noon. Can we talk about this bloke you found in the field? Jennison. Weird that you've got yourself involved, isn't it.'

Thea had several objections to this phrasing. 'I didn't do it on purpose,' she said.

'No, I didn't mean it like that. Just small world kind of stuff.'

Thea moved to the door, already disliking the turn the conversation was taking. 'Let me fetch Hepzie, first. She'll be feeling neglected.'

James's sigh was inadequately concealed. 'Go on, then.'

'And coffee. I'll do coffee.'

She left him flicking the catch of his briefcase, impatience palpable in the air. Thea was aware of a wave of irritation towards him that came as a complete surprise. In this context, so different from usual, he was changed, and not for the better. It wasn't clear just why he'd come, or what he wanted from her. It was an intrusion, with overtones of judgement, and not the simple brotherly visit she'd anticipated at all.

Hepzie was still subdued, and reproachful about being shut in. 'Come on, then,' Thea invited. 'But don't jump up!' She led the dog back to the living room, and watched as she trotted towards James, tail slowly wagging. This was not the usual joyous exuberant animal. 'Be gentle with her,' she told James. 'She isn't feeling her normal self at all.' Then she returned to the coffee.

James launched into business the moment she reappeared with the tray of mugs and biscuits. He didn't appear to have much concern for Hepzie, who was crouched obsequiously at his feet. 'Look, Thea – these murders. We're really not at all sure what it's about. Nothing seems to fit.'

'You mean, is it a family thing or something more organised?'

'More or less. There are whispers about this place, but we've got nothing concrete. I don't suppose you've noticed anything?'

If she hadn't been so irritated with him, she might have given the matter some better quality thought.

'What would I have noticed? People selling drugs outside the church? Small children being passed from car to car?'

He looked at her. 'What's the matter?'

'You, James. I don't get what it is you want from me. Either you've got proper leads to something illegal going on in this area, or you haven't. Don't give me that vague stuff, and then expect me to understand what you're talking about.'

He shook his head slowly. 'It doesn't work like that, and you know it. We have to tread so carefully these days, getting all the evidence in place before showing our hand. Everything's political – or at least politically correct. The only area where we have real freedom these days is child pornography – and I can promise you that isn't what's suspected here.'

'I suppose that's a blessing.' She tried to see beyond his words, to get a feeling for what it must be like. 'You mean, like drugs, for example? Nobody's sure what's worth proper investigating any more? Except, if people are getting *murdered* over it, then surely . . . ?'

'There might be a drugs element,' he nodded. 'There nearly always is. But we can't see a link to the Jennisons. Nothing at all.'

'Family stuff, then,' she asserted. 'Must be.'

'Might be,' he agreed.

'And you want me to be your mole? Your ear to the ground?'

James laughed. 'No, no. Please, no. What I'd really like is for you to pack up and go home. Even you must see it's dangerous, with two killings a few yards away.'

'I can't imagine why they'd go after me, though. There's one theory, surely, that the killer waited for me to arrive, just because I wouldn't be a threat or in their way. Honestly, James, I don't feel the slightest bit bothered about it in that respect. I've met some of the family, and my main feeling is of concern and sympathy for them.'

'Very commendable.'

'So I'm staying. I told Clive I would. And that means you should tell me more about your view of the place, and what you see as the important things I should watch out for.'

There was undisguised admiration in the look he gave

her. She could see him take the decision to at least partly acquiesce to her demand.

'Basically, the most significant element must be money. You'd think, driving through these villages, that it was just another agricultural region of England. There are farm buildings, barns, fields, cows, scattered about. But there's not really much proper farming going on. Read the local papers – you don't get columns about farming, no livestock sections in the classifieds, no fat lamb prices. Instead it's all gardening, arguments about new buildings, home decorating. Property prices are obscene. It's a prime tourist honeypot, too. The whole region screams *Money*. And where there's money, there's likely to be organised crime.'

'I see,' Thea said. And of course she did. She'd worked most of it out for herself, already. 'Which makes the Jennisons rather unusual. And maybe the Staceys.'

'Staceys?'

'I was just coming to them,' she said, and told him the minimal amount she knew.

'They employ a lot of casual labour?' he repeated. 'Youngsters, students – that sort of thing?'

'Apparently.'

'Hollis said something about them, I remember. A lot of coming and going – always draws police attention.'

'Hollis?'

'The DS in charge of this investigation. Haven't you met Hollis yet?'

'Am I likely to?'

'Highly likely, I'd say. Now, can you show me this famous field, do you think?'

'Hang on a minute. I haven't drunk my coffee.'

James leant forward, his big head close to hers as she put her mug down on the coffee table between them.

She laughed at his agitation. 'You've got plenty of time. Don't rush me. Ask me about poor Joel. Let me give you my impressions of him: he was single, attractive, bright, witty. It's outrageous that such a nice man should be killed so young.'

James Osborne's face changed. His eyes widened, and his jaw dropped. 'You *met* him?'

She pulled herself back, pressing into the cushions behind her. 'Yes. He came here the afternoon before he died. Didn't anybody tell you that?'

'Only that you found the body. But surely – there couldn't have been *time*? Clive and his missus had only just left.'

'That's right. Joel was on the doorstep about five minutes after they drove away.'

'How very very odd,' he muttered.

'That's what June seemed to think, as well. June thinks he came to tell me something. If he did, I have no idea what it was.'

'June? Don't tell me – wife of Paul.' He hoisted the briefcase onto the coffee table and opened it. Thea half-expected to see a stack of reports and pictures, full of classified information. If James would just pop out to the loo, she'd be able to snatch a quick look. Instead there seemed to be nothing inside beyond a large A4 notepad, which he extracted.

'The briefcase is a new touch, isn't it?' she said, with only a whisper of sarcasm.

'We use them quite a lot in plain clothes,' he said. 'All part of the disguise, if you like.'

She grinned sceptically. 'I see,' she said.

'Anyway – let's make a few jottings. First, Joel Jennison came to the door here, the same afternoon that Clive left. Saturday. What time?'

'A few minutes after four. I told the local chaps that.'

'I haven't seen the whole file. Bear with me, OK?'

'Fine by me. The next thing that happened was a scream in the night. It could easily not have been Joel. A bird, fox, rabbit – anything, really. I was asleep. It was three forty-five am. I can't even say for sure where it came from. I didn't go outside to investigate and the dogs didn't bark. The security lights didn't come on, either.'

James nodded. 'To be treated with caution,' he said, before adding unexpectedly, 'How do you feel about it?'

'What?'

'I mean – do you wish you'd gone outside? Or have you convinced yourself it had nothing to do with the killing?'

'I don't know. I can't say I feel particularly guilty. Do you think I should?'

'Not at all. You feel what you feel, never mind should. You know that as well as I do.'

'Besides, the man is dead,' she said. 'Too late to dwell on how it might have been different.'

'Precisely.'

'But there seem to be questions about *why* he came here, why he died in this field, the same as his brother.' She paused to think. 'How about if he was searching for clues as to his brother's death? That would make it all far less of a coincidence. I don't like coincidences.'

'Nobody does,' James agreed. 'But they do happen.'

'Not here, though,' she asserted. 'There has to be a direct link. They were *brothers*.'

She caught him looking at her with a recurrence of the earlier impatience. 'Sorry,' she grinned. 'I'm just stating the obvious, aren't I?'

James glanced at his watch. 'I'm sorry this is so short. I expected to be able to take you to lunch, but . . . you know . . .'

She frowned. 'I was looking forward to seeing you,' she began, 'but now I'm not sure. You've got me very confused. Hinting at wicked goings-on and not telling me anything for sure.'

'You're right, I've been very unfair. Look, there's still half an hour. Will you please show me the place where you found the body?'

She got up right away. 'Come on, then.'

They set off across the field, Hepzibah at their heels. It was still breezy, but nothing like the previous day. 'Do you know where the brother, Paul Jennison, was killed?' he asked, scanning the whole field in a slow circle, from a central point.

'No idea,' she said. 'Why would I?'

'The hedge his killer wriggled through – it must have been over there.' He pointed towards the next-door fields, where the hedge was tall, but well-kept. 'Nobody could understand how he did it.'

'It was winter,' she said. 'Easier to see where the gaps are. Maybe he'd prepared it earlier, and knew exactly where to go.'

'It was dark. Pitch dark.'

'It can't have been, Jay.'

'Why?'

'Because Clive wouldn't *know* he'd wriggled through the hedge if it was too dark to see him doing it. It was Clive who witnessed the whole thing, you know.'

He paused to consider this very obvious point. 'I'll need to read the notes again. You're right, of course – unless Clive had some sort of searchlight.'

Thea shrugged and returned to the question about the hedge. 'Desperation, then. You didn't come to investigate for yourself?'

He shook his head. 'No reason why I should. I didn't see any of the notes until Saturday. It was the connection, you see. Two brothers, in the same field. It automatically bounced up the list of priorities.' She showed him the pool, each of them standing a respectable distance away, automatically avoiding any disturbance, despite the forensic people having given the all clear. 'Not much to see,' said Thea.

James gave a brief laugh. 'If I was Sherlock Holmes, I'd probably argue with that. As I'm only me, I can't see a bloody thing. Just grass, mud and water.'

'Er – hang on a minute.' Thea had been looking up, listening to a buzzard mewing in the next field, and hoping to catch a glimpse of it. 'Isn't that something caught in the tree up there? Look.'

She pointed some distance along the hedge, up the slope towards the house. The tree was a well grown alder, which had been coppiced some decades earlier, giving it a bristly shape from about four feet above the ground. There was a colourful object hanging from a bough, twelve or fifteen feet up.

'Just a bit of rag,' said James. 'Must have blown here.'

'Maybe it did. Yesterday was very windy. But what if it's important? Can we get it down, do you think?'

James groaned. 'I never was any good at climbing trees.'

'Maybe not, but I was. Just give me a leg up to where the branches sprout out.'

James, to his credit, helped her without further objection. Finding an easy foothold in the unnaturally low crown of the tree, she hoisted herself a few feet higher, and snatched the piece of material caught on a twig. Instantly, she knew what it was.

Without waiting for help, she jumped down, jarring an ankle, but doing nothing to betray the sharp momentary pain. 'It's Joel's,' she said, taking deep breaths as if she'd just run the length of the field. 'He was wearing it on Saturday.'

The silk scarf, patterned in yellow and purple, could not be mistaken, despite the still damp blood stains. When James asked if she was sure, she nodded firmly. 'But I don't think it can have blown up there after all,' she added. 'It's so heavy.'

It was indeed sodden with blood, and Thea badly wanted to wipe her fingers where they'd touched the scarf.

'The policeman said there was blood. Do you know what happened?'

'I do, actually,' James said quietly. 'His throat was cut.'

Chapter Nine

James was a few minutes late leaving, having first made a phonecall to the local police, reporting the discovery. 'What do you think it means?' Thea asked him. 'After all, we already know Joel was in the field.'

'I don't intend to speculate,' he said. 'It'll have to go to the lab before we know how useful it is.'

'But it must be Joel's blood?'

'Never make assumptions,' he told her, automatically. 'Besides there's other stuff on it. It's so mucky, I'm surprised you could identify it so quickly.'

'It wasn't particularly clean to begin with. None of his clothes were. He was such a mess I thought he must be the gardener, at first.'

James wasn't really listening. Thea could see him calculating his next moves, trying to fit everything in efficiently. She became aware of all the things they hadn't talked about; all the questions and gaps and confusions surrounding the events of the weekend. She was very much aware of how badly she was going to miss him as soon as he'd gone.

'I won't have anybody to talk to,' she said aloud, like a little girl. 'I want to try and work the whole thing out, and for that I need somebody to bounce it around with.'

'Lonely business, house-sitting,' he said with little evident sympathy. She could almost hear him add, You should have thought of that.

The lack of compassion was bracing, as James had probably intended it to be. 'I could go and talk to Helen again, I suppose,' she said.

'No, don't do that. Go and see June Jennison. She's the one I'm interested in.'

Thea bridled. 'Then *you* go and see her,' she flashed. 'One minute you're telling me to be careful because there are funny people around here – the next you want me to do your job for you. Which one is it?'

He sighed, glancing yet again at his watch. 'OK, point taken. But you're just as bad. Either you sit here all on your own for three weeks, going quietly bonkers, or you get out and about, meet the neighbours, hear their stories, have a cup of tea here and there . . .' He raised his eyebrows, to check that she understood. 'Right?'

She shook her head slowly, in an exaggerated arc. 'Not really. June Jennison lives in Cirencester, remember. Nobody else seems to be at home during the week. Admittedly there were eight or nine locals gathered at the gate on Sunday, when they realised something was going on – but that was a Sunday. Not one of them introduced themselves, or invited me over for a drink. What you're really asking is that I do an informal house-to-house for you.'

James laughed. 'Wrong. The Gloucester lads did that

days ago. You wouldn't know what to ask, anyway.' He was edging out of the door by this time, showing every sign of a man worryingly late for something important. 'Look, Thee, I've really got to go now. Phone or e-mail me this evening, if you like. Thanks for the coffee. It was good to see you.'

There were moments when he was unbearably similar to Carl. He tilted his head now, with a kink at the corner of his mouth, displaying apology, self-deprecation, helplessness, which was exactly his brother. Thea's heart lurched, and the ragged old curtain of misery and loss came down over all other emotions. She could hardly see James through it.

'Yes, all right,' she said, taking a half-step back into the house. 'Thanks for coming.' He got into his car, winding down the window to stick his head out.

'Bye,' they both said, simultaneously.

For lunch, she made herself some scrambled eggs, washed down with half a bottle of Clive Reynolds' Chardonnay. The Instruction List said, *There are six bottles of wine in the rack in the pantry. They are for your use.* She fully intended to avail herself of all six bottles.

Her mood was an uncomfortable mixture of defiance and frustration. Here she was, ostensibly in the midst of a first class murder enquiry, and yet nobody came to talk to her, nobody told her what was going on, and she saw no way of grasping the first thing about village politics. The house-sitting job, which had seemed daunting on Saturday, had now settled into a routine that left acres of empty time, especially in the middle of the day. Bonzo and Georgie were livelier than at first, but they still seemed to like nothing better than dozing their lives away. Hepzie shadowed Thea, contentedly sitting at her feet, going for walks or riding on the passenger seat of the car. Now she had a sore ear, she was obviously unsettled, sticking even more closely to Thea than before. Like one of those daemons in the Pullman books, Thea thought.

'Well, this won't do,' she said out loud. 'We've got hours before we have to do anything. Come on, Heps, we'll go to Cirencester.' The Chardonnay probably meant there was a suspicious quantity of alcohol in her bloodstream, but what the hell. Getting stopped on a Wednesday afternoon was unlikely enough for her not to worry. And she'd always been able to hold drink much better than most women.

Taking the dog into town was complicated. Unlike those long-suffering collies and mongrels you saw tied up quietly outside shops, Hepzibah would howl and bark without pause if Thea went out of sight. On the few occasions she'd done it, she'd emerged to a knot of reproachful dog-lovers, all trying to comfort the distraught animal. Thus it meant either leaving her in the car, or walking the streets without actually buying anything. Almost no shops admitted dogs through their doors any more. By rights, she should leave her here with the labradors, but somehow that wouldn't do. The spaniel's place was by her side.

She didn't know the town well, except for a vague awareness of a very large park and an imposing church. Plus a lot of Roman associations and a popular open market. She hoped it wasn't market day: that would surely mean difficult and expensive parking arrangements.

As it turned out, she was not to discover whether it was

market day at Cirencester or not. She had driven less than a mile when she changed her mind. There was a pub indicated, named Five Mile House, the other side of the main dual-carriage A417, which she concluded must be her nearest hostelry. Although it was likely to be closed for a break between lunchtime and evening, it was worth a look. There was just a chance that one day in the coming weeks she would be so desperate for company, she'd break the phobia of a life-time and venture unaccompanied into a bar.

The manoeuvring she had to do to reach it almost put her off. It involved driving underneath the main road, and venturing along an uninviting stretch that turned out to be a rather odd cul-de-sac. A large gate barred the way, just beyond the pub. Why, she asked herself, was she doing this? Was it merely that she was so starved for company that the mere suggestion of a pub had her completely distracted?

Five Mile House was decidedly pretty. It had a friendly unpretentious air, which Thea absorbed as she sat in the car outside for a moment. She hoped she wasn't being whimsical in drawing this conclusion; after all, the inside might be completely different, and to be unduly unspoilt and 'local' wasn't necessarily a good thing. She had been into pubs where a handful of silent old men glowered at the intrusion, with malevolent dogs at their feet. Tacky decor and tasteless background music was preferable to that. What she wanted, she realised, was somewhere with some life. A simple need, on the face of it, but Thea sometimes wondered whether she was a sort of jinx, attracting death and solitude to herself. As a young girl she had vowed to surround herself with a big noisy family of children, with jokes and laughter and affection.

But 'You don't really want that,' her father had told her one day, when she'd been about twelve. The quality of this attention had thrilled and frightened her. It seemed that all along he had effortlessly known precisely who and what she was.

'I do,' she'd insisted.

'No – you'll have had enough of all that, with this lot.' He'd made a sweep of the brothers and sisters – Emily, Damian and Jocelyn. 'Take my word for it.'

She had worried and fumed at this unfair prediction ever since. It was as if he had carelessly written her fate for her, against her own will. All the worse because Jocelyn, now thirty-eight, had produced five children, and if it was all right for her, Thea couldn't understand what was different in her own case. She was the third of the four, had always fitted in perfectly well, was on easy terms with all the others. What was it that her father had seen that day? The answer – or answers – revealed itself in the occasional flash of insight, which she generally buried as quickly as she could. So what if she hadn't liked the pain of childbirth, the broken nights, the constant nagging worry of the dependent child? Two or three wouldn't have noticeably increased these negatives, and might have actually diminished them. Carl had been accommodating. 'It's up to you,' he'd always said.

The truth, or part of it, was to do with a kind of spiritual selfishness, which Thea knew she possessed. Much of the time she redefined this as an assertive style whereby she did what she wanted to, followed her inclinations, and sidestepped many of the martyred games other women played.

All of which brought her back to a bewildered sense of

disappointment at her current solitary existence. Was this what she'd always wanted, deep down, as her father had implied? Was she in fact not good at relationships? Was her reluctance to walk alone into a busy pub a symptom of this very defect?

She shook herself, and muttered, 'Stop it, for goodness' sake.' Hepzie looked at her, wondering just what was going on. 'We've no intention of going to a pub now anyway.' Giving it a last considering look, she started the car again, and turned it round.

Coming out of a garden gate a few yards away was a bearded man she recognised from Sunday morning. The man who, with a real effort, she remembered Helen Winstanley had told her was named Harry Richmond. Without thinking, she stamped on the brake, and wound down the window.

'Good afternoon,' she said, with the biggest smile she could muster. 'Remember me?'

He looked at her with an oddly expectant expression, and smiled back. She confirmed her earlier assessment of his age as late sixties. 'Oh, yes. You're the lady looking after Clive's house,' he said lightly, as if amused by being asked the question.

'That's right.' Now what? Why the hell had she stopped, anyway?

'Will you come and talk to me for a few minutes?' he invited, with a very direct look. His eyes were a shade of brown that was almost yellow. They had a quality to them that Thea couldn't quite identify. Not exactly fierce, or defensive, but full of energy and intent. With surprise, she realised she liked this man.

'OK then,' she said, and turned off the car engine. 'Is this your house?'

'Handy for the pub,' he said, with a weariness that revealed the words as having been repeated so often they'd lost any meaning. He didn't strike her as much of a drinker. 'Do you mind leaving the dog in the car? I have a cat who passionately dislikes dogs.'

She followed him through the garden gate, noticing an exuberant lilac tree just inside the hedge, awash with deep purple blooms, impossible to ignore. Across the front of the house a clematis clung and spread, with a thousand small pink flowers. The effect was of bounteous excess, not just in colour and texture, but scent, from the lilac. The rest of the garden was equally overflowing. No lawn, but narrow paths between beds overflowing with clumps and clusters, buds and boughs, all packed closely. In the summer it must be chest high with delphiniums and lupins and daisies and a dozen other things.

'Wow!' she breathed. 'I love your garden.'

He ducked his chin, as if accepting what was due. 'Come on in,' he said, and pushed open the front door.

It was dark inside, as they stepped into a windowless inner hall. The man took her into a room on the left, where the light was dappled by the clematis outside, which straggled halfway down the window. They were in a sitting room furnished with plump armchairs and a deep-piled red carpet. Thea tried to find evidence of a wife, but the search was inconclusive. There was no sign of the dog-hating cat.

'I should introduce myself,' he said. 'Harry Richmond.'

'Thea Osborne. Pleased to meet you.' She held out her

hand and he took it in a dry assertive grasp. She felt the loss when he let go again.

He didn't bustle or dither, but directed her to a deeply comfortable chair and left her to put the kettle on for tea. He was back in less than a minute. Thea only had time to scan the row of books on a built-in shelf beside the chimney breast. Wilbur Smith and Ruth Rendell seemed to feature most prominently.

'I'm sorry if this seems rather odd,' he said, sitting down in the opposite chair. 'I promise I haven't abducted you. We're supposed to be careful about approaching young women these days.'

'Wasn't that always the case?'

He smiled. 'Of course. Even more so at times, actually. It's just – I suppose we didn't *talk* about it so much then.'

She waited, rehearsing things to say, and rejecting them all. If this was some sort of game, then the next move was surely down to him.

'Do you know this area at all?' he asked.

'Oh, yes. I only live in Oxfordshire. I know Gloucester quite well, and Cheltenham. I hadn't actually been to the Duntisbournes before, though. It's very pretty round here.'

'So you don't know anybody?'

'No, not really. I've spoken to Helen Winstanley a couple of times.'

'And you went to visit Barrow Hill, I gather?'

Was the gentle hint of reproach all in her imagination? 'I did, yes. I felt so sorry for the farmer, old Mr Jennison.'

'Really?' The wry amusement on his face was a shock. 'And how did he receive your sympathy?'

117

He was definitely playing with her. 'You probably already know I never managed to speak to him. I still haven't seen him.'

He got up from his chair, with no sign of stiffness. 'I'll just go and make that tea. Do you have milk? Sugar?'

'Just milk, thanks.'

She waited impassively for his return. He had an agenda, which she did not. She didn't think he wanted to upset or frighten her. It could simply be that he'd understood her loneliness, and wanted to assuage it. He couldn't have known she would come driving past his gate, so he must have acted very swiftly to get into position as he had. Thinking about that, she realised he must have noticed her drive past, towards the pub, identified the vehicle, and decided to present himself as she returned – knowing she had no choice but to come back the same way.

Cleverly, he hadn't flagged her down as she returned, but merely stood where she could see him, giving her the chance to recognise him and stop. This explanation made sense as far as it went, but it still seemed riddled with coincidence and unexplained motivations. He came back with two mugs of tea. No tray or biscuits, no saucers or teaspoons. This was a man who had kept up with the times. She suspected he hadn't used a teapot, either, but merely dunked a teabag into first one mug of hot water, then the other. The tea did not look very strong.

'I should reveal my interest,' he said. 'You must be wondering what I'm playing at.'

She took the mug he offered, and set it down on the floor beside her. 'Go on then,' she invited.

118

'You met June and Lindy at Barrow Hill. It was Lindy who described your visit to me. She's my great-niece, as it happens, and we're the greatest of friends. We have a regular date every Tuesday evening, when we play chess and catch up with the gossip. Nothing can keep us from it, not even the sudden violent death of her uncle.'

'Or the sudden violent death of her father, two months ago?'

'Well, we did miss two weeks then,' he admitted. 'He died on a Saturday, and wasn't buried for a while afterwards, with all the police work and so forth.' He shook his head. 'Lindy's the one you should be feeling sorry for, not her blasted grandfather.'

Thea tried to work it out. 'Is he your brother?'

'Not likely! No, my sister was married to him. Muriel, her name is.'

For the first time, Thea gave a thought to this woman whose two sons had been killed in rapid succession. Was her heart not broken? How on earth must she be feeling? And as if this belated sympathy had shifted something inside, she felt a surge of real horror at what had happened. She gasped with it, aware in that moment of how successfully she'd so far kept herself detached from the emotions involved. It hadn't been her problem; the people were strangers to her. Now this defence crumbled, and sadness rushed in.

'Poor woman!' she said. 'What must she be feeling?'

Harry Richmond eyed her consideringly. 'Do you have children? Sons?'

'A daughter. Jessica. She's twenty-one.'

'And you're a widow, I gather?'

'Right. Did Lindy tell you that, as well?'

'To be frank with you, I knew already. Clive Reynolds and I are friends, you might say. We're both on the Parish Council, among other things. He talked a little bit about you, trying to reassure himself that the house would be in capable hands. He's a worrier, poor old Clive.'

Thea struggled not to be diverted. 'So the Jennisons, Paul and Joel, were your nephews. June said your sister ran off?' It sounded impertinent, but there'd been an unspoken pact from the start not to be unduly polite. She didn't think Harry Richmond valued politeness very highly.

'It wasn't an easy thing she did, leaving those boys. There are people who will never forgive her, never even speak to her, because of it. That's after more than twenty years.'

'Did she have more children?'

'A girl. She's twenty-one now, too. Like your Jessica.'

'Is she still with the man? The one she ran off with?'

'He died, as it happens. Last year. He was older than her, by some years. Got the dreaded prostate trouble, which went into his pelvis. Very unpleasant, poor chap. Didn't know where to put himself, in the last few weeks, for the pain.'

Thea lapsed into one of her familiar reveries, in which she compared the different ways of dying and tried to decide which might be preferable, given a choice, which of course you weren't.

'Where is she now?' she asked, eventually, aware that the woman Muriel was the key element in this conversation.

'Oh, she's not far away.' He looked into her eyes, challenging her to join in the game he was playing. Thea was hooked, wondering whether she was about to hear that

Muriel was landlady of the pub up the lane, or head teacher at the nearest primary school.

She cocked her head and widened her eyes, knowing how pretty she looked when she did that. Harry Richmond responded as men generally did, with a slight tension, a slight upward lift, as if a magnet were drawing him towards her. He didn't take his eyes off hers. She didn't want him to.

'My sister lives in Bisley. Do you know it?'

Thea shook her head.

'It's only two or three miles, as the crow flies. The lanes make it further, but you could say she's local, still.'

'Brave lady.'

He shrugged. 'She'd never get on anywhere else. Some people are like plants – you can't uproot them without killing them.'

Thea wondered at the paradox of this. The woman *had*, after all, uprooted herself from Barrow Hill, in a manner that even these days was exceptional, and twenty years ago was close to blasphemy. Not a lot of women abandoned young sons as well as a husband. She urgently wanted to know more about Muriel Jennison – or whatever her surname was now. She wanted to know what sort of person had produced that very pleasant Joel, and was sister to this seductive elderly man.

'So – the killing of Paul and Joel. Are you trying to say it's somehow a family matter?'

'Whoa!' He blinked and shook his head. 'Have a care.'

It was such an odd old-fashioned caution that she smiled. 'Sorry,' she said. 'I'm still trying to understand.'

'Of course, in one sense, it's obviously a family matter.

They were brothers, after all. The police set out with the attitude that Paul must have been shot by some travelling person, poaching a long way from his own home patch. They couldn't find a match for the threads and hairs and stuff from the hedge. It was a horrible tragic thing to happen, left everybody sick and frustrated – but it suited us to imagine it'd been a stranger that did it, probably by accident. He certainly didn't panic – thoroughly cleaned the gun of fingerprints and left it by the body, before running away. Tried to make it look like suicide, you see, though not very convincingly. Clive seems to have disturbed him by charging out with his torch and his stick. We were just starting to settle down again, thinking, well, he'll never rest easy in his bed, to his dying day, whoever he might be. Saves the taxpayer the cost of a trial. Won't bring Paulie back. One of those things. Then Joel got himself killed, and it's as if everything came back, fifty times over.'

'Everybody was so *quiet*, on Sunday morning, standing by my gate. It was uncanny.'

'Not *your* gate,' he reminded her. 'But I know what you mean. We were stunned senseless. When Helen phoned me, I just couldn't believe it.'

'But why did everybody turn up like that, and just stand there? It was uncanny – or worse than that. Ghoulish. Like gawpers at a motorway crash.'

'I imagine there are as many answers to that as there were people gathered. Young Johnny Baker was just passing on his bike. Martin and Isabel would be concerned merely on the grounds of living so close by. Virginia and her friend might have persuaded themselves they could do something useful.'

'And you? Why were *you* there?'

'That's something I asked myself, as soon as I arrived. Helen said something about more trouble at Brook View, which I believe I heard as trouble for the Jennison family, almost from the start. I've never been a very patient man. It seemed intolerable to sit at home and wait for news.' He shook his head, with a rueful smile. 'I can't really explain, if I'm honest.'

'You were very concerned about that Monique girl. What was all that about?'

He scratched the back of his neck. 'In actual fact, I was just looking for an excuse to break up the crowd. I didn't think it was very wholesome the way they all just stood there. Not very nice for you, after such a traumatic discovery, either.'

'Oh, I'm used to shocks,' she said. 'Immune, probably.'

'Nobody's immune, my dear. It always catches up with you eventually. Sometimes the second time's even worse than the first.'

Thea shook her head. 'Only if you've sidestepped it the first time around.'

'Balderdash!' he said, with a self-mocking smile. 'Utter baloney.'

'So how was it for you?' she asked, knowing this moment had been coming all along and wondering whether everyone in this secretive little village had a tragic tale to tell.

'Wife had motor neurone disease. She died two years ago, inch by horrifying inch. Nothing unusual. She was seventy-two. It was just an unhappy twist that her mother outlived her.'

'Offspring?'

'Just the one. He's thirty-nine and homosexual. We find it hard to understand each other, but he has a very good heart, as Grandma always said. I consider myself fortunate, compared to a lot of people.'

'We still seem to be talking about families,' Thea mused. 'Do you think that's the way the police are looking at the murders now? Something in the family?'

'I'm not privy to how the police are thinking. I gather you're better placed for that than I am.'

Aha! Of course! Now she knew why he'd flagged her down, why she was so interesting. It was James. Clive Reynolds had passed on the fact that she had a senior policeman as a brother-in-law. She almost laughed with relief at having settled that particular question. It did nothing to diminish her liking for and interest in Mr Harry Richmond.

Who had not actually flagged her down; he hadn't needed to be so unsubtle. She had the feeling he'd given the matter a lot of thought. She might almost be persuaded that he'd sent out some sort of magic spell that made her divert her route past his garden gate.

Well, he deserved a reward for his patience. 'Actually, James seems to think it's something rather more sinister than that,' she said.

Chapter Ten

It was not unlike waking from a deep dreamless sleep. A sleep you knew you oughtn't to be having, because it was morning and you should be somewhere. It was like rewinding a video and watching it again properly, putting aside the ironing or newspaper that you'd used as distraction. This time you turned up the sound, watched for every little detail, realising how inattentive and unobservant you'd been before.

Why had the police allowed her to get away with so much? Their questions had been vague, their sense of her importance minimal. She had merely been the individual who discovered the body. 'Found in woodlands by a man walking his dog' had always been one of the less interesting lines in reports of a corpse turning up. The man was never publicly interviewed, or named or given a leading role in the proceedings. Did he receive counselling afterwards for his trauma? Did he dream of decomposing flesh and fingers mistaken for sticks to throw for his Jack Russell?

Joel Jennison had not told her anything during his fleeting visit that could possibly be construed as a cry for help, a warning or a clever clue as to whatever dreadful crimes might be going on in the village. He had been relaxed and friendly. He had asked her whether Thea was short for Dorothea or Anthea, in a funny clever way. So June's suspicion that he had been visiting for an urgent reason seemed wrong.

He hadn't handed her a small important package, or passed on any messages. If he was in a state-sponsored spy ring, she had completely failed to notice. If he was trying to alert her to a midnight assembly of the local coven in Clive Reynolds' orchard, it had apparently never materialised.

Instead, he had got himself into the field behind the house, during the night, losing his neckerchief and his life in the process.

And now, five days later, Thea was feeling deeply distressed by this. She bitterly mourned the cheerful young man, who'd been full of life and humour. She conceived a rage against the faceless nameless killer who had slaughtered him and then dumped the body face down in a muddy pool. And she acknowledged a determination to do all she could to bring this monster to justice. All this, and more, Harry Richmond had elicited from her before she left his cottage. She had even told him the full story of Carl's accident, and the helpless hatred she still felt for the careless lorry driver who had sent him to his death. Neither of them had needed to articulate the consequent desire to prevent another killing from going unavenged.

He had given her another mug of tea, this time with buttered toast and honey. It was two hours before she remembered the dog in the car, clapping her hand to her mouth with self-reproach. There had been no sign of Harry's cat, but he did not invite Hepzibah in. Instead he'd just waited for her to leave, standing in his hallway, smiling gently.

'Come again,' he'd said. 'Any time.'

Thursday evening was disjointed. Remembering her duties to the Reynoldses, she vacuumed the living room and stairs, checked for telephone messages, inspected the sheep in the fading light, and organised a brief romping game for the labradors on the side lawn. Then she e-mailed James, despite there being no message from him.

It was good to see you yesterday, sorry it couldn't be longer. Have met an interesting man, name of Harry Richmond, related to the Jennisons. I hope he's not a police suspect. Are they (you?) getting anywhere? Everything seems terribly quiet.

Rain's forecast for tomorrow, darn it. But I've survived nearly a week here now, and haven't spent more than a pound or two of my own money, which can't be bad. Even with corpses turning up, this is rather a good way to earn a crust.

Anyway, hope to see you again soon. Love to Rosie, and I hope the back's eased up now.

Thea.

It had taken some careful thought to strike just the right tone. Cheerful, self-sufficient, and mindful of poor Rosie, but not letting him off the hook regarding the police enquiry. If his visit the day before had been motivated by a wish to pick her brains, then she'd earned the right to be kept informed. The extent of his concern for her welfare was a matter of some doubt, in her mind. She'd been tempted to hint at nervousness, but in the end decided against it. It was too risky a path to venture down, playing the woman in jeopardy. The last thing she wanted was to start believing it herself.

Vulnerability had never been an attractive trait in Thea's eyes. Her father had taught her to be confident and realistic. 'Very few people in the world are actively out to get you,' he'd said once. 'They've all got more pressing things on their minds.'

Carl had embraced very much the same philosophy. 'Nobody's going to stick the knife in just for the hell of it,' was his line. 'You have to provoke them first.' As far as she knew, he hadn't provoked the driver of the juggernaut that killed him. The man had simply misjudged a bend, letting the vehicle drift over into Carl's lane, swatting his car almost carelessly into a fatal roll. He'd been very upset about it afterwards, and had lost his job over it, albeit temporarily.

But that was another story, another time. Thea banished the familiar wave of frustrated misery and focused on the present. She had a project now, which could well fill the coming two weeks and give her considerable satisfaction. If it turned out to be dangerous, then she'd deal with that too. Whether or not Joel Jennison had knocked on her door with the intention of asking for help, he was going to get it. Too late, perhaps, but nobody could blame her for that.

Except, they could. Because she hadn't got out of bed that night, when she heard the terrible scream outside. She hadn't grabbed a torch and called the dogs, and raised a commotion, which just might possibly have saved poor Joel Jennison's life.

* * *

Obviously, the first place to call, on a drizzly Friday morning, was Barrow Hill Farm again. She had yet to meet old Mr Jennison, and convey her condolences to him directly. Perhaps he could use some practical help, if June and Lindy had gone home, and the relief milker was only doing the cow-related tasks he was hired for.

Finding a pair of Wellington boots in the back room, she pulled them on. 'You stay here,' she told the dogs, who seemed relieved to be spared the uninviting weather. The early morning walkies had been briefly functional on all sides.

For a moment, Thea considered taking the car, but it seemed likely to arouse contempt, given the trip was not even half a mile, door to door. Arriving on foot was more neighbourly, less formal, and somehow suggested a firm intention rather than a casual whim.

True to June's promise, there were no longer cattle in the muddy yard. Nor was there the sound of a tractor engine, any sign of a car or any evidence of a human presence. Thea plodded across the yard and up the short front path to the house door. She knocked, waited and knocked again.

There was a sound behind her, and she turned to see what it was. A man was standing at the gate, one hand leaning heavily on the stone wall separating the little front garden from the yard. He was breathing hard, as if he'd been running – but Thea thought she'd have heard him if that were the case.

'Oh! Hello,' she said, moving towards him. 'I'm sorry to intrude again. I'm Thea Osborne—'

'I know who you are,' he said, scowling.

'Yes? Oh, good. I came to see if you needed—'

'You came from nosiness, the same as all the others,' he accused. 'Can't leave a person alone, can you?'

'Mr Jennison, I'm really sorry—'

He interrupted her yet again. Was he never going to let her finish a sentence? 'Why should you be sorry? You didn't kill him, did you?'

'Of course not.' She stared at him, controlling the urge to be as rude and aggressive as he was. 'Isn't June here?'

'Why would she be? Moved out a year or more ago. There's no place for her here.'

Despite the rough breathless delivery, his accent was almost as much of a surprise as his son's had been. And yet she knew that these days farming took brains, determination, manual skills and familiarity with paperwork, if it were to prosper. Except, she reminded herself, the Jennisons had not been prospering. Far from it. And every farmer she had ever met of this man's generation spoke with a regional accent.

'Mr Jennison, I'm very sorry if you feel I shouldn't have come. The fact is, I did find the body of your son in the field of the house I'm caretaking. I can't help feeling some sort of responsibility for that. Furthermore . . .' she drew in her chin and squared her shoulders, '. . . I was rather upset by it. I feel at a tremendous disadvantage, not knowing any of the people involved, not understanding what it is that's been going on. I didn't just come to see if I could help you – I was rather hoping that you'd have something to offer me.'

It was a gamble that showed no sign of paying off. Aware of the incongruity of facing the man as he approached his own front door, as if he were the visitor, she held her ground. It would be awkward to push past him, anyway. Instead she maintained eye contact, eager to spot any softening on his part.

He made a sound not unlike *Harumff* and shifted his weight. It did seem that he had a severe problem with one or both hip joints. Grooves on his face spoke of constant pain, suffered with absolute stoicism. Pity, however, did not seem to be the appropriate response. Thea began to appreciate the impatience she'd heard in June's voice and words, concerning her father-in-law.

'They tell me he came to see you, that afternoon, before milking,' he said, firing the words like missiles.

'Yes, he did.'

'What for?'

'I have no idea. He seemed to be just paying a polite visit. Except he was wearing his work clothes.' She deliberately risked elaboration:

'I thought he must be the gardener.'

'Gardener! They haven't got a gardener.'

'No, I know that now. But that's what he looked like. Scruffy, if I may say so.' The garden-party diction was catching. Maybe everybody around here spoke like this. Perhaps, like the source of the Thames, this was also the source of True English. The idea almost made her smile.

'The police think it was me that did it,' he said, with a slight lapse of syntax. 'Damned fools.'

'Have they said so?'

'Not directly. They'd have to arrest me then, wouldn't they? But they keep coming back, asking all about the boys'

131

mother, who owns the land, why Paul went off when he did. As if I could . . .' He inhaled deeply, his knuckles tightening on the top of the wall. Thea couldn't let him go on standing there.

'Here, I'm in your way,' she said, and moved to one side. 'Go in and sit down. June said you had a bad hip.'

He gave her a stony look. 'What has my hip to do with you?'

She began to speak, but checked herself, before starting again. 'I told you why I think this whole business has something to do with me. I've been dragged into it, whether I like it or not. I don't know why you're being so belligerent about it.'

In a Hollywood movie, this would have been the moment when he thawed, spilling out his pain and misery, confiding his terror for the future and his bewilderment at what had happened. Instead, he moved stiffly past her, without turning his head. At the door of his house, he threw a final remark over his shoulder.

'This has nothing to do with you. You're a stranger here. Leave us to our own business, will you!' And he closed the door with some force.

Perversely, the reaction of Mr Jennison Senior only made Thea more determined to get involved. The contrast with Harry Richmond had been so stark that she wondered whether the farmer might actually have killed his sons, as he said the police believed. He certainly did not seem to be a very pleasant person. Even taking into account his painful hip and the disastrous loss of Paul and Joel, he still came across as churlish, unyielding and suspicious. Worse – the look in his eyes had been unnerving. It was rare to find such a demeanour in a sane person. The blank gaze of gum-chewing adolescents was annoying and unsettling at times; the defensive sideways glance of youths with a guilty conscience likewise – but this was different in kind. This man had problems beyond the obvious, and Thea wanted to know what they were.

She also wanted to make a report of some sort, and that could only be to James. Trudging back up to the road from the still mucky farmyard, she rehearsed the e-mail she would send him. Or would it be wiser to telephone? People made such a fuss about e-mails being insecure, although she couldn't understand how anybody else could see them unless you all worked together in a big office. She'd never liked making phonecalls; the person was always busy or out or distracted. E-mail it would be – but she'd use James's personal e-mail address – the one he accessed only from home. If he didn't see it until the evening, then nothing would be lost. It was hardly a matter of life and death. 'At least, I hope it isn't,' she muttered to herself.

The computer waited invitingly on the living room coffee table, reminding Thea she hadn't indulged in a game of Scrabble for three days now. There'd been moderately interesting offerings on TV the past few evenings, as well as an absorbing book she'd got into, which tempted her to earlier nights than usual.

It had taken her less than a year to appreciate the pace and freedom of living alone. The lack of routine suited her better than she'd ever expected, with nobody to explain to, nobody saying, 'But you *usually* go to bed at eleven . . .' if she suddenly wanted to go at nine thirty, or one in the morning. It became a habit to avoid habits. She automatically followed whims, having a bath at teatime, staying up to watch a film into the small hours, drifting about in a bathrobe all morning. It was so good she seriously doubted whether she could ever live with anybody again.

Me again, making my report, sir. I've been busy here, meeting people. Chiefly Jennison Senior. The man is a churlish beast, more or less slammed the door in my face this morning. He seems in a bad way with painful hips, but that's not enough reason to be so rude. Seems to think the police suspect him of killing his sons?

No sign of any detective work going on. No sign of anything, come to that. Life carries on invisibly, as far as I can tell.

I haven't said much about Harry R, have I? He knew who I was, and seemed a bit concerned for me. He has a lot of contact with Lindy, Paul J's daughter. He knows about you as well, and I think he might have been probing for some inside information. I'm afraid I might have given him a bit, too.

I know you didn't exactly ask me to report to you, but I feel rather out of my depth, to be honest. I'm not sure what I can do, or what you want me to.

I can see Helen Winstanley again, and maybe her husband (another James, as it happens) will be there.

Only two more weeks to go until Clive and Jennifer come back. Funny, I have a sense of a big blank sheet of paper waiting to be written on, with the events of those coming two weeks. Ignore me, I'm being fanciful.

See you sometime. Love to Rosie.

Thea.

* * *

Then she played a game of Scrabble with a person called Shelby in Australia. The people logged on varied geographically according to the time of day or night. Morning in Europe meant late evening in Australasia, evening in the UK meant morning in America and Canada. She seldom played with other Brits, purely because she had chosen to use the American dictionary. It gave more spelling variations, and fewer 'cheat' words like *zo* and *qi*, which she disliked to use. Bad enough that the American version permitted *jo*, *oe* and *ut*.

She and Shelby were neck and neck right to the end, but Thea eventually lost by ten points, being left with a D when Shelby placed five remaining letters in one deft move. It reduced her overall points rating by a very unfair 12, which annoyed her.

It was still only a little past midday when she was finished. Outside it remained damp and grey and uninviting. The heating had switched itself on in response to the drop in temperature, and the dogs were all revelling in the warmth. She wished the house had a view that included at least one other dwelling, from the back or the front. It recalled the peculiar dread she had frequently suffered from as a child, coming out of school at the end of the day with a sudden conviction that the world had ended and nobody had informed the school. She blamed it on a premature reading of *The Day of the Triffids* when she was nine.

Now she experienced the same sensation. How would she know if everyone had been struck dead across Gloucestershire, if not the whole of the planet? Well, Shelby in Australia was still alive, of course, but that was small comfort.

There were, she reminded herself, houses in three directions, less than half a mile distant. It was simply that the sloping terrain and thick growth of trees closed in the vistas. Each house was cut off from its neighbours by the way the land was arranged, aided by the interventions of mankind, cutting lanes through deeply wooded corridors with high hedges on either side. There was none of the openness she'd noticed on the road down towards Cirencester; none of the bland featureless modernity of the A417, slashing its brutal way through the landscape. Here, just a couple of miles away, all was secret and small and separated.

And beautiful. The human impact had been almost entirely in harmony, she was forced to admit. This, she realised for the first time, was the charm of the area, the reason people came thousands of miles to see it for themselves. Nothing could prepare them for the reality of the warm, almost edible-looking stone, the odd angles, the quirky surprises like the ford through the centre of Duntisbourne Leer, and the barn door covered in public notices, for lack of a Post Office or shop or even Parish Council-sponsored notice-board. Things were not as they seemed, and Thea suspected a person could live here for ten years and never quite feel they'd grasped the spirit of the place.

The delight was in the villages. Bigger than might at first appear, there was nothing brash or materialistic about them, despite the tendency for brash materialistic urban individuals to buy the properties that composed them. It was pleasing to think that the place wove a benignant spell over the people, turning them into softer, slower creatures, content to tend their gardens and enjoy the quiet beauty around them without competing or boasting about their wealth.

Pleasing, but probably inaccurate. People in the Cotswolds were probably just the same as people anywhere else. How, she wondered, was she ever going to find out for herself just how true this was?

'Let's go and see Helen,' she said to the spaniel, after a five-minute lunch comprising a cheese and salad sandwich. 'And if she's not in, we really must go and visit Cirencester. Apart from anything else, we need some proper shopping.'

They walked up the road to the Winstanleys' house, Hepzibah on a lead. The hedges were high on both sides of the lane, planted into banks that were already burgeoning with wild flowers. Thea flipped absently at them as she passed, not in the mood for appreciating nature. She was aware of a smouldering anger, directed at people who killed other people. The ultimate theft, one of few acts that could never in any way be rectified. The same could of course be said of rape – and arson perhaps. Any act of violence brought about irreversible change, but to kill someone sent the world spinning off its axis for large numbers of survivors. It turned black to white and hot to cold. Her head filled with images of Carl, mangled in his car, and Joel Jennison, sodden in the pool, and she raged inwardly. Two good, funny men wiped out for nothing. Whether by accident or design might be relevant, but was not central. The central thing was that they were gone, and could never ever come back.

She arrived at Helen's front door with her eyes smarting and her cheeks wet. The dog was drooping, her damaged ear apparently causing some discomfort, to judge by the odd head-shaking she kept doing. 'We're a right pair,'

Thea said to her. 'Maybe Helen can cheer us up.'

Helen took some minutes to answer the door. When she did, she was in a long blue dressing gown and bare feet. Her hair was tangled; her face smudgy and creased. 'Errghhh,' she said, clasping her hands together and pushing, in a sort of reverse stretch. 'What time is it?'

'Quarter past one,' said Thea. 'Sorry. I'd better go away again.'

'No, don't. It's nice to see you, even if you have caught me being such a slob. You won't tell anybody, will you?'

Thea took this as a joke until she gave Helen her full attention, and realised she was serious. 'Who would I tell?' she asked, genuinely wondering.

'Come in, anyway. How's your ear?' The last part was addressed to the spaniel, who gave no reply.

'I think it hurts a bit,' Thea answered for her. 'But she'll be OK.'

'And your hand?'

Thea had forgotten her hand. Or rather, she had absorbed the fact of the pain as merely part of her overall experience. There was always pain, after all. She made sure of that. 'Fine,' she said, without even looking at it.

'You look a bit rough,' Helen observed. 'Though not half as rough as me, I'm sure.'

'Late night?' Thea ventured.

'Something like that. James gets home tomorrow. I'll have to pull myself together by then. You probably know how it works – doing just the opposite of what you know you're supposed to?'

'Sort of. It depends who's doing the supposing,' said Thea,

striving for accurate empathy. 'It's not quite like that for me.'

'No. Well, I'm tempted to say lucky you, but that would be appallingly insensitive of me.'

They were in the kitchen, and Hepzie jumped onto an old chair that looked as if it was intended for a dog. It stood beside a handsome dark red Aga that gave out a heat that was far too much. Thea disliked Agas for this and several other reasons. Carl had wanted one when they moved to Witney, and she had resisted.

'That looks like a dog chair,' she said, stepping around the minefield of female survival strategies, but realising too late that this could well be another booby trap.

'Oh – yes. We had a dog until a few weeks ago. Sammy. Nice old chap.' Helen spoke lightly, while fiddling with the lid of an electric kettle.

'What happened to him?' When it came to dogs, Thea needed to know.

'Oh, we gave him away. Funnily enough, he's the father of Binnie's pups. He lives with the Staceys now. It wasn't right for him here, nobody playing with him. He needs a bit of company. There's always someone to play with at Fairweather. He does them some good, too, apparently.'

'Don't you miss him?'

Helen turned and gave Thea a straight look. 'I see plenty of him,' she said. 'And he comes back here now and then for a visit.'

'Ah.' Thea took a chair and rested her elbows on the kitchen table. Everything was clean and tidy, the air smelling of some chemical freshener, the windows sparkling. The hand of a cleaning lady was very evident.

'I'm here for another two weeks,' she said, looking at the pine table top. 'That's a long time to stay in the dark.'

'You want more gen about the Jennisons?' Helen chuckled at her own word play.

Thea nodded without a smile. 'I probably wouldn't care if I hadn't met Joel. It feels as if he drew me in, just in those few minutes.'

'Not to mention finding his body,' Helen suggested.

'Right. *Right*. I *am* involved, like it or not.'

'You could have killed him,' Helen said, with a slow thoughtful delivery. 'They might think you did it.'

'What – that I'm a paid assassin? I don't think the police suspect me.'

'They might just be waiting for you to give yourself away.'

Thea wasn't sure how seriously to take this. 'I have wondered, now and then, how it might be to kill somebody. What level of rage or hatred you'd need. I've never met a murderer.'

'They're usually quite pleasant people, I gather.'

'Well, Helen, I promise you I didn't kill Joel Jennison. But I do quite badly want to know who did, and why, and how. Every day that feeling gets stronger. But I've got no idea how to find out the answers. I've never seen myself as a private detective. I don't think they really exist in this country, do they?'

'Only to follow adulterous wives, or chase up bad debts, I think.'

'Mmm. But you know the people. You're not working. You could help me.'

'How do you know I'm not the killer?'

Thea did smile this time. 'Good question. I never thought of that.'

'You're not going to be very good at this, are you?'

'Give me time. I'm just a bit of a slow learner.' She looked into Helen's eyes. 'Did you kill Joel and Paul Jennison?'

The reaction was interesting. Helen flushed, and her gaze flickered away from Thea's. She put her hands together, palms at right angles. 'No, Thea, I didn't,' she said, in a low quiet voice.

'Do you know who did?'

Helen shook her head. 'I don't think so.'

'Do you think it's likely that it's somebody you know?'

'I can't answer that. I haven't yet lived here long enough to understand all the background stuff. Things go back for generations in a village like this. Plus you get all these incomers, like me, stirring things up, skewing the whole community. Trampling on the old patterns. It probably shouldn't be allowed.'

'Do you know Harry Richmond?' Thea was beginning to enjoy herself. How easy it was to ask questions!

'A bit. He was at your gate on Sunday morning.'

'I know he was. I've met him again since then.'

'Is that the end of my cross-examination?'

'I doubt it. There's something with the Stacey people, isn't there?'

Helen flushed again, more deeply than before. 'It isn't relevant.'

'So who are Monique and Paolo?'

'Casual workers. They help Martin with packing his herbs, seasonal jobs. There's always something. Loads of people work for him on and off.'

'And he provides accommodation, does he?'

'For a few. Some bring tents or caravans, if they live too far to come daily.'

Helen's answers came ready-formed, as if rehearsed. 'Monique didn't look the type, somehow. She's living in a tent, is she?'

Helen grew irritable. 'I don't know. She might be in the house. There are two spare rooms at least. She'll be gone by next week. Why worry about her?'

'I'm not worried about her. I'm interested, the same as I am in Virginia and Penny and everybody else living round here. What are they all like?'

'They're just people. A mixed bunch. No obvious saints or sinners.' Helen spread her hands in a gesture of defeat. 'There are more of them than you might think from a first glance.'

Thea thought about her brother-in-law's tentative hints. He seemed to suspect the presence of one or two sinners. It was still hard to credit, or even properly understand.

'Well, I'd better stick to the people I've met, for now,' she decided. 'Old Mr Jennison, June, Lindy, Harry Richmond, you and . . . that's about it. Not a very comprehensive list.'

'I can introduce you to some others, but it would be at random. No suggestion that they'd got any reason to kill the Jennison boys.'

'Did Joel have a woman?' Thea wondered why this question hadn't occurred days earlier. It suddenly seemed a glaring omission.

'He did have, until last summer. Then they broke up.'

'Did she live with him? Were they married?'

'No, she kept on a flat in Gloucester, but she was here most of the time. She was at your gate on Sunday, too. Susanna, with the woolly hat.' Watching Helen's face, Thea noticed the shadow flickering over it at the utterance of the name. Unless she was much mistaken, Helen had some sort of feeling for this Susanna person. Feeling that had been hidden beneath the brisk account of the woman's presence, until she'd been forced to name her. Thea knew the signs. Even now, it stung to utter the word *Carl* aloud.

She remembered the tall quiet young woman who had been instructed by Martin Stacey to take the pale Monique back to the farm.

'Why did they break up? Susanna works for Martin as well, does she?'

Helen pushed out her lips consideringly. 'She only comes at weekends and summer evenings. She's got her horses on Martin's land. Mainly she comes to see them – rides around the bridleways. Various theories flew around about the breakup. Nobody really knew for sure. The old man's difficult to get along with, although I gathered he quite liked her. There was some talk of another chap.'

'That's another thing – the old man. He was very rude to me this morning. Is he like that with everyone?'

'He isn't the most tolerant person in the world. A man of very strong views, you might say, and doesn't care who knows it. That's the main thing about the Jennisons. They used to be quite strict churchgoers and we went along one Sunday, just for good form, really. Felicity – my wretched daughter – was with us, wearing some outrageously short skirt and whatever the fashion was then. Spiky green hair, probably. Anyway, the old man made no secret of his disapproval. That might not have been too surprising, but his sons joined in. I mean, boys not yet thirty, dressed up in suits and ties, like Mormons, looking down their noses at poor Flick.'

'I can't imagine Joel in a suit.'

'No, well, they mellowed a bit since then. And the farm's gone down the pan, just about. Lionel was never very good at it. Not born to it, you see.'

'Oh?'

'No – hasn't anybody told you? He came into money when he was twenty-one, and bought Barrow Hill with it. His dad was a bank manager in Bournemouth. I think even then Lionel was a misfit. He's never been able to accept the way ordinary people behave.'

Thea remembered Joel's invitation to call in. *Dad always likes a visitor*, he'd said. Was that a bare-faced lie, or what? Had they become so isolated that old habits had changed? If so, Mr Jennison had quickly reverted to type, if that morning was anything to go by.

Chapter Eleven

It was after four when she got back to Brook View and there were dogs to see to, washing to get sorted, thinking to do. After all that, she was hungry. Bored with scrambled eggs and cheese sandwiches, she inspected the freezer, mindful of Clive Reynolds's invitation to take anything she fancied. How to feed oneself was a factor in house-sitting that she hadn't thought of at first.

There were six packets containing 'Fisherman's Pie' or 'Ocean Bake', both of which she was partial to. Reading on the box that they took 45 minutes to heat through in a conventional oven, Thea decided to use the microwave. This was courageous, since she had never possessed such a gadget herself, and was hazy on the detail of how to use them. She was utterly defeated from the outset. The instructions told her to 'remove the foil tray'. However, the pie was inextricably welded into the tray. Getting it out was impossible. Perhaps the thing had defrosted somewhat during the journey home from the shop, and become unduly sticky when frozen again. If so, the same was true of the next one she examined. The only conceivable course of action would be to hack the foil away in strips, using strong scissors. But before that, she read the next sentence on the box. 'Place onto a microwaveable plate.'

Was ordinary china microwaveable? She thought so, but couldn't be certain. If it wasn't, would it explode, or simply poison her? Thinking about it, she concluded that it must be all right, because people put coffee mugs in, when they let their drinks go cold. This, in fact, was the only usage that had ever tempted her to get a microwave for herself. She almost settled to some foil-stripping, until checking the rest of the instructions. They comprised a line of words, with numbers beneath. It appeared that you had to opt for either 800w or 650w, combined with an E or a C. And then you had to let the thing cook for eight (or nine) minutes, stand for one minute and cook for three more minutes. This was considerably longer than she'd bargained for. Allowing for all the preliminaries, it wasn't a huge improvement on 45 minutes in the oven. She could pop a baked potato in as well, and perhaps find the wherewithal to make a nice sponge pudding. In fact, she was beginning to feel decidedly enthusiastic at the prospect of some proper cooking.

She turned her back on the incomprehensible microwave and switched on the oven.

The doorbell rang just as she'd assembled everything for the pudding. The Ocean Bake was sitting unworryingly inside the oven, alongside the potato. It was the policemen again. They were almost like old friends, and she asked them in with a sense of being mildly pleased to see them. 'How's it going?' she asked.

The response was a shock. 'We're not at liberty to say, madam,' replied the one who customarily did most of the talking. Thea wished she'd taken more notice of their names – this third encounter felt like high time they started on a more amicable footing. Except this didn't appear to be a mutual wish.

Their faces were severe to the point of wooden. It seemed strange, after all the police dramas featuring detectives in plain clothes, that these same two uniformed men kept showing up. Wasn't she important enough to warrant a detective inspector wearing a worn sports jacket and brown shoes? Should she complain to James about being undervalued as a witness?

She needn't have worried. 'Mrs Osborne, we'd like to you come to the station with us, in Cirencester. Detective Superintendent Hollis wants to have a word with you.'

Detective Superintendent! She almost laughed. 'What? Now? I can't – I've got something in the oven. It's half past five – why *now*?'

'Turn the oven off, then, madam. It'll still be there when you get back.'

'Why doesn't he come to me? Isn't that the usual way it happens?'

'He'll explain all that when you see him.'

Curiosity prevented any further argument. She turned off the oven, suddenly aware of how hungry she was. Well, that would have to wait. There wasn't any instant food in the house, apart from handfuls of dried fruit, or a slice of bread and jam. She'd just have to hope that the Hollis man offered her a cup of tea and a biscuit.

* * *

She took very little notice of the police station as she was hurried down a corridor and into a small empty room. She was left alone for over ten minutes before a man joined her, followed by a young uniformed policewoman. Explanation, at least in part, was no longer required, once she was face to face with the man. After a terse introduction ('I'm Detective Superintendent Hollis and this is Police Constable Herring'), 'I should have come to you by rights,' he said. 'We wouldn't normally send out a car for you like this. But –,' he indicated his leg, which she had already observed. ' – I'm in plaster for another five weeks, and it makes getting out and about a bit tricky.'

'Shouldn't you be off work?'

'Probably. But I can still function well enough to be of some use here. And this is *my* case.' His chin jutted out like a schoolboy's. Thea diagnosed a severe case of stubbornness.

'Well, how can I help?' she asked. 'The blood-soaked scarf, I suppose?'

The chin jutted even further. 'You found it in a tree, I understand.'

'That's right. We thought it must have blown up there, but then we decided it was probably thrown. *Hurled.*'

'In point of fact, we tend to the latter interpretation. It does not, however, assist very much with our failure to discover the exact scene of the killing. There must be a considerable quantity of blood somewhere.'

Thea said nothing. She had not come across a pool of blood and had no helpful suggestions to make.

Hollis drifted off the subject. 'Your brother-in-law called me yesterday. He's worried about you.'

'Oh,' Thea flapped a hand. 'That's a permanent state, I'm afraid.'

'He thinks you don't take enough care of your own personal safety.'

'Well, I'm still here, aren't I?'

'Apparently. But I'm not giving you the full picture. You're here as a witness, not as a vulnerable potential victim, whatever your brother-in-law might think. Now, let's get down to it – there's another reason it was better for you to come to us – we wanted to have the gadgets to hand. And I'm afraid we're working rather long hours just at present.'

She was reminded of the microwave and the undesirability of gadgets.

'It's not a lie detector test, is it?' she joked nervously. Hollis was her sort of age, broad-shouldered, sharp-jawed, clean and tidy. His accent was from somewhere not far north of Birmingham, and his eyes were brown. He frightened her, which was unusual. She was very seldom frightened of men.

'It's about that scream,' he explained. 'We're going to try to work out just what it was. That's all.'

She leant back in the chair a little, feeling her shoulders loosen.

Of course – what else did she have to contribute, after all? 'It's been almost a week,' she said.

'Yes, yes. Very remiss of us. It's been busier than it looks, believe me.'

She was tempted to remark that that wouldn't be very difficult, but thought better of it. This wasn't a man to banter with.

'We've got a few tricks to help you remember. Nothing

very sinister – just recordings of different sorts of scream, to help you pick out the kind of thing you heard.' He was standing beside a small table on which an electronic machine sat winking a red light at him.

'Aren't you worried that that might give me wrong ideas?'

He looked at her without a trace of humour or very much patience. 'It sometimes works very well,' he said.

'All right then. Ready when you are.' The bravado was slipping, but she refused to let it go altogether. She threw a quick glance at the Herring girl, wondering what her nickname was likely to be. The glance was caught and exchanged, but with ill-concealed boredom. She was merely there as chaperone, a role assigned to the junior female officers, Thea supposed.

'It might help to close your eyes, and try to think yourself back to that night. Tucked up in bed, dark outside. A strange house, all on your own. Probably not sleeping too well.' His voice was low and slow, switched into a totally different timbre. Before she knew it, Thea was leaning forward on her elbows, propped on the table, face in her hands, eyes closing.

'That's it. Let yourself drift back through the days to Saturday. You've only arrived that day, it's all new to you. Your dog isn't sure what's going on. You've got a whole lot of things needing doing. So you want to get a good night's sleep. It's half past three, quarter to four. Something wakes you up . . .' The sound of a hooting owl filled the room. 'Was it something like this?'

'No,' Thea muttered. 'Nothing like that.'

'Good. Well, something else woke you. Maybe a different sound . . .' The sudden high-pitched inhuman screech of another type of bird made her jump.

She had to think about it, listening for the echo as it faded inside her head. 'Well, that's more like it,' she said.

'Fine, fine. Similar, but perhaps not quite right.' She was ready when the next recording came up. It was an unearthly high-pitched single-note yowl. Thea recognised it. 'That's a fox,' she said. 'I get them a lot at home.'

'It's a disconcerting sound, in the dead of night,' Hollis suggested.

'True.'

'Could it have been what you heard?'

'I think not. I wouldn't have been so startled if I'd heard a fox. I'd have realised what it was, right away.'

'OK, then.' He flicked the switch for the next piece of tape. Thea listened to a girl screaming, a stylised Hollywood scream, obviously acting. 'Nothing like it,' she said, with a dismissive shake of her head. 'That's a girl. I heard a man.'

'Did you?' He was trying to keep the eagerness out of his voice, trying to maintain the soothing hypnotic tone. The fifth sound seemed horribly authentic after the one before. A man howling, uttering the word *No-o-o-o!* within the howl. It didn't sound like acting at all, and yet how could the recording have been made? She tried not to pursue that line of thought.

'I heard a man. He wasn't howling like that, but screaming. With physical pain. And fear. That tape's a sound of sadness and despair. Mine had other things.'

She sat up and looked round at Hollis. 'A man screamed outside Brook View at three forty-five on Sunday morning,' she said.

'Thank you,' said DS Hollis, switching off the machine. 'That's what I hoped you'd say.'

Everyone seemed to exhale at once. The air quality changed, and Hollis came close to smiling. 'Thank you,' he said again.

'How does it help?' Thea felt drained, as if she'd been there for hours under intensive grilling.

'It confirms that Mr Jennison was attacked within earshot of your bedroom. With the window open, and a still night, that could have been in the field, or even the road at the front of the house. It's still a wide area, but not as wide as it might have been.'

'But it's not the whole story?'

'Of course not.'

'At least you don't think I killed him,' she quipped. 'Or do you?'

'You *could* have done.' He gave her another direct look, his eyes locking onto hers. 'You're just about the best placed person, after all.'

'True. I could have planned it all in advance. Got the job as house-sitter deliberately to be close to the Jennisons. I can't prove I never knew them until Saturday afternoon. And if I did do it, you're hoping I'll give myself away by saying something about how he died.'

The man smiled coldly and said nothing.

'I have no idea precisely what killed him,' she went on, with a sense of increasing recklessness. She could even envisage Hollis reaching out and slapping her, or pushing her off the chair. There was a tightness about him, a lidded violence that might blow at any moment. 'I mean – a knife, or razor or piece of broken glass.' She faltered, beginning to feel foolish and much too talkative.

'There's no proof that he came to visit you on Saturday afternoon. His father finds the idea astonishing.'

'So did his sister-in-law,' Thea agreed. 'But it did happen.'

'You didn't recognise him when you found his body.'

'He was face down in mud, wedged under some brambles. How would I?'

'You were unusually calm when you dialled 999 and when our people arrived.'

'I was widowed suddenly a year ago. I'm unshockable now. And I didn't feel personally involved with that body. I felt rather sick, and useless, and sad, but I didn't panic. There wasn't any point. He was dead.'

'Hmm,' Hollis said.

And that appeared to be that. Perhaps mindful of all the things awaiting him in another room, he switched off his scream machine and jerked his chin at Constable Herring.

'Well, thank you for coming,' he said to Thea. 'We'll probably be in touch again soon. Somebody will drive you home now.'

The Ocean Pie had gone very dry in the slowly cooling oven, and the half-baked potato was unappetisingly wrinkled. Intending to throw them away, Thea nevertheless dipped a fork into the crust of the pie to test whether it had gone quite cold. The taste on her exploring tongue was good enough for her to dip again, and soon she had eaten most of it, standing in the kitchen, wondering how to spend the rest of the evening.

Joel Jennison's face came and went in her mind's eye. The outlandish costume, the quick wit floated back, and she struggled to identify any hint of fear or anxiety in his manner, any hidden message, any appeal for help. There had been nothing of that sort. He'd been confident, friendly, informative. But there must have been something in his timing, his sudden absence from the Barrow Hill milking parlour where he should have been.

She sat down in the living room, close to the window and looked out onto the front garden, trying to think. She needed to jump the rails, approach from a different angle, put herself in different shoes. What if Joel had wanted to check her out? What if he thought she might be somebody he knew? Somebody planted by the Reynoldses? What if he needed to satisfy himself that she wouldn't get in the way of some sort of covert activity he had planned for the weeks of Clive and Jennifer's absence? Perhaps he even needed to be sure her dog wasn't going to tear his throat out if he ventured into Brook View property at night.

She mentally laid out all the information gleaned thus far: Joel's brother had been shot with his own gun in the field behind this house, and his killer has escaped undetected. Joel's mother, Muriel, lived close by, a survivor of two marriages, sister to a remarkable man who had apparently lived all his life in the area. Joel's father was a wounded lion, a curmudgeon hitting out in blind agony, driving away anyone who offered sympathy. Joel's sister-in-law, June, was disconcertingly composed, in the circumstances, although Thea understood only too well how that could work. Hadn't DS Hollis just accused her of the very same thing?

The whole story screamed *family*, whichever way she looked at it. Only James, a distant, world-weary senior police officer, seemed to think there was a wider picture. Something to do with drugs or farm subsidies or pornography or illegal cash crops – every time she tried to guess, the list got longer. And less relevant. If there were something like that under investigation in Duntisbourne Abbots, somebody would surely have hinted at it by now. Helen or Harry, informed by local gossip, would have directed their disclosures that way, instead of focusing on relationships and lost loves and old jealousies.

It was both a handicap and a help not to have had any close encounters with most of the character list. Thea had no great faith in her own judgment of human nature. She was no better at detecting a lie than anyone else. What she was reasonably good at was noticing patterns, making logical deductions and hearing underlying messages.

Harry Richmond wanted her help, as did June Jennison. Joel Jennison had wanted something from her, too, even if only reassurance that she was harmless. Helen Winstanley was a loose cannon, involved in something with the unknown Staceys, as well, perhaps, as the estranged Susanna. Helen Winstanley was damaged goods, sitting on a compost heap of secrets, and with uncomfortably little to lose. The old man had already lost everything. He, if anyone, was the ongoing victim in the story.

A horrible idea began to sprout; an idea that seemed to answer quite a few of the most immediate questions.

Chapter Twelve

She went back to see Harry Richmond on Saturday morning, after a ten-minute dog-exercising duty, plant-watering and rapid head count of sheep. She didn't phone Harry first, and she didn't take Hepzibah with her.

He showed no surprise when he opened the door seconds after she'd knocked. She was almost disappointed not to have more time to savour the lilac and the profusion of the flowerbeds, which seemed to have come on noticeably in two days.

'I'd really like to meet Muriel,' she said, very early in the conversation. 'Would that be possible? I know I've got no good reason to intrude like that . . .'

'But I've already pulled you in,' he said. 'You're involved now. We can go and see her right away, if you like.'

It was ten o'clock. Thea had a silly notion of a Jane Austen-type encounter, calling on the woman in bonnet and gloves, in the knowledge that morning tea would be standing by, ready for just such an eventuality. There would be calling cards and polite smiles, and smartly upholstered dining chairs.

'Why not?' she said, unable to shake off the impression that she'd just fulfilled an expectation on Harry Richmond's part.

Mrs Muriel Isbister, widow, bereaved mother and runaway wife, was in reality not a million miles from a Jane Austen character; a discovery that Thea found unnerving. Small, restless, twittery, Muriel was completely unlike her brother, who laid a calming hand on her elbow and tried to make her listen to who Thea was. 'You know Clive Reynolds? And Jennifer? In Brook View . . . ?'

'Of course I remember Brook View,' Muriel interrupted him. 'How could I forget dear old Mrs Whimslow, she was always so kind to me. She sent me a note, you know, when I left Lionel. But she must have died ages ago . . . ?'

'Listen,' Harry ordered his sister, with a very effective thread of authority in his voice. 'This is Mrs Osborne – Thea – who's looking after Brook View while Clive and Jennifer are away.'

Muriel reared back as if suddenly confronted by a snake. 'Uh!' she gasped. 'Then you must be . . . it was you who . . .'

'Found Joel in that pool – yes,' Harry filled in. Thea was relieved that the woman had evidently been given the whole story, though irritated with herself for thinking it could have been any other way. She was, after all, Joel's mother.

'The police never came to tell me, you know,' she said, jittering around the room on shoes with high slender heels. She wore a neat two-piece outfit in dark blue, as if dressed for a funeral. Her white hair was tidy, her face carefully made-up. 'I had to hear it from June.' She looked accusingly at Harry. 'Why didn't you come to tell me?'

He shook his head, and pulled an exaggerated expression of regret. 'I can't really answer that,' he said. 'Not without hurting your feelings.'

Her eyes flashed and Thea could sense echoes of age-old sibling spats. 'You mean I didn't come top of the list. You had to go off and pander to that girl before me. Or play your part as grand old man of the village, interfering in everybody's lives, playing your stupid games.'

Harry cast an anxious glance at Thea, evidently concerned for his image. Too late – she was already revising her impression of him, fitting the accusations with what she'd already experienced. The 'girl' was presumably Lindy – though that was an unusual way of referring to one's grand-daughter.

'And why have you brought this woman here?' Muriel went on. 'What are you hoping to achieve? She's got nothing to do with me, or you, or any of us. She's not working for the police, is she?'

Thea felt it was high time she spoke up for herself. 'I wanted to meet you,' she said. 'I do feel involved, mainly because Joel came to see me the afternoon before he died, and I can't just pretend it's got nothing to do with me. Especially since it was me who found him on Sunday. Try to put yourself in my shoes – visits from the police, worries that there might have been something I could have done to save him. I need to understand what happened, and why, as much as you do.'

Muriel laughed bitterly. 'Oh, I understand what happened, well enough. Somebody's doing it to get back at me. They're punishing me for running off and leaving the boys the way I did. First Paul, and now Joel. What else am I supposed to think?'

'But *who*?' Harry Richmond spoke impatiently, as if to a very obtuse child.

Muriel's eyes narrowed. 'I'm not such a fool as to name names,' she muttered. 'But I would have thought it was obvious.'

Thea felt shaky at this veiled accusation, wondering whether there was another large piece of the picture she had not yet grasped. She hoped, in a way, that there was, because otherwise Muriel Isbister's words had just uncomfortably echoed the direction her own thoughts had been tending.

If two brothers were killed, without any obvious motive, the conclusion that somebody wanted to hurt those who most loved them seemed inescapable. Or if not hurt, then to damage financially.

Harry Richmond interrupted her thoughts. 'It's no good casting aspersions like that on Lionel,' he said. 'He's lost everything in this. You think he's gone on hating you all these years, but you're quite wrong. He's a wrecked man, now. He'd never have laid a hand on either of the boys, and you're a damned idiot for thinking he would.'

'No, Harry – you're the damned idiot,' she said. 'I wasn't talking about Lionel, of course I wasn't.'

Harry's composure slipped. Thea could see him reproaching himself for saying too much, and her view of him shifted yet again. 'Well, then,' he blustered. 'I don't know . . .'

Muriel turned to Thea, deliberately ignoring her brother. 'So you feel *involved*, do you?' she said, with strong sarcasm.

'Have you no family of your own with dirty secrets and vendettas? How long are you here for, anyway?'

'Another two weeks.'

'And then you can just float back to where you came from and never give us another thought. Meanwhile, you want to be some sort of Miss Marple or fairy godmother and put everything straight for us sad little village people? Is that the way it works?'

Thea almost enjoyed the attack. 'I hadn't thought of it in that way at all,' she said.

'Well, maybe you should.' Muriel continued to flutter about the room, but now with angry twitches, pulling at the shoulders of her jacket, stamping her heels down hard on the slightly shabby rug. Thea couldn't imagine her at rest, let alone asleep. There was an energy inside her that seemed relentless.

'If you think you know who killed the boys, have you said anything to the police?'

'They wouldn't believe me. They asked a string of fatuous questions about Paul's political activities, years ago, and whether I'd seen Susanna lately . . .'

Politics! Thea's heart sank at this possible link to James's hints at wider matters. How dull. And what an unlikely motive for murder. All the same, she felt duty-bound to pursue it.

'Political activities?' she echoed.

Muriel tossed her head violently. Thea half expected to see it go spinning off her shoulders. 'Oh, he was in the Socialist Workers' Party when he was young, that's all. The police had a file on him, because of it.'

160

Thea was impressed by the easy way this unexceptional little woman uttered the words Socialist Workers' Party. At least she hadn't said SWP, which Thea was certain she would not have understood. Was it possible that the murders could have had the remotest connection with something that sounded like a normal phase in Paul's development?

But how did that sit with Helen's description of the Jennisons as upstanding churchgoers wearing suits and judgmental faces? Socialist workers wore long hair and ragged T-shirts. The only common factor was a tendency to extremes, and perhaps to a certain sort of misanthropy.

'Was he still a member when he died?' she asked, deliberately not evading the word. Passed away was a phrase that made her want to scream.

'Of course not. He dropped all that before he was twenty-five. He went the other way after that, under the influence of his father. I'm just trying to explain to you what fools the police are.'

'Um . . .' said Harry, from a position at some distance from the two women. They both looked at him.

'Mrs Osborne's brother-in-law is in the police,' he elaborated.

'I don't care if he's the Home Secretary,' Muriel flashed back. 'They're quite evidently fools. I have more than enough proof of that.'

'Perhaps because people like you don't give them the assistance they need,' said Thea. 'After all, everything they do has to be based on information from the public. Without that, they're pretty well helpless.'

'They don't *listen*,' whined Muriel. 'They just stick with

what they think they know. If somebody's got a criminal record, they think that says everything about the person.'

'Paul had a criminal record?'

'Yes. I said so, didn't I?'

Thea didn't argue the difference between a file and a record. She found herself wishing that Harry would take a more active role in the encounter, and wondering why she'd walked into this muddle in the first place. She also noticed that no tea or coffee had been forthcoming, which rendered Muriel Isbister rather less of a Jane Austen figure than had first seemed to be the case.

'I don't understand why you've come,' shrilled Muriel, taking a series of short sharp glances out of the front window. Her house was in the main street of the village of Bisley and people passed regularly along the pavement outside. Opposite was a high wall with a garden on a bank above it, with the obligatory clematis and lilac spilling over the top.

'I'm afraid I can't explain it any better than I have already,' Thea said. 'Call it common human decency. I know what it's like to lose somebody. In my personal experience, there's some comfort in the sense of being in a community, where good and bad things happen to everybody, and we can offer a helping hand here and there.'

'Community? You're not a bloody *nun*, are you?'

Amusement came as a relief. Thea smiled widely. 'No, I'm not a nun. I didn't mean it like that. It's a jargon word these days, isn't it. I didn't even mean the people where I live – just random people stopping for a minute to tell me they cared about what had happened. You can never get enough caring, I find.'

'I wouldn't know about that.' Muriel sniffed, and Thea was reminded of the woman's first husband, Lionel Jennison, rejecting sympathetic advances in much the same way. He and Muriel must have been quite a well-matched couple, at least in that respect. She devoted a few moments to trying to imagine the early days of the Jennison family, the abrupt swings of fortune, as the mother abandoned them and the farm slid into penury. Paul's extreme public manifestations could perhaps be explained in terms of his domestic experiences, if only the chronology could be sorted out.

'Come off it,' scolded Harry, sounding much less indignant than the words themselves suggested. 'I care about you, you silly thing. And so does Daisy. And you know Susanna's been a lot of help, ever since Fred died.'

Daisy? Thea had to think hard before she remembered the daughter, twenty-one, offspring of Muriel's fertiliser salesman – who was presumably Fred. Susanna she knew to be the erstwhile girlfriend of Joel Jennison, and a subject of rapidly growing interest. Mentally, she placed Susanna at the top of the list of people she still very much wanted to get to know better. The list continued with the Staceys, along with the mysterious Monique and perhaps Virginia-and-Penny-from-the-village.

Muriel was still fluttering and pecking when they left, her agitation distressing to witness; her sharp momentary attacks disconcerting. 'Is she always like that?' Thea asked.

'She's a bit more nervous than usual, but she never has been exactly serene,' Harry said. 'We used to call her Birdy when she was small, and it fits just as well now.'

'You're not a bit alike.'

'Siblings seldom are, in my experience. Don't you find that they deliberately choose to be different, right from the start?'

Thea laughed. 'I'm going to have to think about that one, but I dare say you're right.' Her sister Jocelyn came to mind, with her rowdy brood and incurious attitudes.

After a pause, while he turned the car round outside an historic-looking pub by the name of The Bear, he said, 'I think she rather liked you, believe it or not.'

'How could you tell?'

'She's only unpleasant to people she likes.'

Thea accorded him an appreciative look. 'Does she know you've grasped that about her?'

'I doubt it. She doesn't waste much of her attention on me.'

'She sounded lonely.'

'Most people are lonely,' he said, pushing down on the accelerator as they left the village.

Back at Brook View before midday, as she was shoving dog blankets into the washing machine, the doorbell rang. Her initial feeling was of intrusion. She didn't want to talk to anybody, to offer them lunch or answer questions. Whoever it was was bound to want some or all of the above.

Her mood did not substantially change even when she discovered it was James and Rosie. James and Rosie, paying her a visit without prior notice. Highly unusual and more than a little sinister.

'What's the matter?' she demanded, before she'd even let them into the house.

'Nothing,' James replied with too much heartiness. 'What would be the matter?'

'Something to do with Jessica,' Thea said, knowing as she spoke that this was a foolish anxiety.

'Heavens, you're in a state, aren't you,' said Rosie. 'Not that I blame you, with murders going on all around you.'

'One murder, actually,' Thea said. 'Or two if you go back a few months. I'm not really in a state. I'm just not very good at sudden surprises. Why didn't you phone me?'

'We didn't have the number of this house, and you didn't pick up the mobile. We left a message on it.'

Thea remembered that the mobile was upstairs, in her bag. She also remembered, by instant association, that she had failed to keep her promise to phone Julia Phillips in Minchinhampton about house-sitting in July. The whole thing had gone out of her head. 'I didn't check for messages,' she admitted.

Rosie was giving the impression that she would do much of the talking, which must imply that they hadn't come to discuss the Jennisons or the secret criminal activities in and around Duntisbourne Abbots. But she was wrong. These were just meaningless preliminaries.

'We're taking you out to lunch,' James said. 'Somewhere a few miles away. You could probably do with a change of scenery.'

'*This* was intended as a change of scenery,' she pointed out. 'I've only been here a week. I'm not bored with it yet. I've still hardly seen the village itself. Things keep conspiring to deflect me from exploring it.'

'I gather the church is worth a look,' said Rosie. 'Maybe we could pop in there after lunch. We're not in any hurry.'

'Can Hepzie come?'

James glanced out of the window. 'Only if we sit in the pub garden, and it's a bit cool for that.' Thea couldn't tell from his tone or expression what he thought of the suggestion. She'd never been sure what he thought about her dog, in spite of the animal's lavish affection towards him.

'Better leave her here, love, if you think she'll be all right,' said Rosie. 'Has she settled in OK? Do these big boys play with her? How's her poorly ear?'

Rosie was easier to read. She gave dogs her full attention, but would take no nonsense from them. Constantly heedful of her fragile back, the prospect of a large animal jumping at her and knocking her over was too dire to contemplate. She had therefore developed an authoritative voice which invariably worked. Most dogs liked and respected her, and Thea always felt that more or less summed it up from Rosie's end, as well.

'She'll be fine here,' she agreed. 'I'll take them all for a nice run when we get back.'

'It's a magnificent garden, isn't it,' Rosie approved. 'Have you got to cut that grass?'

'I think it's on the list, yes. I wasn't going to bother until a day or two before the people come back. I haven't even found the mower yet.'

'You'd think they'd have a gardener, wouldn't you?'

'Oddly enough, I thought poor Joel Jennison was the gardener.' Thea stopped, realising it was exactly a week ago that she'd met him. The poignancy affected her for a few seconds.

'Come on then,' urged James. 'Before they get too full.'

'You have somewhere in mind?' It wasn't really a

question. James never left anything to chance. The idea of driving around in the aimless hope of lighting upon a likely pub was not his style at all.

'Wait and see,' he said, with a smile that struck Thea as a trifle forced.

The pub was near Coates, no great distance away. The Tunnel House Inn was, apparently, a discovery that James had made a few years earlier. 'He'll make any excuse for another visit,' Rosie teased. 'He thinks it's the most romantic pub in the world.'

'You haven't explained properly,' James reproached her. Turning to Thea, he said, 'It was burnt down in 1952 and not restored until fairly recently. But that isn't really why I like it. You'll understand what I mean when you see it.'

'Well, it's news to me,' said Thea, wondering how the place could hope to live up to such a billing.

As it turned out, she liked it a lot, at the same time as wondering why she'd never known about it. The tunnel it was named after was a canal running under the hill at Sapperton, which had a romance all of its own. A glorious stone façade marked the entrance to the tunnel, exuberantly decorated, for the sheer fun of it. The canal had barely a foot of water in it, and notices explained how the Canal Trust was painstakingly restoring the length of the Cotswold Canal, yard by yard, to include the full extent of this tunnel. 'Hey!' she cried with delight. 'I've never seen this before. How on earth have I missed it?'

'How indeed?' smiled James. 'And you an expert, too.' The tease was justified. Thea could name every canal in

Britain, with dates, traffic levels and primary purpose.

'It's the *history* of them I focused on,' she defended. 'Mostly, anyway.'

'Well, there's a lot of restoration work going on over here,' he said. 'Bringing the past into the present, or something.'

It was deeply nostalgic. Thea and Carl had taken many a narrowboat holiday with Jessica and the dogs, in the early years of their marriage, before she did the history course.

'It's beautiful,' she sighed. 'You are clever, James.'

James grinned his agreement. 'What'll you have to drink?' he asked.

They did sit outside, but Thea refrained from pointing out that Hepzie could have come after all. 'So – what's all this about?' she asked, once they'd settled at a table with views over open fields. Rosie had lowered herself gingerly onto the wooden bench, automatically leaning her weight on her forearms, to avoid any strain on her back. Thea knew from past experience that any comment would be inappropriate. Rosie's back was a given, and nothing could be gained by referring to it.

'So, why are we here?' Thea demanded. 'What's all this about?'

'What do you think it's about?' James parried.

'Murder, organised crime, screams in the night,' Thea listed, with a hint of impatience. 'All the things I hoped you'd fill me in on when you came over here on Wednesday.'

'Yes – sorry about that,' he blinked at her, in a boyish expression of humility. 'My timing was off that morning.'

'For God's sake don't tell me it was all very delicate,' Thea warned him. 'Delicacy doesn't cut much ice with me. It just makes me feel left out and frustrated.'

'And resentful, I should think,' added Rosie.

'It's not delicate now, anyway,' James cut in. 'Just desperate. The investigation isn't getting anywhere, and everybody's admitting it at last. I gather you made the acquaintance of DS Hollis?'

'I did.'

'And? What did you think of him?'

'I was scared of him.'

James jerked in a spasm of amazement. 'Surely not?' he said. 'That's the last thing I expected you to say.'

'He struck me as a man with very little to lose. He showed me no human feeling, no hint that he even understood that I was an individual with my own life to live. I was just a receptacle of possibly useful information. I can't imagine how he got so far up the ladder – aren't police officers meant to have some sort of empathy these days?'

'I don't think he was always like that,' James said softly, with a glance at Rosie.

'He's had a very unhappy life,' Rosie said. 'I knew his sister, years ago, funnily enough. It's terrible how changed he is since, well—'

'But not actually the point,' said Thea firmly, not wanting to hear about the Hollis calamity, whatever it was. 'What's the problem with the investigation? The Hollis man sounded pretty confident yesterday.'

'For one thing, they're wishing they'd brought Clive and Jennifer back when they had the chance. The Chief isn't too happy about them being out of the picture for so long.'

'They can speak to them by phone, can't they?'

'It's not the same.'

'What else?'

'Somebody made an anonymous accusation, which has to be followed up. Forensics are complaining there's practically nothing to go on. Old man Jennison won't answer any more questions. And there's still no hint of a motive.'

'Why aren't they back at Brook View, combing the place again for clues, then? Somewhere there's a great pool of blood. Except it'll all have soaked away by now, or been washed off by the rain.'

'They assume they'd have found it on Sunday, if it was there to be found.'

'Stop it!' Rosie pleaded. 'I'm not liking this.'

James and Thea ignored her.

'Poor man,' Thea murmured. 'If that was him screaming, he must have known something about it before they killed him. Isn't that horrible?' Rosie's clear blue gaze flickered from her husband to her sister-in-law and back, distancing herself from their excessive interest in the details of murder. This wasn't the first time she'd had to interrupt such conversations.

Thea went on, 'Which is all the more reason why we should be doing everything we can to find out who did it.'

'And bring him to justice,' supplied Rosie, parodying the official words. She made her mouth round, producing a sonorous tone that achieved its intended effect. James and Thea both laughed.

'I knew I shouldn't have come today,' Rosie went on. 'James talked me into it. I haven't been anywhere for weeks, except the library.'

'I did warn you,' James said. 'This isn't just a social visit.'

'Hmm,' was all his wife replied.

Thea leant towards him across the slatted table. 'Who made the anonymous call?' she asked, before realising the absurdity of the question. 'I mean – what did they say?'

'Something about old Jennison threatening his boys that if they didn't stick to his rules, he'd make sure they never got the farm.'

'What were the rules? Do we know?'

'He was a stickler for decent behaviour. Clean living. But that was all years ago. It doesn't seem like much of a lead.'

'Joel had a girlfriend. Was the old man trying to prevent him from sleeping with her? Is anybody still as old-fashioned as that?'

James laughed. 'I'm not privy to that information,' he said.

'What else have you come to tell me, then?' she asked. 'Are you going to give me an assignment?'

'Essentially I want to urge you to be careful. There's a lot of hypothesising that Joel went to see you for a reason. If the killer thinks you know something, then – well, I don't have to spell it out.'

'Surely that particular danger's past now?' Thea said. 'They'd have bumped me off by now if they were going to.'

'Why would you think that? It's barely a full week yet.'

'Maybe, but if I'd had any vital information, I would already have passed it on to the police, so killing me now would be pointless.'

James shook his head. 'I thought you understood the law better than that. If you're not there to give testimony, it's hearsay evidence, and inadmissible. Unless it's in a signed statement or on tape, of course.'

'Which it would be, wouldn't it? James, you're being melodramatic, and frightening Rosie. What else am I supposed to know? Let's get on with it, and have a nice lunch without upsetting our stomachs. For Rosie's sake, at least.'

James sighed. 'You're not being very cooperative, are you?'

She narrowed her eyes at him, losing patience. 'What?'

'Look, having you here ought to be a big asset for the police, being connected to me the way you are. You could be getting to know the locals, listening to the gossip, all that. Instead you seem to be huddled in that house with those dogs, not doing a bloody thing to help.'

Thea swallowed hard. 'James – have I been set up here? Was something going on long before Joel got killed, and you planted me, without saying anything?' She tried to remember the sequence of events leading up to her selection as house-sitter for the Reynoldses. She had discussed the idea with James, but no more than that. She'd advertised her services, and Clive Reynolds had answered the ad. But Clive had already known James. It was obvious. 'You did, didn't you?'

Rosie chimed in. 'Oh, James! Is she right? Why didn't you tell her?'

He shifted irritably. 'All I did was mention to Clive that you'd be available for the job. I had no idea about any criminal activity here.'

'Come off it, you liar. Am I supposed to believe you didn't know about Paul being killed behind Brook View?'

'I knew a man had been killed, probably by a poacher or gypsy. But I had no involvement in the case. It never entered

172

my head that it would impinge on you if you took the job. Believe it or not, I was trying to *help*.'

'You're shifting your ground,' she accused. 'I don't know what to believe. And I have no idea what more I can do for you than I've been doing. I've met the father, niece, ex-girlfriend, uncle, mother and sister-in-law of the dead brothers. I've also got friendly with a close neighbour, and gleaned a snippet or two about another neighbour. I think that's damned good progress for an amateur, and a stranger in the area. When I tried to tell you how it all looked to me, you said you'd got to rush off, and barely gave me a minute to speak. Now you come down here again with no warning, and start talking about throat-cutting and pools of blood. Rosie wants to change the subject and I'm beginning to think this is the lunch outing from hell. Now I'm going back in there for another drink. Does anybody else want one?'

James and Rosie both proffered empty glasses, with visible relief. Neither offered to go with her to help.

When she got back with the drinks, James was some distance away, apparently admiring the view. Rosie took her glass, and cocked her head conspiratorially. 'He's working up to saying sorry,' she explained.

Thea rolled her eyes. 'He doesn't need to. I think I said a bit too much. After all, it is a good job. Money for old rope, as they say.'

'And the rest,' Rosie said, with a sigh. 'Rather you than me.'

'Is there anybody else you've met?' James asked, when he came back to the table.

Thea tried to think. 'A girl called Monique. She's staying at the Staceys' farm. A student, I suppose.'

'Student of what?'

'I have no idea.'

'Because, as you must be aware, students are mostly at college at this time of year. Unless she's doing an agricultural course, I'd want to confirm that she really is a student.'

'For heaven's sake! Maybe she's working there in a proper job, then. I'm only guessing. There's somebody called Paolo with her, I think. It's a herb farm, or something. There must be plenty of work.' She knew she was babbling in order to drown out the inner voices that were clamouring *Illegal immigrants*, *asylum seekers* and similar alarming suggestions.

'Thanks,' James said calmly. 'Now let's change the subject.'

Chapter Thirteen

'The truth is, we haven't got enough to do,' Thea told
Hepzie on Saturday evening. 'Nothing on the telly, bored
with Scrabble, everything fed and watered, and still only
nine thirty.' She didn't often talk aloud to the dog, but there
were times when it seemed to come naturally. Hepzibah
responded with sympathetic spaniel glances and desultory
tail-wagging. The labradors ignored her. She wondered if it
was her imagination, or were they both gaining weight under
her ministrations? Despite some energetic stick-chasing in
the garden, she realised she hadn't taken them for a single
serious walk since her arrival. Clive had made so little of
it that she felt she'd had permission to neglect this aspect
of their care if she wanted to. She had the impression that
neither Clive nor Jennifer routinely route-marched them over
hill and dale. The warnings about letting them into the field
had also been open to interpretation. The message seemed
to be Take them in there at your own risk. More than once
she'd been tempted to try it, only to lose confidence at the
last minute. What if they ran off and never came back?

She had tried to phone Jessica, forgetting it was a Saturday and her daughter was sure to be out with friends, the mobile switched off. Then she'd thought of Celia, who'd be wondering how she was getting on. She could be sure of catching her in, whatever day it was. Celia almost never went out in the evenings, unless it was high summer. She was afraid of the dark, and could not be convinced that it was safe to drive at night.

But Celia would ask questions, and Thea would start the story of Joel Jennison and his family, and the odd silent village. It would all take hours, and leave her feeling unsettled. Better to postpone all that until she got home again, and could recount the whole episode with hindsight. By then, even if the police had made no progress, it would not be Thea's business any more. It would just simmer quietly at the back of her mind, until eventually she forgot all about it. One day it might even qualify as an amusing tale for dinner parties – how I was house-sitting and guess what, a man got murdered the first night I was there, right in the next field! Well, no, that was never going to sound all right – but at least she wouldn't be so worried and confused and curious about it as she was now.

Throughout her life, Thea had had difficulty with roles. Never properly engaged in an identifiable long-term career; more friend than wife to Carl, more mate than mother to Jessica; seldom acting her age or doing what was expected – she mostly thought of herself as an observer, watching people from outside. Perhaps as a defence against any anxiety that *they* might be watching *her*, this had become her habit.

But she wasn't very confident of her own powers of

observation. She certainly didn't believe she possessed any of the deductive qualities of a Miss Marple. She was simply caught in the middle of something violent and hate-fuelled and she thought it ought to be stopped. More than stopped – since there were no more Jennison sons to be murdered, it might well have stopped already. She actually wanted the killer located and punished. Killing Joel Jennison by pulling a blade across his throat was an act worthy of retribution, in anybody's eyes.

The ringing phone startled her, at the same time as giving rise to a surge of anticipation. It didn't matter who it was – it would be good to have somebody to talk to.

'Hello? This is June Jennison,' came the surprising announcement. 'Would it be all right if I popped in to see you?'

'Of course. When?'

'Now. I'm just down the road. I thought I should phone first, in case you were scared by somebody knocking at the door.'

'That's very thoughtful. I'll see you in a minute, then.'

Despite her gracious words, Thea was irritated by the assumption that she would be scared by a knock on the door at nine thirty pm. These repeated signs of apprehension across the nation, as well as large parts of the wider world, always disturbed her, putting her in a gloomy mood. She wanted to believe it was all hysteria and over-reaction, media-induced and groundless – but hard facts would persist in intruding. A man had been killed close to the house; burglaries happened everywhere; violence and hatred ran riot. The aberration, she sometimes suspected, was in her, not in the security-conscious mass.

June, when she arrived, was as neat as ever in a tailored jacket and well-pressed blue trousers. Thea was reminded of Muriel Isbister, mother of June's murdered husband, and concluded that Paul had followed the stereotype and married a woman like his mother – at least as far as her attitude towards clothes was concerned.

Or maybe it was a feature of the Cotswolds, and all the women dressed like this.

'Come in,' she invited, trying to prepare herself for whatever might follow. This could hardly be dismissed as a casual passing visit.

'You'll think I'm off my head,' June began, 'coming at this time of night. I'm sure it's a crackpot notion – but the idea wouldn't go away. I just had to be here at the same time as Joel was killed last week.'

'Like a police re-enactment?' Thea said, wondering how such a thing could possibly work.

June shook her head. 'I know it doesn't make sense. We don't know what happened out there, and anyway the weather's different tonight, and the moon's in a different phase. But I've got to do *something*. It's all just drifting away, otherwise. The police have said we can bury Joel any time from the middle of next week, nobody ever even mentions Paul any more, the papers are full of the usual rubbish about children with leukaemia and corruption on the Council. Whoever killed them will get away with it if we don't find some sort of new evidence.'

It was a heartfelt speech, and Thea found herself in sympathy with most of it. 'But I don't see what you can achieve by coming here.'

'Will you come outside with me? I suppose "re-enactment" isn't quite the word, but I want to try and work out what Joel was doing. I bet the police haven't been back for a look at it in the dark.'

'I don't think they have. Come to that, we still haven't checked the security lights – I mean, I know they work, but not exactly where you have to be to trigger them. Come on, we can do it now there's two of us.'

June expressed a silent question.

'They didn't come on that night, you see. Or I'm fairly sure they didn't. Let's do it now. You go out and set them off, and I'll go upstairs and see what I can see from the window.'

Without further query, June did as instructed. Thea went to her room, switching off the lights on the stairs and landing as she went. For extra verisimilitude, she lay down on the bed. A yellow glow was evident. Probably not enough to wake her up, but unmistakable once awake. The lights lit most of the garden at the front and side of the house. She hurried down to June, who had come back into the house.

'The lights didn't go on. When I heard the scream, it was dark – cloudy, I suppose. There wasn't any moonlight. Which means the person knew how to avoid triggering them, or it was happening further away than we think.'

'So what does that tell us?' June asked.

'Probably not much more than we know already. Joel was attacked within earshot of my room, then dumped in the field pool some time later. And somewhere there's a lot of blood – although it might have gone by now.'

'Blood?'

Too late, Thea realised that it couldn't be assumed that

the family knew just how Joel had died. Nobody had warned her not to tell them, though. Once again, the issue of roles cropped up. Was she meant to be a police informer, or a friendly sympathiser? Didn't everybody want the same thing, anyway – apart from the killer? Who could, in theory, be June.

'They haven't told you.'

'What?'

'His throat was cut. He'd bled to death before they left him in the water.'

'Oh yes, they did tell us that. They had to, really, didn't they? We've a right to go and see the body, after all.'

'Have you? A right, I mean.'

June gave her an impatient look. 'Yes, of course. Gramps, me and Lindy. And Muriel, I suppose. Close family. We could just phone the undertaker and ask to see him. I went to see Paul, anyway.'

'But not Joel?'

June shook her head. 'I decided I could give it a miss. Nobody else wants to, either. The point is, we knew how he died. The Coroner's Officer told us, actually.'

'That's all right then. I don't want to have to keep secrets.'

'Didn't it occur to you that they'd hardly tell *you*, without telling us as well?'

Thea wriggled, aware of further confidences. 'I suppose that's right,' she mumbled.

June was becoming more confrontational. 'You heard him scream.' It was an accusation, and Thea took it on the nose.

'I think I did, yes.'

'And you didn't do anything. You didn't even call the police.'

'No. I listened for a few minutes, to see if it would come again, and then I went back to sleep.'

'You didn't even go outside for a proper search the next morning.'

'No. I went for a walk with my dog. It was nearly midday when I found him.'

'Don't you feel *terrible*? Knowing you might have saved his life?'

Thea wove her fingers together, squeezing the knuckles, watching the fingertips turn red. 'I try not to think about might have beens, and what ifs. I think most people would have done the same as I did. I was lazy, that's all. I am trying, in my own small way, to assist with the investigations. Some people would have packed up and gone home, after a thing like that. I'm not very good at it, but I really do want to see if I can discover who did it and why.'

Her hands throbbed when she let them fall apart. It was a favourite trick, acquired accidentally during Carl's funeral.

'You're not scared, are you?' June was watching her closely. 'Unhappy, perhaps, but not scared. I can see it would take a long time to understand you.'

'Don't bother. I'm only here another fortnight.'

'And then what?'

'And then I go somewhere else.' Belatedly she remembered again the Minchinhampton woman. What was it that prevented her from phoning when she had the chance?

June seemed to give up. 'So let's go outside, shall we?'

'You're assuming I'll participate in this plan, are you?'

181

'That's right.'

June led the way through the house and out of the back door. The garden sloped slightly downhill towards the road, with a shrubbery of rhododendrons and other evergreens between the lawn and the front hedge. A winding path led to the ornamental pond in the north-eastern corner. The field gate was some distance to their right. Most of the paths were of old stone, kept ruthlessly clear of weeds and moss. June seemed quite familiar with the layout. 'Which window is your bedroom?' she asked.

Thea considered a moment, before pointing out an upstairs window overlooking them. 'There, I think.'

'Which suggests he was on this side when he screamed. If he'd been in the yard, you probably wouldn't have heard him.'

'I expect I would. It was night, when sound carries. And I don't think it was as close as just here.' The idea appalled her – that the murder could have taken place right outside her bedroom window.

'Did you have your window open?'

'Just a bit, yes. I always sleep with a window open, if at all possible. That means I'd have been more likely to hear him from a distance.'

'Or perhaps it means you'd be more likely to be woken up if there was a noise just here. Are you a deep sleeper?'

'Fairly. But it was my first night in a strange bed. I don't think I was very deep asleep.'

She thought about the police experiment with the tapes, and wondered whether she should tell June about it. From the way she was talking, it almost seemed that she knew already.

As if to confirm this idea, June began to speak, in a fluent monotone, only half addressing Thea. It was more like someone rehearsing the story so far, checking it through for inconsistencies or overlooked clues.

'Raymond Barnfield – he's one of the cops who've been talking to you – was a friend of Paul's. He's been keeping me updated. He's a nice chap.'

'Which one is he?'

'Probably the one who didn't say much.'

'Right. So what's he been telling you?'

'They're stumped. They're coming to the pretty obvious conclusion it was the same person who killed Paul and Joel. That means they think it had some kind of family motive. Money, jealousy, hurt feelings, so they see me as a key witness. Me and the old man. They're not too worried that anybody else is at risk, and that means they're going about it all at a snail's pace. Endless forensic work, going through the bank statements; checking everybody's alibi. They won't listen to me when I keep saying they've got it all wrong.'

They had moved down to the gate behind the house, and stood leaning on it, looking out into the dark field. Thea had a sudden sense of wilderness – deep countryside, where anything might happen. Like the outback in Australia, it sat there pretending innocence, when the reality was of an unyielding hostility towards humanity. The field sloped down to the brook, and from there more fields spread out, with no lights to indicate human habitation for some distance.

'How far is the next house in that direction?' she asked June, pointing an indistinct finger.

'Probably nearly a mile. Of course there's the

Winstanleys just up there,' indicating to the left, 'and the Normans down the hill, plus the Staceys over the road – and us, of course. It's not exactly isolated – it just feels that way sometimes.'

Thea had noted the *us*. Hardly surprising that June still regarded Barrow Hill as her home, of course. But did it also imply that she intended to move back there now?

They stood for a silent three minutes, listening to the faint sounds of distant traffic, a dog barking, a night bird singing. 'I still don't know how you could just ignore a scream,' June said, dropping the remark like a big stone, right onto Thea's foot.

The tone wasn't aggressive, but nonetheless, Thea felt the full impact. She could have saved the man's life. Perhaps. She was never going to know. The wound made her speak rashly.

'But his throat was cut. It must have been over in a few seconds. There'd have been no hope of saving him, even if I'd rushed outside, and managed to find the right place.'

June was grudgingly agreeable to this defence. 'That's true, I suppose. Could a woman have done it, do you think?'

Thea paused. There was a significance to the question that seemed to be taking them into new waters. 'I don't know,' she said. 'Possibly if he was taken by surprise, pulled backwards. I really don't know.'

'Tell me,' Thea switched to a fresh topic, 'would you have come over here like this if the Reynoldses had been at home?'

'What?' Thea couldn't see June's face at all, but her tone was bemused. 'Well, yes, of course. At least . . .'

'Would this have happened if they'd been here?'

June made another sound reminiscent of being strangled.

'That's what we'd all like to know, isn't it,' she blurted. '
now? Why here? Why him?'

Thea made no attempt to provide answers, but took the
initiative of pushing away from the gate and starting back
towards the house. 'Come on,' she invited. 'We're not doing
any good here. If Joel's ghost is going to show, it won't be for
a few more hours yet.'

It was flippantly said, but seriously received. 'You believe
in ghosts?' The hope in the voice was unmissable.

'Oh, well, not really. I mean – I've never seen one, and
never met anybody who has. Surely you don't think . . . ?'

'Don't mock.' June's voice was low and hard.

'I'm not. I know it's a basic human need. Believe me, I do
know all about that.'

'Never mind *need*.'

Thea kept on walking, her feet drifting off the path at
one point, stepping into the bare soil of a rosebed. Thorns
snatched at her trousers. 'Who does the gardening here,
anyway?' she asked, aware of the inconsequentiality, but still
curious to know.

'Jennifer. Jennifer gardens obsessively. Always did. Even
at school she had things growing in the classroom.'

'School? You were at school with her?' The casual twist
almost made Thea laugh. 'But surely she's years older than
you?'

'She's forty-seven and I'm nearly forty-five. We were at
Cheltenham Ladies' together.'

'I don't believe you,' said Thea, meaning something
slightly different. Jennifer Reynolds had seemed at least ten
years older than forty-seven. 'She must be older than that.'

'She married a man twelve years older than herself, and I married one eight years younger. Funny what a big difference that can make. We were day girls.'

'Best friends?'

'Not at all, no. I never really liked her. She was prissy and thin and obsessed with botany. I was plump and jolly and sporty. But it made us very *aware* of each other, living here as neighbours. I suppose in a small way we kept each other's secrets.'

Thea's frustration expressed itself in a small groan. 'What? What's the matter with you?' June demanded.

'It's hopeless. I'm never going to grasp the links between all these people. However do the police manage to make sense of something like this? It's impossible.'

'They work backwards.'

'Backwards?'

'First they get the forensic stuff – hairs, footprints, mud, DNA – you know. Then they match it with everybody they can think of who could be the killer. Quite often that's all they need. The motive jumps out at them as soon as they make the arrest.'

Thea laughed. 'It ought to be me telling you all this, by rights. I'm the one with a policeman in the family.'

'Don't forget Raymond. He fills me in on the procedure now and then.'

Thea remembered again that June was a recent widow. Remembered, but scarcely credited it. There was nothing about her that chimed with Thea's own experience. If anything, June was still plump and jolly, if not visibly sporty. The murder of her husband had left little discernible scar tissue. 'Did you love Paul?' she asked, on the very threshold of the back door. In the harsh light of the house it would not have been possible to frame such a question.

'Ah!' June inhaled as if preparing for a struggle. 'The answer to that could take all night.'

Chapter Fourteen

They sat in the living room, with Jennifer Reynolds' biggest fern watching over them, and Hepzibah ignoring them from the comfort of the hearth rug. Bonzo and Georgie remained voluntarily in the kitchen, as human males might do. Not for them the sighs and tears and sudden clashes of two emotional women waiting for ghosts in the night.

'It isn't only Joel's anniversary,' said June, as Thea opened a bottle of not-very-cold Hock. 'It's ten weeks today that Paul died, too.'

Thea struggled to remember what ten weeks felt like, only managing to come up with a memory of her daughter at that age, suddenly showing animated responses to words and songs. She'd made a point of noting down the landmark that had been ten weeks – but in no way did it translate to a similar period of widowhood. Unless perhaps it did mark a kind of emergence, a better sense of proportion, a setting in a wider context. 'Ten weeks,' she repeated. 'Dear me.'

'I didn't go to pieces or anything, when they came to tell me. I had to be brave for Lindy's sake, but that wasn't it.

I think women in this country are brilliant at coping with death, for some reason. I suppose we've had to be – with babies dying like flies, and the First World War taking all the men, and all the rest of it. There's no patience with any nonsense. You can't go loopy, and pretend it hasn't happened. You can't howl and scream and pull your hair out. You've got to choose a coffin and write thank you letters and fill in all those bloody forms for the bank.'

'I didn't cope brilliantly,' said Thea. 'I fell apart. That's what it was like – a string puppet with all the cords severed. Arms, legs, head all lying on the floor in a jumble. I was, to be honest, *wrecked* by it. The sheer bloody *pain* of it.'

'Pain?'

'You didn't get the pain?'

June shook her head, screwing up her mouth in a mock wince. 'Not that I remember. It was definitely a huge *surprise*. I'd never dreamt he'd get himself murdered. And I missed him, as a presence. As somebody to talk to. I kept starting to ask him something, and he wasn't there. Still do it, now and then. But not pain, no. Sorry.'

Thea changed tack. 'So what about ghosts? Do you think they do happen?'

June shook her head again and rubbed a knuckle into a corner of an eye, like a child. 'I can't explain,' she said. 'It isn't a yes/no sort of thing. I just felt that if there was something to learn, this would be the best night for it.'

'Maybe the killer will return to the scene of the crime,' suggested Thea, again feeling inappropriately flippant.

'Maybe he will.'

The Hock was girlishly sweet, making Thea feel

unsophisticated and therefore almost embarrassed. You weren't supposed to enjoy such stuff. June showed no such qualms, holding out her glass for more, and asking worriedly whether there was another bottle.

'Were you at school with Helen Winstanley as well?' Thea asked.

'Helen is a good ten years older than me,' said June, with a severe look. 'Don't be silly. Anyway, she's an incomer. I hardly know her at all.'

'The Staceys?'

'What about them?'

'Anything about them.'

'They grow herbs, mostly. Very labour intensive. Always youngsters there, working for a few weeks then off again. Isabel does the paperwork, I think. Martin's away a lot – meeting buyers and stuff, presumably. He goes to London, off down the M4, like most other people round here.'

With a sense of irresponsibility, born no doubt of the wine, Thea asked, 'Is there anything between Helen and Martin?'

June's face seemed to lengthen with stunned surprise. 'You're joking!'

'Oh, well – she just seems to spend quite a bit of time there.'

'That's because they're in partnership, you idiot.'

'Partnership? What sort of partnership?'

June looked at her suspiciously, for signs of teasing. 'The herb farm, of course. It went through a bad patch a few years ago, and Helen baled them out. She needed an interest, and she's stuck with it. It's doing all right again now. There's some gossip about them expanding.'

'What sort of herbs?'

'Oh, I don't know. You name it, they grow it.'

'Have they got glasshouses or polytunnels and all that? A packing shed? I haven't noticed anything like that.'

'Not glasshouses, but just about everything else. It's on the far side of the house from here, with an entrance on the other road. They had a monumental job getting permission for it all. The villagers went bonkers about it. Now, of course, nobody turns a hair. It doesn't affect them much at all. Lindy was telling me the locals are all quite happy about it now. Martin's in favour with everybody again, for some reason.'

'Don't they even object to the lorries? Surely there's a lot of traffic connected with something like that?'

'Actually, there aren't many, as far as I can see. A lot of it gets sent in boxes in the post. Dried stuff – seeds, I suppose. One of the supermarkets was taking plants in pots for a while. Tarragon and sage and basil. Hundreds at a time. But you can get a lot of little herb pots onto one lorry. The truth is, it doesn't impinge on the village at all.'

'What about James?' Thea suddenly thought to ask. 'Helen's husband.'

June laughed. 'What *about* him?' It was beginning to feel like a party game.

'Is he involved? Was it really his money that went into the herbs? What does he think about it all?'

'James Winstanley is not a man to express his feelings carelessly,' said June, her tone betraying a degree of inebriation. 'James Winstanley is a stuffed shirt, a blithering bore, a bloodless buffoon. He should have been smothered at birth. He's a waste of space. We do not like James Winstanley, Mrs Osborne. Please remember that.'

'Right. I think I've got that. Does Helen feel that way about him, as well?'

'Obviously. Doesn't it show? Poor cow loathes his guts.'

'It's beginning to seem as if happy marriages are somewhat thin on the ground round here.'

'You can say that again. Can't think of a single one.'

'Not even you and Paul?'

'Not even me and Paul,' said June Jennison.

Somehow it was astonishingly midnight and June was still there.

Two empty wine bottles stood on the stone hearth, where the spaniel lay, enjoying the long evening of company and generous heating. A somewhat old-fashioned electric fire stood in the grate, augmenting the central heating. Thea had developed the habit of putting it on once darkness fell, wantonly heedless of the running costs for a change. What the hell, she decided – the dog likes it.

The conversation had drifted into various backwaters: jobs, their daughters' talents and character, thoughts about the future. Thea had asked about Harry Richmond and his sister, and been told they were a funny pair, not particularly forthcoming, although Lindy clearly found something appealing about Harry. Thea could detect no undercurrents there, just a gap where feelings should have been.

'And Joel,' she said, at last. 'What about Joel?'

June's head flopped forward, melodramatically. 'Don't make me talk about Joel,' she pleaded.

But then she started doing just that. 'Joel was a lamb. A little lost lamb. You've seen his mother, the woman who walked out on her boys. And his father, the selfish old bastard . . .' She caught herself then, listening to a mental rerun of her own words. 'No, that's not really fair. Lionel's not bad, when it comes down to it. He's clever, and straight with people, although it's usually to tell them where they're going wrong. But he was a lousy father, and isn't a brilliant farmer, to be honest. I've got the measure of him, after all these years, and he's fond of me and Lindy, though he'd never show it. But the only one who watched out for Joel was Paul. We thought Susanna would be good for him, at first, but she blew it. Two-timing him, she was. But he'd probably have stuck by her, even then. He went to pieces when she finally dumped him, following her about, pleading with her. Didn't care who saw him or knew about it. All Joel ever knew, really, was abandonment and neglect. All things considered, he turned out all right. Maybe a bit judgmental, like his dad. Intolerant of people's weaknesses. But basically he was the sweetest boy. Soft and smiling, nice to everybody. Looking for love, and never quite finding it.'

Thea said nothing, remembering the friendly open face, the amused indignation at being mistaken for a gardener. Remembering, too, the air of composure and self-possession. He hadn't struck her as a lost lamb, but a young man rooted in his little world, conscious of the tasks ahead, steady in their performance.

'If it wasn't for the way it happened, I'd have easily believed that Joel killed himself,' June added. 'He didn't really have very much to live for – not after Paul died.'

'It's midnight,' said Thea.

'And the ghosts have come,' said June. 'Can't you feel them?'

Sadness was the background to Thea's existence, so much so that she simply assumed its proximity without thinking. But that Sunday morning, when she woke late with a head like a much-kicked leather ball, sadness consumed her. The murdered brothers had become increasingly present in the house, as June talked about them and Thea sank into a familiar contemplation of loss and abandonment. But they came no closer to solving the mystery of who had killed them. Indeed, the question receded into the shadows, pushed there by grief. 'I *liked* Paul,' June insisted. 'It's just that we didn't make a very good fist of being married. We never really understood how it was meant to go.'

Thea had pointed out the inconsistency of June's liking him, but feeling no pain at his death. 'Maybe I'm still numb,' said June. 'Maybe it hurts so much I can't even feel it yet.'

They opened a third bottle of wine, with some trepidation. 'How'm I going to get home?' June wondered.

'You're not,' said Thea.

Now, as far as she knew, the woman was still stretched out on Clive and Jennifer's bed. *Please God, don't let her have been sick on the duvet*, she prayed.

Slowly she went down to the kitchen and put the kettle on. Strong tea, toast and Marmite were her favoured morning-after breakfast. The dogs had been unnaturally quiet, given the long wait they'd had to be let out. 'Good boys,' she murmured. 'Very good boys.' Then she opened the back door and let them out, to go wherever they liked. In the process she realised she hadn't set the burglar alarm the previous night. She didn't think she'd put the dogs out, either, for a bedtime widdle – but it seemed to her now that she must have done. The last hour or so before bed was a disconcerting blur.

'Errghh,' came a voice from the top of the stairs. 'What time is it?'

'Twenty past nine.'

'God! What's Lindy going to say? That's if she's there, of course.'

'At home, you mean?'

'Yeah. She stays at Barrow Hill sometimes, or goes to see my mother. She's pally with the Staceys as well. I can't keep track of her.'

June came down the stairs looking much fitter and fresher than her sluggish tone implied. The only hint of the previous night's excesses was her unbrushed hair. Thea half-remembered finding her a large T-shirt to wear in bed – but there was no sign of that now. She was wearing the previous day's clothes, showing no sign of creases or crumples.

'You look great,' Thea said. 'How d'you do it?'

'Clean living,' June laughed. 'Good genes.'

Thea heard this as *jeans*, and glanced at the dark blue trousers in puzzlement before realising. Wits are slow today, she told herself.

'Is there any coffee?' June asked, making for the kitchen. 'Just a quick cup and then I'll go.'

Thea experienced a surge of relief at this announcement.

She was uneasy in June's presence, almost guilty at the way they'd made free with the house. She'd spend the day vacuuming and dusting, she promised herself. And making sure the master bedroom was just as Clive and Jennifer had left it.

The coffee evidently completed June's restoration, and with no sign of a headache or remorse or grief or embarrassment, she took her leave. Only then did Thea wonder how she'd got there the night before. She saw no sign of a car.

'You're not *walking*, are you,' she asked. 'Or is there a bus?' Didn't June live in Cirencester, seven or eight miles away?

June laughed. 'No, I don't think there's a bus. I left my car down at Barrow Hill. It's in the yard.'

'But won't the old man be wondering where you are?'

'I don't care if he is. But no, he won't worry. He's got more than enough on his own plate to wonder what I'm up to. He probably hasn't even noticed it.'

Left alone, Thea began to feel busy. Not just cleaning, but contacting her daughter, and perhaps James. Giving the dogs some quality time, too, after days of skimping on that particular duty; watering the plants; sorting the mail that was scattered untidily on the hall table. And making a close inspection of the sheep, which had been even more neglected than the dogs. She was not earning her pay, she concluded. The Reynoldses would not be very happy if they knew how little attention she'd given to their domain throughout the past week.

On the other hand, everything was still alive, which felt

like a minor triumph. And there were still two weeks to go, during which everything could be handsomely polished, cherished and supervised.

The phone had not murmured for several days, and she had not made any outgoing calls. There were, perhaps, messages on the facility. One of her clearly stated duties was to note all communications, and then delete them, to leave space for more. She remembered, dimly, the sense of being admitted into the Reynoldses' lives, trusted with their phonecalls. It had felt pleasingly intimate, and potentially interesting. That had been when things had appeared simple and innocent; when she'd assumed invitations to garden parties, rotas for the church flowers, changes to the bridge club calendar – not the drama of murder and the mysteries of marital infidelity.

Again, she felt an urgent need to sit down and think. She had been drawn into something disturbing, to say the least. People on all sides were assuming that she was not merely involved but concerned enough to actively participate. They *wanted* something from her. Even James. *Especially* James. The suspicion, successfully buried over the past days, resurfaced. The suspicion that she had been deliberately placed here by a conspiracy between James Osborne and Clive Reynolds. That there was a bigger, blacker reason for this than merely a benign wish to find her some paid occupation.

But surely neither James nor Clive had known there'd be a murder the first night of her occupancy? At least, James could not have known. Clive might have done. Clive might have paid somebody to kill Joel, while he himself had a cast iron alibi. The network of links between just about all the people she had met so far, as well as a few she hadn't, was hurting her poisoned head. She tried to remember everything June had told her: the factual stuff, if not the stated or implied emotions. Jennifer Reynolds was younger than she looked, and had been at Cheltenham Ladies' with June. Lindy, although only fifteen, was allowed to wander the countryside without supervision, staying the night with one or other of her relatives. And Lindy certainly had a lot of relatives to choose from. Not just her paternal grandfather, but a maternal grandmother and a great-uncle. And a paternal grandmother, too, although she seemed almost entirely detached. Did June have a father somewhere? Or siblings?

Helen Winstanley was in business with Martin Stacey. At least that settled a clutch of questions. Except . . . a number of June's revelations had sat uneasily with Thea's own observations. Joel as a lost little lamb; Jennifer as only forty-seven; Lionel as misunderstood. She had skated over the Staceys and their herb farm as if completely uninvolved in it herself, and she had claimed that the Winstanleys were miserable together. Thea found a lot of this quite difficult to absorb.

She sighed, but not unhappily. She sighed with a sort of contentment. Another week was stretching before her, in which she would learn more about the Jennisons and the Staceys and the Winstanleys. Spring would be in full flood, and the dogs would be made happy. She would go back to Duntisbourne Abbots and admire its extraordinary beauty. She would visit the other Duntisbournes, in their straggling string down the valley, and perhaps take some photographs. She would seek out the goodness in the creamy, honeyed, syrupy stone, savouring the solid history behind the buildings.

Absently, she squeezed the fingernail that had been a source of suffering all week, and found that it no longer hurt.

The morning passed with a vaguely satisfying sense of having things to catch up with. Radio 2, a channel she chose when feeling self-indulgent, kept her company. It soothed her head and contributed a feeling of the world being essentially benign. How this could be possible at the scene of two unpleasant killings was not a question she chose to explore.

When the doorbell rang at mid-day, she went to answer it expecting the pleasant atmosphere to continue.

She was not disappointed. Harry Richmond stood there, dressed in a mauve jumper and pale grey slacks. There was a jauntiness to him that made her smile. Easily, she invited him in.

'No, no. I've come to take you out to lunch. We're going to my favourite pub.'

She'd forgotten, totally and utterly, how that could feel. To have a man come calling, with a ready smile, and whisk you off to a place of his choosing was intoxicating, and all the more so for the scratchy and suspicious experience of the day before with James and Rosie. The contrast told her quite a lot about her feelings towards Harry Richmond.

But above all, it required a complete absence of analytical thought, which was the biggest relief of all. 'Give me three minutes,' she said. And then, 'Can Hepzibah come? She likes a good pub.'

'Welcome,' he said.

They drove sedately in his middle-aged blue Renault, winding through villages she'd never heard of with rarely more than a mile between them. Signposts pointed the way to a string of others – names that came and went before she could fix them in her memory.

The denseness of the English countryside struck her – the ancient rich textures, with settlements around every turn, layered in patterns almost too complex to interpret. She had never been one for excessive conservation; if an old bridge had outlived its usefulness, she was happy to go along with its replacement. But these stone buildings seemed to have become part of the natural scenery in a way she suspected was unique in Britain. Perhaps the adobe houses and churches in New Mexico might compare, but she could think of few instances where the materials for the buildings were so evidently taken from the ground close by. Mostly, it seemed, mankind strove to do the very opposite. She recalled the grim corrugated iron roofs of Australia, the incongruous Italian marble of west coast America, the man-made amalgams of most of the former Soviet countries and rejoiced to be where she was.

'It's lovely, isn't it,' she said.

'Not bad,' he agreed. 'The trees are good around here, too. And the tilting ground. There are no right angles anywhere – had you noticed? Everything curves and leans, even the houses. The corners of the stone look soft, the tops of the walls are odd shapes. And there are countless colours in every single stone.'

'We're being very poetic.'

'Must be spring. Oh, here we are. It always catches me by surprise.'

'Where? Where exactly are we?'

'It's called Oakridge Lynch, and its claim to fame is a pub called The Butcher's Arms. Wait and see.'

Thea gave up trying to visualise just where they were on the map, and followed Harry into the pub. It had a massive car park, to which it stood at right angles, the entrance approached down a path. Facing it, across the path, was a sheltered garden.

'Can we sit outside?' she asked. 'It's quite mild today.'

'Of course. I always sit outside.'

With some difficulty, and expectations of a long delay before the food arrived, they settled at a garden table, facing each other across the wooden slats. The spaniel lay quietly at Thea's feet. She spoke idly. 'I was planning to go and walk around Duntisbourne Abbots again today. It's a week since I was there. It seems daft when I'm living less than a mile away.'

'A mile's a long way around here,' Harry said, with a sententious note.

'Harry, I seem to be getting more and more involved in Joel's death. I can't seem to help it. It keeps cropping up.'

'Does that surprise you?'

'I suppose not. But it's all very odd. There's no sign of any panic, the fields aren't crawling with police. People don't phone up or even visit me much. It's all going on invisibly in Cirencester, I suppose. At least I was taken there on Friday for some questions – but since then I haven't heard a thing.'

'What did they ask you on Friday?'

'They wanted to talk about the scream I heard in the night . . .'

'What did you tell them?'

Belatedly she wondered if it was wise to reveal the details. Harry was such a warm friendly man, it was hard to keep anything back from him. The calculations she might ordinarily make in this sort of conversation were mostly abandoned in the face of his interest. There were no jagged edges, no danger signals between them. She wanted to nestle up to him and lean her head on his chest. She wanted to tell him everything.

'Only what I'd said already,' she said. 'I saw a man called Hollis. He seemed terribly focused on the job.'

'I know him. He's a cold fish.'

Thea giggled. This was one of the phrases she and Carl had sometimes mocked. After all, there weren't many warm fish. And Hollis had not seemed very fishlike to her. More a wolf or a snake.

'You don't like him?'

'Not much. But I quite respect him. He's a professional.'

Thea was reminded of something. 'I gather he's had some sort of personal tragedy?'

Harry took a long draught of his beer, and gazed around the garden as if expecting to see somebody he knew. 'Yes. He had a daughter who died after taking Ecstasy at one of those dance things. She was fourteen.'

'When?'

'About three years ago. It's made him touchy about drugs. Not sure he should be in the job, as a matter of fact.'

'I don't suppose there's too much of that sort of thing out here?'

'More than you might expect.'

'Besides, most people cope perfectly well with Ecstasy. Surely more kids die from alcohol poisoning, and you never hear that making the headlines.'

'I didn't bring you here to discuss the pros and cons of drugs,' he said, with a little shake, as if reminding himself of something. 'Tell me more about yourself. What line of work were you in before you took up house-sitting?'

'I was a part-time cataloguer at the Bodleian Library. It used to impress people, but it was never what I wanted to do. I just stuck it because I couldn't see any good reason to quit. I used Carl's death as an excuse to pack it in.' She paused, hearing herself. 'Gosh, yes. I've never said it like that before, but that's exactly what I did.'

Harry laughed, and encouraged her to share a few anecdotes. But before long, she'd returned to more pressing matters. 'How old is Lindy exactly?' she asked him.

'Um – let me think. She must be fifteen. She had a birthday last month. March 22nd. Yes, she's fifteen. Why?'

'Her mum gives her a lot of freedom.'

He lifted an eyebrow. 'You don't approve?'

'Well – it's unusual these days. How does she get about? She's too young to drive.'

'People give her lifts. I'm one of them. And she's a very sensible girl. Just like her mother.'

Thea thought back to the previous evening, and kept her counsel. 'Well, I know the dangers are overstated. Even so . . .'

'Don't worry about Lindy. She's got more friends than anyone else I know. Somebody's always going to be there to make sure she's safe.'

Thea squashed the flash thought that there could be something unwholesome in the relationship between Harry and his great-niece. Such suspicions were a blight of the times, she was convinced, but no easier to avoid for that.

The food arrived sooner than she'd have believed possible, giving rise to a flurry of activity centred on struggling with sachets of mayonnaise. 'I loathe these things, don't you,' said Harry. 'Even here – where the food isn't at all bad, they can't provide ordinary jars of Hellman's.'

'Something to do with EU regulations, I expect,' Thea said, feeling young and placid. She could hardly remember a time before the small unopenable sachets.

'You're not afraid of anything, are you?' he said, without looking at her. He thrust a forkful of ham into his mouth, and chewed deliberately. 'I remember being like that, although it didn't last for very long.'

'I'm not terribly good with daddy longlegs.'

He smiled a thin smile, not at all deflected. 'It must worry your family. Did you say you had a daughter?'

'She doesn't worry. James does, a bit. Well, quite a lot, I suppose. But James worries about everything. He spends a fortune on insurance. He tries to anticipate everything that could go wrong years and years in the future. I don't think he counts, being like that. And it's ironic in a way. Carl died with an insurance policy we regarded as a sort of joke, and never really wanted.'

'And now, without him, you don't feel you've got much to lose.'

'Obviously. Jessica and Hepzibah is about it. I'm afraid of losing either one of them.'

Harry cocked his head to see the dog under the table. 'Only a certain sort of person can abide living with a spaniel, you know. All that adoration and constancy can get on your nerves.'

'It suits me very well.'

'And yet dogs only live a dozen years or so. Doesn't that worry you?'

'Cockers go longer than that. I don't have to think about it for ages yet.'

'Thea – there have been two murders close to the house where you are now staying on your own. You could easily have seen or heard something that will help the police catch the killer. You must surely have some sense of danger?' He spoke with an earnestness she found engaging, but also confusing. What did he want her to do?

'The police haven't said anything like that. They don't appear to have any concerns for my welfare. I don't go out in the field at night. I've got the dogs. Surely it's far more likely that the person who killed Joel was waiting for Clive and Jennifer to go, and considered me to be no problem.'

'So you don't regard yourself as any sort of amateur detective, trying to work out who did it and why?'

'If I did, I'd have to spend much more time and energy on it than I am doing. It would be hopeless. How could I ever work out all the relationships and histories of everybody involved?'

'Sometimes a fresh eye can see through the superficial tangles and grasp just where the truth lies.'

She shook her head. 'It doesn't feel remotely like that. I expect the police will work it out in their usual slow meticulous way. It's probably somebody from outside the area, poaching or something. They shot Paul, and then possibly got the idea that Joel knew who they were, so they came back that night and got him as well.' The sheer feebleness of this scenario gave it a sort of reassurance.

'They?'

'I didn't mean it as a plural. Just "he or she".'

'Shall I get you another drink?'

She hesitated, more from a concern for her still slightly fragile head than any fear of getting drunk. 'Just a lemonade and lime, thanks. I had too much last night.'

'Oh?'

'Yes, I told you. With June.' And then she remembered she hadn't actually told him about June's visit. He could hardly have deduced it from her remarks about Lindy. Harry's puzzled expression reinforced her sense of foolishness. 'Sorry – I didn't, did I. June came round last night and we had some wine.'

'I see. Lemonade and lime, then.'

While he was in the bar, Thea did some hasty thinking, despite the discomfort it brought her. Had Harry been warning her about something? If so, why not come right out and say it directly? Was she seeing conspiracy and subterfuge where there was nothing more than friendship? Something was making her uneasy, when all she wanted was a friendly lunch out with a man she found very appealing. A man who seemed to feel the same way about her. Perhaps that was it.

She looked across at the pub, but the windows were too small and dark to see into the bar. The garden had a rather odd box hedge, four or five feet high, growing down the middle, effectively creating two distinct areas. It was impossible to look over at anybody the other side. Hepzie had got up when Harry did, and was pulling at her lead, tied around the leg of the table. Thea reached down to pat her. 'Hey, you. What's the matter?'

The long tail wagged, and the tongue lolled from between the smiling jaws. Thea followed the animal's gaze and focused on Helen Winstanley walking slowly across the path from the pub with a man, who was carrying a tray holding four pint glasses. Thea had not seen him before. Several thoughts struck her at once:

Why was Hepzibah so enthusiastic, when this woman had been partly involved in the injury to her ear?

Was this some sort of prearranged meeting between Helen and Harry?

Had they been sitting the other side of the hedge and able to hear her conversation with Harry?

Was the tray-carrying man James Winstanley, home from his business trip?

Should she call out to them, or wait for them to see her?

Who were the other two glasses for?

Answers came quickly. Helen noticed the wagging dog, and Thea attached to it. With a show of delighted surprise, she diverted her route to Thea's side of the hedge and identified the man as, indeed, her husband James. When Harry Richmond returned with two further drinks, Helen greeted him with more muted enthusiasm. 'We're sitting round the other side,' she explained. 'We've got Susanna and Lionel with us. Do you want to come and say hello?'

Harry shook his head, but Thea got up, towed by

Hepzibah. As soon as she was in sight of the other table, she wondered what on earth she was doing. But it was too late to go back.

There was some turbulence as drinks were distributed, nods and smiles exchanged, connections made. Thea was hustled over to the table and after shaking hands with James, was reintroduced to Lionel and Susanna by Helen, in a manner that seemed deeply insensitive, given the link between them. 'I think you two saw each other last weekend, at Brook View,' she said, referring to Susanna. Thea gazed at the younger woman, struck by the vivid red hair, blatantly dyed as unnatural a colour as any purple or green. This, then, had been Joel's girlfriend. Similar in age to him, at least. Relaxed in the company of people much older than herself, who she apparently knew well. And about to consume a chunky baguette oozing bright yellow egg mayonnaise. At least that probably boasted some Hellman's, Thea thought.

Susanna looked up and flipped a hand, with a brief smile. She was sitting beside the farmer, trying to interest him in a plate of Sunday roast. Thea remembered Mr Jennison's rudeness and assumed he did too. He didn't look up at her or acknowledge her in any way.

'Well, it's good to meet you all,' said Thea, after a strained minute or two. 'I'd better get back to my lunch before the girl takes it away. Nice to see you, Helen. Drop in any time. I'm usually there.'

James Winstanley gave a loud guffaw at that. 'Making free with the homestead, aren't you?' he said, in an accent Thea hadn't heard anywhere but in old films and archive footage. Dumbfounded, she looked at him, wondering if he was play-acting. Surely nobody actually spoke like that any more?

The red-haired girl giggled. 'Come off it, Jim. Stop pretending to be the local squire.' Her own accent was plain and classless, if on the squeaky end of the tonal scale, but her delivery was confident. She didn't care whether or not Winstanley thought her rude.

Thea felt torn. She couldn't just abandon Harry, but she was beginning to wish she could stay and witness the crosscurrents at this crowded table. Dutifully she left the foursome and rejoined her escort.

Having finished her lunch, Thea went to the Ladies in the pub, and lingered on the way back, examining again the people in the other part of the garden. It was a fascinating group: the old man sitting hunched and expressionless, sipping Coca Cola in a tall glass, but not eating anything; Helen very upright, leaning slightly away from her husband on the slatted seat beside her. The Susanna person kept up a constant chatter, scattered with shrill little laughs, encouraged to some extent by James. Thea couldn't hear the words, but the impression was of inane superficial babble.

'I didn't know they'd be here,' Harry said. He sounded almost sad, and Thea was instantly remorseful.

'Rather a coincidence, then.'

'Not really. There aren't too many pubs that offer such a variety – food, garden, space. This one's become a bit of a habit with several of us lately. I've been here with June a few times, and Joel. Surprising to see old Lionel, though. I've never known him to go to a pub.'

'Trying to cheer him up, I suppose.' Thea remembered some deeply unfortunate attempts to do the same for her, when Carl died. Her sisters had been the worst – they'd actually bought tickets for a Stratford performance of *The Taming of the Shrew* three weeks after Carl's funeral, thinking, bizarrely, that it would improve her mood.

Harry seemed to read her mind. 'Poor chap,' he murmured.

She turned her attention fully onto him. 'I'm sorry,' she said. 'I'm being rude, aren't I. It's just so interesting, seeing them together. I mean – I've never seen James before. And Susanna! She's unreal, isn't she.'

'The hair, you mean. Horrible.' He shuddered, exaggerating the disgust for comic effect.

'Not just the hair. It makes her skin look odd, as well. Like a doll. And her lips. Do you know what she's really like?'

He shrugged. 'If I'm being unkind, I'd just say she was a typical girlfriend. That's what Lindy called her, and it's rather accurate. I don't think we tried very hard to get to know her as a person in her own right.'

'What does she do?'

'Oh, heavens, now you're asking. Something in an office, I think. In Gloucester. Possibly to do with a newspaper.'

Thea couldn't imagine the woman as a journalist. 'Selling advertising space,' she decided.

'Very likely,' Harry agreed.

'And James Winstanley – she called him Jim just now. Very familiar. What's their connection?'

Harry drank an inch or more of his beer before replying. When he did, it was with another question. 'Oh, Thea, give it a rest. Is this part of some amateur sleuthing, spying for your brother-in-law? You're never going to see any of these people again, now are you? Why don't you let it all go, and just enjoy the moment?'

It gave her a jolt. 'You make me feel like the flying Dutchman,' she complained.

'Well, isn't that what you are?'

She understood, then, what had made her uneasy earlier. It was to do with Harry Richmond's attentions. As if he had dropped everything that was already going on in his life, at the appearance of a pretty woman, apparently unattached. It made her wonder what he'd been doing before – what he would be doing if she had never turned up. Why, in fact, he had so much time for her, was so eager to get to know her.

People who latched onto newcomers with such enthusiasm often turned out to be social misfits, in her experience. They'd used up everyone locally, bored or frightened or embarrassed them all to the point where they no longer associated with him or her. Could this be true of Harry Richmond, with his open friendly twinkle? Or did he have a more sinister motivation?

Neither possibility seemed to work. She looked into his face, noting the laughter lines, the direct gaze, and merely found her liking for him reinforced.

They drove back another way, almost equally scenic. 'Come back for a bit,' he invited. 'We could take the dog for a little walk.'

That was another thing – he had been completely relaxed about taking Hepzie in his nice clean car, letting her sit on the back seat without fussing over hairs on the upholstery.

Thea admitted to herself that this had been a small test for him, which a great many people would have failed. So what if she gave the message *Love me, love my dog*? She wasn't so desperate for a new relationship that she'd give up the faithful company of the spaniel, anyway.

He found a grass verge for the car, and took them on a walk through the middle of Duntisbourne Abbots, offering to show Thea its attributes from a more familiar perspective. He led her into the church, where she admired its unusual layout, and flipped incredulously through the visitors' book.

'My God! Look at this – New Zealand, Italy, Nottingham, Texas, Vancouver, Montrose, Ramsgate, Helsinki and Truro – all on one page! I have never seen such a cosmopolitan list. It's amazing!'

Her whole idea of the village changed, as she tried to visualise this stream of visitors from all corners of the globe. Suddenly it was the hub of something huge, a quiet centre into which everyone rushed, and wrote down their names and addresses to prove it. 'I'm stunned,' she said.

'They come quietly, in little groups,' he said. 'And then they forget all about us. Most people just see the church, and the general prettiness, and leave it at that. They overlook the history and the quirkiness of the setting.'

'But the church and the views are basically it, surely?' She was half serious, half teasing, hoping he'd come up with something surprising.

'Maybe if you're just passing through, that's enough.' He sounded wistful, as if coming to an unpalatable conclusion. 'Maybe it is, at that.'

'Everywhere's got history. Human lives. Tragedies and miracles. Is this place anything special?'

'Possibly not. I can't pretend to any expert knowledge, and haven't heard of any dramatic stories. But look at these gardens, the way they've been fitted into every nook and cranny. Look up there – fancy perching a house that size on the side of a hill. Imagine the problems! And see how it looks as if it's always been there, growing out of the ground. Doesn't it thrill you?'

'It's lovely. It is lovely. I never questioned the beauty – how could I? But what lies beneath the chocolate box imagery? Why is everything so quiet? Where *is* everybody?'

'Obviously, a few of these cottages are holiday lets, or second homes,' he said, with mild irritation. 'And where would you expect them to be? Wandering about the street in local costume? Shepherding their shaggy sheep back and forth? It's Sunday afternoon. Either they've taken the kids to the pictures or some sports thing in Cirencester, or they're watching the telly, or playing computer games. Look – there's somebody!'

Almost sounding relieved, he pointed to a woman in a garden, bending over a tidy flowerbed with a trowel. She looked up at the sound of his voice and stared at him unsmiling.

'Too many tourists come through here, just gawping, and expecting some sort of entertainment. That's what she thinks we are.'

'Doesn't she *know* you?' Thea asked. 'You only live half a mile away.'

'I know very few people in the village itself,' he said.

'There's no shop, you see, or post office. Nowhere to congregate and get to know each other.'

'That's awful. They can't have much sense of community, or belonging, living like that, all in their private boxes.'

'Isn't it like that where you live?'

She hesitated. 'Well, I know most of the people living within half a mile of me. Four or five of them are quite good friends.'

'Well, you can't have everything. At least most people here have deliberately chosen it for its visual appeal. I think that shows something about them. Good taste, finer feelings, that sort of thing.'

'And the ones who were born here?'

'Are mostly out of the village and working their fingers to the bone. Different kettle of fish entirely.'

'That's enough clichés,' she laughed. 'Why don't you come back to Brook View for some tea? I ought to be exercising those labradors, the slobs. And I rather like acting the hostess in someone else's house.'

'So James Winstanley had a point,' Harry flashed. Thea took a moment to get the allusion, and then gave him a quick look of surprise. She had been sure he hadn't heard the exchange in the pub garden.

Chapter Fifteen

Harry Richmond took a cup of tea, but no biscuits, after accompanying Thea and the three dogs around the garden at Brook View. 'This must be over an acre,' he said, with envy clear in his voice.

'And the field is another nine, I think. Must be worth a bit.'

'Astronomical. A goldmine.'

'They've been here some time, haven't they?'

'Twenty years at least. The boys were young, I remember. I had charge of them as Boy Scouts for a while. Seems an age ago, now.'

'Isn't there any sort of gardening club in the village? With people like you and Jennifer so keen?'

He laughed. 'Keenly competitive, you might say. No, I don't think either of us is the sort to join a club like that.'

'You make yourself sound like quite a curmudgeon.'

'Not really. At least, I hope not.'

He only stayed an hour. On the doorstep he turned and gave her one of his long looks, meeting her eyes. 'Thank you,' he said, and put both arms around her in a hug that caught her completely off guard. 'Thank you for a lovely day. You're a very beautiful woman, Thea Osborne. It's been a treat to spend time with you.'

Belatedly she returned the hug, savouring the warmth, the male scent, the broad chest. 'My pleasure,' she said.

Telling herself she was being silly, she could not suppress a burst of euphoria that lasted the rest of the day. Neither could she deny the erotic charge that had flooded through her at the contact with a new man's body. It brought back memories from twenty years ago, when she'd been aware that somebody new was almost always immensely more exciting than a familiar lover. She had felt vaguely guilty about that, but fully accepted that it was so. It had been one of her worries when she agreed to marry Carl. Would she be able to stay faithful to him, when there were so many desirable men in the world?

As it turned out, she had been pregnant within six months, and so preoccupied with the baby for so long that other men faded from her consciousness. The idea of adultery simply never floated up. Carl was exceptionally good at being married, which helped. He skilfully maintained the balance between admiring her independence and being there when she wanted him. He told her when he was angry or anxious, seldom leaving her to develop unhealthy fantasies about other women or loss of affection. He was funny, and generous and . . . *Stop it*, she ordered herself. We're not thinking about Carl, just at the moment.

It made her smile to think that a man close to seventy, a

solitary gardening widower, should be the one to rekindle the coals. A smile that turned rueful, when it struck her that Harry was only a few years younger than her father, and could very easily have been older. Obviously there could be nothing in it, no future, no further development. If he thought her beautiful, then that was well and good. He wouldn't be the first person to mention it, and Thea had come to regard it as a simple statement of fact. She looked like Kristen Scott Thomas with a touch of Amanda Burton for good measure. It was a quirk of her skeleton that everything was in proportion, her eyes deepset and clear, her jawline sharp against a long neck. It would be folly to take any credit for it, or to think it meant anything.

Still in the same aroused mood, she e-mailed James.

Good afternoon. How's it going? I've had a very nice day, taken out to lunch by Harry Richmond, who you will recall, no doubt. Saw several other locals, even though we were some miles away from the village.

June Jennison was here last night, visiting the scene of the crime one week on. Is she a suspect? In my humble opinion, I would say not.

I can't see this murder investigation getting much further. If everybody closes ranks and protects each other, it'll never get solved. Even old Lionel was at the pub today. Is HE a suspect, I wonder?

June was at school with Jennifer Reynolds, did you know? I don't suppose it matters. And Helen Winstanley is as odd as ever. Another of today's pub people. Still haven't talked to the Staceys.

Give DS Hollis my regards if you see him.
Hug Rosie for me.
Love, Thea

It amused her to list murder suspects in e-mails to James, hoping it would irritate him. She hadn't forgiven him for being so obscure and contrary when he last came to see her. It felt now as if he'd really come to check that she was safe and unafraid, and not to recruit her into his team as an undercover agent at all. This might be kind of him, but it was disappointingly unexciting. It left her wondering just how much he cared about the Jennison brothers – were they just small local murders, possibly connected to larger criminal activities, but just as possibly not?

She tried again to reconcile the idea of unspecified but serious misdemeanours with the facts as far as she knew them. An obvious one would be stealing valuables from the affluent homes in the area and then disposing of them profitably. Obvious and rather dull. Not to mention difficult in these times of paranoid security and registration of any object worth more than a hundred quid.

Child pornography would be considerably closer to the mark, if only James hadn't explicitly ruled it out. Unsuspected in this polite and civilised corner of England, and therefore all the more possible. Anything could be going on behind those firmly closed, electronically alarmed front doors. Everybody had computers and scanners and digital cameras. They could be uploading horrendous images to each other to their hearts' content, and nobody would ever guess. In fact, it was virtually certain that many were doing precisely that, given the statistics. Thea tried to avoid knowing about such depravities, but there were inevitably moments when the radio or television forced it on her.

Giving it up, she treated herself to a nice leisurely game of Scrabble, a 25-minute game, which allowed ample time for cheating on both sides, if she or dezzyduks had felt so inclined. She hadn't brought a dictionary with her, and didn't search for a Reynolds-owned one, either. But she hardly had need of it these days. She knew by heart a vast assortment of improbable words, and also knew when to take a risk on something. YOWE had turned out to be allowable, which was a surprise. Her opponent put KOTO, which she challenged, as surely not on. But it was. Koto? *Koto*? Maybe, she decided, it was lazy American spelling for kowtow?

She successfully placed RAJAH in a high-scoring position, quickly followed by TOQUE, which was a personal favourite. But in the end she lost by 15 points, when dezzyduks used all his/her letters near the finish, with a very boring REDRAWN.

The day drifted on, with the inner contentment still intact despite Scrabble defeat. Outside the light was fading and it was getting chilly. The penalty for a clear sky in late April. 'Come on, dogs, let's have some air,' she invited. 'Time to count those sheep again.'

At last she plucked up the courage to take the labradors into the field. They'd earned a good run, and she couldn't think of anywhere else to take them, in the failing light. It seemed reasonable to assume that they would more willingly stay close if it was getting dark. She promised herself that she would keep a close eye on them, and whistle them back if they went too far towards the hedge. Being in the field, in any case, was not completely relaxing, after the previous weekend's discovery. She found herself glancing over her shoulder, up into the trees, and down into the ditches. The chances of finding another body – or of becoming one herself – were clearly infinitesimal, but reason was famously adrift at times like this. It wasn't, she assured herself, so much that she was afraid as that she really didn't want the complications that would ensue from another murder. Actually, she decided, she was much more worried about being considered a potential murderer by the police, than she was of being killed herself.

When she caught a sudden movement, she believed for a moment that it was pure imagination. Only when Bonzo, followed by a daftly exuberant Hepzibah, suddenly charged towards the same spot, did Thea trust her own eyes.

A figure had been standing in a shadowy part of the hedge, she realised. If he or she had kept still, Thea would almost certainly never have noticed anything. But it might not have seemed like that to the person concerned. The movement she now watched with disbelief was an odd diving motion, the body bent at the hips, then down on its knees and *gone*!

This was so exactly how the killer of Paul Jennison had been described as behaving that Thea's heart started to thump wildly. What on earth was going on?

Bonzo reached the spot, and she called him to stay. Rather to her surprise, he obeyed, but her own foolish spaniel ignored her call. Georgie had trundled off on some business of his own under the hedge near the top of the field, and was blissfully unaware of any excitement.

Thinking mainly about her dog, Thea strode to the spot,

and bent down to look. 'Hepzie!' she called sharply. 'Come back here this minute.'

There was another field beyond the hedge, which was at least preferable to a road in this poor light. All around was silence. She peered at the vegetation, certain she was in the right place, and eventually a kind of tunnel manifested itself, very low down. Little more than a fox run, it had clearly been used regularly, the roots and twigs framing a hole that was difficult to see. But not so difficult that the police could be excused for missing it, surely? Heedlessly, Thea pushed her head and shoulders into it, and found herself tumbling like Alice down the rabbit-hole into the adjacent field.

So like Alice's experience was it, that she almost laughed. She was now lying flat out in a much deeper ditch than the one on her side. Looking back, she couldn't see the hole at all – just a thick clump of brown ferns, with the small new shoots of this year's early growth at their roots. Perhaps, she surmised, the police had tried to be clever, and examined the hedge most carefully from this side. If so, they'd made a big mistake.

'Your dog's OK,' came a voice. 'You were brave, coming through like that.'

Maybe she was in Wonderland after all. The voice seemed to be coming from above her. She blinked and squinted, and identified the silhouette of a girl against the indigo sky.

'Lindy?' she ventured. 'Is that you?'

'Yeah, it's me. I didn't think you'd see me. Why'd you come following me? Now everyone's going to know about the secret hole.'

Thea climbed awkwardly out of the ditch and brushed

at her trousers. 'But – isn't this where your father's – er – attacker, disappeared? It matches what June told me.'

'What if it is?'

'Well – doesn't that mean it isn't really so secret, after all?' A nasty thought occurred. 'I mean – that's assuming you weren't – I mean, didn't . . . ?'

The girl snorted.

'In any case, I doubt if I could find it again.'

'Somebody did find it though,' Lindy went on. 'The person who shot Daddy. It's right what you said. I forgot that.'

'It's very neat. Is it a fox run or something?'

'No, it isn't. *Daddy* made it. For me to use to escape from horrible Mrs Reynolds.'

'Look – come and have a cup of tea with me, and tell me all about it,' Thea ordered. 'If we can get back into my field, of course.'

'It's not *your* field, and no, I don't expect we can. It's very important not to squash the bracken on this side. It only works if you sort of roll through, without breaking it. You managed that quite well.'

'Purely by accident, I assure you. What about the dogs?'

'We'll have to go round by the road and call them. They'll be all right. Yours is nice, isn't she?'

For the first time, Thea noticed that Lindy had Hepzie slung without dignity over her shoulder. The dog hated being carried, her centre of gravity never quite right, and no position entirely comfortable. Now this girl seemed to have effortlessly worked out the way to do it. 'She doesn't like being carried,' she said. 'Put her down.'

'No,' snapped the girl. 'She *does* like it.'

The abrupt change of tone came as no surprise to Thea. It wasn't long ago that her own daughter was this age, and she still remembered the inconsistent swings from child to adult and back, from minute to minute. 'Well, if she starts wriggling, I want you to let her go.'

'She won't wriggle.'

And it seemed she didn't. They arrived at Brook View, having gone out onto the road through the field gate, and walked back to the house up a gentle slope. By the time they arrived it was very nearly dark. Miraculously, Bonzo and Georgie were both standing forlornly by the gate between the field and the garden, waiting to be allowed home again. Thea let them through, with a relieved pat for each one.

'I love being out at night, don't you,' said Lindy.

'It depends.'

'Huh.' The scorn was all the more chastening for its lack of elaboration.

'I don't suppose you drink coffee?' Thea led the girl into the kitchen and then stood indecisively in front of the cupboards.

'Milk, if you've got it, thanks.'

There wasn't very much milk, and what there was had been sitting around for days. Thea had bought four litres from a garage some while previously. She still hadn't properly got to grips with the shopping.

'I can't really care about Uncle Joel, you know,' Lindy said, sitting down at the kitchen table. 'I used up all my caring on Daddy.'

'That makes sense.'

'Does it? Harry said that when a second awful thing happens, it often feels twice as bad as the first one. More than twice as bad, sometimes.'

'I think that's usually when you haven't really faced up to the first one. I mean, if you've just told yourself that it isn't really so terrible, and you're coping all right, and it's not OK to make a fuss. Then if there's something else, even years later, you're overloaded, and all the stuff you should have felt the first time comes bursting out, and you're knocked flat.'

Lindy frowned. 'You mean I got it right with Daddy?'

'Well – I wouldn't put it like that, quite. It's not such a deliberate thing as that. You're lucky if the people around you are talking about it, and showing their feelings and not making up rules on how to do grief. It depends on the whole family, I think.'

Lindy laughed her understanding. 'Nobody made up any rules,' she said. 'It was like being dropped onto another planet where you've got no idea at all what you're supposed to be doing.'

'Your mum was here last night. She talked a bit about your dad.'

'She tells lies about him.' It was a plain unemotional statement.

'Oh?'

'She says she can't have loved him properly because she hasn't cried about him dying. She thinks she wasn't a proper wife, because she can get along so well without him. But she's got it all upside down.'

'How?'

'She doesn't see that he was her best best friend. She told him everything she did, what she was reading and thinking, who she'd met, what they said to each other. She listened to him, the same. Wanted to know where he'd been, who he'd seen – not in a jealous way, but *interested*, you know? So now, she keeps going into the living room, or upstairs or out into the garden, to tell him something, her mouth already open to say it, and then she remembers. And *of course* she doesn't cry. It's not a crying thing – it's just a great big hole where he used to be. And she *desperately* wants to know who killed him. She used to phone the police every single day, for weeks, asking if they'd found out any more. But she *looks* all right. She laughs and smiles, and does her hair and gets the food in and cooks things, like a normal person. I'm the one who does the crying.'

'He was a good father, then?'

'Whatever that means. He loved me.' Tears started flowing, with no change of expression, and no sound. Just running down her face, of their own accord. Thea's heart contracted.

'And you want to know who killed him, too?'

'Sort of. It won't make any difference, will it. I'm not going to hate them, or try to get revenge or anything. I want to know if it hurt him, if he saw the person, if he knew he was dying. I think I can understand some of that. You see, when I was nine, I was nearly killed by a car. I mean – it didn't hit me or hurt me, but I was so close to being hit by it. I felt the wind, and *imagined* it had killed me. Like – there was a parallel reality where it did kill me, and I could get into that reality for a minute. Enough to know what it would

225

have been like. Sounds crazy, I know. It's hard to say it, the way it was – but it showed me that being killed isn't so bad for the person themselves. It's all over before you have time to know about it – unless you've got cancer or something. Or if you're being tortured to death, or burnt or strangled. But other things, like being shot, aren't so bad.' She took a deep breath and sat up straighter, the tears abating. 'Gramps understands. He knows *exactly* what I mean. Poor Gramps.' She sighed.

Thea was aware of a sense of privilege. How had she managed to unleash such intimate revelations? The answer came instantly.

'And you – you probably understand it as well, because you're a widow, aren't you? Mum was quite chuffed when she heard that. She's the same age as you, I suppose, and wanted to come and talk to you. And I did, as well – because most people haven't had anybody die like that. Not when they're still quite young, and not ill or anything.'

Thea quailed at this. She had no excuses; after all, she'd encouraged these confidences from the outset. 'My daughter wasn't much older than you when my husband died,' she said, aware of stretching the truth a trifle. Jessica had in fact been nearly twenty, which was immensely older than fifteen. Lindy watched her, not reacting to the thickening in Thea's voice, the frequent swallowing. 'And I don't think we took it at all the way you and your mum are doing. It's hard to remember now, exactly how it was. You tell yourself the story, a thousand times, and every time it changes just the tiniest bit, until it's probably nothing like the truth. But just now, it came back – how it was in those first days. Jessica wouldn't talk to me at all. She seemed to turn into a lump of wood. And I was angry with her for being so useless.'

'That's not what you said just now.'

'No. No, it's not, is it. I was fibbing just now. Just saying what I thought would be good for you to hear. What I *hoped* was true, I suppose. I mean, really, if we're honest, we can't help anybody else. We can't say "I know how you feel" because we're all different.'

'Did you talk to Mum like this, last night?'

'Not at all. We were a bit manic, I think, both of us. We talked about men, and ghosts and we drank a lot of wine. We thought we were being very grown up.'

'Ghosts?' Lindy's eyebrows went up, her eyes widened. Hope, Thea diagnosed miserably.

'Not the way you think. Just memories, really, and presences. We carry them inside us. I would think a daughter does that more than a wife. After all, you're made out of him, aren't you. Jessica sometimes has such a look of Carl, it's as if she's possessed by him. As if he's there behind her eyes, in her voice.'

'You haven't asked me why I was in your field.' If she was disappointed, she didn't show it.

'I assumed it was the same reason as your mother's. You wanted to be where they died. As I said – ghosts.'

Lindy snorted. 'I don't think so. I wanted to check the burrow – and look for clues. The police haven't any idea what to look for. They're so *stupid*.'

'I expect they need you to explain it to them. It can't be easy for them, trying to work it out from scratch.'

'I tried to explain, but they don't listen to a kid, do they?'

'Well, try me instead.'

Lindy gave her a calculating look. 'OK. Well, you know we used to live here, until last year. Dad didn't want to move, and he used to come back to help Gramps, at weekends mostly. I came with him sometimes. You know, I suppose, that the field over there, the other side of this one, is our land? We're on both sides of the road.'

Thea blinked. 'No, I didn't know that. Where do you mean, exactly?'

'I'll show you.' Confidently, Lindy led the way through to the dining room, where a large window looked over the back garden and field beyond. Outside all was darkness. Lindy giggled. 'Oh! Well, anyway, it'll still work.' She waved her left arm. 'On that side, I mean. Where the brook goes. Where the pond is, at the bottom. Well, the other side of that is Little Barn Field. It's actually rented out at the moment, but we still go in it. There's a fox earth in the far corner, and a big blackthorn that's good for sloes. Dad always made sloe gin with them. There were mushrooms in it last year, too. It's got a good fence, but we made a place where we could climb over it.'

'But the burrow, as you call it, is on the other side of Clive's field.'

'Right. We used to cross his field to get to the crab apple tree.'

'Did Clive let you?'

'He didn't know. We'd walk around the bottom hedge. You can't see it from the house.'

Thea took a few moments to appreciate the images of country life conjured by the girl. Father and daughter helping themselves to the bounty of the hedgerows, making free with other people's property, forming secret routes, like wild animals. Something about it did not ring true. She looked closely at Lindy.

'How long ago was all this?'

'Oh! Um . . . a few years. I mean, when I was quite little, mainly. But we did it sometimes, right till when he died.'

'You crossed this field, keeping out of sight, to pick crab apples?'

'Mostly, yes.'

'Mostly?'

'And to see what the Staceys were doing. That was after we moved. Mum didn't know about it.' Lindy wriggled, and rubbed a hand around the back of her neck. There was a strong impression of unburdening.

'What? Explain.'

'You can see across to their place from there, without them seeing you.'

Thea tried to work this out, realising that she hadn't explored in that direction; realising too that she'd already calculated that Fairweather Farm must have a front entrance a little way down the road to the west of Brook View.

'You were spying on the Staceys?'

Lindy blushed. 'Only Paolo,' she admitted. 'He's so lovely. But I think he's gone now,' she added sadly.

It began to come clearer. 'You mean you've been watching him through the hedge. I see. How long has this been going on?'

'Not long. About a month.'

'Do you know who Paolo was? Where he came from? Where he's gone now?'

Lindy shook her head. 'I think he was Turkish or something. Very dark, with gorgeous deep brown eyes.'

'Did you ever speak to him?'

'Course I did. He's in the network. We're *all* in the network. All except Mum and Gramps.'

Thea didn't have to ask. Lindy clapped a hand over her mouth, and stared wide-eyed at Thea. It was perfectly plain that she had said too much, and feared for the consequences. She took her hand away, and laid it on Thea's arm. 'You won't tell anybody I said that, will you? We're not supposed to say anything about it. Don't worry – it isn't illegal. Isabel and Martin promised us that, when it started.'

Thea chewed a lip while she considered this. 'Just tell me – were your dad and your uncle Joel in the network?'

Lindy took a step back. 'No!' she almost shouted. 'That's the whole thing, you see. They wouldn't have anything to do with it. That must be why they died.'

Chapter Sixteen

Thea could get no more out of the girl, despite a barrage of questions. 'Have you told the police about this?' was one of the more urgent ones. Eventually Lindy said, 'There's no point. They wouldn't understand, and anyway it would wreck everything. There's a lot at stake.' The solemn adult words sounded like a quote to Thea.

'But – if it helps them catch the person who killed Paul and Joel . . . ?'

'It wouldn't. We don't know who it was, and we've decided we don't *want* to know. There's a lot at stake,' she repeated.

'I think your mother wants to know.'

'Then let her work it out for herself.'

'Lindy, you'll have to go home. How did you get here? Shall I give you a lift?'

'I'm staying with Gramps tonight, and helping with the milking tomorrow. I will go now, thanks for being nice.'

'What about school? You've got school tomorrow, haven't you? It's not half-term or anything, is it?'

'Tomorrow's a bank holiday,' Lindy said, as if the knowledge had been at the forefront of her mind from the start. 'That's why the relief isn't here. He was booked to do another farm.'

How rare, Thea thought, to find a girl so collected, so competent and focused. It was more than a little disconcerting, too. She had been quite unaware of the bank holiday, and wondered inconsequentially where she would find more milk. The garage again, she supposed.

She let Lindy go, watching her from the gate until she was out of sight, the beam from a small torch bobbing ahead of her.

Illegal immigrants, she concluded, with a slew of mixed feelings. *They must be harbouring illegal immigrants*. Martin Stacey would be taking cash for his part in a major operation to get people into Britain. Some of the neighbours would be getting a cut for services rendered, but the Jennisons, for whatever reason, had not been trusted to take part, and had been kept out of the secret. Perhaps they'd made threats or were regarded as dangerous, and that was the reason they'd been murdered. It all made perfect sense, and Thea resolved to deliver the whole discovery to James Osborne first thing in the morning.

She woke to sunshine, and remembered quickly that it was a bank holiday; the first Monday in May. An obscure sense of duties unperformed hit her. Not merely the duty to pass on what she had learnt the previous evening, but a duty to go out and enjoy herself just because it was a bank holiday. It was the same anxiety that made single people flinch at the prospect of a solitary Christmas, even when it had been their favoured option. Somehow it was against the rules to fail to take advantage of these special days when the world invited you to be free and happy and self-indulgent. That is, provided you went out, mingled, spent money and ate ice cream.

As if to reinforce this unease, her daughter phoned as she was drinking her morning coffee. The mobile sang its mindless tune from her bag in the hall, summoning her from the kitchen.

'Mum? How are you? Why haven't you phoned me? What's it like in the stately home?'

'It's not a stately home, you fool. It's just an ordinary house. It's nice enough. The dogs behave themselves, and I hardly bother with the sheep. Hepzie's having a nice time, except for being attacked by a collie and having her ear torn. She soon got over it.'

'There was something on the news about Duntisbourne Abbots. A man was killed.'

It seemed extraordinary to Thea that she hadn't told Jessica about Joel Jennison. And even more amazing that it had been on the news, without her realising. 'When?' she said.

'Last weekend. I kept thinking you'd phone and tell me the whole story. I bet you've been getting involved, haven't you? Making friends and trying to work it all out.'

'Have you been talking to James?'

'Not since I sent you that e-mail, saying he wanted to tell you something. He sounded worried. But then I remembered he always sounds worried.'

Thea laughed. 'I still can't make him tell me just what his problem is. He's not directly involved in the murder investigation; that's a man called Hollis. I met him during the week.' She paused, undecided as to how much to reveal. 'I've met some of the murdered man's family, actually.'

'Oh yeah?'

'He came from quite near here. It's not really in the village, you see. It's a bit more remote, and less – well, you know.'

'Pretentious.'

'No, no. That isn't fair. The village people aren't *that*. They have a lot of money, and they keep their houses neat and tidy, but it's more a matter of *absence*. On a normal day, there's hardly anybody around. They all seem to commute to work, miles away. A lot only come here for weekends, I think. It leaves a feeling of emptiness.'

'Sounds rather nice. This place could do with some emptiness. It's bedlam today.'

'Even on a bank holiday?'

'That's why. No lectures or anything. But it's lovely and sunny, so we're all outside, pretending to revise, but really just chatting and messing about.'

'It's only ten o'clock. I'm amazed you're even out of bed.'

Jessica laughed. 'Force of habit. Most people get up on a Monday. Anyway, you're OK then, are you?'

'Of course. Are you?'

'Yeah, yeah.'

'I'm not sure you sound it.'

'Yeah, I am. It's just Finals, and jobs and decisions and that stuff. Stressy.'

'You'll be fine. We'll both be fine. Thanks for ringing.'

Thea firmly curtailed the call, before it became any more maudlin, and ruined her mood completely.

Finding something to do became more urgent, thanks to Jessica's call. The usual old platitudes about single women having to amuse themselves at weekends and holidays came surging in, all too horribly true. She couldn't go and visit Helen Winstanley because her husband had come back, and it was axiomatic that you did not intrude on couples on a bank holiday unless very convincingly invited. She might try Harry Richmond, but that required a lot of careful thought beforehand. She didn't know how to contact June Jennison, and really there was nobody else. She hadn't made enough of a bond with Muriel, mother of the murdered brothers – and wouldn't much want to spend time with her, anyway.

And all that was in reality a diversion away from the news she had to impart to the police. Initially she had only thought of telling James, but then it struck her that there would be far more sense in passing it on to DS Hollis in Cirencester. He would listen, and then take a team of officers to Fairweather Farm, where the entire property would be comprehensively searched for evidence of wrongdoing. The chances were that blood, knife, threads, DNA would all turn up and indicate clearly who had killed Paul and Joel Jennison.

But the more she rehearsed this process, the less inclined she was to set it in motion. For one thing, was it credible that the farm had not already been searched? Next door to Barrow Hill, the scene of fairly public and surely strange goings-on, it wasn't possible that the police had ignored it in their investigations. They would have heard of the existence of Monique and Paolo and the others, whoever they were.

They had probably interviewed them. If they were there illegally, it would have been discovered, and the appropriate procedures performed.

Had Lindy been making it all up, or had she, Thea, jumped to unwarranted assumptions? Was the 'network' something the girl had invented from nothing – a few kind looks from visiting students, some e-mails perhaps, a system of financial support and repayments from the herb farm that looked like something it wasn't?

Whenever she had asked about Fairweather, the answers had been freely given. Helen in particular had tried to explain how it was there. People – Helen especially – had invested in the herb business, and helped out with seasonal work. Nothing sinister in that. The Monique girl had shown herself without obvious signs of reticence, in a group of local people. If she'd been part of something illegal, would she have done that? The only cause for suspicion was her foreign name and arguably foreign looks. And if Paolo was Turkish – well, so what? As far as she was aware, Turkish Kurds were welcomed in Britain as genuine refugees from ill-treatment.

Besides, it was a bank holiday, and she should not bother James with her flights of fancy at least until the next day. Worse than that, the prospect of trying to contact DS Hollis and explain herself to him was deeply unappealing. He hadn't seemed like a man who would take kindly to being told how to do his job.

Despite the familiarity of the mood swings, she hated the sudden dip into glumness. The world turned grey, there was no prospect of a better future, nobody cared about her and she'd stupidly blundered into something very puzzling going on right outside her temporary gate. She gathered her spaniel onto her lap, and absently combed her ears, looking for grass seeds or burrs that might be entangled there. The damaged ear had a three-inch split in it that was healing around the edges, but not knitting together. The dog would always have the marks of her stay in Duntisbourne Abbots. She'd never win a dog show now, Thea thought, with a self-mocking little smile. Entering dog shows was not an activity she had ever seriously contemplated.

But the stream of consciousness took a new turn from there. My trouble is, I don't have a proper hobby, she told herself. Something to lose myself in, with other people similarly obsessed. It could, after all, be anything. Astronomy had occasionally appealed, or a concentrated study of Arabic. Not ballroom dancing, although she had a friend who swore by it. Not pottery or feltmaking or book-binding, because they would all lead to a great deal of clutter and mess. Not cookery because that would make her fat. Possibly painting, although she was very sure she lacked all talent in that direction. The only thing that had her even mildly hooked was pathetic solitary anonymous online Scrabble. Most of her opponents maintained a complete silence. If they did say anything it was usually just hi, gl, and at the end thx gg. As human intercourse went, it was about as dull and minimal as it could get.

And so, more or less by default, she started yet again to consider the details of the killing of Joel Jennison. At college, where she once took a short extra-mural course in philosophy, which included a Logic component, she had acquired a habit of argument backwards, from effect to cause, more as an exercise than anything really useful. She tried it now. The chief effect of the deaths of the brothers had been to cause havoc at Barrow Hill. The old farmer could not manage alone, his daughter-in-law was showing little sign of long-term commitment, his ex-wife was out of the picture and his grand-daughter too young to be up to the task of keeping things going. Was all this the intention, or merely an unimportant side-effect, in the mind of the murderer? If the latter, then what else had changed with the two deaths?

Unless June and Lindy moved back, and actively participated in running the farm, it looked as if it would have to be sold. There was likely to be a prospective buyer waiting in the wings, salivating at the prospect of acquiring the acres and the not insubstantial farmhouse. The acquisition of property was a well-established motive for murder, after all. But Thea wasn't sure she credited it with plausibility in this particular instance. Being a prospective buyer was too vague a role. Unless you were guaranteed to inherit the place, it seemed just too long a shot for comfort.

Which took her back to Fairweather Farm. The Staceys might well be the impatient would-be buyers, perhaps even given verbal assurance in the past that they'd have first refusal if Barrow Hill were ever for sale. The herb farm could expand conveniently to the adjacent land, along with any other enterprises they had in mind. Martin had the strength and the opportunity to kill the brothers. He could easily have the motivation. Thea just doubted that he had the necessary ruthless streak to plan and execute something so vicious. Granted she had scarcely met him, and knew herself to be a shaky judge of character, but there had still been something in his eyes that told more of benevolence and concern than vice and greed.

Acknowledging the inconclusive results thus far, Thea pressed on. What *themes* were emerging, in connection with the killings? Cheerless relationships and families with sad histories, going back to that between Lionel and Muriel, which had broken up twenty years ago. Joel and Susanna had separated more recently. Helen and James Winstanley didn't appear to like each other very much, and June had admitted her ambivalence towards her Paul. Finally, Clive and Jennifer Reynolds had some unhappy history between them, for which this expensive cruise was intended as a remedy. Only Harry Richmond claimed to have loved his wife, and to have grieved for her loss in a normal and dignified fashion. And, interestingly, the Staceys gave every sign of getting along amicably.

Then there were the odd alliances: Helen Winstanley and Martin. The Winstanleys and the red-haired Susanna. Harry Richmond and Lindy. There were probably others which Thea had not yet observed. She had a feeling that Muriel Isbister lived quite near Susanna, and that there'd been some reference to the young woman when Harry had taken Thea to meet Muriel.

There were loose ends. The peculiar telephone message for Jennifer Reynolds from a man she thought was Martin Stacey; the apparently half-hearted police investigation into Paul Jennison's death; the doubtful level of competence of old Lionel. These and more might or might not have anything to do with the murders.

Murders . . . she repeated the word to herself, startled by the sudden power it carried. The huge fact of death, which washed over her at odd moments, without warning, was here again. It came at random times and places: driving through open countryside and suddenly seeing a freshly killed rabbit on the road; hearing a news report on the television; being told that her sister's dog had died unexpectedly. Man or beast hardly seemed to matter – it was the horrifying cessation of life that impacted on her. The inability to relax and trust that what was here today would not be gone tomorrow, which kept a perpetual tension in her chest. She seldom admitted to herself that she'd detached, at least in some secret central part of herself, from her daughter, as well as from friends and wider family, because she didn't think she could survive if one of them died as well, unless she somehow steeled herself for it.

The abrupt and senseless killing of the pleasantly friendly Joel had reinforced this fear, she understood now. And it meant, of course, that she would never find the courage to get any closer to Harry Richmond. The man was approaching seventy, for God's sake. Due to die in no time, just as she might permit herself to love him.

She prepared herself a lonely little lunch, comprising a piece of frozen haddock and some frozen peas. Chips would be too much trouble and there didn't seem to be much else available. Raiding the Reynoldses' freezer was becoming a habit, through the past week, and it was already beginning to look very depleted. Had they really meant for her to eat all their stores, she wondered belatedly? Was it just something people said, without expecting you to act on it? Should she go and buy replenishments before the end of next week? They were, after all, paying her rather handsomely, and here she was, using their electricity, eating their food and making a somewhat rudimentary job of exercising their dogs.

This last could at least be rectified. The dogs needed stirring up, with balls to chase and romps to enjoy. Feeling rather like a nursery school teacher, she rounded them up and urged them out into the garden. It was breezy but mild and dry – the morning sun disappearing behind a light covering of cloud. Not bad for a British bank holiday, she decided.

Stricken with a persistent guilty conscience, she played strenuously with the dogs for almost half an hour. Their energy levels seemed to rise the more she threw the ball and stick, and she began to wonder whether she'd cruelly cheated them by merely strolling around the garden with them in the past few days. Eventually, she took Bonzo and Georgie back to the house, and invited Hepzibah to join her in an inspection of the sheep.

The Cotswolds were contentedly gathered under a tree, looking rather warm in their thick fleece. They eyed Thea warily, but made no attempt to get up and flee. The lambs had surely grown since she arrived, and she experienced the small pang of pride that shepherds must habitually feel at the health and fitness of their charges. Never particularly interested in sheep, she indulged in a few moments of contemplation of their nature. Passive to the point of imbecility, she had always assumed, and these specimens had done little to alter that impression. Their lives were routine, their instincts defensive. There was something pathetic about their lot, raised for their flesh or fleece, with scant consideration for their eventual fate. She was aware of the unpleasant final hours of their short lives, in most cases: the lambs bundled into terrifying trucks and lined up to be shot and skinned, dismembered and displayed in sterile supermarket trays. Platitudinous stuff, perhaps, but real for all that.

There was an incongruity to the Reynoldses keeping sheep that had nagged at her ever since she arrived. Clive and Jennifer did not present as natural shepherds. If they had rented out their grass to farmers in need of pasture, that would have made sense. But Clive had been very clear that these animals were his own. He'd even admitted that they had names, although he wasn't always guaranteed to know which was which without a close examination. He had given her at least as many injunctions on how to care for them as he had for the dogs. It made Thea further doubt her own assessment of character, as had other encounters during the week. Who was trustworthy, and who was not? Who had honest motives and who did not?

The person at the heart of these questions was, of course, Harry Richmond – but he was closely followed by Helen Winstanley.

Chapter Seventeen

Her scrutiny of the sheep continued, despite the impatient dartings back and forth on the part of the spaniel. The afternoon was far warmer than any day of her stay so far, and it seemed folly to return to the house and waste the sunshine. Inevitably the events associated with the field began to intrude yet again, beginning with the sudden realisation that these sheep had almost certainly witnessed the slaughter of Joel Jennison and the dumping of his body in their watering hole. It was an unsettling idea. Had the animals rushed to a distant corner in a panic – or had they dozed on as usual, ignoring the strange inscrutable human behaviour? Could you perform one of those bizarre Victorian experiments and analyse the contents of their brains or the impressions on their retinas, to glean the facts of the matter?

There was a moment in early May when all the trees were in full fresh leaf; the birds in full throat; the hedgerows full of energy and colour; a moment when it would be criminal not to simply pause and *experience* the full glory. Thea had learnt, through grief and fear, how to do this. Wise words from a distant ante-natal instructor came back to her, again and again: 'If you're all right now, in this present moment, then you're all right. No more to be said or feared. Animals live by this maxim, and so should we.'

It wasn't entirely true, or always by any means achievable, but it helped. Now was one of those moments when it was not only easy but obligatory. Thea breathed the balmy air, smelt the natural smells, watched the passive sheep and let her own bloodstream take over.

The downside, she had learnt, was that such moments were impossible to recapture later. They were by definition transient. Joy left the most fleeting memory trace, and was elusive when needed. Only pain could be reliably accessed on demand and Thea could see no escape from this harsh truth.

And so her mind regained control, and back came the darkness. The face of the crushed old farmer, the loss of both sons an injury beyond tragedy, beyond hope or understanding. A loss infinitely greater, Thea forced herself to admit, than her own. And her own had been, after all, an accident. Nobody had willed it, with black vengeful motives. By contrast, somebody had deliberately removed Lionel's reason for living – or so it appeared. Nobody had hinted at disharmony between the father and his sons, at conflict over property or morals, decisions or methods. The farm was struggling, but it had sounded as if the struggle was a shared one, the goal freely agreed on.

It was a new pain, this contemplation of the man's distress – and perhaps its very newness gave it a vigour she found energising. For the first time in several years, Thea wanted to rescue somebody, to ameliorate their suffering and find answers to at least some of their problems. Perversely, she realised, the churlish ingratitude of the man had only increased her concern for him. He was a wounded old fox, with dignity and independence the only things left to cling to. She recalled the image of him slumped morosely over the Coke in the pub garden, and wondered at the unkindness of taking him there in the first place, to parade his misery in public.

Which took her thoughts back to Helen, and her galumphing husband Jim. One of those men who hammered so hard on their computer keyboards – which they resented having to use, because surely typing was always women's work – that it was impossible to forbear from imagining them in the bedroom, equally heavy-handed and insensitive. Men who have to be laboriously taught how to watch out for other people's delicate spots, and where not to make jokes or references – and still they got it terribly wrong more often than not. For decades the blame had been wryly placed on the British boarding school system, but somehow that no longer quite hit the mark. 'Oh, all British men are Aspergic,' was a mantra Thea had begun to hear, rather to her irritation, despite the grain of truth it contained. Except it hadn't fitted Carl, and she didn't think Harry Richmond lacked sensitivity, either.

She started a circuit of the field, with no particular purpose in mind. The remembered presence of June Jennison, and then her daughter Lindy, gave rise to a flood of thoughts about the killing of Joel and Paul in this very place. There were no traces, either physical or spiritual, to be discerned. The elusive pool of Joel's blood seemed unlikely to materialise now. Instead it would merely become a part of the normal processes that characterised the long history of human activity in Gloucestershire. The chances were that quite a few people had died within a hundred yards of where she was standing – some by violence, some by quiet and natural causes. Death, as she often tried to persuade herself, was part of life. It happened constantly, predictably, *normally*. It wasn't some extreme outrage, some exceptional piece of bad luck or calamity. It happened *all the time*, to everybody. Why, then, was such a tremendous fuss made about it? Thea did at least know the answer to that, and so did the grieving June, whether she admitted it or not. Or if she didn't now, she very soon would.

The sun was briefly covered by a billowy white cloud, and a light breeze blew. 'Time to go in,' Thea said, looking round for the dog. She scanned the centre of the field in a few seconds, before turning closer attention to the hedgerows bordering it. She was never going to forget this patch of land, and the encounters she'd had in it. There it sat, a tiny part of the pattern across the county, well-proportioned, gently sloping, a delight for the senses, mutely providing sustenance for the incurious sheep. But for the moment it appeared to have swallowed up her spaniel, and this was mildly worrying.

'Hepzie!' she called. 'Come on in now.'

Normally the white tip of the animal's ludicrously long tail betrayed her whereabouts, even in the longest grass. Now there was no sign of it. Thea's breath was caught by the reminder of vulnerability, here of all places. Shooting, strangling, drowning – what unforeseen disaster would befall her beloved pet?

'Hepzie!' she shouted again, her voice sharp. 'Come here.'

And there she was, trotting obediently across the grass, head held awkwardly high so that the thing she carried would not drag on the ground. Even as she wondered with foreboding what the thing might be, Thea observed with a pang how lovely the spaniel was.

It's a cliché, she told herself. Dog digs vital piece of evidence out of the hedge. Probably never happens in reality – and anyway, we already found Joel's scarf in the tree last week.

'Drop it!' she ordered. Dropping things was not one of Hepzibah's talents. She was never disposed to release her trophies. Thea inserted a finger between the soft jaws, and levered. It was something rigid with caked soil and the ravages of long exposure to winter weather. Something basically made of cloth, but so shapeless and colourless now as to be unidentifiable. She couldn't believe it was anything significant, or related in any way to either of the murders. Just an old rag, discarded months ago – or even longer.

Except that people like Clive and Jennifer Reynolds probably didn't chuck old rags into the hedge. They would bring everything back to the house and dispose of it responsibly. She worked at one corner, flaking off the mud, and scratching the surface with a thumbnail to try at least to ascertain what kind of cloth it might be. And then a piece seemed to detach itself and dangle towards the ground. Curiously Thea examined it, and found a lead weight tied onto a length of tape, sewn securely to the body of the cloth. It meant nothing to her, but did raise her interest to a new level. She was going to have to show it to someone; someone who would know what it had been for. She tried to recall the direction from which the dog had come, and concluded it had been the hedge not far from Lindy's burrow. It seemed reasonable to suppose that the cloth had been hidden in the undergrowth, or even partly buried in the softer leaf mould of the hedgerow.

'Come on,' she ordered the spaniel, who was sitting prettily, watching Thea's handling of her new treasure with concern. 'No, you're not having it back. It's mine now. Good girl for finding it, though.'

She did nothing with the discovery, just laid it out on a sheet of newspaper, where the dogs couldn't reach it. If it did have any links to the murders, she knew she ought to leave it as untouched as possible. She was, however, frustrated at not knowing what it was. Somehow she felt she ought to, that it was obvious to any real country person, and she was being ignorant and suburban in not being able to work it out.

She played four games of Scrabble that evening, with Americans who were not having a public holiday. At the end of that marathon, she felt sated, and slightly disgusted with herself, as if she'd drunk a whole bottle of solitary wine, or indulged in a frenzy of masturbation. But she had discovered a few new words. *Insoul, Gleet* and *Carnie* had all been used to good effect by opponents. What in the world, she wondered crossly, did *gleet* mean?

'Almost halfway now,' she told the dogs next morning, having counted the days on her fingers, twice. All of a sudden she found herself wishing it was time to go home. She was lonely in Duntisbourne, after the solitary bank holiday. Lonely and sad, she admitted. This was not how it was supposed to be. She'd been intending the three weeks as a restorative interlude, enjoying the glories of the countryside and abandoning the muddle that was her own daily life at home.

She'd got up slowly, and was actually still in her dressing gown when someone rang the doorbell. The dressing gown was an indulgence she'd only recently adopted. It was big and warm and bright red in colour.

The red matched, almost exactly, the hair of her visitor. 'Hello,' she said. 'Aren't you Susanna? You were at the pub on Sunday.'

'Right. Can I come in? Is this your little dog?' The visitor seemed unaware of the informal attire and resolute in her aim of entering the house.

Thea stood back and let Susanna have her way. There was something off centre about this visitation, a misfitting piece of the jigsaw. Thea thought of Helen Winstanley and the way her voice had altered when speaking of Susanna.

Susanna hesitated in the hallway, waiting to be shown into a room, and Thea surmised that she hadn't ever been inside Brook View before. This gave rise to a flicker of anxiety. Was she *persona non grata* then? Had she some feud with the Reynoldses, which effectively banned her from the place? She remembered that there were two Reynolds sons, either of whom might conceivably know this woman, or even have had relations with her. The yawning chasm of ignorance was frustrating. Worse, it was alarming. She could so easily say or do the wrong thing, betray a confidence, permit the breaking of a taboo. But of course everyone already knew that. They

249

would be deliberately exploiting her if anything like that happened, and thus she was automatically exonerated. She couldn't be blamed for what she didn't know.

Susanna was about five feet eight, and underweight. Her shoulders stuck out, and her trousers looked like a size ten at most. There was a girlish awkwardness to her, which Thea was aware of exaggerating with her own smaller and more feminine physique, which suffered very little from being wrapped in a shapeless red garment. As a general rule she felt sorry for tall women, especially when surrounded by those of average height. They could never just blend in and be one of the crowd.

But for all that, she didn't warm to this person. In possession of sisters and a daughter, Thea was good at quick and easy intimacies with other women, but this one was an exception. Something brittle and insensitive about her put Thea on her guard. She remembered the braying laugh, the casual flirting with James – Jim – Winstanley, the sad bowed figure of Lionel Jennison, and wondered what that had been about. Had a well-intentioned kindness gone sour? Had it been the Winstanleys or Susanna who had been struck by a surge of goodwill towards the bereaved farmer? Whose idea had it been to winkle him out of his misery and display him to the world in a pub garden?

'When are they due back?' Susanna asked.

Thea made no pretence of not understanding. 'A week on Saturday.'

'Nearly halfway, then.' The echo of her own earlier thought was unsettling. Did this woman read minds?

'That's right.'

'Are you having a good time?'

'It's beautiful countryside. I'm planning several more long walks, and some exploring of the other Duntisbournes.'

They were moving into the living room, in a slow drift, where Thea was trying to lead the way, but somehow found herself herding Susanna towards the door. Eventually she said, 'Let's go in there and I'll make some coffee.'

'A bit formal, isn't it?' It became apparent that she was reluctant to do as invited, and preferred instead to sit in the kitchen. Thea gave in with good grace.

'You don't mind the dogs?'

'Course not. I spend my life among horses and dogs.'

'Do you? I thought . . .' Thea paused, realising it might be rash to reveal that she'd been filled in on Susanna. At least she knew some history, and what she did for a living.

'What? That I work in some office in town? Well, I do, but I've got animals as well. I have to work to feed the horses, bloody things. You're not into riding and all that, then?'

'Not really. I've never quite seen the attraction, if I'm honest.'

Susanna laughed, the same upper-class noise that could almost have come from a horse rather than a human being. Thea wondered just who she was. There was something patrician about her, as if she expected to be recognised and acknowledged. The daughter of some local millionaire, perhaps, or slightly down-at-heel aristocrat. The red hair a defiant gesture towards Daddy; the concern for old Jennison a sort of *noblesse oblige*. And yet she seemed a trifle old for defiance, too assured and world-weary.

There was still no hint as to the reason for the visit. If

Susanna worked in an office, why wasn't she there now? If she wasn't an intimate of the Reynoldses, then what was she doing calling on their house-sitter?

Again, the mind reading. 'I've got this week off, as it happens. I'm supposed to be going with June and Lindy to arrange Joel's funeral tomorrow. They've released the body – did they tell you?'

The tone was unforced, with no discernible emotion. Thea paused before replying. 'Not his father, then?'

Susanna's eyes narrowed, and Thea could sense a desire for a cigarette or a swig of alcohol. 'He's not in any fit state,' she said with a carelessness Thea couldn't entirely credit.

'Will it be a burial?'

'Right. Easier, after a murder, apparently. If they get new evidence, they can dig him up again for more investigations. Not that that happens very often.'

'Do you have a date?'

'Why? Thinking of coming along?'

'I might. I did meet him, after all. And I found his body. I can't help feeling involved.'

'It's likely to be Monday next. You'll still be here. Feel free to come. The more the merrier.'

Thea made coffee without consultation. Strong, instant, milky coffee. She pushed a half-full sugar bowl across the kitchen table, but Susanna ignored it, predictably.

'My husband died, you know. Nearly a year ago.'

'Sorry to hear that.' The offensive *So what?* hung in the air between them. 'Joel and I were finished ages ago, but that doesn't mean I'm not devastated by his death. I'm still like one of the family – and that's why I'm helping them now.

Actually, if you must know, I'm doing it for his mother. I always had a fellow feeling for the daft old thing. I gather you've been taken to meet her? Dear old Harry, he's always trying to keep her in the loop. Can't imagine why.'

'Did you come to tell me about the funeral?' Thea frowned, hoping to convey a measure of disapproval at the flippancy, while at the same time understanding it. Just another coping strategy – how many of the damned things were there, anyway? And why was it always women who proved so inventive with them?

'Oh, no, not really. Mainly I was curious to find out what you're like. We're all nosy round here. The rich incomers hate it, of course. We spend half our lives trying to ferret out their stories, and guess how much money they've got. They build their fences higher and higher and put up their security systems, and we run rings round them. It's a local pastime.'

'You were born and bred here, then?'

'Course I was. I think I'm descended from whoever the Roman bloke in charge of Cirencester was. Salt of the earth, me.'

It was a contrived display. Anything further from the usual image of 'salt of the earth' would be hard to imagine. But Thea felt her guesses had been largely accurate, all the same.

'You mean your family's always lived here?'

'More or less. Daddy's been in the Army, actually, until a year ago. The family house is here, of course, but he's been posted to all sorts of places.'

'Don't tell me,' said Thea, before she could stop herself. 'You were at Cheltenham Ladies' College – as a boarder.'

'I was, as it happens.' Susanna's eyes narrowed further. 'How did you know that?'

'Lucky guess,' said Thea. 'Now, if you've finished your coffee, I ought to get dressed and see to all the jobs. I'm not being paid to sit about chatting all day.'

'Ha!' Susanna crowed. 'I thought that was exactly what you were being paid to do.'

But she didn't resist Thea's unambiguous dismissal, and was gone within five minutes.

'What was *that* all about?' Thea muttered to the dogs, before hurrying upstairs to get dressed and take them out for some exercise. The weather was cloudier than the previous day, but still quite acceptable. The activity made her hungry, which reminded her that she ought to go and do some shopping. The sense of having a list of tasks, some of them almost urgent, lifted her mood. Today she would not be lonely or sad. Today she would bustle about, getting food and perhaps a newspaper. Clive had explained that they'd cancelled their usual copy of *The Times*, not wanting to waste it if it wasn't her usual paper. He was only partly right. Thea didn't read a regular daily newspaper, but when she did buy one, it was as likely to be *The Times* as anything else.

Leaving Hepzie behind, on the grounds that it would be too hot for her in the car when she had to go shopping for food, Thea finally left at a quarter past eleven, heading once again for Cirencester. As she passed the entrance to Barrow Hill Farm, she automatically glanced down the drive, trying to see into the yard and identify Susanna's vehicle. She'd noted that it was a rather modest dark blue Toyota, and not the ostentatious sporty model or hearty four-wheel-drive that might have been expected. In any case, although she couldn't see the whole of the yard from the road, there was no sign of any vehicle at all.

The shopping was brief and dull. A circuit of the town centre revealed, at first glance, no food outlets at all. But then she followed signs to a car park and found it was attached to a medium-sized supermarket. Feeling this was a more major exercise than she'd intended, she took a basket and quickly skimmed down two or three aisles, picking up milk, yoghurt, tinned soup, biscuits, bread, breakfast cereal and a pack of ready-cooked chicken. The basket would hold no more, and she decided this would keep her afloat for another few days, given that there were still plenty of basics in the Reynoldses' fridge.

Paying a quick visit to the Ladies' in the car park, she took a wrong turn when she came out, and found herself in a small square, looking towards a large craft centre. Perhaps she ought to have a look for something for Jessica's birthday, coming up at the beginning of June. Perhaps she would do just that, but not today. The place looked interesting, but daunting. Its wares would be expensive. She needed to feel decisive and relaxed, which did not describe her current mood. Instead she was on edge, impatient, distracted.

And so, without giving the town anything like the proper inspection that was its due, she drove back to Brook View. But, stupidly, she missed the small left turn that took her to the upper road, avoiding the village. Instead she found herself in the middle of Duntisbourne Abbots, trying to decide how best to rectify the situation. Knowing it was a warren of tiny roads, with little logic to the way they were arranged, she did her best to project a mental map onto what she could see. By carrying on a little way, and hoping to find another left turn, she would probably come out on her familiar home road, just a bit beyond Brook View. From the walks she'd done, and the rides with Harry, this seemed quite feasible. And if it wasn't, she'd just have to retrace her route until she got back to the larger road, and use the missed turning.

It worked out almost as planned. The narrow roads pitched up and down, giving occasional open views across patchworked landscape, before closing in again, with great trees looming overhead.

She found herself swinging round a tight bend, going slightly too fast. If her sense of direction had not deserted her, she ought to see the house ahead – but she did not. Instead there was a farm opening on the left-hand side of the bend, with a colourful painted sign announcing:

HERBS FOR HEALTH
Fairweather Farm
M.& I. Stacey

This, then, was the main entrance of the nearest neighbours to the west. At last she'd located it. Remembering Lindy Jennison's story of spying, Thea looked across to the fields on her right, wondering if she could work out just what the girl had meant. There was a wooden gate a little way ahead, which looked as if it was almost never opened, to judge by the long grass and other vegetation growing around it.

Still slowing, but with an uncomfortable feeling of inadequate control, she was alarmed, when she looked back at the road, to see a dark blue car emerging from the farm entrance on the left. Visibility was bad – why in the world had they put their gate on a blind bend like this? – and the driver was craning forward to look to her left, as the car kept moving out into the road. Thea was approaching from the right. She tried to swerve, but caught a glimpse of another vehicle approaching around the bend.

She didn't hit it very hard, but both cars cried out in distress. It was like being in a very aggressive version of the fairground dodgems, for a few seconds. The car slewed, and bucked, with a clash of thunks and scrawks, tinkling glass and hissing airbag. The airbag inflated with impossible speed, and then, its work done, it went down again, hanging obscenely from the middle of the steering wheel. Thea felt bounced and bumped, but nothing actually hurt.

She was, however, aware of a desperate need to get out of the car, but as she fumbled for the door handle, it miraculously opened. Outside, a man was standing, looking down at her with an angry expression. It was Martin Stacey. 'Is she all right?' she demanded. The blue car and the driver's bright red hair had left her in no doubt as to whom she had hit. Nor that there was a modicum of fault on both sides. 'She pulled out right in front of me,' she said, congratulating herself on having the wit to take the offensive.

'You were going too fast,' he said, stating a plain fact without accusation. 'I saw you.'

'How? Where were you?'

'I was in the field just there. I saw the whole thing.'

'Help me out,' she said. 'And why don't you ask me if I'm hurt.'

'I can see right enough that you're not.'

'And Susanna?'

'My wife's seeing to Susanna.'

Thea discovered two women standing beside the Toyota, which had somehow spun round and seemed to have come into contact with the hedge. It was tilted, and there was a gash along its side. Shaking her head, she tried to work out where her own vehicle had come to rest. Was there a risk of being hit again by oncoming cars?

'Am I in the road?' she asked. 'I mean, will something hit us?'

'Not a lot of traffic along here, this time of day,' said Martin. 'But best get out, to be on the safe side. I've phoned for the police.'

'Oh, no!' said Thea, with feeling. 'Why did you do that?'

'Law,' he said.

'No, it's not. Not if nobody's hurt.'

'Who said nobody's hurt?'

'What d'you mean? Why are you bothering with me, if somebody's hurt?'

'Get out, and then I'll explain.' He took an arm and levered her up and out of the vehicle, leaving the flaccid airbag to dangle over the seat she'd vacated. She worked her neck, fearful of whiplash, then flexed her legs, noting a soreness on one knee. Then she looked around her.

Another car was nose first in the opposite hedge, most of its length on the reasonably generous grass verge. Its driver was standing beside it, leaning over the roof, his head in his hands. Thea wondered for a moment if she had blacked out. A lot seemed to have happened in an impossibly short time.

Then, with no warning at all, her knees buckled. Half in

the road, she sprawled, all energy simply drained away in a wholesale collapse. Somebody cried out, but nothing else happened.

It was a dream sequence from then on. Remembering her dog, Thea repeated that she was unhurt, just shocked, and must go back to Brook View. People came and went, earnest faces looming close to hers, demanding immense efforts to convince them that she was undamaged. A police car materialised, and orders were issued, questions asked. The ambulance only had space for two, and there was no immediate prospect of another. The man from the other car was bleeding, Susanna had a possible broken wrist. Thea's airbag was praised, after all her vital signs were assessed. Eventually, the decision was made to send her home, with the promise of a medical visit at some later point in the day.

'But somebody must be with you,' came the stern injunction. 'You might be concussed without realising it.' The fact that Thea was silently and embarrassedly weeping did not help her argument that she was in no need of supervision.

A silence followed, until Martin Stacey agreed to drive her back and sit with her, until someone else could be summoned. His wife, in a tone that could only be described as frosty, asked what she should do.

'Phone June or somebody. Helen, maybe. She knows this woman, doesn't she? The police'll sort these cars out. What a bloody mess.' Martin Stacey showed signs of impatience, and Thea cringed at the sacrifice he was making on her behalf. The prospect of an afternoon under his supervision was not one she relished. It seemed, however, that she was to be given no choice.

He's being kind, she kept reminding herself. He didn't have to drop everything and come back with me like this. Stacey had loaded her into his big old estate car with some gentleness, and driven her the quarter-mile to Brook View. On the way, she tried to assess her condition methodically. Definitely no bones broken. Everything flexed and waggled as it should, including her neck. The unheralded collapse was, therefore, more of an emotional thing. And she knew, then, just what that was.

'My husband died in a car crash,' she said, in a voice that felt forced, obstructed. 'That man, leaning over his car – that's what did it. I've only just realised.'

'Hmm,' was the only response.

He unloaded her with the same light touch, and walked her into the house. Thea was beginning to feel quite silly, but couldn't deny the shakiness of her limbs. Strange images came and went, quite against her will. The ambulance, not calm and sedate as today's had been, but frantic and noisy as they'd told her it had been for Carl. Broken heads, tearstained faces, the bottomless black pit of knowing nothing could be all right again.

'This won't do at all,' she insisted, from the sofa where he'd made her lie at full stretch. 'House-sitters aren't *allowed* to be ill.'

'It's only the dogs, isn't it? Anybody can come in and see to them, a couple of times a day. You're not indispensable.'

'Maybe not – but I want to do it. I'm going to do it. I just need an hour or two, and then I'll be back to normal.

Except' – the bottomless pit rushed towards her – 'the car! How will I manage without the car? I can't get to any shops. And there'll be all that business with insurance. What about that man in the other car? Do you know who he was?'

'Some traveller, I think. You know – a rep. Selling fertiliser or cattle feed or grass seed. His car was full of samples and catalogues. It'll be his company's, not his.'

'It wasn't his fault at all. He was just an innocent bystander. *Bydriver*, I should say.' She managed a weak laugh. 'Poor man.'

'He'll be OK. Get a week off work in the sun, and a good story to tell his mates. Things happen.'

'That's true,' Thea sighed. 'What'll they do with my car?'

'You need to phone your insurance people. Are you covered comprehensive?'

'Luckily. Will they let me borrow one?'

'Probably. It works pretty smoothly these days.'

Her guardian went to make her a large mug of tea, sweetening it, as a time-honoured remedy for shock. 'Should have done this ten minutes ago,' he said, coming back to her side. 'Drink it quick.'

It tasted marvellous. She could feel it soothing her as it went down. 'Lovely,' she said. 'Thanks.'

'Look, you just lie there, have a little kip. You'll feel a lot better afterwards, if you do. I'll see to the dogs.'

'Leave Hepzie with me. She's going to wonder what's going on. I don't usually lie down like this during the day.' The spaniel was already curled up at her feet, casting liquid brown glances at her mistress every few minutes, inscrutable canine worries filling her expression.

'Nice little beast,' Martin Stacey said, giving the dog a brief pat.

And rather to her surprise, Thea did drift off to sleep, letting the shame and self-reproach fall away, knowing they'd come back again soon enough.

She was woken by the pressure of a full bladder, with no idea of where she was, what time it must be or who was with her. The disorientation was frightening for a full minute, as she stared fuzzily at the big front window, unable to place it as any bedroom she knew.

Then reality returned, little by little. She'd been very deeply asleep, for what could have been some hours. The light outside was hard to judge, but it was not that of early afternoon. There was a mutter of voices beyond the window.

Heavily, she got up and started towards the downstairs loo, just off the hall. The dog followed, and she turned and told her to stay, in a low voice. For some reason, she felt furtive, a disobedient patient, defying instructions.

In the little cloakroom, before she had time to flush the toilet, the voices came closer. Two people had apparently come into the house through the front door, and were standing just outside the loo, where she could hear every word they said.

'Is Susanna really all right?' came a woman's voice which Thea quickly recognised as that of Helen Winstanley.

'At worst, a broken wrist. But it's more likely just sprained.'

'Whose fault was it, would you say?'

'A bit of both. The Osborne woman was going too fast, and Susie pulled out a bit further than she ought. Bingo! Bad news for the bloke coming the other way.' Stacey gave an unfeeling little laugh.

'But it's not going to change anything?' Her words crackled with anxiety.

'Why the hell should it?'

'Police everywhere again. Susie out of action. It makes things much less predictable.' Helen's voice was hard, giving as good as she got. Thea wished she could grasp the nature of the relationship between these two. More urgently than that, she wished they would move away, so she could get out of the loo without being discovered.

As if granted by a good fairy, a mobile phone began to warble. 'Damn!' said Stacey. 'Not again. I'll take it outside. You'd better go.'

Thea waited until she was sure they'd gone, and then crept back to her sofa. They'd never know she'd left it, never have the least idea that she'd overheard them.

Something, obviously, was going on. Something outside the law, involving Helen and Martin. Lindy's 'network' carried more credibility now. Maybe the illegal immigrant theory didn't stand up, but what about drugs? 'Herbs' was a common euphemism for all sorts of substances. How likely was it that the Staceys were growing something on the banned list amongst their marjoram and dill?

Highly likely, Thea decided. Absolutely likely. They were running a racket where they supplied hash to locals, and probably people further afield. Maybe they even grew some opium poppies and made it into heroin. Thea had no notion of how that might be done, but she didn't imagine it was beyond the realms of possibility.

So – James had been right: there was some sort of organised criminal activity going on close to Barrow Hill, where the murdered brothers had lived. The wrongdoers appeared to include Martin Stacey, Helen Winstanley and Susanna Whatever-her-name-was. How extensive, criminal and dangerous the activities were remained to be seen. But suddenly Thea felt she had a clear mission. For the first time, she had suspects and the bare bones of a credible motive.

The front door banged, and voices could be heard again. Different voices this time. At least, Martin and somebody else. Thea made her preparations.

The living room door opened slowly, as someone tapped on it lightly. Hepzie jumped off the sofa and ran to the newcomer, somewhat spoiling Thea's intended effect. She raised herself and looked over the back of the sofa.

'Mmmm,' she said, sleepily. 'What time is it?'

'This is the District Nurse,' Martin told her, ushering in a stout woman of middle years. 'Come to give you a check-up.'

Thea permitted herself a moment of gratitude at the lengths the British Health Service would still go to to watch over the nation's wellbeing.

'Hello, dear,' said the woman. 'It's half past four, or a bit after. Had a good sleep, have you?'

'Brilliant,' said Thea. 'Amazing. I must have slept for two hours or more.'

'Any headache? Double vision? Temperature?' The woman was at her side, feeling her forehead, peering into her eyes, all briskness and efficiency.

'I feel perfectly all right. It was only the shock made me

go wobbly for a bit. Mr Stacey's been ever so kind. Gosh – you've wasted the whole afternoon watching over me, have you?' She peered around the nurse to where he was still in the doorway, looking quite relaxed.

'No worries.' He waggled his mobile phone at her. 'I've been catching up with some calls. I let the dogs out. They're happy enough in the garden.'

While the nurse took her pulse, Thea examined the man. It was the first time she'd paused to consider him objectively. Three hours ago, he'd been chastising her for careless driving, then he'd dropped everything to come and watch over her – an unusual role for a man, even these days. Next she'd heard him discussing nefarious doings with Helen, and now here he was cheerfully claiming to be quite happy with the situation he'd been landed with.

There was an energy and outspokenness to him which Thea recognised as attractive to women. But for her, everything about him screamed 'unreliability'. His chameleon changes, the singular lack of irritation, the way he offered himself so readily when a nursemaid was needed – it all struck her as much too good to be true. He'd been glad to gain entry to Brook View, where he could make calls on his mobile, and stage an encounter with Helen. For the first time, it struck her that he could easily have doctored the sweet tea he'd given her: that would explain her deep sleep. With her dead to the world, he could have indulged whatever whims he liked during the afternoon.

'Look, I really am fine now,' she repeated, and to prove it she stood up and breathed several deep breaths. 'Nothing hurts. Clear head. Just a few worries about the car, and a bad feeling about the trouble I've caused.' Then, with a delicious sense of cunning, she added, 'Now, if you'll excuse me, I really have got to go to the loo.'

The nurse nodded, and swiped her hands together, as if to delete Thea from her list of concerns. 'You'll be all right now,' she said.

'I can go then, can I?' said Martin Stacey. 'You're sure now?'

Thea put her hand on his upper arm, as she passed him in the doorway. 'You've been extremely kind,' she said. 'I'm ever so grateful.'

They waited in the living room for her to finish in the toilet, and then Stacey took his leave, climbing into his estate car and driving off sedately. 'Do you know him?' The nurse was clearly puzzled.

'No, hardly at all. I don't live here, you see. I'm just the house-sitter,' Thea said. 'The accident was in his gateway, and he saw the whole thing. I suppose he felt he was somehow involved.'

'Hmm. A bit too good to be true, if you ask me,' said the woman. Thea could have hugged her.

Chapter Eighteen

Thea had fibbed about the headache; it was throbbing quite badly by seven that evening, and she felt herself move more and more slowly as she fed the dogs and tried to summon the energy to make herself a sandwich. The shopping from Cirencester had been miraculously transferred to the fridge and cupboards, presumably by Martin Stacey, who must have retrieved it from her car without her noticing. Whether or not he'd drugged her, and arranged his criminal business from someone else's house, he had been thoughtful. She really did owe him some gratitude.

But it was difficult to think warm thoughts when everything seemed so dark. Why had she been driving so badly anyway? It wasn't like her. She of all people knew the permanent lifelong penalties that could be suffered from a few minutes of carelessness. She'd been in a hurry to get back, that was all. She'd been hungry and impatient with the meandering confusing lanes. The bend had been far sharper than she'd anticipated, and she'd over-compensated as the car started to swing across to the wrong side. Or had she? She couldn't recall the exact sequence at all, and that bothered her. The road was wide enough for two vehicles to pass, but only just. Had some sixth sense or unconscious glimpse through the hedges told her there was an oncoming vehicle? Had she hit Susanna as a preferable impact to that with a moving car? For a while she obsessed about it, knowing she would have to make a detailed statement for the insurance people, and knowing, too, that she was never going to escape without the bulk of the blame being laid at her feet.

The senseless argument about the impact of new traumas and losses came back to bother her. It was not that the same old anguish came flooding back with redoubled force, but that it confirmed some thick vein of pessimism acquired when Carl died. Bad things were going to keep happening. Life was not trustworthy or kind. Every time you got up off the floor and relearnt how to smile, there'd be another knock and down you'd go again.

And if a minor road accident could make her feel like this, what would she be like when something bigger happened – as it surely would? Her parents would get ill and then die, she'd have money worries, the dog would die, Jessica would have trouble with relationships, grandchildren would be ill or delinquent. The list was endless.

'Selfish cow,' she told herself out loud. 'Think about others for a change, why don't you? Do something useful. Get a life.'

At least this had the effect of attracting the interest of all three dogs. They stood in a row looking at her, wondering if this was something they ought to be acting upon. And, as if to confirm their impression, the doorbell rang, pealing through the hall and kitchen and somehow setting things going again.

Harry Richmond stood there, comically clutching a bottle of Rioja, an untidy bunch of garden flowers and a pineapple. 'Don't you find,' he said as soon as she opened the door, 'that pineapples can be so *consoling*?'

'Personally, no,' she argued. 'Too much work to get to the good bits. Too much wasted.'

'You're hopeless. What about artichokes, then?'

'Artichokes are immensely over-rated.'

'You're very pale. Let me come in and nurse you. I'm rather good at it.'

'This place is full of caring men. Must be something in the water.'

'Could be,' he nodded, giving her the impression he would agree to anything she said, for fear of upsetting her. For all the overdone sick-visiting act, it was obvious he was worried. He watched her as if she was a piece of fragile old porcelain teetering on the edge of the mantelpiece.

He found a vase for the flowers, and tweaked them here and there, making an extraordinarily effective display. 'You've done that before,' she accused.

'Flowers are my thing. Surely you noticed?'

'Your lovely garden,' she remembered. 'Of course.'

'Can you cope with wine, or are you still too convalescent?'

She put an exploratory hand to her head. It was still aching, but much less severely. 'Give it another hour or so,' she said. 'And don't do anything that'll give me any stress.'

'I can guarantee to be entirely stress-free,' he smiled. 'We can sit and watch programmes about wallpaper, if you like. There's sure to be several to choose from.'

They didn't do that. Harry indicated an interest in Brook View's garden and they strolled slowly round, in the fading light, with Harry tutting about the draconian slaughter of weeds both on the lawn and in the flowerbeds. 'I hate to see bare brown soil between the plants,' he sighed.

'Do you? I think it looks rather good. Especially around the roses.' The roses had been mulched and each one stood in its island of weed-free soil, looking to Thea's eye as if it was well cared for and quite contented.

'Ah, well – *roses*,' said Harry meaningfully. Clearly he held roses in contempt – an attitude Thea found almost sacrilegious.

'What's the matter with the pond?' he asked, as they meandered in that direction.

'What do you mean? I know Clive told me not to turn off the waterfall, but the trickling noise was irritating. I'll put it on again before they come back.'

'Never mind that – look at it.'

Thea looked where he pointed, and saw a brownish stain on the far side of the pond, opposite the waterfall. A rim of colour adhered to the rocks, which could be traced around the edge, so the more she looked, the more she found. The water itself seemed to be lightly tinted with red, as well. The poor light made the colour hard to see, but it was certainly not the normal green of a garden pond.

'It wasn't like that when I arrived,' she said. 'What do you think must have happened?'

'Some sort of weed or pollution, I suppose. It doesn't seem to have upset the water lily.'

'Thank God. That's Jennifer's pride and joy. I haven't

270

topped up the water level yet. I wonder if I should?'

Harry had no contribution to make to this dilemma, and, after a further minute or two of puzzlement, they went back in. The wine was breathing on the kitchen table, the air lightly scented by Harry's profusion of home-grown blooms. Thea noticed dust on sills and ledges that had not been there a week before. She had no doubt it would still be there a week hence – but that she would tackle it before Clive and Jennifer returned.

'I feel better,' she announced. 'Much better.'

'You haven't asked me how I knew about it. Your accident, I mean.'

She pulled a face to express impotence. 'I know what villages are like,' she said. 'No chance of keeping something like that secret.'

'That's not quite true. But in this case, Isabel phoned Muriel and Muriel phoned me. A short chain. I gather you managed to smack into no fewer than two vehicles, on different sides of the road. Quite an achievement.'

'Please don't. You make it sound dreadful.' But she was acting. In reality, the *fewer* had delighted her. Almost nobody still said *fewer*. Just as they didn't say *criterion* or *phenomenon*.

Then she remembered. 'Harry! It's Tuesday. You said you and Lindy always play chess on a Tuesday. Have you stood her up for me?'

'In a manner of speaking, I suppose I have. Don't worry. She'll forgive you – and me. She's got plenty to do at the farm, not to mention mountains of homework the school insists on giving her.'

He stayed until ten thirty, and then firmly ordered her to lock the doors and go to bed the moment he was out of sight. He went with her to escort the dogs on their final circuit of the garden. He hugged her again as he took his leave. A longer warmer hug than before. He rested his chin on the top of her head, reminding her of the appeal of a tall broad man.

'Thanks for coming,' she said, with a slight tremor. 'You've been really kind.'

'My pleasure.'

It all felt soothingly old-fashioned, something from an easier era where there were conventions and forms to follow, tea came in cups with handles and saucers, men brought flowers, and had big white hankies for emergencies.

When he had gone, she felt more vulnerable than at any point since she'd arrived. The sudden arrival and departure of a protective male had shattered her independence, just like that. 'Damn it,' she muttered. 'I'm forty-two, not sixty-two. Tea in cups and saucers had already died out before I was even born. Nearly, anyway.' She scowled at Bonzo, who was lying at full stretch in the hallway, looking rather warm. 'What's the matter with you?' she demanded. He was panting exaggeratedly.

Hepzibah helpfully supplied the answer by carrying the square plastic dish that was used for the dogs' drinking water out from the kitchen. It was completely dry. Thea couldn't remember filling it for days. 'Oh Christ,' she snapped. 'Thanks, Hepzie.' She filled it up, and the labradors jostled for the much-needed fluid. She had to fill it two more times before they were sated. 'Now I suppose you'll want to pee in the night,' she complained.

She went to bed with a sense of foreboding that she fought hard to ignore. When that proved impossible, she tried to rationalise it away. It was obviously the result of the accident, shaking her confidence. It was the result of too much forward planning, rehearsing all the tasks she had to perform next day. Plus self-reproach for her stupidity, and anxiety about whether she should already have contacted the insurance people. She should, of course – but had been defeated by circumstances. She had none of the relevant documents with her, for one thing, including the name of the company. She wasn't sure whether she was with Norwich Union or Friends Provident. It could just possibly even be Direct Line, although she thought she'd remember if she'd actually changed to them, as she'd once envisaged. There had been so many decisions and changes and forms to fill in when Carl died that car insurance had slipped far down the list of things to remember. Indeed, a nasty niggling doubt was creeping in as to whether she'd remembered to renew the policy at all.

When she finally did fall asleep she dreamt about strange aggressive plants, leaning across narrow country roads towards her, with stings and thorns waving in her face.

The next three days were dramatically hot, sun blazing, animals sticking to the shady areas of field and garden. Thea saw herself as a still centre, hardly breathing, waiting, wondering what might happen next.

Oddly, very little did happen. She managed the insurance business with some difficulty, and even more embarrassment. It involved phoning her friend Celia and asking if she could recall the details of the policy. Celia was interested in that sort of thing, constantly watching out for special offers and trying to persuade Thea to go for them.

'Oh yes, you idiot – you're with Cornhill. Remember I tried to make you change to esure, and you wouldn't? Anyway, I did. You said Cornhill sounded more solid, or something. But it's no good calling them without your policy number. Shall I get it for you?'

And she'd gone to Thea's desk, found the document and relayed all the vital numbers. It had all taken a long time, especially as Celia wanted to know all about Duntisbourne and Brook View and people and shopping. Thea had refrained from mentioning the minor detail about Joel's murder on her first night, but there still seemed to be quite a lot to say.

Then she had to wait in for the replacement car to be delivered. Her own mangled vehicle had been collected from the Staceys, not before he or his wife had thoughtfully removed every item, including the radio, a pair of socks, three crumpled magazines, Hepzie's blanket and the toolkit from the spare wheel compartment. Martin came round with it all.

'They'll probably write it off, you see,' he explained. 'You've got to assume the worst.'

'Was it as badly damaged as that?' Thea was incredulous. All she remembered was the inflated airbag.

'Doesn't take much,' he'd shrugged.

In the evening, knowing she had already ruined her image by being so late, she phoned Julia Phillips at Minchinhampton. When the woman picked up the phone, Thea launched straight into profuse apologies. 'I know I said I would phone last week,' she began. 'It's just that I've been so awfully busy here . . .'

'Oh, not to worry. I began to wonder whether I'd said that I would phone *you*. Then I realised I didn't have a number. I thought you hadn't liked the sound of us, or something.'

The lack of reproach was irresistibly seductive. 'So, do you still want me?'

'Of *course*. Didn't I say so last time? I thought it was all decided. When can you come and see us?'

Thea saw no escape. 'Well, how about tomorrow?' she said. 'In the afternoon, or maybe evening.'

'Lovely. Let's say five o'clock, shall we? Can you get away then?'

'Could we make it five thirty? I feed the dogs at about five.' She needn't have bothered to make herself sound efficient and responsible. Julia Phillips was past caring.

'Have you got a pen? I'll give you directions,' she said.

That was Wednesday. Thursday was spent largely on the laptop, trying to write a concise description of the accident, e-mailing the usual people, plus a few more further afield. Then she wrote a long letter to her parents, making her stay at Brook View sound idyllic and restorative. They had been dubious about the idea, warning her of the loneliness and boredom, and she was determined to prove them wrong.

Despite assuring herself repeatedly that she was unharmed, and that nothing very significant had resulted from the smash, she was aware of doing everything much more slowly than normal. She was wading through an invisible sea of resistance, pushing forward against a tide of foreboding that never seemed to abate. Something else was going to happen. It was the lull before the storm, the eye of the hurricane.

There were moments when she had the physical sensation of holding her breath, her chest tight with the need to exhale and relax.

Her courtesy car arrived during Thursday morning, and she gave it a quick practice run along the dual carriage for a mile or two. It was an automatic, which needed a bit of getting used to. But by the time she got back to Brook View, she was quite comfortable with it.

Navigating through the small roads to the Phillips's houses was complicated, but she managed it without any reversals. Julia and Desmond met her as she drove into their untidy yard. They promised it would be less of a mess by July, and introduced her to Pallo the palomino, numerous hens and ducks and one cat.

Thea confirmed the dates, offered references, made no mention of murder and mayhem at her current placement, and retreated wondering whether she really did want to carry on as a house-sitter. Presumably she did, because the prospect of a fortnight at Juniper Court was far from unappealing. Compared to the obsessive order of Brook View, it looked almost impossibly relaxed. Julia took her on a rapid tour of the house, indicating a girl's bedroom that would most likely be hers. 'Of course, I'll make her tidy it up,' the woman laughed. The room was a blur of scattered clothes and possessions which Thea deliberately refrained from examining.

On Friday, the phone came alive. James Osborne called her at nine in the morning, wondering what was happening. 'If anything,' he added.

'I meant to e-mail you yesterday,' she said. 'I had a little contretemps with my car. Very embarrassing, actually. I suppose I ought to find out whether the other people are all right.'

'I'm sure they'll let you know if they're not,' came the dry retort. 'Nothing more on the Jennisons then?'

'Not really.' A surge of resistance to discussing the Jennisons, or even thinking about them, washed through her. 'It's Joel's funeral on Monday.'

'Yes, I know. Will you be going?'

'I might. I'll speak to June about it first.' The visit from the flippant Susanna seemed an age ago, and no longer felt like a credible invitation to the ceremony. 'I'm worried I'd feel like an interloper.'

'So you're all right, are you?' The query came belatedly, and Thea felt it as a somewhat casual concern.

'Yes, I'm fine,' she lied. 'No harm done at all.'

'Nice weather. I s'pose you're out on that lawn with a book all day long, getting toasted?'

'Something like that.' Even Thea had begun to heed the alarms about ozone depletion and skin cancer. She was not especially dark-skinned and the sun certainly did seem to burn more fiercely than it used to. 'The dogs are feeling the heat rather.'

'Rosie loves it. Says it does her the world of good.'

Thea bit back the *Well, bully for Rosie* she was tempted to utter. It would be unthinkable to say such a thing. Even having it on her mind's tongue was deeply disturbing. 'Oh, well, better get on,' she said instead. 'Thanks for calling.'

'Thea, wait. Hollis contacted me. He might want to speak

to you again, and walk the field and garden for himself. He didn't say much, but it's only reasonable to assume the main evidence has to be around the place.'

'But their forensic people must have found everything there was to find? It's nearly two weeks ago now. What would be the point?'

'I can't answer for Phil, Thea. I'm just telling you what he said to me. I'll have to go now. I'll be seeing you.'

'Bye.'

Her thoughts inevitably turning to the garden and field, two memories floated up. The pond with its strange red colouring, and the cloth the dog had found in the field. Both demanded action – both could possibly be of some interest to the police. Furthermore, after the hot weather, she surely ought to be adding some water to the pond, as Clive had requested.

She looked around the kitchen, expecting to see the muddy cloth still laid out on the worktop where she'd left it days ago, and then forgotten about it. She couldn't find it. Spinning around, scanning all the available surfaces, she was forced to accept that it was gone. The dogs had to have taken it – although the dogs had never once jumped up to steal anything. She searched the floor, their baskets, the living room, and the lawn outside.

It was nowhere to be found.

Chapter Nineteen

Late on Friday afternoon, she walked to Fairweather Farm, home of Martin and Isabel Stacey. She left the dogs behind, still wondering whether they were responsible for the missing cloth, and whether it mattered.

Her ostensible reason for the visit was to thank the Staceys for their kindness, and apologise for the disruption she'd caused. Her real motive was to snoop and spy and listen for careless revelations.

She approached through the back entrance, which was very much closer to Brook View than the front gate was, and involved hardly any road-walking. Over the stile in the hedge a short way down the road, down the bridle-path, and in through the gate where Binnie the collie had torn Hepzibah's ear. The echoes of the dog's howls still rang in her ears as she drew near. Glancing around, she caught sight of chimneys in a hollow behind her – which could only belong to Barrow Hill. The Jennisons and the Staceys really were close neighbours, then, with the Reynoldses completing the triangle. Even in stand-offish rural England, the three families must surely have close links, going back over time, necessitated by shared boundaries and occasional urgent needs.

And then there was Helen Winstanley, more remotely situated perhaps, but clearly very involved with Martin Stacey. Thea permitted a mildly optimistic feeling that some new understanding was almost within her grasp.

It was good to have a purpose, in any case. The three days of gloom had been wasted time, missing the improving weather and the delights of the area. Clive and Jennifer would be home in a week, and she wanted them to return to a gleaming house and happy dogs. A neatly resolved murder investigation would be the icing on the cake.

The back gate to Fairweather Farm was firmly closed. A spring-loaded latch nestled in a hole bored into the stout gatepost. To open it, you had to pull sideways against the spring, which was an unusual action requiring a strong wrist. Thea gripped it with both hands, and forced it back, grimly reminded of having to do something similar to the collie when its jaws were clenched onto Hepzibah's ear. Once through, she had to repeat the process to return the latch to its hole. If anything, this was even more difficult, since the gate had dropped a few millimetres, and had to be lifted at the same time to make the alignment. The completion of this task left her feeling foolish and annoyed. Why, she asked herself crossly, hadn't she just climbed over the damned thing?

The process had been additionally stressful for knowing there was a defensive collie bitch somewhere on the property, which might well appear without warning and start attacking her as it had done Hepzie a week earlier. With luck, it remembered the damage to its jaw and was cowering in apprehension in a barn somewhere at the arrival of its assailant.

Once on Stacey property, she felt nervous of proceeding for other reasons, too. Knowing that there was something nefarious going on, but hoping not to reveal this knowledge, made it difficult to strike the right attitude. With a sense of being watched from dark interiors and shadowed windows, she headed for the house, which she could see beyond a large open-sided barn. The ground underfoot was dry, the general impression one of tidiness and under-usage. There were no signs or smells of livestock; no bawling calves or squealing piglets. No hens or cats or pigeons. In fact it hardly seemed to qualify as a farm at all, by normal definitions. The barn sheltered a tractor, and some odd-looking implement she could not identify. An even larger barn away to the left was well-maintained, with closed doors and new roof. Thea increasingly scented money in the air as she approached the house itself.

In rapid succession, she noticed a burglar alarm, security lights, satellite dish and decidedly tasteless gold-painted weathervane incorporating a silhouetted horse – all as she scanned the upper part of the house. None of these items were particularly unusual on modern farmhouses, of course, but the contrast with the Barrow Hill house was dramatic. She recalled the muck, the lack of maintenance and air of disintegration on the Jennison farm, and concluded that whatever Lionel and his family were doing wrong, the Staceys had managed to avoid the same pitfalls.

The back of Fairweather Farmhouse was augmented with a clutter of small outhouses and sheds, some actually attached to the house, others forming a row at right angles to it. The place was a warren, like so many farms. It presented the common impression of a secretive settlement, where only the initiated came and went without challenge. Just about anything could be going on here, and nobody from the outside world would ever get to know about it.

Thea decided it would be more politic to approach from the front. Another gate separated the yard in which she stood from the driveway that led down from the site of her accident. This time a simple catch lifted to open the wooden gate, and she walked the gentle slope along the side of the house, and then down across a gravelled sweep to the front door.

Built of the usual Cotswold stone, the house had been positioned on uneven ground, so that one end was against a bank, while the other looked over an incline that had been grassed over and looked quite tricky to keep mown. The neatness was even more noticeable than that at Brook View. Surely somebody had to be employed to keep it in such immaculate condition? More signs of affluence, Thea presumed.

She had also begun to presume that the place was deserted, bereft of man or dog, wife or child. Not that there'd been any reference to a child, nor could she see any toys. It struck her as wasteful for a youngish couple to live here without a family around them. She *hoped* there was a child.

The doorbell rang inside the house, and nobody responded. No barks, either. Had Binnie gone off, abandoning her offspring? Was it possible that Helen had lied, and there never were any puppies? Thea had reached the point where she was quite willing to believe such a deceit had taken place.

With thundering heart, she turned to give the place a closer exploration. Where were Monique and the shadowy seasonal workers that had been referred to more than once? Was there some large workshed further afield, out of sight and sound of the main buildings? She would say she was looking for Martin or Isabel if anybody caught her. Wouldn't anyone do the same – just take a peep into a few of the barns and sheds?

But it proved impossible to just 'take a peep'. There were padlocks on the doors of the large stone barn and the first shed she tried. The shed had a window, but she soon discovered that it was covered by some sort of blind. Suspicious in itself, of course, but not helpful in assembling evidence against the Staceys and finding cause to connect them with the murders of the Jennison brothers. Stacks of pallets were standing neatly against the barn wall, but she found no other visible evidence of herb production.

With a strong feeling that she should make an escape while she could, she started back towards the metal gate with the stiff catch. This time she was going to climb over it and avoid another struggle with the fastening.

She was literally perched on top of the gate when the dog rushed towards her out of nowhere. The same dog she had fought with previously, and every bit as unpleasant as before. It leapt at her, teeth bared, and she kicked at it, holding tightly to the top rail of the gate, knowing she was going to lose her balance. The rail was a smooth round metal pole, impossible to grip properly whilst under attack.

Where was the damned animal's owner? At this rate it was going to develop into another bare-handed conflict between Thea and the dog, and this time it might be less easy to win. One leg was on the farm side of the gate and both hands clung tightly to the rail. That left a single foot and leg with which to fend off the snapping animal. If it managed to get a grip on that leg, she'd be pulled off the gate and was sure to land in a vulnerable sprawl on the ground.

Leg and voice, she realised, immediately starting to shout at the dog. 'No! Get down! Down!' She tried to make her voice low, with sharp authority overlying the growing fear. Collies were famously obedient, after all. And Thea *liked* dogs. She understood them and wanted their friendship. She could hardly blame this one for attacking her: she was an intruder on its territory, and she had hurt it in the recent past. Two good reasons for going onto the offensive, in Binnie's mind.

'Binnie!' she tried. 'Go! Go back!'

She would never know just which of the many ensuing elements were most effective, but events combined to save her. The dog's jaw was evidently still not fully restored, after Thea's rough treatment the week before. Snapping and snarling were clearly proving uncomfortable. The firm orders, associated with her name, seemed to register – and a woman finally appeared from the direction of the village, along the bridlepath, too breathless to call out, but apparently claiming some connection with the dog.

It was Isabel Stacey.

'Get her off me,' Thea ordered, although the dog had already retreated to a much safer distance.

'What are you doing here?' Isabel grasped the dog by the scruff of its neck, in the absence of a collar. 'Binnie's only protecting the property.'

'Mrs Stacey?' Thea jumped down from the gate, managing, she hoped, to retain a vestige of dignity in the process. 'I came to thank Martin for his kindness on Tuesday. He doesn't seem to be here.'

'No. He's out all day today. God, I'm puffed. I ran all the way from the top of the village when I heard you yelling.'

Thea gave this some thought. The top of the village was almost half a mile away. Surely she hadn't been shouting at the dog for more than a minute? If this was so, Isabel Stacey had just broken the world record for the half-mile. Obviously, she exaggerated. Or perhaps she was very much fitter than Thea had first assumed.

'Well, no harm done,' she said.

'Not this time. The poor thing still can't use her jaw properly. It takes her ages to eat her supper.'

Thea began to see herself through this woman's eyes: attacker of dogs, careless driver, nuisance and intruder. Little wonder there was scarcely any light of friendship on her face. 'How are the puppies?' she asked, hoping to thaw the ice a little.

'Gone. All but one, that is.'

'Oh? You found homes for them, then?' Thea tried to work this out. Helen had implied they were still only a week or two old when she'd been here before. If that was true, they couldn't possibly have been of an age to go to new homes yet.

'Actually no. Martin drowned them.' The casually cruel

285

image of rural folk was, of course, legendary, but Thea had often suspected it to be at odds with the reality. Some of those weeping farmers on the news during the foot and mouth catastrophe belied the image, for a start. On the other hand, non-productive livestock were culled without sentiment, and millions of beasts every year were slaughtered by conveyor-belt, shipped off from the farms without a second thought.

But drowning puppies was a new one on Thea. 'Does Helen know?' she asked, without due reflection.

'Of course,' Isabel Stacey shrugged. 'Why not?'

There was no answer to that. Thea began to feel at a very bad disadvantage, with the Stacey woman giving no quarter. 'You've been into our yard,' she said. 'What were you doing there?'

'Looking for Martin or you, or Helen. I wanted to thank you for helping me – I've told you already.'

'Why would Helen be here?'

'Because she was here last time I passed this gate. She told me she comes here quite a lot.'

Isabel manifested impatience. With an easy flick of the wrist she unlatched the gate and ordered the collie through it. 'Well, you've done what you came to do. I'll tell Martin. And for your information, Helen Winstanley hardly ever comes here. She's got practically nothing to do with us, these days. When are you leaving, anyhow?' The last question was darted at Thea with a host of implications trailing from it.

'End of next week.'

'Then you've got nothing to worry about, have you? Our funny little lives are going to carry on quite happily without you. You can forget all about us.'

Thea cracked. 'Oh, yes. I can just forget two murders, a car accident, my dog's ear being ripped by your bloody sheepdog, and a pseudo farm where God knows what's going on behind locked doors.'

The last bit was foolish, as she realised the moment it was out of her mouth. As always when she lost control like this, she regretted it within seconds. Micro-seconds.

'Hey! Hold on a minute. You're not trying to make a connection between our *perfectly normal* business and the murders, are you? Because if you are, we'll have you for slander by the end of tomorrow.'

'I didn't mean there was a connection.' Thea's voice was stiff. 'I'm just listing the things it will be hard to forget.'

'I'm sure you'll manage, if you try hard enough.'

Unfriendliness on such a scale was rare, and Thea tried to rationalise it, as she walked back up the bridleway to the road. The woman obviously had things on her mind. She was anxious and irritable. Running home so fast at the sound of shouts and barks implied that she was afraid of some specific identifiable threat. Nothing to do with Thea personally. She'd just taken the brunt of a whole lot of unrelated stuff. And, she reminded herself, the woman's husband had been perfectly affable, even kind. The fact that he was involved in something underhand, to which Helen Winstanley was party, didn't necessarily connect him to the murders.

But, damn it, it certainly put him and his bad-tempered wife well and truly in the frame.

A car drew up beside her almost before she'd turned out into the road. Somebody's got fast reactions, she thought, before she could see the driver or recognise the car.

'Hi!' It was Susanna, her red head leaning across the passenger seat, peering up in that awkward fashion that people in cars always had to adopt. Thea had to reorder her thoughts rapidly. Shouldn't Susanna be angry with her? Wasn't it much more to be expected that she would snap and snarl, rather than Isabel and her dog?

'Oh, hello. How *are* you? What about your wrist? I didn't think you'd be driving again so soon. And the car! I assumed it'd be a write-off.'

'No, no. We're both tough. I got my mate Nigel to hammer out the dent. He did it yesterday. Needs a new coat of paint, and then it'll be fine.'

The point of impact was on the other side of the vehicle, and Thea wondered whether to go and inspect it. Somehow she was reluctant to do so. From her hazy recollections, there had been more than a 'dent' in Susanna's motor.

'I hope the insurance people will be able to work something out. It sounded quite complicated. Are you covered comprehensively?'

Susanna shrugged. 'Leave it to them, I say. That's what we pay them for. No hard feelings at all. Anyway, must dash. See you at the funeral?'

Oh, God, the funeral! 'What time is it?'

'Eleven, in the village church, then burial. Do come. We all want you to.'

It would be an even worse ordeal now than she'd originally supposed. She'd openly linked the Staceys with the murders, which would make it very hard to look them in the eye. And they might easily tell other people about the calumny, though presumably only if they were innocent and able to prove it beyond any doubt. But Joel's friendly face floated before her, and her intimate connection with him, via his dead body, made it almost obligatory. She would learn more about him from the funeral, and she might achieve some sort of closure by watching him being laid in the ground.

And, of course, she might find it all too much to bear, with the reminders of her own husband's funeral just a year before.

Chapter Twenty

She did not want to spend the weekend in depressed isolation, but her options for company were limited. Harry, of course, would be her first choice. The comfortable but increasingly auspicious relationship was not something she wanted to abandon just yet. On the other hand, Helen Winstanley, who had initially seemed such a soulmate, was now tainted with suspicion and confusion. June and Lindy would be immersed in preparations for the funeral of their brother-in-law and uncle, and Thea held out no hope of a rapprochement with old Lionel, despite his being the neediest of all the people she had encountered.

And there was brother-in-law James, who might turn out for a visit if she pleaded with him. Somehow she did not relish that idea. She had parted from him a week ago feeling annoyance and frustration towards him. Some of those feelings persisted.

But she need not have worried. At nine thirty on Saturday morning, a police car drove through Brook View's gate, and she instantly understood that Mohammed had come to the mountain. DS Hollis emerged from the rear of the car, plastered leg foremost. He stood on the gravel, finding his balance and looking all around. Thea went to meet him.

'Nice morning,' he said.

Thea recognised the young PC Herring as the driver of the car and entertained the notion that these two had some special relationship. The girl looked as bored as before, standing idly by while Hollis got on with whatever it was he'd come for.

'Just a few things I'd like to check for myself,' he said. 'Would you walk round with me, in case I've got any questions?'

He was remarkably relaxed, she thought. 'Your leg's getting better then?' she said.

'Thank you. It's more a case of getting used to it, I think.'

'Where do you want to start?'

'Underneath your window might be the best, and work out from there. I can't help feeling we've missed something.'

'Were you here? That first Sunday, I mean?' She tried to remember all the comings and goings, the different faces of all the officials.

'Oh, yes, but I didn't stay for long. The SOCOs were doing a good job, and I soon got the lie of the land.'

They stood where Thea and June had stood, a week earlier. The Saturdays seemed to be coming around with some rapidity. Only one more, and she'd be discharged from Brook View duties.

Hollis looked up, down, right, left, considering all the angles, listening to the background sounds. He limped to the field gate, inspecting the stone path closely. Thea wasn't sure whether this was due to anxiety over slipping, or a search for missed clues.

'Have you come across anything odd?' he asked her.

She gave this some thought. 'Well, only the pond. It's gone a funny colour.'

Hollis looked over the gate towards the far corner of the field, and Thea thought she detected a small sigh.

'No, not that one. The ornamental pond, down by the road. It has a little waterfall thing, but I turned it off. Your men might have missed it – it's down behind those shrubs.'

Hollis appeared to consult some mental notes, looking into PC Herring's face as he did so. She waited passively, like a well-trained nurse in the wake of the top consultant. Thea wondered how much of the detail of the murder Herring was party to. Could she supply names and times and connections, backing up the senior man's memory?

'I don't remember anything about a pond.'

'It's down there, behind the rhododendrons,' she repeated. 'The land slopes towards the road.'

'Show me, please.'

Thea led the way along the winding garden path, thinking that if it hadn't been for Clive's express instructions, and the annoying splashing, she might never have found it herself.

Hollis overtook her, the moment he saw their goal. He stood on the far side of the pond, his injured leg stuck out at an angle, obviously wondering how to proceed. 'Let me help, sir,' said Herring, trotting after him.

'I need a sample,' he said. 'Can you scoop some of that red stuff out for me?'

Herring knelt on the grass and leant over the water. She

gingerly scooped some of the red scum onto a fingertip and proffered it at Hollis. She made no suggestions as to what might have caused it.

He bent down and sniffed the girl's finger, then touched it with his own. The intimacy was all incidental to the science. Thea felt a lurch inside her.

'Good God – it's not *blood* is it?'

'Could well be,' said Hollis. 'Why didn't the SOCO team find this, though?'

'They'd probably not think to examine a garden pond,' Thea said, realising at once that it was not her place to defend his forensic people. She carried on, just the same. 'If it is Joel's blood, I imagine it would have settled in the middle, under the water lily, for a day or two, before being dispersed to the edges, over the following days. Don't you think? The waterfall was running the night Joel died. I turned it off on the Sunday morning. It makes quite a noise, you see.'

He looked at her slowly. 'When did you first notice this?'

'Oh – Tuesday, I think. Tuesday just gone, I mean. I thought it was odd, but it didn't occur to me until now that it might be blood. Have I got it all wrong?'

'Take a sample, Herring,' the man ordered. Herring produced a small plastic pot, and filled it with the red stuff. 'Let's have a think,' Hollis said. Thea was increasingly aware of him as a clever, unemotional but essentially approachable man. She no longer felt afraid of him, and wondered, with hindsight, just what that had been about.

'Let's say, then, that the murder happened here. The victim's throat was cut, in or beside the pond, and much of the blood loss went into the water . . . *all* of it, possibly. He would then have to be carried down the field to the *other* pond, where the body was found.

'How did they carry him? How long between being killed and the disposal of the body? The post-mortem showed he was left lying for some time before he was moved.'

Thea experienced a thrill at being party to this thinking aloud. It was like being taken backstage or onto the flight deck. She refrained from contributing any suggestions.

'It explains most of the unanswered questions,' he went on. 'Why we couldn't find any blood, in particular. And why you didn't hear a struggle. This running water would have masked some sounds. If he screamed as the knife went across his throat, you wouldn't have separated out a splash as he fell from the general splashing already going on. If he and his attacker had been speaking beforehand, you weren't woken by it.'

'If I'd gone outside to investigate, I would never have thought to come down here.' She looked around her. 'If they came in through the road gate, then along the fence, that would explain why the security lights didn't go on. They probably never went near the house.'

'They? Do you think Joel and his killer came in together, like friends?'

She put her hands up defensively. 'I have absolutely no idea,' she said. 'I'm just guessing.'

He started to limp around the whole of the pond. In shape it was a long thin oval, the rocks and channels of the waterfall at one end, the red staining mostly accumulated at the other, perhaps ten feet away at most. 'Just big enough for a body to lie in,' Hollis mused. 'But then quite a job to fish him out again and move him to the field.'

'One person couldn't do it, sir,' said Herring. 'There's a liner, look. They're dreadfully slippery. You can't get a purchase on them.'

'So let's assume he was left on the grass, with his head in the water, so he could bleed discreetly, and not leave any marks. Then they arranged him in much the same way down in the far pond.'

The implication of a multiplicity of killers made Thea feel suddenly vulnerable. 'Do you think there was more than one?'

'No reason to think it was the work of just one person. Never make assumptions,' he told her. As he talked, he was staring at the ground, searching, she supposed, for flattened grass or drops of blood.

'They might have used the wheelbarrow,' Thea said, on a whim. 'It's a good big one.'

'Show me.'

She led the way back to the yard, passing the front of the house. Hollis limped awkwardly, with no regular rhythm. The barrow stood upended against the wall of the barn, where it had been when she first arrived two weeks before. 'Herring,' said Hollis, with a flick of the head. The police officer took thin plastic gloves from a pocket, pulled them on, and lightly grasped the handles. She set the barrow down, and all three gazed at it.

There were smudges of mud up the sides, but no more than that. A dead body would have overflowed, arms and legs dangling over the sides, but it was certainly sturdy enough for the task. 'Could they have got it over the field?' Hollis wondered. 'Is it very pitted?'

'Not really,' Thea said. 'And there are little paths across it, that the sheep have made.' She expected him to go and look, but he made no move.

'We'll have to take this for examination,' he said, looking dubiously at the barrow. It wouldn't go into the police car, as they all quickly realised. 'Or maybe I'll send someone out to collect it.'

'I can check it for prints now, sir,' offered Herring. Hollis nodded.

'Well, this looks like progress,' said Thea, feeling rather chirpy. 'Wouldn't it be splendid if you got the murderer's fingerprints!'

'It would be incredible,' he said, with none of her optimism. 'But I agree we've found a few more pieces of the puzzle.' Then he scowled. 'No thanks to that bloody SOCO team.'

'Shall I make some coffee?' she asked, feeling they'd concluded the main purpose of his visit.

'Thank you,' he said.

In the kitchen, making coffee for Hollis, while Herring stayed outside with the wheelbarrow, another belated memory came to her. 'Oh, I ought to tell you about the cloth we found,' she said, handing him the coffee, and trying to make him sit at the table. 'In the field.'

She described it as best she could, and he listened closely. 'Sounds like a barrel cleaner,' he said. 'For a gun. You drop the lead weight down the barrel and pull it through. Did it smell of cleaning fluid?'

'It didn't smell of anything. It must have been outside for

ages. It was stiff with mud. I think someone had tried to hide it in the hedge.'

'Would your dog have taken it to play with? After you brought it indoors, I mean?'

'She might, but I put it out of her reach. And the labs don't jump up – they're too well trained. I can't think where it's gone.'

'Have there been any people here since you found it?'

Thea tried to recapture the sequence of events for the past five days, with considerable difficulty. 'Oh, yes, lots. I had a bit of a car accident, which threw everything for a while . . .'

'Yes, we heard about that.'

'I suppose you would have done. Anyway, Martin Stacey brought me home and stayed with me for a bit. Then there was a District Nurse who turned up to check that I wasn't concussed or anything. Then Harry Richmond popped in. I think that's everybody.' She paused. 'Except Helen Winstanley, who was only here a little while on the day of the accident.' She caught herself, and devoted a few seconds to wondering just why she'd added this final nugget. She had betrayed Helen with those few words, wantonly revealed something that the woman would almost certainly wish to be kept secret. It was the mere presence of the police, she realised. Burly male shoulders inviting her to unburden herself. James had long ago convinced her that the police were in fact not stupid. They operated under major handicaps a lot of the time. They were slow and methodical and patient. That made them come across as bovine, very often. But they were also careful and attentive and trustworthy.

Thea had never been seriously let down by a man, never

been attacked or frightened by one, either. She obeyed the law because she saw no reason not to, and the benefits of a clear conscience were indisputable. So, despite a certain impatience and even occasional scorn towards the police, she was merely following a built-in injunction to tell them as much of the truth as she could muster, when asked a direct question.

'This car accident. There's no way it could have been a deliberate attempt to injure you?'

Thea laughed. 'Absolutely not. I probably shouldn't admit this, but the truth is that it was almost entirely my fault. Susanna had pulled out a bit too far, but if I'd been going at a proper speed, I could easily have avoided her.'

'She seems to want to take a share of the blame on herself.'

'That's very sporting. It'll be a knock-for-knock job, then, will it?'

'Except the driver of the third vehicle isn't quite so relaxed about it.'

'Oh? Who is he, exactly? I haven't heard any details.'

'He's a travelling salesman, who lost some business, and says he's been having severe headaches since the collision. He's planning to sue you, I fear.' It was taking on the atmosphere of a casual kitchen chat, Thea noted. Perhaps it was the effect of the coffee, or the general influence of Saturday morning sloppiness.

'Well, I'm not going to worry about that now,' she decided. 'It doesn't seem very important compared to a murder.'

'I agree. So we have to allow for the possibility that somebody deliberately removed that cloth, thinking it might give us some sort of information. Probably used to clean fingerprints off the gun. Have you given me the full list of people who've been here since you found it?'

She tried to think carefully. 'I think so,' she nodded. 'But the days have got a bit blurred. I'm not even quite certain just which day I did find it.'

Hollis leant back in his chair, wincing slightly. Thea understood that he liked her, enjoyed talking to her, wanted her to be safe and free from harassment. She wondered again at her earlier reaction to him.

'Do you think much about pain?' The question hurtled out of his smile, catching her right between the eyes.

She floundered for an answer, but managed little more than a gasp or two.

'Sorry. That was unfair.'

'You've been speaking to Helen Winstanley,' she accused. 'What did she tell you?' It was clear from his raised eyebrows and forward motion across the table that she'd got it right. Hurriedly she groped for the logical thread that she'd thought was securely between her fingers. If Helen had discussed her so intimately with the police detective, did that mean she, Helen, was immune from his suspicion, with regard to the Jennison murders? Did it mean that she, Thea, had got things badly wrong? Could she ever hope to go back to the time when she'd liked and trusted Helen?

'She told me you'd found an unusual strategy for coping with the death of your husband. She told me you were still so raw from that loss that you were unlikely to be taking proper care of yourself.'

This was so far from the expected line of questioning that Thea could do nothing but sit still and hold herself together, literally, with arms clutched across herself.

'Look, you're only here for another week. You've stuck to your post, let the Reynoldses enjoy their cruise, and made some good friends in a short time. You've been an excellent citizen, in very difficult circumstances. Several people are worried about you, alone in this house, next to the scene of a murder. Two murders. To be absolutely honest with you, I wonder a bit about your brother-in-law. He's allowed you to put yourself into danger, and if anything encouraged you to increase your vulnerability.'

Thea held up a hand. 'Please stop,' she said, in a small voice. 'You're making me feel awful.'

He reached a hand out and took one of hers. 'I didn't mean to do that,' he said.

She pulled her hand away, slowly. 'I'm completely confused,' she admitted. 'Just when I thought you were going to make things fall into place for me.'

'No need to worry. What I would really like to say to you is – forget the murders. Enjoy your week as if nothing had happened. But it probably isn't going to be possible. Not entirely, anyway.'

She shook her head, trying to clear the confusion.

'There's still a lot I don't understand. James hinted at some sort of organised crime, that you were already investigating. I suspected – still do, I think – that I'm here as a result of a setup, between you and James. Is that right?'

He smiled. 'I couldn't possibly comment. I did know you were coming, and that you were connected to James Osborne. That's all I'm going to say on that matter.'

That felt like a dismissal and she got up to take Herring

her coffee. He spoke to her retreating back. 'This whole case is about pain,' he said softly. 'My broken ankle is just a small highlighter on that central fact.'

She looked back at him. 'Hasn't it occurred to you yet that the whole of human life is about pain?' she said, as gently as she could.

The experience left Thea having to sort through a complicated set of feelings. A sense of privilege at being so closely involved in the top man's procedures; a frustration at not seeing through the mist to what had been going on with the Jennisons; and a subtle complacency at having elicited that attentive smile from him, before he left. The smile she expected from most men she met, and which left her uneasy until it came.

Helen had obviously betrayed her by talking about her use of physical pain to quell the emotional anguish she was prone to. What if Hollis started prattling to James about that stuff? She'd never have a moment's peace, with lectures and homilies and suggestions of counselling or some other sort of therapy. And it would all be futile. She knew what she was doing, what worked for her, and how much recovery she was capable of. There was nobody in the world who could affect the process or change its course. Sitting pretty in a lonely Cotswold house, besieged by the bewildering elements of a sudden death, was as good a therapy as any. Better than most. Besides, there was nothing she could learn from any therapist. She knew, after a year, that the self-torture was not merely an effort to overwhelm the pain of Carl's loss. It was more subtle than that. The whole truth was that she was afraid to let go of this latter pain. With each week that passed, Carl became more shadowy, the memories of life with him more elusive. The loss actually did hurt less than it had at first. And Thea wasn't happy with that. It felt like a wicked betrayal of a man who should not have died when he did. She could not yet permit herself to be happy or easy or free from suffering. Not yet – but in recent days she had come to believe that one day, she just might manage it.

It was, however, necessary in some opaque way, to go and see Helen. There had been a brief point where June Jennison had felt more of a friend, a more likely soulmate, in the shared widowhood and articulate analyses of her condition. But the darker realms inhabited by Helen Winstanley were more directly appealing to Thea regardless of an apprehension that Helen might become clinging and needy. In some ways Helen embodied the spirit of the Cotswolds as they now were, despite, or even because of, her comparatively recent arrival there. Helen had the aesthetic taste, the money, the tangled background that typified much of the area's population in these times. People who knew to their bones that they were privileged to live in a place of utter beauty, and struggled daily to do justice to their good fortune. Thea felt a kind of pity for them, burdened with the duties of care and conservation that went with the package. Every stone was cherished, and rightly so. No manmade change could enhance or embellish what was there already, settled so perfectly into the landscape by past generations who might easily not have realised just what they were doing. And thus Helen herself was caught in the amber of this perfection. It was as if she and all the other residents were holding their breath, afraid to shout or cough in case something lovely became dislodged. And, of course, their own untidy family relationships couldn't hope to match this flawlessness.

Which explained, Thea suddenly saw, why this whole murder business had been so very *quiet*. Everything was quiet and careful around here. Even the charabancs of American tourists, making a quick detour on the way to Stratford, nosed their way down the little lanes with acute delicacy. They disgorged in Stow or Bourton, for a brief invasion of the souvenir shops and tea rooms, but even there they behaved with decorum. The place insisted that they did so, with the force of its atmosphere, its very modesty. Once in Stratford the tourists could start shouting and jostling again, in the sub-Disney mess that the town had become. The Cotswold villages were made of stronger stuff. With no famous Bard to celebrate, they simply offered up themselves and their dull history of wool production, handsome profits, excellent climate and sheer geographical blesssedness.

So Thea went to see Helen, not caring that it was a Saturday, and still lunchtime. Not caring if she walked in on the less than happy couple eating their pasta or pie in a state of weekend laziness. There was an urgency upon her born of the knowledge that in precisely one week's time, she would have to leave this place. This she could not do without understanding much *much* more about how and why and by whose hand poor Joel Jennison had died.

303

Chapter Twenty-One

She had been right to follow the gut feeling that took her up the road to the Winstanleys' house. Helen was in the front garden, beside the beautiful stone wall, the sun on her face, the perfectly proportioned house behind her. The husband was not in sight.

'Helen,' Thea said, not sure whether or not her arrival had been noted. 'I'm asking you again – do you know who killed Joel?'

Helen's head slowly turned. It wasn't clear just what she'd been doing. There was a trowel in her hand, but she hadn't been bent over a flowerbed – merely standing upright, as if in profound thought, face lifted slightly to the sun.

'I'm trying very hard not to know,' she said.

'Which means you do. I've just been talking to the Hollis man.'

'Oh yes. Philip. A good man. Broke his ankle, I hear.'

'Helen, he said you'd seen him since he broke it.' The obvious lie produced a surge of fury in Thea. She wanted to shake the woman.

'Well I haven't,' Helen said. 'I've spoken to him on the phone, that's all.'

'Oh.' Thea scanned back through the morning's conversation, and concluded that this did in fact fit with what Hollis had said. In fact she understood that she had knitted up a complete scarf and glove set from a few implications and facial expressions. 'OK.'

'You seem to be in a bit of a state. Shall I get some sherry or something? We always have sherry on a Saturday. Isn't that weird.'

'Whatever you like.'

'Go and sit down, woman.' Helen waved towards a garden table and chairs set out on a small paved area under a big cherry tree. 'I'll be back in a minute.'

The fury had rapidly turned to affection and something close to amusement. She couldn't imagine Helen Winstanley ever becoming seriously, deeply upset, at least in public. She'd find a flippant comment, a wry acceptance that life was mostly crap, and all you could do was find the sweeter bits. Sherry was an interesting example. Thea hadn't had sherry for at least a year and was already savouring the prospect.

'Where's James?' she wondered, when Helen came back with a small tray.

'Not here. He'll probably show up soon.'

'For his sherry?'

'Precisely.'

'So what you just said means that you do know who killed Joel.' Thea spoke with a slow unemotional delivery.

'Not at all. And if I did I wouldn't utter a name. You know, catching a murderer isn't at all the way people think.

Everybody can know quite well who did it, but unless there's proper evidence and witnesses and so forth, you can't do anything about it. It's like catching a snake. There are so many narrow crevices and holes it can go down that you have to prepare well in advance. You have to stop up all the exits, but without it realising you're doing it.'

'Is that what's happening?' Somehow Thea didn't believe it. She'd seen no sign at all of such activity. 'Is that how they catch snakes?'

'Probably not. Bad analogy. But you know what I mean.'

'I assume I'm not involved in any of this? I'm just in the way – an inconvenience.'

'I think that part is unclear. The timing suggests you might be significant.'

'Helen, you're not helping. It's all whispers and mirrors, smoke and shadows – whatever it is they say.'

Helen shrugged. 'I didn't want to have this conversation, Thea. I'm sorry if you think I've been going behind your back somehow – you do think that, don't you?'

Thea considered. 'A bit, yes. Telling him about my finger thing surely wasn't necessary.'

'You don't know his story then?'

'Yes. Harry told me. His daughter died after taking Ecstasy.'

'She did, yes. And seven years after that, his son was convicted of child abuse, and he's still utterly certain of the boy's innocence. He's in the most ghastly trap, whichever way you look at it.'

Thea tried to grasp the full import of these multiple disasters in one man's life. There was an obvious implication that his wife was no longer with him, either. 'You mean because he's in the police, he has to believe in the system?'

'Partly. It's more that he has no credible options. Technically, it seems there's no doubt the son did what he's accused of. But he was a victim as much as the girl. It all came down to drugs.'

Thea was reminded of her first visit to Helen. 'Does this connect in any way with your daughter?' she asked. That would perhaps explain Helen's evident intimacy with Hollis, for one thing.

Helen turned away without answering – which in itself felt like an answer. 'Tell me,' Thea pleaded. 'What's so secret about it?'

'I'd never be able to make you understand.' Helen turned back, and met Thea's gaze. 'You can't have any idea what it's like. And the law is no help. It's worse than useless. Hollis knows that, you see.'

'I don't see at all. Has this got anything to do with the Jennisons?'

'That I couldn't say. That's where it all begins to unravel.'

Thea remembered another corner of the incomplete jigsaw. 'The network!' she said. 'Something to do with a network.'

Helen put a hand to her mouth. 'I'm going to pretend you didn't say that,' she mumbled.

Thea ground her teeth, feeling the muscles harden in her jaw. 'Come on! You've got to explain it to me now.' Suddenly the whole thing was becoming farcical to her. Village people playing some distorted game to relieve their dull little lives.

'I haven't got to, Thea. It's none of your business, and

it would hurt too many people if I told you about it. Now let's just change the subject. Will you be at the funeral on Monday?'

'I suppose so. Will you?'

'Oh yes. Who would dare to miss it? It would look like guilt.'

Thea entertained this piece of logic for a few seconds. There was some sort of Catch-22 at work, which she couldn't fully grasp. If you didn't go to the funeral, you looked guilty. So if you were guilty, you'd obviously go. So anyone not there was actually very likely to be innocent. Something like that.

The day was gloriously sunny, the air full of birdsong and spring scents. The cherry blossom had almost finished, but there was an exuberant lilac growing against the stone wall, attracting bees and hoverflies. Every few minutes, a car passed along the road, leaving a more noticeable silence behind as it disappeared. Thea determined to surmount the insult she felt at being told to mind her own business. 'Isn't it wonderful here,' she said.

'England at its best,' Helen nodded. 'Pity about the people.'

Thea tilted her head thoughtfully. 'That's not right, though, is it? I mean, this area is beautiful mainly because of what people have done here. OK, so the trees are fabulous, and the way the land lies, but it wouldn't be much without the buildings and hedgerows, let's face it.'

'They had a lot of help, though. What really does it is the stone. Handed them on a plate, you might say.'

'A happy conjunction,' said Thea, with a smile.

'Quite.'

They sipped the sherry and refilled the glasses. Thea found herself not wanting to talk any more. There was a process going on that she didn't grasp, but which she felt she might be able to trust, when it came down to it. The killer snake was slithering confidently towards its crevice, little knowing that Hollis or Helen or somebody had already blocked it up. A light of confidence in Helen's eye gave her reassurance that things were in hand. She didn't have to bustle about being a detective, after all. She could proffer odd bits of evidence, and stand guard over the house that still seemed to be at the centre of the story.

She was just preparing to get up and leave when she heard a car engine approaching, the gears changing down. 'James,' said Helen tightly. 'There's James.'

She spent Sunday diligently pursuing the chores for which she was being paid. A team of police officers showed up and crawled around the garden pond for a while, but did not call at the house.

Before they left she went out to them, intending to ask if she could top up the water level for the sake of the lily. Instead, she found that they had virtually emptied the whole pond, with shiny aluminium buckets brought for the purpose. The water was now in a matching aluminium tank, which they must also have brought. There was no sign of the water lily.

'Good God! What have you done?' she cried.

'What we should have done a fortnight ago,' said one man, ruefully.

'Did you find anything?'

Nobody gave an answer to that.

'Well, can I top it up now?' she insisted. 'If you've taken everything you want out of it.'

'No, madam. Please leave it as it is. We might have to come back again tomorrow.'

Thea gave up. After all, Jennifer Reynolds could hardly hold her responsible for the demise of the precious water lily.

It was obviously sensible to walk to the funeral, rather than take the car and try to slot it into a space on the grass verge with dozens of others. There was to be some food at Barrow Hill afterwards, but Thea had no intention of putting in an appearance there. Whatever her duty might be – and this was hazy even now – it did not extend to mingling with close family and friends at the home of the deceased.

The path to the church was knotted with people, none of whom Thea recognised. It was also bordered with ancient headstones, removed from graves that were presumably destined for reuse. Feeling self-conscious, she devoted a few moments to an inspection of these stones and wished she'd had the sense not to come. She was wearing black trousers and a green shirt. Packing for a funeral had not been part of the process when she'd set out. It was a sheer fluke that she had any dark clothes at all, and the lack of a skirt was just too bad. She spotted two other women in trousers, which reassured her.

The church door stood open and Thea followed a small group inside. Most of the pews were already occupied. People whispered in the dim light, and Thea slid into a half-empty row, almost at the back, alongside two men, who looked at her briefly, and then ignored her.

In front of her a woman wearing a dark blue hat with net covering it was saying to her neighbour, 'You never know, do you, whether you're meant to go in first, or follow the coffin in a procession.' The other woman inclined her head but said nothing.

The church was three pews wide, and Thea could see almost everybody present. The front pew was empty, suggesting that the immediate family were going to follow behind the coffin when it entered the church. She remembered Carl's cremation with a terrible vividness: the four of them walking behind him into the sterile beige building, with its sterile inoffensive music and the heavy blue curtains drawn back so the coffin could be placed on a kind of stage, the focal point of the whole procedure. When those curtains had slowly ceremonially closed, shutting him away forever, she had felt giddy with abandonment.

Who would feel like that about Joel Jennison? No wife or child, a mother who had deserted him decades ago, a girlfriend who showed no sign of feeling. The answer to the question was obvious, even before the procession came through the door at the back of the church. Old Lionel, grieving father of two lost sons, was the locus of suffering. The truism that no loss could be as desperate as the loss of a child must surely apply here. She had permitted herself to glimpse the man's agony a few times over the past fortnight, and flinched away again in horror. How could he carry on with such a gaping wound? Who could even come close to assuaging the pain? Who could willingly inflict it upon him, surely knowing just what they were doing?

Detective Hollis's words came back, 'This case is all about pain.' It meant more to her now, was more specifically true than she had acknowledged when he said it. She had even come to the same conclusion, over a week before, and then let it go again. Was it not indeed probable that the person or persons who murdered the brothers actually had the primary motive of inflicting suffering on Lionel?

When the coffin and its followers finally arrived, the reality of the Jennison family group sprang into relief for Thea. She had not previously seen them together, and the connections between them had been shadowy and lopsided in her mind. Now, in three dimensions, a lot was clarified.

Lionel, a shambling bowed figure, was supported by June, his daughter-in-law. Her concern and affection for him seemed absolute. She held her arm in a gentlemanly crook, and Lionel clung to it. The impression was of dignity and a combined strength. Behind them came a threesome – the girl Lindy flanked by her grandmother and great-uncle. She was holding tightly to Harry's hand, but not touching Muriel. Muriel, who ought by rights have been in front, arm-in-arm with the father of her dead sons, gave every sign of being there on sufferance. She held her head high, eyes darting agitatedly, feet almost dancing in her impatience to get to the front and sit down. Muriel, who Thea understood was really not quite right in the head, made a jarring note. She could not be trusted to behave. Her feelings were impossible to guess. She had quite evidently forfeited her natural right to be present at all, let alone in the family procession. Thea witnessed an impatient glance from June, thrown over her shoulder at this woman who was officially her mother-in-law. Another missing piece fell into the jigsaw – the relationship between these two women was not a warm one.

The bearers laid the coffin on the velvet-covered trestles, and edged invisibly away. Lionel, June, Harry and Lindy pressed into the front pew on the right-hand side of the church. There was no room for Muriel, who stood in horror at her exclusion. Deftly, a hand reached out from the row behind, and guided her into an empty space. Thea could see a bright red head, uncovered by hat or scarf, and realised Susanna, one-time girlfriend of the deceased, had come to the rescue.

The vicar was clearly very familiar with Joel and his family. He made a competent job of the eulogy, alluding fleetingly to the murky details of how the man had died. Death was death, he seemed to be saying, and how you got there was secondary to the eventual reality. Thea thought about this with some intensity. There were of course a million different ways to die. Silent, noisy, painful, easy, violent, disgusting, lonely, public, accidental, self-inflicted – she calmed herself by making a mental list that seemed to go on and on. It was surprisingly soothing to follow such thoughts, and to accept that death was indeed death, and the dead don't care how it happened in their particular case.

The vicar made no hint at the general appetite for retribution that must surely exist amongst those who knew Joel. No Biblical quotations about eyes for eyes or turning cheeks. Understandable, Thea judged. What in the world could he say on that subject, anyway? Knowing there was

313

every chance that the killer was sitting there in front of him, it would be hard to start down that particular path.

It was not so unlike the traditional gathering in the library for the final climactic unmasking. Thea scanned the rows, trying to pick out the few familiar faces who had featured in the Jennison story as she understood it. Helen and James Winstanley were sitting in a pew all on their own. Martin and Isabel Stacey were with a woman Thea hadn't seen before. Virginia and Penny, the women who had been at Brook View's gate on the Sunday that Joel's body had been found, sat close together halfway down the church. A man she had noticed every morning and evening, driving past the gate in a silver Mondeo – dark hair, old-fashioned black moustache, pale skin. Helplessly, she realised the murderer could be any of these people she'd never met, or someone far away and overlooked, never to be caught and punished.

She had been no kind of detective, after all. Just a bewildered bystander, caught up in events that made no sense, even now. All that had happened was that she'd been forced to think about death, when that had been the last thing on her agenda for the house-sitting interlude. She had been scrutinised and understood by Helen; hugged and kissed by Harry; shouted at by Isabel Stacey; comforted by her husband Martin; confided in by June and Lindy: all far richer and deeper than anything she had anticipated.

She thought about Harry Richmond, wondering what she really felt about him. Would she deliberately let him go when she left? Forget him, put him down as a small step towards recovery and nothing more? It would be too much of a fairytale for anything else to happen between them, surely?

314

Would she even see him again after today? There were only four days left of her sojourn, and they would be busy. She had a sense of him waiting for her to make the decision, ready to abide by whatever she said.

Suddenly it was all over. She had stood and sat and pretended to sing the hymns, and listened to the vicar, and that was it. The bearers rematerialised and carried the coffin outside to the waiting hole in the ground. Thea hung back, along with four or five people who apparently also considered themselves too distantly connected for participation in this final phase. People were strung out along the route from church to grave, looking awkward, saying nothing.

The Staceys, who Thea hoped to avoid, were side by side, very much the united couple, in contrast to the Winstanleys who had separated by some margin. Helen was close behind Susanna, who had followed watchfully behind Muriel. James hovered uncomfortably, leaning one hand on the top of a gravestone, seeming to need the support. As Thea watched, he shifted his weight and she saw that one leg was hurting him. And yet he had seemed so upright and powerful when she'd seen him in the pub garden at Oakridge Lynch. Was it just cramp from the hard wooden pew? His gaze was directed intently on the interment going on, a harsh frown on his face, the hand on the stone clenched tight.

Had James Winstanley murdered Joel, Thea wondered with a growing anxiety. Was that what Helen had been trying to say on Saturday? That she strongly suspected it was so, but didn't dare look too closely? Helen clearly had a habit of making friendships amongst the neighbouring farmers, if Martin Stacey was anything to go by. Had she grown so friendly with Joel that James had taken umbrage? If Thea put it to her, would she confirm or deny or merely laugh?

There was a flurry at the graveside as Lionel was assisted in throwing the ritual handful of soil onto the coffin. A choking cry rose up, shocking everyone into paralysis. 'No-o-o-o!' he called, sending his voice out like the harsh cawing of a crow, addressing the cosmos, the cruel universe that had brought him to this. Thea felt tears flood her eyes.

When she looked again, there had been a regrouping. A striking tableau caught her gaze: three women standing together, an inward-looking arrangement where each could look the others in the face. A triangle of female emotion. Thea could see two of them clearly – Isabel Stacey and Helen. The third was Susanna.

Thea knew about female threesomes, being in possession of two sisters. There was always one on the outer edge, excluded from a special intimacy between the other two. But the alliances constantly shifted, in order to sustain the basic group. This was where the magic lay. Nothing in human society was as powerful as a trio of women; they very often frightened even themselves.

In this case, Susanna was the misfit. Isabel and Helen were both looking at her with a complexity of emotions that Thea could only glimpse. Anger, pity, collusion all seemed to be there. It was also a surprising grouping. She would have expected June to be involved, and she was oddly aware of the absent Jennifer Reynolds. She could have formed another trio – former pupils of Cheltenham Ladies' College – with June and Susanna.

But none of this supplied any half-credible explanation

316

for the deaths of the Jennison brothers. Complicated scenarios involving jealous rivalry for the men's affections came and went. Had something momentous happened the previous year, when June and Paul moved to Cirencester, and Susanna split up with Joel, initiating a chain of events culminating in two murders? Trying to recall all the snippets and snatches of history she'd heard, Thea felt she might have hit on something there.

And there'd been something else. She rummaged for the memory, and finally found it. Jennifer and Clive Reynolds had had their big falling out at that same time. Their marriage had almost collapsed, and this cruise was by way of celebration or confirmation that they'd come through the crisis and were still together.

The obvious explanation for this was that Clive had been carrying on with June, and not the nameless woman in Helen's account. June and Paul had moved away, to give both couples a chance to recover, and to distance the errant lovers from each other.

It fitted so neatly that Thea instantly believed it to be fact. Further than that, it suggested that Clive and Paul would have been in a state of mutual animosity, perhaps to the point where Clive shot the farmer one night, having seen him lurking in the field behind his house.

She shook herself. People were leaving, and she was standing alone in a rather too prominent spot. It was time to go home.

The house was definitely dusty. The cushions looked tired and crumpled, the corners of the kitchen silted up with dog hair

317

and fluff. Thea had not been a very good housewife during the past two weeks. This didn't bother her. The labradors and the plants were all alive and healthy. The sheep appeared to be contented. The garden was not within her brief, but the few new weeds wouldn't take long to eradicate. There had been no burglaries, fires, breakages or floods. Only a little murder, in the garden pond, to disturb the peace; plus, of course, a tragically devastated water lily, which was, in the circumstances, not too great a price to have paid.

Several cars passed the gate throughout the afternoon, coming and going to Barrow Hill, she supposed. She remembered from a year ago the sudden drop in tension when everybody finally departed, the funeral concluded, the new circumstance confirmed. Thea and Jessica had looked at each other warily, conscious that they had no choice but to reconstruct their lives without the keystone that was Carl. Carl had balanced his wife and daughter, according each of them his attention, but in different ways. He had skilfully avoided giving either cause for jealousy or insecurity. He had smiled tolerantly whenever they ganged up against him, as they often did. Without him, they simply toppled over, like two playing cards kept upright only by the third one placed at just the right angle.

But it wasn't like that for the Jennisons. Their house of cards had been a more complicated one. Lionel would have been as much the keystone as the one in need of support. June had already suffered her own cataclysmic loss when Paul had died. Losing Joel couldn't possibly be of equal significance. Lindy, likewise, was left isolated, a great hole knocked through the generation above her, and nobody of her own age to cling to. The pattern was of a single representative surviving in each age group, calling in reinforcements in the shape of Harry, Susanna and the very odd Muriel.

The afternoon passed restlessly. Something was coming to a head. Some observation made at the funeral was surely the key to the mystery of Joel's death. There was something about hatred and female revenge that niggled at her. A sense that most of the women she'd met did in fact dislike each other. She herself disliked Isabel Stacey, after her rudeness, but she liked Helen and June, in spite of an acknowledgement that either of them might just have been the killer. Either or *both*, given the new discovery that Joel's body must have been lifted and carried some distance.

It was an exercise not dissimilar to juggling the seven letters of a Scrabble game. The permutations initially seemed to fall into only three or four different patterns, but the chance adjustment of a single element could introduce completely unexpected possibilities. Thea was tempted to put her musings into hard copy – give each individual a letter and start juggling them. Harry, Martin, Susanna, Lionel, June, Lindy and Helen. That was a lot of suspects, and it ignored Muriel, James Winstanley and the host of neighbouring villagers who hadn't made themselves known to Thea. And including Lionel seemed unjustified. Even rather cruel, she felt, on reflection. Who could ever believe that the poor old man would murder his own sons?

But before she started cutting out paper squares and laying them out in various formations, the will went out of her. Suddenly it all seemed foolish. She wasn't going to catch a murderer like that. There wasn't enough objective evidence to make one scenario more plausible than any other. Anyone watching her would laugh at the futility of what she was planning to do.

The abrupt plummet into the dark hole of futility was familiar enough for her not to panic. Instead she went into the kitchen and rummaged in the freezer for a carton of chocolate chip ice cream, which she had previously noted, but not so far sampled. She took a bowl of it outside, and sat on the lawn, trying not to think. Hepzie sat beside her, contented to play the faithful hound, while Bonzo and Georgie loped and sniffed about the borders and beds.

How much, in the end, did it matter to her who killed Joel Jennison, she asked herself. Just as it hadn't seriously mattered who had been driving the truck that slaughtered Carl. The knowledge wouldn't change anything; retribution was undoubtedly over-rated and justice a very abstract concept. Could she, though, just leave at the end of the week with the whole business still unresolved? Could she somehow act to hasten the denouement? Was it in her power to identify and expose the murderer? It was impossible to answer such questions, but the slow procession of them through her mind, as the sweet ice cream slipped down her throat, returned her to a sense of proportion. There were things she could reasonably do: well-intentioned and responsible things. She had time and brains to assist her, and a detached standpoint from which to observe the participants.

And, above all, she had almost nothing to lose.

Chapter Twenty-Two

Aware of the rapid passage of time, Thea devoted Monday evening to hatching a workable course of action. Making a number of dubious assumptions, she devised a plan containing several alternatives, depending on the outcome at each stage. The sense of taking charge and precipitating events was intoxicating. There was no return of the moments of bleak futility as she gained confidence in what she was about to do.

The basics were simple enough, time-honoured and fairly obvious. Bluff and counter-bluff, setting the players against each other and sowing mistrust. It took nerve, and would scarcely have been possible if she had been one of the community, intending to continue to live amongst the people concerned. Many of them would never be able to forgive her for her treachery. James Osborne would be appalled and DS Hollis outraged. Perhaps, in the morning she would again change her mind, and pretend the whole idea had been a foolish fantasy. But she hoped not. In the course of her preparations, she had come to certain tentative conclusions, considering as she had the persons under scrutiny, assessing the probabilities of each one as murderer. Given the gaps in her knowledge, she could not be sure. But she did think she had a workable hypothesis. And the whole thing about hypotheses was that you had to put them to the test.

On Tuesday she got up at seven thirty, and vigorously exercised all three dogs on the lawn, before taking Hepzie around the field to count the sheep. The sun rose delicately, mistily through the trees at the edge of the field, reminding Thea of the bolthole through which Lindy had burrowed. It was on the western boundary of the field, and Thea found herself looking directly at it without being able to see anything unusual. It was one of many details in her careful construction of a plan of action.

Back in the house, she sat down to think things through one more time. She had to watch and react and stay in control, without safety nets of any kind. She wondered whether it had been wise to omit her brother-in-law from the exercise, or any other members of the police. As her anxiety level rose, she reached for her laptop, and quickly connected the modem.

James, I did go to Joel's funeral. Very sad. Everybody was there. Odd groupings.

I'm only here a few more days. It feels like I've been here a lifetime. I'm going to have one last try at solving these murders for you, starting this morning. Nothing ventured, or something. Hollis came over on Saturday – I expect you're up to speed with what we found? We have a murder scene now, which seemed to please him.

Love

Thea.

At least it hinted that she was planning something, which made her feel more resolute and slightly more secure. There were times in life when one's behaviour diverged from the ordinary routines, and took a plunge into stuff much closer to the edge. Thea's experience to date had not ventured far into these peripheral regions, but she had always known they were there. She knew because her brother in his youth had twice been arrested for using cocaine and once for having sex in a car in broad daylight. She knew from once seeing a young woman jump off a high bridge, as she, Thea, drove across it. She knew from reading ordinary daily newspapers. The edge was much closer than anybody would admit, and to cross it and fall over into the underworld of violence, madness, law-breaking and chaos was much easier than the normal world liked to pretend. Thea was deliberately marching towards this frontier, heart pounding as she went.

The heavy duty thinking she had done the previous evening had produced two large areas of confusion and concern, which became so closely linked in her mind that she began to wonder if they were the same thing. Firstly the network that Lindy had inadvertently mentioned, centred on Fairweather Farm. Secondly, the scattered allusions to young people hooked on drugs. Tied in with this was the pale-faced silent Monique, and the invisible Paolo, as well as the strange young couple she had encountered that first weekend and never seen again. In a further flight of fancy, Muriel's daughter Daisy was slotted into the picture, too.

But Lindy had said the network was why her father and uncle had died. That they wouldn't have anything to do with it, which made them outsiders, victims, a threat of some kind. One disconcerting conclusion to draw from this was that just about everybody had risen up and slaughtered the brothers from a collective outrage at their non-participation. But Thea couldn't credit that idea for long. She would have heard more commotion outside her window, and even Hollis's imperfect SOCOs would have noticed a dozen sets of footprints in garden and field.

The first stage of the plan was inevitably to explore the scene again, this time with no dogs and no distractions. She would conduct the re-enactment that had never really happened when June had come for her one-week follow-up.

She began at the garden pond, which PC Herring had taped off, and which had been left drained and desolate by Sunday's white-overalled men. Then she went through the gate into the field and cut diagonally across to the burrow under the hedge. It was not easy to locate. After several minutes she got it and, with a strong sense of unreality, she dived through it, once again falling three or four feet into the deeper ditch on the other side.

Picking herself up, she looked around, knowing she was trespassing. This field was empty of livestock, and seemed to have been neglected for some time. 'Set aside,' she muttered to herself, only dimly aware of what that actually entailed.

In full daylight it seemed smaller than it had on the evening of Lindy's appearance. The side bordering the road was a curving wire fence, with clumps of untended grass and other things growing up on the field side. A good-sized oak tree had been circuited by the fence, and used as a support for it, staples hammered into the bark. The wire seemed to sag just there. Carefully, Thea examined it all. Not until she looked up did she begin to understand the parts of the story that Lindy had omitted. The tree had a fork, only eight or ten feet above the ground. About halfway between the ground and the fork was a block of wood nailed to the tree, projecting about three inches, not immediately useful for anything. Perhaps only a lifelong tree-climber would understand its purpose.

Placing a foot on the sagging fence, she hoisted herself up. Instantly the block of wood became an obvious foothold, and Thea used it. That gave her access to a stout branch with which to haul herself easily into the fork in the tree. From there she could see a scuffed area of bark, a foot or two out along a main limb. This, she suspected, was a well-used vantage point from which to spy on Fairweather.

Wishing she had brought binoculars, she scanned the view before her. The first thing she noted was a long low green-topped building, some distance from the main buildings of Fairweather Farm, but clearly on their land. A track ran up to it from the house. 'Just as I thought,' she murmured to herself.

The distance was hard to gauge, but it had to be two or three hundred yards. It would not be possible to see faces without the assistance of binoculars. But anyone wanting to monitor comings and goings without being seen could very easily do so.

Below her the road passed just beyond the fence. In winter a spy sitting in the tree would be visible to anyone glancing upwards from a car – but probably only to a passenger. Drivers seldom looked at trees, especially on a bend in a small country lane. Wearing dull-coloured clothes and keeping very still would probably be all that was needed to remain undetected.

Had Paul Jennison sat here, as well as Lindy and Joel? Why would they? What did they expect to see? Lindy's story about the delicious Paolo had sounded convincing, but now Thea wondered. Paolo had been a transitory element, the way she'd heard the story, whereas this network business had struck her as more permanent and far-reaching.

Had Joel been sitting up here the night he was killed? Had he been discovered and pursued back to Brook View's garden? Had he been lured there by someone he thought was a friend? Had he been on his way to the tree, and been intercepted? The possibilities were legion and Thea felt weary before she'd properly started.

She remembered the scarf, caught in quite a different tree, and the barrel-cleaning cloth. Would their part in the story ever be fully understood? Was it ever possible to assemble scraps of evidence and supposition and create a complete picture – even if you found the killer and forced a confession from them? Wouldn't there always be discrepancies and omissions?

She sat there, letting random thoughts come and go, hoping to trick them into supplying connections and insights of their own accord. But nothing made much sense without understanding the nature of the network, and the goings-on at the Staceys' farm.

A movement caught her eye, and she focused more carefully on the green-roofed building. A vehicle was driving up to it, along the track she'd missed during her last visit there. It looked like a minibus and, as she watched, it stopped and several people climbed out. She counted seven, as they stood in a ragged group, apparently waiting for something. Frustrated by the distance, she tried to work out what was happening from their body language. There was something unusually passive about most of them, contrasting with one figure which carried an energy and purpose in the way it marched to the door of the building, threw it open, returned, and apparently spoke. An inescapable conclusion formed in Thea's mind. Surely these had to be illegal immigrants, or desperate asylum seekers? People who had travelled far, weary and drained of all initiative. Packing them away into a building that looked like a hostel, out of sight of the road or the main farm buildings, was an obvious clue. It would be reasonable to refer to such an enterprise as a network – although why the whole community should collude in something that was surely anathema to the comfortable residents of the Cotswolds was less easy to explain. And the sense she had had of a rather flimsy police interest in the whole business was at odds with her conclusions. The government was genuinely agitated by the issue of immigration, and the police would not lack persistence when it came to any hint of such activity. What's more, Lindy had insisted that the network was not conducting any illegal business.

And another inconsistency nagged at her: Joel Jennison had not struck her as a man to jeopardise this sort of endeavour. If he was threatening to report the network, then Thea believed – on the basis of a ten-minute encounter – it was because it was doing something he couldn't stomach.

She spent a little time considering this angle and chastising herself for jumping to such a conclusion. What, after all, did she really know about Joel? She recalled his use of the words 'even now' when referring to Hepzie's long tail. An implication, which had struck her at the time, of a man not fully integrated into his time and place. A vein of disapproval at the ways of mankind, which persisted even now, when the general view was that all was well in the world – or at least in Duntisbourne Abbots. So, Joel was uncomfortable, unsettled. Helen had described the whole family as obsessively clean-living when it came to social behaviour. The mucky farmyard clearly didn't count as decadence or depravity, whereas much of modern human activity probably did. She caught herself up – almost all of this was groundless supposition, sparked by two insignificant words.

She climbed lightly down from the tree, and retraced her steps to the house. Things were coming together, and the next step had to be planned carefully. Resisting the powerful urge to phone a long list of witnesses, to plead with them to tell her all they knew, she continued with the strategy of examining and checking for herself. It was, at least, safer this way, and much less embarrassing. The previous evening's reflections had shown her that she was not a good interrogator, anyway. She had at least twice forgotten important details when in conversation. The worst of these was her failure to mention the network to DS Hollis, so distracted had she been with the way events had unrolled during his visit. She had a butterfly brain, she concluded, and any diversion sent all her thoughts flying off in every direction but the right one.

But there were things she had to check, and the only way to do that was by asking questions. Or was it? A flash of inspiration led her to the laptop, and the wonders of the internet. Her hands were shaking with excitement as she booted it up, and connected the modem.

She began with the local paper, keying in Jennifer Reynolds as the first search, remembering the odd message left on the telephone during her first day at Brook View. It popped up effortlessly, the whole story.

'Mrs Jennifer Reynolds was booed when she spoke at a public meeting last Wednesday at the Duntisbourne Abbots Village Hall.

The meeting had been called to discuss the renovation of local footpaths, and the proposed resiting of the path leading into the village from the southern side. Mrs Reynolds is said to have raised a different matter in the course of the meeting, which led to impassioned debate on all sides. The exact nature of the issue has not been reported, but when contacted, Mrs Reynolds (47) would only say that she did seem to be at odds with village opinion, at least for the moment.'

Scrolling backwards, Thea ascertained that the story was on a page entitled Village News Round-Up, sent in by local contributors. She wondered at the undercurrents, the something-and-nothing of the report as it appeared, and the mischief implied. Why had the contributor mentioned the disagreement at all, if its subject couldn't be given? Was it too fanciful to think that he or she secretly agreed with Jennifer, and wanted to raise the profile of the whole thing?

Another thought came out of the blue. The phone message would still be saved in the 1571 facility. She ran to listen to it again, jittering impatiently at the measured tones of the recorded woman listing dates and times, which seemed to go on forever.

The voice, when it came, was now almost familiar. The estuary English of Martin Stacey was loud in her ear, both actual and remembered. Martin had phoned to sympathise with Jennifer Reynolds. Thea had no idea what to make of this, but it filled another hole in the picture.

She went back to the laptop, eager to find more background. She keyed in Helen Winstanley then Fairweather Farm, followed by Lionel Jennison, Paul Jennison, Joel Jennison, Harold Richmond and finally for good measure DS Philip Hollis.

Some bore fruit, and others did not. She followed red herrings and false trails. It all took a long time, as she copied sections of text and pasted them all into one Word file. She had not brought a printer with her, so she noted down the most salient details on the jotter pad that the Reynoldses had placed beside the telephone.

It was both exhilarating and appalling just how much information could be gleaned about ordinary village folk, who now and then happened to get their names included in one thing or another.

When she'd finished, she did not have her murderer, or a picture of any great clarity. But she was close. She understood a great deal more than she had before.

Chapter Twenty-Three

She spent the rest of Tuesday on the project. She was still up at midnight, absorbed in it all. The last thing she did before crawling up to bed was to forward the Word file as an e-mail attachment to her brother-in-law James.

She awoke on Wednesday morning with patterns and guesses and intentions still whirling around her brain. The sense of urgency persisted, but with it came a loud warning to proceed with caution. There were still several points at which she could make a wrong assumption, and the course of action open to her was by no means obvious.

The answers to most of the remaining questions lay firmly at Fairweather Farm, and Thea felt simultaneously reluctant and inclined to walk over there and investigate. But the mixed feelings were paralysing. Weighing up the arguments, she recalled the unfriendly manner of Isabel Stacey. Whatever the reason for it, Thea felt there was little scope now for a civil exchange between them. She had utterly failed to endear herself to the woman, and saw little prospect of changing her attitude. Another factor on the negative side was a niggling suspicion that her earlier thoughts about the Jennisons still had some mileage in them. Thoughts centred upon old Lionel and his unmistakable pain; the obvious fact that by slaughtering his sons, somebody had been at best careless of his wellbeing. Perhaps it would be a better idea to turn right at the front gate, towards Barrow Hill, and follow up a hunch that something would manifest itself as a result.

June had implied that Lionel was naturally curmudgeonly, but Harry and Joel had both given him a rather better character assessment. There were a lot of people making excuses for each other, Thea noted. A network of loyalties and affections that tinted the whole sorry story with something surprisingly warm and good. She had not expected that at all. Her researches implied that there was one and only one malevolent individual pretending to be part of the universal fellowship that she had unearthed. Someone who nursed grievances or psychoses, unsuspected and unobserved. Motives traditionally stretched back into the past, but this wasn't always the case. Hot revenge, sudden alterations, opportunism – all produced flashes of violence without premeditation.

Abandoning any attempt to understand motivation, she did not argue with the inner prompting that made her leave the house, without the dogs, and turn right at the front gate.

The track down to Barrow Hill farmyard was becoming familiar.

The thistles in the fields, the grey stone house positioned to escape most of the day's sunshine, the weedy corners and pungent smells all reminded her of the first time she'd visited. The afternoon when she'd skirted the yard because of the muck, and met June and Lindy in the first shock of their bereavement, vividly recurred to her.

But today there was a dramatic difference. The yard, hitherto thronged with bullocks, was now dense with sheep, all making indignant noise. *May 10th*, she remembered. The day Joel had told her was scheduled for shearing. The day Clive's little flock were also meant to be having their fleeces removed, God damn it. Well, how was she meant to remember that? It was extraordinary that the Jennison sheep were actually being done, in the circumstances. Who was in charge? How was it being organised? She had to find someone and ask if they would fetch Clive Reynolds's sheep, before it was too late.

There was a faint sound of a motor running in the large barn, and a loud voice somewhat closer. Thea took the plunge and dived amongst the heaving hot woolly beasts, heading for the sounds across the yard. The voice she could hear seemed unnaturally angry. Why would shearing sheep give rise to rage, Thea wondered, with a flicker of amusement at the mysteries of agriculture.

There had to be two or three hundred sheep. Smaller than those at Brook View, they also seemed much wilder and more terrified of human beings. Penned in by a complex arrangement of gates, they were being funnelled into the barn. Expecting to find the source of the angry voice, she pressed on, noticing a lot of naked white sheep in a field beyond the yard. Clearly the shearing was well under way.

There were two men just visible in the shadowy interior of the barn, one bent over a captive animal, one standing by, holding the next victim. The shearing machine was clattering, the sheep were bleating. It seemed unlikely that the men could hear anything going on outside. It was quite evident that these were not the shouting people. Thea skirted the barn, moving along the side of the house, beginning to feel that something important was going on.

She came upon a tableau of violence that startled her into rigidity. The old man, Lionel Jennison, standing crookedly, one arm raised. In the uplifted hand was some sort of metal weapon, a curved blade that chopped downwards as Thea watched. Its intended goal was plainly the head or neck of a woman, crouching against a low stone wall, hands defensively wrapped around her face.

But despite the hidden face, it was obvious from the first who she was. The bright red hair gave her away. The weapon found its objective, but only the tip made contact, striking the protective knuckles of Susanna's right hand, the wrist of which was still bandaged from the injury sustained in the car accident of the previous week. She screamed, and scrambled further away. Blood began to trickle from the cut, a much deeper red than that of her dyed hair.

Thea wakened from her moment of catatonia. 'No!' she shouted, as she lurched forward to prevent the man from striking again. She hardly need have bothered. He wobbled as his damaged hip took his weight, and then shifted rapidly back to his previous position, with a moan. As Thea reached him, he began to list, his balance gone, and she caught him with difficulty. The hook fell from his hand. She realised that he was weeping.

'She did it,' he babbled. 'It was her, the sly little bitch.'

Susanna made no attempt to regain her feet, but watched

Thea's face with narrowed eyes. Her bloody hand went to her mouth. She was an animal at bay, dangerous and unpredictable.

Hampered by the old man leaning most of his weight on her, Thea began to worry. The shearers couldn't hear or see them, in this angle between yard and house. The sharp hook was on the ground within Susanna's reach. Sliced laterally, it could do immense damage to a human body. Thea trembled for her own vulnerable throat or thigh or calf.

But Susanna made no move towards the implement. Instead she reached across her own body with her left hand, and fumbled something out of her trouser pocket.

'Watch her. That's a knife!' Lionel's mind was obviously less incapacitated than his body. 'The one she used to kill Joel.'

'Shut up,' Susanna snarled. 'You *stupid* man.'

Stupidity didn't seem an adequate explanation for such ferocity, Thea thought. Surely he'd committed some far greater sin in Susanna's eyes than that?

'What's he done to you?' she asked, her curiosity so strong that the question came out with laughable normality. They could be sitting in Brook View's living room.

Susanna merely shook her head, and flicked out the blade of the knife. Thea wrestled for rational thought. 'You won't use that,' she said. 'The place is full of people. They'll stop you.'

'She'll use it all right,' said Lionel, unhelpfully. Thea felt her sympathy for him evaporating.

'He started it,' Susanna snarled. 'I came over here to help with the sheep. June asked me to. I couldn't very well refuse.'

This went beyond normality. If Thea's grasp of events was

correct, the killer of the farmer's sons had casually turned up as requested, to assist with the shearing. 'What went wrong?' she asked.

'The gun cloth,' said Lionel. 'She's got the gun cloth.'

Thea blinked, letting the neural connections work their lightning magic. '*She* took it! When she came to tell me about the funeral. It never occurred to me. But *why*?'

'It was Paul's. She shot him with his own gun, and cleaned it afterwards.'

'I buried it in the hedge. How did you find it, you bloody pest?' Susanna glared at Thea, with genuine curiosity. Even in this moment of potential cataclysm the detail seemed important to her.

'The dog dug it out,' Thea said, hoping for a moment that an ordinary explanation might calm things down.

'I never thought –,' Lionel choked on his words. 'Paul *and* Joel. I knew you weren't right, but I never thought – Not until I saw you with the cloth.'

The old man's deductions seemed to have come too quickly to be credible. There had to be more than a bit of material. 'You mean you recognised it just now?' she asked him.

'She was trying to hide it over there.' He lifted his chin towards a scruffy corner strewn with rusty buckets and misshapen lumps of concrete.

Susanna's gaze flickered between her antagonists, waiting for them to finish speaking. Thea thought she looked much less certain of her next move than she had a minute earlier.

'And you took that to prove she killed Paul?'

'Why else would she be doing it? And I saw her face, like a cunning vixen. The same look she had when she was running off with that Clive, behind his wife's back. I saw her then, too.'

'You told Joel,' Susanna said, as if that explained everything. 'And he told Jennifer. It was all down to you, you old bastard.'

Lionel's eyes bulged and his hand on Thea's arm was like a claw.

She did not follow up anything he had said. There were more pressing considerations. Susanna's failure to deny the charge demonstrated guilt beyond further doubt. The immediate goal was to get out of this mess without injury.

'Look,' she said, trying to keep the quiver out of her voice. 'You'd better be sensible and put the knife away. We can go in the house and . . .' And what? Get Lionel into a chair, for a start. His weight was pushing her over, and she staggered a little.

'Shut up!' Susanna flashed the knife across Thea's face, three inches away. 'I could cut your pretty looks to ribbons, just like that, if I wanted. Why not? What have I got to lose?'

'What would be the point?'

'I *like* it, that's the point. It feels good. Blood spurting out, people dying at my feet. I *like* it.'

'But that isn't why you do it. You're not completely insane. I haven't done anything to you.'

'You have. You're taking his side. You had Joel running over to meet you two minutes after getting here. You stuck your nose in. You talked to Helen and Lindy about me. You crashed your car into me.'

Thea said nothing. There was an acute risk of bursting into uncontrolled laughter if she opened her mouth.

337

It felt as if the three of them had been there for hours, ignored by the world carrying on a few feet away. Something had to give. Lionel seemed to feel the same. He eased himself back onto his good leg, and then slowly tested the bad one. Thea felt suddenly unburdened again, free to move. It didn't appear that Susanna had noticed the adjustment.

'Put the knife away,' Thea ordered more firmly. 'It's not doing you any good.'

'It's scaring you, isn't it? Both of you?'

'Not really.' Something shifted inside Thea, and she swiftly bent for the hook, snatching it by the greasy wooden handle. As she'd hoped, Susanna was too startled to react. Pushing Lionel aside, Thea swung the curved blade towards Susanna, who was still not fully upright. For a ghastly second, Thea feared she was about to cut the younger woman's head off. That hadn't been her intention, although the sudden bloodlust was shockingly intense. She hadn't known she was capable of such rage.

Susanna rocked back, out of reach, and then scrambled to her feet. The ensuing duel was clumsy and inconclusive, thanks in part to Susanna having to use her left hand. The knife was much less threatening once Thea understood the problem. But damage might well have been inflicted if rescue hadn't finally arrived.

Chapter Twenty-Four

Rescue in the shape of a flurry of black and white, at knee level, which did not initially do anything constructive to help. Hepzibah was jumping up at her mistress, distracting her from the immediate task, and causing stunned confusion in both combatants. Then Susanna saw what was happening, and made another more businesslike lunge with her knife. It caught the dog somewhere in the ribs, powerful enough to penetrate hair and skin, and wrench the weapon out of the woman's hand.

Thea blindly lashed again with the hook, before letting it go and grabbing the spaniel in her arms. The dog was staring up at her wide-eyed. The knife fell away, clattering in a sudden silence. The shearing machine had stopped. Nobody spoke, until Lionel began to shout.

'Here! Come here!' he called in a deep voice of authority that could not fail to be obeyed. Then he put a hand on the dog's side, examining the wound more by touch than by sight.

'Punctured lung, seems like,' he said. 'Have to get her to a vet quick.'

Thea's gratitude at his shared perception of where the priority lay made her want to hug him. But before she could move, obedience to Lionel's shout became manifest. Four men came into view, two from one direction, two from another. Thea looked at them in bewilderment.

'James!' she squeaked. 'Oh, James. Take me to a vet. We've got to save Hepzie.'

Lionel asserted himself again. 'Rog – you phone Hendersons and tell them there's a dog with a collapsed lung coming. Get ready for surgery. Tony, you run them in, will you? You know where it is, and your truck's outside the gate already. Unless this lot've boxed it in.'

Thea ignored everything except her suffering pet. The agony was unbearable, thinking about the soft innocent animal's possible demise. Following the greasy sweating Tony to his truck, she cast a glance back at Susanna, aware of an overflowing hatred towards her. The woman was sitting on the ground again, clutching her upper arm, which seemed to be pouring with blood.

'Did I do that?' Thea asked, as she paused momentarily. 'Good!'

The sea of sheep seemed to part effortlessly for her and Tony, but another man blocked her way. 'Go now,' he said. 'But I'll want to talk to you as soon as this is sorted out.' He nodded down at the dog, with a true Englishman's concern.

'Thanks, Mr Hollis,' Thea said, before wondering whether it was proper protocol to call a Detective Superintendent Mr.

The file that Thea had sent to James read as follows:
'Missing person, Felicity Winstanley, aged 18.

340

Reported missing by parents Helen Winstanley and James Winstanley October 2001. Known to use Class A drugs.'

'Fairweather Farm. Refuge for recovering drug addicts.

Unclassified, unregistered. Address not disclosed. No questions asked. Telephone 07712 455677.'

'"Why Drugs Must Not be Legalised" by Paul Jennison. Abstract – drug addiction is the single biggest cause of crime in the UK, and police tolerance is exacerbating this. The perceived problem of the cost of sustaining the addiction leading to theft of goods and money is the wrong approach. Legal drugs would still be expensive. Thefts would still take place and lives still be ruined. The only solution is to remove the incentive to use drugs. Full article appears in the *Big Issue*.'

'"I owe it all to Fairweather Farm." Susanna Hawker, 34, speaks to Jenni Murray on *Woman's Hour* in March 2002 about her problems with drugs since her late teens. A secretive establishment in the heart of the countryside is credited with Susanna's full recovery. "At Fairweather, people are given the confidence and freedom to recover in their own way. Not everybody succeeds, but the friendships can last forever. I show my gratitude by working there in my free time. The Farm is run by a dedicated couple, who frequently go to London and other towns and cities to invite addicts living rough to spend some time with them. The whole thing runs on a shoe-string, with no grants, but active local support. It operates outside the usual Social Services or NHS provisions, because several of the users are in trouble with the law."'

'E-mail from anonymous listener to *Woman's Hour* on

message board: I spent a few weeks at Fairweather Farm last year, at the suggestion of my mother, who lives nearby. It worked for a while, but is not really an answer to the problem. Susanna means well, but there are many things I didn't like about the place. It felt like being part of a cult, at times.'

'Missing person. Monique Puyere. Aged 22. French. Last seen in London, Camden Town. Reported missing by her older sister, with whom she was living until recently. Known to be user of Class A drugs.'

Thea waited at the vet's while they performed emergency surgery on Hepzibah. The waiting room was deserted, except for one girl on reception, who repeatedly had to answer the phone. Tony and Rog had returned to finish their shearing, but not before supplying her with a mobile phone and a promise to send somebody to be with her.

Her mind was blank to begin with, but slowly the pressure of recent events broke through the protective wall and flooded her head with questions and explanations.

She had worked out the balance of hostilities between Fairweather Farm and Barrow Hill. The Jennisons – or Paul, at least – had disapproved of the illicit 'rehabilitation' going on under the controlling hand of Martin and Isabel Stacey. The precise motivations of the Staceys were still not apparent. Perhaps simply to acquire free labour for the farm, or to implement sincerely held ideas about how best to fight the scourge of drug addiction. The implication that they collected addicts from the streets of London fitted in part with the glimpse she had gained of the arriving minibus.

The further suggestion that one of their inmates had been Helen Winstanley's daughter had caught Thea up short. Who else in the area had errant offspring who were taken to Fairweather? Did they get special preferential treatment? Had it been personally affected locals who set the thing going in the first place?

Susanna had some strong personal investment in the place, which the disapprobation of the Jennisons clearly threatened.

The hostile reception of Jennifer Reynolds's speech at the public meeting was very likely on the same topic. Had she questioned the activities at Fairweather? Were the villagers actively in sympathy with it? Did they collude to keep it from the public gaze and the attentions of the police?

Just how altruistic was the whole exercise? At first Thea had believed it to be a network of benevolence and charity. Now she wondered if it had more sinister aspects. Was it all down to money? Did it involve blackmail or extortion or organised fraud?

But oh, the poor little dog. Nothing mattered as much as this terror and guilt that surged through her at the image of the innocent animal trying to save her from danger. Except, she had to admit, that wasn't really how it had been. Hepzie didn't understand threat or malignancy. She'd just been jumping up at Thea in a frenzy of delight at finding her mistress again, after being shut indoors. She had been indiscriminately joyful, leaping and wagging and smiling, expecting to be greeted and hugged by anyone she approached. It had been an act of the most wanton evil to stab her like that.

The door opened, and Harry Richmond came in, almost on tiptoe. His expression, as he focused on Thea, was of profound concern and distress. 'How is she?' he whispered.

'They're operating. It's been ages.'

'I'll stay with you, shall I?'

'That'd be nice. Thanks.'

They sat in silence, listening to the receptionist answering calls from pet owners wanting appointments, or advice on their cat's scratched head. Nothing sounded urgent or even interesting.

'Did you know about Fairweather?' she asked him, when the silence began to weigh heavily.

'Oh yes. How did you find out?'

'Lindy. Spying. The internet. It eventually came together. Did you suspect Susanna?'

He shook his head. 'I was quite sure Clive had organised it. Paid somebody to assassinate Joel while he had a perfect alibi.'

She thought that over. 'But the Reynoldses and the Jennisons were on the same side.'

'Were they?' He shook his head. 'I doubt that.'

'But—' The door at the end of the waiting room opened, and a white-coated woman emerged. 'Mrs Osborne?'

Thea got up. 'Is she all right?'

'I think she'll be fine. The lung's inflating on its own again now. She'll be conscious in a few minutes.'

'Can I see her?'

'Better not. You might get her too excited.'

Thea had an image of the comatose dog recognising her

344

and trying to jump up and cover her with tail wagging and licks. 'Right,' she agreed. 'When, then?'

'Leave her here overnight. She should be almost back to normal by the morning.'

Harry took her home. The borrowed mobile phone trilled while they were in the car, and Thea answered it.

'Thea? It's James. How is she?'

'They think she'll be all right. I'm coming home now. They're keeping her in overnight.'

'You've got a bit of a reception committee here. They all think you're a hero.'

'That sounds ominous. Can you send them away?'

'I'll try. But I doubt if I can shift them all.'

Thea relayed this to Harry. 'Who does he mean? What do they think I've done?'

'Got them off the hook, perhaps?' That gave Thea plenty to think about as they covered the last few miles. Who could possibly think that? Susanna had been acting in defence of the Staceys, hadn't she? Didn't that implicate them in the murders? Helen had a daughter who fitted into the story somewhere. June, Lindy and Lionel had never been on a hook, as far as Thea could see.

James sat her down with a large mug of tea, and did his best to explain. The network had never been the object of close police scrutiny, because nobody had made any complaints and there was no indication of criminal activity. It was, however, flagged up against the name of Duntisbourne Abbots as something to be aware of. The double killing of the Jennison brothers had brought it to the forefront of police attention, but still with no obvious law-breaking activity. The Staceys provided wobbly but acceptable alibis, and the handful of youngsters in the hut were all able to produce identification and reasons for being where they were.

This immunity from serious police attention was, it was beginning to appear, largely due to the protective offices of most of the population, who had been convinced from the first that Fairweather was providing a highly desirable service.

'But *how*?' Thea demanded. 'I'd have thought they would have hated it. Drug addicts roaming around their precious homesteads. Surely they'd be horrified?'

'Ah, but that isn't the way they see it. Not at all.' Here James looked to Harry for confirmation. 'As far as the village is concerned, the Staceys were keeping their own kids safe. Once Martin had found and rescued Felicity Winstanley, and got her off the crack, he could do no wrong. He gave priority to local people, you see. Daisy Isbister was headed off before she could get seriously hooked, and her friend Monique – you remember Monique, I suppose? – was a dramatic success story. Virginia's boy, Kenny, was brought back from a ghastly squat in Birmingham. And so it goes on.'

'It's true about Daisy,' said Harry. 'Martin worked hard on her, and now she's a model citizen.'

'But Susanna?'

Harry shook his head. 'We all thought Susanna was doing fine. It seems we were wrong.'

Thea snorted. 'She's a complete psychopath. She's off the scale.' Thea's fists clenched, and she began to sweat. 'I never saw anything as evil as her when she was holding that knife.'

'She was very badly addicted to heroin in her twenties. It probably did permanent damage.' James spoke gently, almost, Thea felt, reproachfully.

'Are you *defending* her? She killed two young men. She stabbed my dog!'

'She wanted to save Fairweather Farm,' said Harry, slowly, as if assembling his thoughts as he uttered them. 'She owed her life to it. She was devoted to Isabel and Martin. It was the first time anybody had given her any responsibility, and it matured her remarkably. She was a dreadfully spoilt little girl – I remember it only too well.'

'If you're talking about Susanna, I'll second that. She was a holy terror at school, according to some of the Old Girls I know,' came a voice from the doorway. Thea turned to see June standing there, holding a teatowel. Their eyes met. 'Hello, Thea,' she said. 'I've been in the kitchen. I thought I'd let you talk to your brother-in-law for a few minutes.'

Thea didn't reply. She was still sweating as well as beginning to shake. The mug rattled against her teeth when she tried to take a swig of tea.

June went to her, squatting on the floor putting an arm across her legs. 'Steady!' she advised. 'It's all OK now.'

'But—' Thea didn't know what to say.

'Let me tell you about Susanna,' June said. 'She was famously badly behaved all through her teens and twenties. Her father bought her a fast car, a horse and a husband. She destroyed all of them, in the process of destroying herself. People did everything they could to stay out of her way. Then the Staceys arrived, and somehow got through to her when nobody else could. We never worked out how they did it, but it looked like a miracle. That was ages before the network got going, but it probably sowed the seeds for it. When Susanna took up with Joel, we were worried, obviously, but it all seemed to be working out. She inherited money from an uncle, and put it into Fairweather – the same as Helen and others did. They were always getting donations from grateful families.

'But she was always pushing Joel – and Paul – to do more for the place. She wanted them to give an evening of their time to working with the addicts. The system involves learning new skills, understanding that there's a world full of possibility waiting for them – that sort of stuff. But Joel and Paul were both completely unconvinced. They disagreed with the whole basis of the way it operated. Paul dabbled with pot when he was younger, and had plenty of friends who were into drugs. He wrote an article about it—'

'Yes, I know,' said Thea, with a glance at James. 'It's on the internet.'

'Good grief! Well, his ideas only got stronger, and Joel shared them. When Felicity Winstanley went back on the crack and dropped out of sight, that proved to them that the Staceys were charlatans.'

'But not Helen? Helen stuck with them?'

'She hadn't much choice. It was her only hope of finding her daughter again.'

'And you knew all this? About Susanna and everything? What about her affair with Clive?'

June rested her face lightly on Thea's lap. 'I never even dreamt,' she mumbled. 'Not in a million years, that she shot Paul. And the thing with Clive was blown up out of all proportion by Lionel. He should never have told Joel about it, silly old sod.'

'So he never suspected her of killing Paul?'

'Not at the time. He never liked her, but he didn't ever connect her with Paul's death. We *all* thought it was just some poacher from town.'

'But why Joel? I mean, why such a long gap between them?'

'We're still guessing, but we think she must have believed he was going to try and get the place closed. He had made some threats. Jennifer was involved, trying to force Fairweather to go public, get the Social Services to take it over, and have the whole thing properly registered and monitored. Ironically, nobody on either side wanted that. She put herself right out on a limb.'

Thea looked at James. 'Then you've got your woman? Is Hollis happy?'

James sucked his teeth in prevarication and glanced at Harry Richmond. 'I'm not sure *happy* is quite the word.' He looked around the room. 'None of you knows this yet, but Susanna almost had the last word. She picked up the knife, as you were running off to the vet, and stabbed herself with it.'

The collective gasp seemed to empty the room of air. 'Is she dead?' June whispered.

'Not quite, last I heard. I called Hollis just before you got here. She's in intensive care.'

Thea groaned at the tangled ironies and ethics, unable quite to utter the thought that Susanna might well be better off dead.

'And there's somebody by her bedside who won't let go of her hand,' he added. 'The person, we believe, who helped her wheel Joel's body down the field and into that pool. The person, perhaps, who Susanna was most fiercely defending all along.'

'Martin Stacey?' Thea supplied.

'No, not Martin,' James told her. 'Isabel.'

Thea almost let it lie there, but remembered images prompted her to seek full clarification.

'You don't mean they were lovers? Do you?'

'Not that, no,' June said, with a glance towards Harry for his confirmation.

'Right,' he said. 'Nobody doubts the strength of Isabel and Martin's marriage. No – it's a closer bond than a sexual relationship. Isabel understands Susanna's pain, you see. And, more than that, Susanna understands Isabel's.' He looked down at June. 'You tell her,' he said.

'It was eight years ago. Susanna was at her lowest point. She was out in her fast car, driving like a lunatic, when she turned it over in a ditch. Isabel found her, and hauled her out before the car caught fire. Saved her wretched life for her.'

'Wow!' Thea breathed.

'That's not the point, though. Isabel was pregnant at the time, about eighteen weeks, after a string of early miscarriages. She was supposed to take it easy. She lost the baby. She's never conceived again since then. These druggie kids are a kind of substitute for her. It isn't surprising that she'd fight to keep the whole thing going.'

Thea closed her eyes, tasting the reproach, the guilt, the

sheer unspeakable agonies. She reached blindly for Harry Richmond's warm hand.

'I see,' she said. 'Poor people.'

Harry gripped her fingers, giving them a little shake. 'Hang on,' he urged her. 'Isabel's going to gaol for a while, but I bet you Martin's not going to give up. It's good work they do, and now it's all going to be out in the open, some good people will come forward to help.'

Thea smiled shakily. 'Like you?'

He shifted on the cushions. 'Better than me, I hope.'

James Osborne cleared his throat. 'Harry's right,' he said. 'In the long run, this might all be for the best.'

Thea looked slowly from face to face, absorbing the concern, the reassurance and admiration they were all showing her. 'Thanks,' she said.